Murder

Among The Tombstones

Kim Carter

Published by Raven South Publishing
Atlanta, Georgia 30324, USA

Cover Design by www.mariondesigns.com
Library of Congress Control Number: 2018933816
ISBN 978-1-947140-03-5 paperback
ISBN 978-1-947140-02-8 e-book

Dedication

This book is dedicated to my mother, Mary, and her best friend, Billie Sue, whose friendship spanned the better part of fifty years and inspired the characters of Clara and Iris. I had the privilege of riding in the backseat of the car, as both a child and an adult, as they went on many of their adventures, most of which involved searching for the perfect piece of antique furniture desperately in need of stripping, sanding, staining, and varnishing. This usually occurred on Saturday mornings and was fondly referred to as antiquing.

I am now the proud owner of one of my mother's prized pieces, an oak buffet, which held my father's Scotch, a mason jar of white lightning moonshine that he only brought out on special occasions, and my mother's linen napkins used faithfully at every meal. My fondest childhood memories are of Billie Sue's home which always smelled of a pound cake in the oven because someone in town was always feeling poorly or had just lost a loved one, and of my mother working in her lovely flower gardens, either weeding them or planting bulbs which would surely delight everyone later as they bloomed in all of their glory. There is a little of each of them in both characters. Oh, what fun to have known the real Clara and Iris!

Acknowledgments

No book is ever written without the help of others who are kind enough to share their knowledge and expertise. This novel is certainly no exception.

Many thanks to the following:

First and foremost, a big thank you to my husband, Julius who never stops encouraging me. Because of him, I know I'm never on this journey alone.

A special thank you to my dear friend and fellow writer, Terry Kinder who sent me literally encouraging words every day as I struggled to make a deadline and doubted myself relentlessly. Without reservation, this book was completed because of her.

Thanks to, John Cross Deputy Director of the Fulton County Medical Examiner's Office (GA) for his continuous efforts through the years. Looks like we've pulled off another one, John!

Thanks to Sergeant Liane Lacoss with the Atlanta Homicide Unit who met with me and graciously answered numerous phone calls. Her job is certainly a tough one, and I have the utmost respect for her, and all the law enforcement officers who put their lives on the line to make our world a safer place.

Thanks to Captain Mike Whitlow Fayetteville Police Department (GA), whose help was immeasurable in this novel. I couldn't begin to thank you for taking every call and answering a ridiculous amount of questions. Without you, Clara and Iris would've had a very hard time!

Thanks to my two dear friends and road buddies, Carol Jones and Sandi Miles, who went on numerous field trips with me, most of which were to cemeteries. But we have fun wherever we go! I love you both!

Thanks to, Lynn Daniel former Atlanta Homicide Detective and old friend for all his help and insight.

Thanks to, Wesley Thomas and Ronald E. Yates for doing me the honor of blurbing this Clara and Iris novel. For my books to be read by such tremendous and celebrated authors is certainly nothing I take for granted. Eternally grateful for our friendship!

Thanks to my besties and loyal road dogs who continue to encourage and love me even on days when I know they find it difficult…Lisa Mobley Putnam, Kelly Keylon, and Greg Headrick. Words are simply inadequate when feelings run deep.

Thanks to David and Carrie Ann Pitts for their support and belief that Clara and Iris could become so much more than a novel. In memory of Carrie Ann Pitts who passed away on April 15, 2018, after a valiant battle with brain cancer. One of her true loves and passions were the survival of sea turtles and their habitats. Consider donating to this cause in her memory at https://conserveturtles.org/

Last, but certainly far from the least, I thank Raven South Publishing for the great honor of finding my work worthy of your label.

Other Works by Kim Carter

Sweet Dreams, Baby Belle

No Second Chances

Deadly Odds

And The Forecast Called For Rain

When Dawn Never Comes

Prologue

Nineteen-year-old Jasmine Baines ran with all her might until her legs felt as though they were nothing more than exhausted limbs, mindlessly carrying her weary body even further into the woods. Each breath she took sent out another billowing cloud of steam as the heat from her body met the starkness of the cold night air. Her efforts to scream were lost as she struggled to maintain her footing.

How much longer can I keep this up? It was only a matter of time before her predator would close the gap between them, and she could only imagine what he had in store for her. His eyes promised no mercy.

In the midst of his cruel, relentless pursuit, she knew he was toying with her. He could've caught up with her many strides ago, but he found the chase more amusing. He felt no pity for the young girl. She was just another in a string of endless victims. This one, however, he would allow to be found. It was fascinating every now and then to see the authorities scramble to find such a ruthless killer.

Pressing on, he soon caught up with her weakened frame. She hadn't been much of a challenge, but that wasn't the point.

"Please…" she pleaded, more calmly now. "Please don't kill me."

"Oh, but it will be such fun." He grinned, his perfect, white teeth glistening under his well-formed lips.

"But, why me?" she whispered, allowing her lithe body to give in to the tiredness.

"Need you ask?"

"I won't tell on you. No one would believe me anyhow."

"On the contrary, they might," he said with a sinister laugh, doubting seriously they ever would. "Take your clothes off."

"But I'll freeze to death," she begged.

"That's the least of your worries."

He had no intention of molesting her. That would be revolting. Then again, he thought. *It would have the cops scrambling for a false lead.* The thought humored him.

Chapter One

Detective Pitts sat behind his cluttered desk in the Homicide Division of the Atlanta Police Department. He was a good detective, but much better in the field than with the mounds of required paperwork. A lukewarm cup of coffee sat on the edge of his desk, along with a honey bun from the vending machine in the lobby. Pitts was like a bored fifth grader when it came to tedious tasks that didn't interest him. There weren't any playmates in the surrounding cubicles to distract him, so he stared absentmindedly at an open file before finally folding it shut.

One down, a bazillion to go, he thought with a sigh as he literally closed the case.

Now, all that remained was the trial, where justice would hopefully be served for the sake of the victim and the family left behind. Pitts enjoyed happy endings, unfortunately, they were few and far between in the homicide business.

He took a slug from the Styrofoam cup, swished the tepid liquid around in his mouth, and fought the urge to spit it out in the metal trash can beside his desk. Just as he stood to get a fresh cup, the desk phone rang. "Pitts, Homicide," he answered.

"You at the office?"

"Hell, Nettles, where do you think you're callin' me?"

"Oh, yeah. Anyway, we got a body over at Oakland Cemetery."

"*The cemetery*, really? I bet you'd find more than one if you looked hard enough," Pitts added sarcastically.

"You're a funny guy. Sarge has you down for the lead on this one," Detective Matthew Nettles added. "I'll meet you there."

"Give me ten."

The celebration over his closed case was short-lived. At the very least, another case meant two straight days of lost sleep. Just as The First 48, a documentary currently filming with the department stated, if there weren't any leads in the first forty-eight hours, the case had the potential of growing colder than the stale coffee he'd just swallowed. That was the last thing Pitts wanted to happen.

The detective grabbed his leather jacket from the back of his desk chair and paused briefly at the hat rack where numerous fedoras dangled. Pitts knew which one was his, but he studied them all concisely before reaching for his own. He allowed his fingers to rub the softness of the brown felt before placing it firmly on his head.

The stylish hats had long been a tradition among Atlanta's Homicide Division. It was quite simple really, solve a case, earn a hat. It was a fervent reward for a rookie detective who cracked his or her first homicide, and they were always presented and purchased by experienced officers. It was a rite of passage, quite the honor for hours of long, often unappreciated work.

It was a fairly brisk day for mid-October in Georgia. Atlanta seldom saw any harsh weather, but when snow or ice did fall, it virtually debilitated the inexperienced city. It was rare for anyone to require a jacket this time of year. Pitts threw his hand up to greet several officers he passed. A couple of minutes later, he slid into the vinyl seat of his department-issued Ford Taurus. Exiting the parking lot, he turned right onto Peachtree Street and passed the slew of bonding companies that made their living by rescuing the men and women who faced the unfortunate circumstance of ending up in the City of Atlanta jail.

Homeless men congregated in front of their businesses in hopes of snagging a free cigarette from a stressed-out friend or family member anxious to get someone out of the pokey. The vagabonds and worried relatives all paused to watch his undercover car pass, mindful of the dark fedora perched upon his head. Pitts nodded slightly while they took long drags from their cheap cigarettes and wondered among themselves who else had been murdered in their city.

Making a left onto Memorial Drive, he sped through the yellow light before it changed to red. Oakland Cemetery was less than a mile from the heart of downtown, and depending on traffic, not more than five or ten minutes from his office. Noted as one of the city's crown jewels, it was known as the final resting place of many of Atlanta's settlers, builders, and most noted citizens. Among the winding paths, overwhelming magnolias and elderly oaks were elaborate mausoleums in varying styles of architecture ranging from Greek Revival to Gothic. It also boasted an impressive section for Civil War soldiers—battle casualties resting eternally under small, weathered tombstones.

Pitts turned onto Oakland Avenue and pulled through the black iron gates attached to the red brick walls surrounding the graveyard. He could see the reflection of blue lights flickering at the back of the property, so he wound his way through the one-lane roadway, not intended for more than a small golf cart.

As far as cemeteries went, Oakland was undeniably beautiful, even though Pitts wasn't a big fan of visiting them. The land had been allocated for burials in the mid-1800s, and Pitts was sure it'd been a remarkably peaceful place for quite a long time. It still offered unprecedented views of the city skyline and the old Fulton Cotton Mill, but the surrounding streets now boasted low-end convenience and liquor stores, as well as some seedy tattoo parlors. Indeed, it was not what the prominent citizens had expected when they spent their fortunes on family crypts.

The detective placed his car in park, stepped out, and immediately spotted his partner. Detective Nettles was a beefy man with a round face and thick black hair. His clothes seemed to be a size too small, and he was always perspiring and frustrated. Pitts liked him, plain and simple. He knew Nettles was a good cop and a good man.

"He's just a diamond in the rough," Pitts always said when defending him to their superiors. Now, he found Nettles yelling at one of the newest patrol officers, waving his thick hands around in exasperation.

"Okay, what've we got?" Pitts asked, ignoring the ongoing dispute.

"What the hell took you so long? Did you stop for a cappuccino?" Nettles asked loudly.

"Got here as fast as I could," Pitts said calmly, waving the patrol officers away while securing the scene. "Do we have an ID on the vic'?"

"Appears to be a female, but all we can see is a small, barefoot. The toenails are painted although that doesn't mean a damn thing these days," Nettles scoffed. "The cemetery sexton found her about thirty minutes ago while making his rounds. She's Caucasian and judging by the visible foot, appears to be young."

Pitts walked closer to the small body that had been so carefully wrapped in a pale pink blanket. "Well, this cover's clean as a whistle. She must've been dumped here. Is Upshaw on his way?"

"Yep, called him before I called you. He's two blocks closer. I figured he'd beat you here."

"Maybe *he* needed a cappuccino fix," Pitts answered with a wink.

"Very funny."

"Well, I'm sure he'll be here soon. In this town, Upshaw's a busy man."

"You got that right."

Travis Upshaw, the medical examiner Pitts preferred to work with, was a young man, presumably in his early thirties. He never left a stone unturned. That was a feat in itself considering he was one of only five MEs working for Fulton County. Not only were they tasked with performing autopsies for Georgia's largest county, but for the City of Atlanta as well. Upshaw was tall and lean but solid as a rock, and his blond hair was always tousled from running his hands through it when he got overwhelmed. He wore tortoise-shell glasses whenever he could find them, which wasn't often.

"I didn't touch the blanket," Nettles said as he snapped on a pair of latex gloves. "Figured this might be a weird one, so I decided to wait on Upshaw before I did anything."

"Probably a good idea. It's bound to be a homicide, but our killer must've had regrets and covered her to ease their conscience."

"No doubt about that," Nettles said, calming down a bit. "Wonder why somebody dumped her here? Maybe it's some sick ritual killing or a serial killer. Perhaps it has some inside meaning."

"It doesn't make sense," Pitts countered, shaking his head. "I've never heard of a signature like this, but then again, I'm not a profiler."

"Cemeteries are all about death," Nettles pressed.

"Yep, but we could be overanalyzing it. If I were to make a guess, I'd say it's some type of domestic. Perhaps the death was an accident, and the boyfriend or spouse felt remorseful and knew someone would find her here. Otherwise, he or she could've just dumped her in the woods somewhere to decompose," Pitts said, looking around anxiously. He was relieved to see Upshaw's car pulling up.

The three men exchanged brief pleasantries before Travis kneeled on one knee and slowly pulled back the plush, chenille throw. The scene became eerily quiet as was often the case when a victim was revealed. The men audibly gasped as the beautiful young girl became visible. The world seemed to stand still for several painful seconds before Upshaw motioned for the investigator from the ME's office to come forward with her camera.

Kim Carter

Then, thankfully, the group was able to quickly detach themselves and get to work.

Upshaw pointed out the stomach, thighs, breasts, and the left side of the face blanched white from lividity. "She was left somewhere before this, lying face down for several hours. Get some good photos of these blanched areas, Tess," he softly ordered his coworker.

Tess Dyer had only worked for the ME's office for a couple of years. Everyone liked her and had confidence in her work. She'd graduated from The University of Alabama with a degree in Criminal Justice, and often caught hell from her peers who considered anyone who pulled against the Georgia Bulldogs a traitor. She, like Travis, was quiet and was so tiny people often weren't even aware of her presence. She quickly snapped a number of photos before stepping back for further instructions from her superior.

"How do you know she was somewhere else for so long?" Pitts asked, pointing to the victim.

"She had to be left in another location for hours," Travis continued. "The blood pooled under her, leaving these white patches. Even when she was relocated here and placed in another position, the lividity had already set in the tissues." Everyone remained silent as he inspected her neck and throat, taking the time to brush her strawberry-blonde hair away from her face. "Damn," Travis said, shaking his head. He motioned for Tess, Pitts, and Nettles to kneel beside him. "Of course, we'll have to do a full autopsy," he said quietly. "But I'm almost certain we're going to find out that the cause of death was asphyxia. Look at these chin abrasions," he continued. "Appears there was some manual strangulation. She was lowering her chin in an attempt to protect her neck. Probably scraped against the perp's hands..." He paused as Tess took photos. "Note the combination of fingernail markings. That son-of-a-bitch strangled her from behind. The poor thing didn't have a chance." He waved his hand around her small, pale neck as he continued the anatomy lesson. "These bruises are from his thumbs pressing into her, and the semicircles are from his fingernails, embedded in her neck as he squeezed harder. The scattered scratches must've been from her attempts to pull his hands away, so she could catch a breath. She really did some damage, clawing at her own neck. She fought like hell. Hopefully, we can get some DNA from under her nails."

"Why do you suppose our killer took the time to wrap her in this blanket, almost lovingly, and relocate her?" Nettles asked.

"That's for you and Pitts to figure out," Travis answered honestly with a shrug. "I'll start the autopsy as soon as I get back to the office. I have to admit, it's rather odd, but people have been known to do things in a fit of anger, only to regret it later."

"That was my first thought," Pitts added. "The killer definitely wanted her to be found. Probably couldn't stand the thought of her lying out in the elements but didn't want to chance getting caught and going to jail."

"She's completely nude, and there are no identifying marks that I see now," Travis said. "You can run her fingerprints right away, but she doesn't look like the type to have a record. No tattoos on the body, not even a single piece of jewelry."

"We'll be here for at least a couple of hours," Pitts added. "I'd like to interview the sexton and see if he saw anything else on his rounds. I'll be by your office later, Upshaw."

Chapter Two

"I do declare, Iris, you're going to Windex those letters right off our front window," Clara Samples said fervently.

"Well, what else do you propose I do with my time?" Iris responded firmly. "With no customers, I've gotta find something productive to do."

"We've only been open for two days. The business will come."

"Honestly, I think we've lost our minds, Clara. What were we thinking when we opened this private investigation business, old as we are?"

"Well, I suppose we could've just sat at home and crocheted afghans for shut-ins."

"Stop poking fun at me," Iris said flatly. "If we were gonna do this. Why'd we have to set up in such a seedy part of town? I'm a little uneasy, I must admit."

"How many times do I have to tell you?" Clara asked. "This is all we could afford…and it's actually an ideal location. The seedier, the better, in our line of work."

"How do you figure that?" Iris asked as she let out a heavy sigh and plopped down in the chair across from Clara.

"Look, Jefferson Street maybe a little shabby, but we're right around the corner from the county jail, and there's a lot of traffic rolling through here, so we're bound to get some clients."

"And what in heaven's name are we gonna do if we *get* some?" Iris said, then laughed in spite of herself.

Actually, the whole situation was pretty laughable, like some sort of makeshift sitcom. Iris Hadley was a retired hairdresser and enjoyed nothing more than a bit of juicy gossip. She was plump and sassy, to say the least. Profanities slipped out of her mouth more often than not, and whatever crossed her mind soon escaped her lips. Her partner and best friend, Clara Samples, was her polar opposite. Tiny and neat in appearance, she was a retired nurse, and much more on the dignified, restrained side. Both ladies were in their early seventies and had been widows for the better part of a decade.

Before Clara's recent retirement—a rather quick departure from her position as a nurse and office manager for a cardiologist, the two women had discovered they had quite a few investigative skills. They were smart and inquisitive enough to determine that Clara's boss was running a Ponzi scheme, squirreling millions away in offshore accounts. That was enough excitement to steer them in a different direction and give them a new lease on life. Frankly, they both found retirement dull, and neither was ready to head to assisted living.

"You know what, Iris?" Clara asked, looking calmly at her partner in crime-solving. "We've come this far, so let's just see how it goes. We paid for six months' rent upfront, so the worst that can happen is we lose that money. Anyway, let's face it. What else do two ol' bats like us have to do?"

The longtime friends sat in comfortable silence until the bell chimed, signaling a visitor. It was a young, African American woman, probably in her early twenties with braids that hung almost to her slender hips. She was tiny, barely five feet, and her energy filled the room.

"Good morning, Dear," Iris said, standing to greet their guest. "How can we help you today?"

"My name's, JaQuita, but Quita will do just fine. Where's the private investigator? I need some help."

"You're looking at them, Dear. I'm Iris Hadley, and this is my partner, Clara Samples. What can we do for you?"

"Huh?" she said, looking at the two gray-haired women incredulously. "You can't be serious! I mean, no disrespect, but you, uh…"

"Don't look like PIs?" Clara finished for her. "Yes, we're aware of that, but looks can be deceiving. Now, what can we do for you today?"

"It's my sister, Nikki," Quita started.

"Why don't you sit down, Hon'?" Clara said, motioning to a chair. "I'm going to sit at my desk and take some notes."

"I've gotta be straight with ya," the young woman said. "I don't have much money, and—"

"Let's hear what the problem is," Clara persisted, cutting her off. "We'll talk money later."

"Okay, well, Nikki's having a hard time with her baby and all, and the baby daddy, Denard, won't pay her nothin'."

"That shouldn't be a problem, Quita," Clara said kindly. "Fulton County has an office to enforce child support payments."

"Yeah, right. We've been that route before. He either finds work where he gets paid under the table or when they try to garnish his wages, he just quits."

"What a no-good—" Iris started with a fervor.

"Excuse me, Iris. There'll be none of that."

"You're exactly right, Miss Iris," Quita cut in. "He's good for nothing. My sister works hard, but she only makes minimum wage, and she struggles to buy diapers, even with assistance. That's all she's askin' for, some diaper money."

"Where's this Denard working now?" Iris asked.

"For a construction company over near Juniper and Tenth, but he'll just quit as soon as they send over a child support order."

"His baby's got a right to clean diapers, for God's sake. We'll go over and talk to him," Iris said.

"Iris Hadley!" Clara spat. "You'll do nothing of the sort."

"I don't see any harm in it," Iris insisted. "We'll be in public, right, Quita?"

"Yes, Ma'am."

"What are we waiting for then?" Iris asked, reaching for her coat and purse.

"Oh, good Lord," Clara said, grabbing her keys. "This is *not* what I had in mind."

"Quita, you ride up front," Iris insisted, then scooted in and belted herself in the back seat. "Clara drives most of the time. I have trouble merging onto the interstate, and Lord forbid should we drive up on some construction. It's part o' being old, I tell ya. It's nothing to look forward to."

"Iris, really," Clara interrupted. "We don't need to go into all that. You'll only depress the poor girl more."

"I don't want Quita to think I can't drive! I'm totally fine going to Walgreens or the Piggly Wiggly. It's only the interstate driving that gets me."

"Iris, please!" Clara scolded, rolling her eyes in the rearview mirror. "Quita, can you give me directions?"

"Yes, Ma'am. We're only about ten to fifteen minutes away."

Until they reached their destination, Iris continued her rant about inconsiderate drivers and speed limits she swore, "*Were established to boost reckless behavior.*"

"There's the superintendent's trailer," Clara said as she pulled up and parked in front of the work lot. "Now, Iris, let's not be rude. Leave the talking to me."

The tan construction trailer looked as though it'd traveled to numerous sites over its lifetime, and the interior didn't appear much better.

"We're here to see the manager," Clara said firmly as she stood on the doorstep, tapped lightly on the door frame, and peeked inside.

"That'd be me, name's Jeff. What can I do for you?"

"Apparently, you have an employee by the name of Denard. Is that correct?"

"Yes, Ma'am, we do. Is there a problem?"

"He owes some child support, and we'd like to see that he pays it."

"I'll need a letter from the State to garnish his wages. That's a real pain in the ass, and…oops, sorry. Please excuse my French."

"We're not from the State. Apparently, Denard has a history of leaving jobs before he'll support his own child. We don't want that to happen. It'd be greatly appreciated if we could just work out a little deal for him to purchase diapers every week, then we'll be on our way."

"Are you attorneys?" he asked quizzically. "I'm afraid I don't understand."

"No. We're private investigators."

He shook his head but didn't comment further. "So, what do you want from me? I understand the predicament, but I hardly have time to deal with this sort of thing, and it isn't really my problem unless the State gets involved."

"I'd just like to speak with him. Maybe we can talk some sense into him, come to some sort of…agreement."

"All right," Jeff said. He motioned them inside and picked up a radio. "I'll call him to the trailer. Please have a seat."

Less than five minutes later, the deadbeat Denard walked in. He was a puny-looking fellow, and both women wondered what any young woman would've seen in him. Jeff stood and motioned toward the three women.

Denard recognized Quita right away and puffed his chest out in protest. "What the hell is *she* doing here?" he asked loudly.

"Actually," Iris began as she stood and bravely faced the angry, young man, "We're here concerning some diapers."

"What are you talking about?" Denard all but spat at Iris. "Are you trying to get me fired?"

19

"No, we're trying to keep you working, so you can purchase some much-needed items for the child you fathered. Let's make a deal, shall we? Then you can get back to work like any responsible father would."

Clara held her breath. She wanted to stop Iris from tongue-lashing him but knew if she did, they'd never get anywhere with Denard.

"Who are you anyway?" Denard asked snidely.

Iris rummaged through her purse for what seemed like an eternity until she found her PI shield. She rubbed it against her wool cardigan, as if to shine it, then thrust it in his face.

Denard looked at it quizzically, then laughed. "Are you packin', old lady?"

"Huh? No, I'm not packing up, because I'm not ready to go anywhere just yet. In fact, I'm not leaving until I get some cash for this baby…and a signed IOU for the future."

Iris's naïve comment drew bursts of laughter from both Denard and Jeff this time.

"I meant, are you packing a weapon?" Denard said as his face softened a bit. "Lookout, world, Granny's got a gun!"

"I don't need a weapon, but I am one second away from turning you over my knee and wearing your little ass out."

"Iris, please," Clara said, finally stepping in. "Listen, Denard…I'm sure you want to provide for your child. We're not here to cause you to lose your job. We're only asking for you to provide some necessary things for your child. Your boss here doesn't want to fool with garnishing your wages any more than we do. It seems like you've got a decent job. Why don't you just leave some money here every payday and Quita can pick it up for her sister?"

"Sounds pretty fair to me, Denard," Jeff said. "You know I don't like drama on the worksite, and I'm not too fond of men who don't step up to their responsibilities. You can start by leaving fifty bucks with me every Friday. If things work out and you stay for a while, we should be able to up that."

"Um, I guess so," Denard said hesitantly. "But that bi—"

"Hey!" Iris screamed, halting him. "You'll not disrespect the mother of your baby in front of me, young man."

"Right," Denard said, rolling his eyes. "She just damn well better not spend my hard-earned money on nails or weaves," he said as he glared at Quita.

Posturing ensued, making it clear there was no love lost between them, so Clara stepped in again, speaking softly but firmly. "You don't have to worry about that. The money should cover diapers and a few other needs, which is all we're concerned about. We appreciate it, Denard, you're doing the right thing by your baby." She then turned to the supervisor. "I think we're through here, Jeff, and we appreciate your willingness to help."

"And we don't expect any trouble from you, Denard…or any contact with our friend Quita here. You got that?" Iris asked, crossing her arms and casting him a hard stare.

"Yes, Ma'am," he answered as he looked down at his shoes like a child taking a scolding. "Can I get back to work now, Boss?"

"Yeah, no problem. As long as you drop off the fifty dollars every Friday and continue to work hard, you'll have a job."

Denard quickly left the small confines of the cheap trailer as the women let out a sigh of relief.

"You sure come out guns blazing, packin' or not, don't you, Miss Iris?" Jeff asked as a smile spread across his face.

"I don't know if you're making fun of me or not," she retorted. "I swear, I don't understand this generation."

"Neither do I, Miss Iris. Neither do I."

Chapter Three

As suspected, Detectives Pitts and Nettles spent the next three hours scouring the cemetery for leads. The cold weather had caused the ground to be hard, and it was covered with thick grass, leaving them without any footprints to cast. Obviously, the perp had driven his vehicle down the paved, one-lane roadway, which didn't give them the luxury of having any tire tracks either. They took notice of the surrounding family plots, in case there was any significance as to where the body was disposed.

The sexton was a soft-spoken, older gentleman who'd worked for the cemetery for over forty years. His pale, arthritic hands were still trembling from finding the dead girl, and he was inhaling heavily from an unfiltered Pall Mall.

"I...I don't understand it," he said, emotion cracking in his voice. "We don't ever have any problems here. I hear tales of folks vandalizing cemeteries, but it's never been the case on our grounds. Everybody here has always rested in peace."

"Tell me...Mister Mason, is it?" Pitts asked.

"Yep, Stuart Mason."

"Mister Mason, what time did you find the body?"

"I was on my golf cart this morning, takin' my regular ride 'round the property. I do that first thing, just to get my agenda in order for the day."

"I understand," Pitts said soothingly. "This is quite a big place. I bet there's a lot of upkeep."

"Yes, yes, there is. Folks don't understand that. My work's never done, and on top of everything else, I've got employees to supervise. It ain't an easy job."

"I'm sure it isn't, Mister Mason. What time did you make those rounds?"

"Um, let's see," the old man said, looking down at his Timex. "I'd say it was about nine-fifteen. I saw the blanket and wasn't sure what it was." His hands started to tremble again, and he sucked deeply on the cigarette to calm himself.

"A quarter after nine? Okay, now what did you do when you saw the blanket, Mister Mason? Please think clearly. This is very important," Pitts insisted.

"I got off my golf cart and walked over to it, err...to her," he stammered.

"Okay," Pitts continued, ignoring Nettles' growing impatience. "So, you walked over to her? Did you touch the blanket or pull it back?"

"Oh, no Sir," Mr. Mason said adamantly. "I never touched anything. I saw the poor child's foot and knew she had to be dead. I had my cell phone on me," he said, pulling it from his coat pocket as if to verify he owned one. "But I was so nervous that I forgot all about it. I got on the cart and drove straight to the bell tower where I called 9-1-1. I was nervous as a cat, I tell ya. I felt like I shouldn't leave her alone. I guess that sounds sorta weird, but it didn't seem right to me. So, I drove back here and flagged down the first cop I saw."

"Okay, to verify again," Pitts said. "You never touched the blanket?"

"No, Sir, I *never* did."

"What time do you open the front gate, Sir?"

"In the winter months, we don't officially open till ten o'clock, but I get here anywhere between eight and nine, just to get an early start on my day."

"So, you open the main gate when you arrive?"

"Correct," he said, pausing briefly to take another long drag from the Pall Mall that was quickly disappearing.

Pitts glared at Nettles daring him to speak. They needed to keep the older man calm to ensure getting as much information from him as possible, and one of Nettles' flaws was that he was too impatient.

"I can't imagine anyone being able to carry a body back this far, to say nothing of getting her over the brick barrier," Nettles said.

"The side gate on Memorial Drive is always left unlocked. We don't advertise it, but we have a lot of early-morning walkers. They complained about not being able to get in, and we figured they were probably jumping the fence to walk anyway, so we decided to leave it unlocked for 'em. There's been sort of an unspoken truce between all of us. They enter and close the gate behind them and get their exercise in, and they've never bothered anything or anyone."

"Was the gate closed, this morning when you got here?"

"I always open the front gate on Oakland Avenue first, then the one on Memorial. It was closed when I got here, but unlocked, of course."

"Nettles, we need to check the security cameras from the surrounding businesses," Pitts said. "Maybe someone has a view of that side entrance." He turned back to the caretaker and suggested, "Mister Mason, you say not everyone's aware of the unlocked gate. Perhaps it was one of your regulars."

The thought of a killer being in his midst, on the turf he patrolled every day, didn't sit well with Stuart Mason. So, he finished his cigarette and lit another before speaking again, "Don't like the thought of that," he said, shaking his head. "We've got a lot of regular visitors—people taking pictures, exercising, and walking their dogs, even kids riding tricycles. I know many of 'em by name, or at least by face. I lived above the bell tower years ago, but it's an old building. The City and the Historic Foundation didn't like the idea of updating it, so I had to get my own place."

Pitts turned to Nettles. "The fact that not everyone knows about the gate being unlocked could narrow down our suspect list."

"I can't be sure who knows about it and who don't," Mr. Mason said quickly. "Word about all sorts of things gets out among those walkers, spreads like wildfire."

"You're probably right about that," Nettles agreed. "Those exercise nuts are quite a clique. One of 'em finds a good place to walk in this congested city, and they share the love. Know what I mean?"

Stuart shook his head and zipped his windbreaker. "Got cold quick," he said. "You men want a cup of coffee? Got some brewin' back in my office."

"No, thanks," Nettles answered abruptly. "We've got a lot to look into. You said you were doing your rounds. Did you see anything unusual this morning, anything thrown on the grass, that sort of thing?"

"No, Sir, and I know this place like the back of my hand. Wasn't even a single piece of trash."

"All right. Go on and get that cup of coffee, Mister Mason," Pitts suggested as he handed him a business card. "This has my cell number. Call me if you think of anything else, anything at all."

"Will do, Officer." Relief washed over his face as he cranked up the old golf cart and rode back to the whitewashed bell tower.

"What'd you think?" Nettles asked.

"About the sexton? Seems a little shaken up, but who wouldn't be?" Pitts countered.

"Yeah, I guess. I'm thinking I should take the lead with the surveillance tapes. I can start on that as soon as we wrap up here."

"Sounds like a plan. Have our CSI boys and girls get clear pics of these surrounding tombstones. Who knows, we might find some links later in the investigation. I'm gonna walk around a little more, then head over to see how Upshaw's coming with the autopsy. I'll check with missing persons, too."

The cemetery was a vast place. With over 70,000 burial sites, it was impossible to cover it all in one day. Pitts did one last scan over the surrounding area, then drove his car around the rest, stopping lastly at the side gate on Memorial. There were a couple of popular restaurants and drinking spots, but he didn't see any outside surveillance. Those places usually applied their resources toward elaborate security systems and interior video recording devices.

Atlanta was currently struggling with a big smash-and-grab issue— young thugs breaking in through the storefronts, grabbing anything of value, particularly flat-screen televisions. Businesses had to bolt them to the walls and lock away their liquor for the night, but that essentially caused even more destruction when the delinquents went in to grab the loot. Juveniles were aware that they'd only get light sentences, the proverbial slaps on the wrists, which only exacerbated the problem. So, the ongoing crime didn't appear to be going away anytime soon. Nettles knew his best bet would be to view the convenience store tapes, but their cameras were, more often than not, vandalized and inoperable.

It was always a crapshoot, and unfortunately, it frequently resulted in little more than the loss of valuable investigative time. Detective Pitts passed Daddy D'z BBQ Joynt, and his stomach grumbled in protest. He thought about stopping for a pulled pork sandwich to go, but he didn't have time to waste.

Pitts had been dating Jessalyn Brock, the young receptionist at the ME's office, for about three months. His heart tended to race a little whenever he had an opportunity to see her at work. His hours were so unpredictable that their dates were often canceled, but fortunately, she understood the ins and outs of his job. For that reason, as well as many others, she was the perfect fit for him. But he often wondered what laid ahead for them? What female in her right mind would ever marry a cop anyway?

It was hard to find a woman his age, mid-thirties, without a lot of baggage. Jessalyn was a rare gem: she'd never been married, didn't have any kids, and understood and coped with his incessant need to find the bad guys. She was perfect for him, without a doubt, but he wasn't so sure he was perfect for her. Unfortunately, on this particular day, he had to head straight over to Upshaw, stopping by to flirt with her would only derail him from a time-sensitive investigation.

Pitts entered through the back and nodded at the morgue attendant in the small office. "What's up, Sugar?" he asked.

"Not much, my man. Upshaw's just starting the autopsy."

"Damn, I was hoping I'd missed it," Pitts said.

Sugar let out a full belly laugh. "You know Upshaw ain't that fast."

Pitts shared a laugh with the lively, Sugar, the bright side of the morgue if there was one to be found in a place of perpetual death. He was the largest man Pitts had ever laid eyes on, close to six-seven and topping the scales at over 350 pounds. Anyone who didn't know him would've been intimidated by his size and approached him with trepidation. He was a black man with a dark complexion, and his hair was always braided in cornrows. His shirts were tight, accentuating his bulging biceps. Sugar had straight, white teeth that sparkled when he smiled, which was often. His real name was Stanley Peters, but everyone called him Sugar because his gentle personality was a sharp contrast to his overbearing appearance.

His office was essentially a small box with a window much like that of a fast-food drive-thru. Sugar always appeared to be crammed in like a sardine and welcomed any opportunity to come out. His job was to sign in and out all the bodies that came and went, living and dead. When the delivery drivers rolled their gurneys up the ramp, Sugar helped them transfer the deceased to the ME's gurney. The two industrial-sized, walk-in coolers opened from the front and the back. The left one was where Sugar rolled in the bodies to be autopsied, and the right one was where the autopsied bodies were kept until someone from a funeral home arrived to pick them up.

It certainly wasn't a position of fortune and glory, but Sugar took it seriously. He was content to deal with his impeccable paperwork and filing system, with no plans to go anywhere. The pay could have been better, but he was a county employee with good benefits and a decent retirement plan.

His coworkers were fond of him, and there wasn't any office drama from the refrigerated corpses.

"Catch ya later, Sugar," Pitts said as he passed the coolers and turned toward the autopsy suite.

He looked through the glass window and saw Travis Upshaw standing over the young victim, positioning the X-ray machine. Tess Dyer was standing on a stepladder, adjusting the lens on her digital camera. He tapped lightly on the stainless-steel door.

Upshaw looked up and acknowledged his presence, inviting him in with a nod.

Pitts pushed the doors open with his hip and went to the center of the room that accommodated seven autopsy stations. He fumbled through the gowns and masks and slipped plastic covers over his shoes. Hoping Travis had already started, he was disappointed to discover that he'd most likely be present for most of the post-mortem. He wished he hadn't rushed over, but there was little else to investigate at the scene. Nettles was busy with the surveillance tapes, so Pitts was where he needed to be, whether he wanted to be there or not.

"Find anything else at the scene?" Upshaw asked as he looked up over his mask.

"No, not really. Our best hope is some surveillance footage or DNA under her nails."

"I'm sure there'll be some. She clawed and fought frantically. There are no signs of past domestic abuse. She was a healthy, young woman, in her late teens or early twenties. Rigor has already come and gone, and there's minimal decomp," he said nonchalantly as if he were discussing nothing more disturbing than a summer rainstorm. "I'd say she was murdered within the past forty-eight hours. There's no bloating or marbling of the skin, but it's pretty cool outside."

"But we don't know where she was lying overnight."

"It had to be a fairly cool place, temperature-wise, I mean," Upshaw clarified. "I haven't done the invasive. That'll tell us much more, but it was definitely manual strangulation."

"Strangling someone with your hands is a more personal crime. My thoughts are it was a boyfriend. It takes a lot of pressure to squeeze a neck hard enough to leave thumbprints."

"Sick bastard," Upshaw muttered under his breath. "We took prints. They're over on the counter. Other than that, I guess you'll have to wait on someone to report her missing. Tess has some good headshots if you can find anyone to identify the body."

"I'm still baffled about that blanket. Why would they wrap her up and leave her lying in a cemetery?"

"Who knows why people do what they do," Upshaw answered.

"It's a crazy world. Listen, there's not much I can do here. Call me when you finish and let me know if you find anything else. I'm heading back to the office."

"It'll be at least a couple of hours. I'll call your cell."

"Okay, Upshaw. Later."

Pitts took off his scrubs and threw them in the cart before realizing he hadn't even acknowledged, Tess. She was so quiet and small that she often went unnoticed. "Hey, Tess," he said. "Thanks for those headshots. I'll contact you if we get a missing person's report."

She looked up from her camera long enough to nod, then went back to work.

Chapter Four

The three women got back in the Buick and clicked on their seatbelts. Clara cranked the car and maneuvered out of the construction site.

"I think that went pretty well," Iris said confidently.

"Iris Hadley," Clara said. "You could've gotten us in a world of trouble with that mouth of yours. What were you thinking, talking to that man like that?"

"Like what? I was just being firm."

"You threatened to wear his little ass out, as I recall."

"You can't let young people think they can walk all over you, Clara. It's a new generation."

"And what would you know about the new generation, Iris?"

"I watch reality television," she said defiantly.

"Actually, I think the good-cop/bad-cop routine was pretty effective," Quita said with a grin.

"What do you mean?" both women asked in unison.

Iris unhooked her seatbelt and leaned toward the front seat, so she could hear her answer more clearly.

"One of you acts like the bad cop, rude and demanding, not taking anything off nobody. Then the good cop, you, Miss Clara, is calm and closes the deal. You kinda made Denard feel like he had some options, gave the arrogant bastard some o' his pride back, so to speak."

"That was never the plan," Clara said. "In fact, there was never a *plan* at all. That's the problem. Things could've gone a lot worse."

"How many cases have you two handled?" Quita asked.

"You're our first," Iris said proudly as if their inexperience were something to brag about.

"Oh my," Quita said. "You ladies are in trouble."

"We're certified," Iris quickly interjected. "And technically, this isn't our first case. We solved a multimillion-dollar Ponzi scheme. The crook was even shot and killed by the FBI."

"Really?" Quita asked as she turned to look at Iris.

"Yep, sure did. That's how we got started in the business."

"I don't know what kind of cases you're expecting, but Bankhead's a foul place. You're obviously not used to dealing with the streets."

"I've already admitted that," Iris said, again taking someone's words too literally. "It's okay, though, because Clara can handle the driving. We'll make it work. I'm more useful in other areas."

Quita shook her head and stifled a laugh. "That wasn't what I meant. I thought you said you watch reality TV. Anyway, you're way too defensive about your driving abilities. Remind me never to catch a ride with you. Anyway, what I meant was that you aren't, um... how do I say this?"

"We aren't very *streetwise*," Clara answered. "You're exactly right. We're older and behind the times."

"Something tells me you never knew much about the streets," Quita said. "But that's cool. I mean, it ain't nothing that can't be learned. You must have somethin' going for yourselves if you solved a big crime like that. What types of cases do you think you'll get with your office bein' here?"

"We're not sure," Clara answered honestly. "Truth is, we haven't thought much of it through. We're just two old ladies who weren't ready to throw in the towel and retire."

"Here she goes," Iris said, rolling her eyes. "Once again, she's going to start doubting our business and feeling sorry for herself. I personally think we've got a lot to offer. Maybe we have a lot to learn, but hey, like you said earlier, Clara, what else do we have to do?"

"I've got an idea," Quita said, obviously taking the time to choose her words carefully. "I just got laid off. Well, I actually walked out. My job wasn't going anywhere, difficult boss, that kind of thing. I happen to have some time on my hands. I don't come cheap, but I've got a lot to offer, and I think I could help you ladies out, show you the ropes—you know, familiarize you with the hood."

"I'm starting to take offense about my shortcomings with an automobile," Iris said.

Quita and Clara both laughed.

"Maybe there's something to your proposal," Clara said. "We weren't counting on having to deal with payroll yet, so the salary will be minimal at best."

"I'm used to that." Quita said, "I think a big title might make up the difference."

"Hmm. How does office manager/consultant sound?" Clara asked.

Quita pondered for a moment. "Perfect! Can I have my own desk with one of those plastic nameplates on it?"

"I don't see why not," Clara answered.

"Then you've got yourselves a deal."

Chapter Five

Detective Pitts and Nettles sat in an empty conference room, comparing notes. It had been two days since the young girl had been found in Oakland Cemetery, and they didn't have any leads or an identification.

"Can't believe we came up empty-handed with the surveillance footage. That would've been a major break," Nettles grumbled.

"I wasn't very optimistic that we'd get anything. Dope dealers hang out on Memorial Drive all night. They've long since destroyed anything that could implicate them and hinder their business. I'm sure it gets pretty damn frustrating repairing those things. It can't be cheap."

"Yeah, I know. I'd be damned if I'd work in one of those convenience stores at night. Makes our jobs look safe."

"The autopsy showed exactly what Upshaw expected—manual strangulation. No drugs or alcohol in her system. She was perfectly healthy…except for being dead," Pitts said as he rubbed his hand across his face. The ringing of his cell phone interrupted the conversation. "Pitts, Homicide." He frowned a bit as he listened to the conversation on the other end of the line. "Really? First hit we've gotten on this case. I'll be up in a sec'."

"What is it?" Nettles asked, his voice hopeful. "We got something? Not sure, but it sounds promising. A young woman is filing a missing person's report for her nineteen-year-old sister."

"I'm going with you," Nettles said as he gathered the few sheets of paperwork they had on the case. "Hope we get an I.D. I hate that such a young girl is just lying there in that morgue. Kinda makes me feel sick."

"Yeah, I know what you mean."

The two detectives remained silent for the rest of the way, lost in their own thoughts about where the case would lead them.

"Morning, fellas," Cassidy Moore said as she looked up from the computer. "Daniels has your girl in room four. I've got to warn you, she's pretty distraught."

"Thanks," Nettles answered. "We want the I.D., but it's hard as hell to tell somebody it might be their sister."

"How's your wife?" Cassidy asked, turning her full attention to Nettles. She knew how hard it was, after all, she saw it every day. *So, what if a little small talk prolongs the inevitable for the young girl in the back? Perhaps she needs a couple more minutes before her life is changed forever?*

"She's good, still teaching. Have to tell ya, I don't know how the hell she deals with a buncha little, snotty-nosed kids. Half the time she's got a cold herself."

Pitts knew what Cassidy was doing and why she was stalling. He appreciated it, but it was time for them to do their job. "Nice seeing you, Cass. You should do lunch with us sometime," he interrupted.

"I might just do that." She turned her attention back to the computer.

Room four was less than ten feet away, but it seemed much farther as the men made their way there. Nettles tapped lightly on the door, then opened it slowly.

Detective David Daniels was sitting across the table from a young redhead who was tightly clutching a box of Kleenex. Several used tissues were wadded up on the table in front of her.

"Morning, Detectives," Daniels said. "This is Ginger Baines. She's concerned because she's been unable to contact her sister for four days."

"Mornin', Ma'am," Nettles said awkwardly as he and Pitts joined them at the table. "Can you tell us about your sister? What makes you think she's missing?"

Ginger looked up at Nettles with tears rolling down her face, they clung desperately to her jawline before dripping down her pale neck. "We're very close, my sister and me. She's nineteen, and I'm twenty-two. It's just been the two of us our whole lives."

"So, you took care of her?" Pitts asked softly, wondering silently and speculating about their childhoods. They ran into all sorts of dysfunctional families in his business with parents ranging from crackheads to spoiled, wealthy, neglectful people who didn't want to be bothered with their kids.

"We were stuck in the foster system on and off for most of our lives. We never knew our dad, and our mother dragged us from one place to the next. Every time we got close to being adopted, she showed up, just sober enough to take us back for a few months. Then it would start all over again."

Pitts fought the urge to reach across the table and wipe the tears from her face. She was a beautiful young woman like her sister. "Do you and your sister live together?"

"No, but we aren't very far from each other. We each have our own apartment near our campuses. She goes to the Art Institute of Atlanta, and I go to Emory."

"Well, I've gotta say, it sounds as if you're both doing well for yourselves, especially without any parents to push you," Pitts said.

"We both worked hard in school," Ginger said, finally wiping the tears from her face. "It was the only thing we could do for ourselves. It was tough being moved from one school district to the next, but we survived. We're both on scholarships and have part-time jobs."

"That's great," Pitts complimented. He'd succeeded in calming her down a bit, only to have to upset her again. "So, uh, tell me…when was the last time you spoke with your sister?"

"Four days ago. I wasn't worried at first. We're both busy with school and work, but after the second day, I knew something had to be wrong. We never go two days without talking," she whispered as the tears began to pour again.

"You said you both work part-time. Where does your sister work?"

"Jasmine works at Greylon Steak House at Lenox Mall. She's a waitress and does pretty well there. It's a pricey place, so she makes excellent tips. It doesn't hurt that she's so pretty," Ginger said as she lowered her head to sob. "Please tell me…has something happened to her?"

Pitts looked at Nettles, and he nodded his head in affirmation. Like it or not, it was time to tell her about the body at the ME's office.

"Ginger," Pitts said, looking her sternly in the eyes. "We have an unidentified body at the Fulton County Medical Examiner's Office. I'm afraid it could possibly be your sister."

"You mean the *morgue*!?" she screamed. "So, she's…*dead*? There's no way! No…it can't be her!"

Daniels patted Ginger's forearm in an awkward attempt to comfort her, but she roughly jerked away.

"Don't you dare touch me!" she barked in between wracking sobs, "He's *lying*!"

The three detectives sat silently as she went through the phases of denial, the ones they'd witnessed so often. They allowed her a few minutes to calm down before continuing.

"Ginger," Nettles said gently. "We aren't saying for sure that it's Jasmine. It's a young woman about her age, who hasn't been identified. Do you happen to have a picture of her?"

She wiped her face with a saturated tissue and dug through her purse to retrieve her phone. She swiped through several photos before choosing one for them to view. "This is the most current I have of her. I took it the last time we had lunch together."

Nettles looked at the photo, then passed the cell phone to Pitts. Both men knew it was the strangled girl in the morgue but didn't allow their expressions to reflect it. She would have to be officially identified, regardless of their assumptions, and there was always the slim possibility they were wrong. They knew corpses seldom resembled the people they were in life with all the color and life drained out of them. Nevertheless, it was too big of a coincidence for her to resemble the corpse and be a missing person too.

Pitts made eye contact with Daniels indicating it wasn't going to be a happy ending. "Ginger are you here alone?" he asked.

"Yes," she said quietly.

"We can drive you over to the ME's office it's just down the street. It's not a very pleasant place, though, and it'd be best if you had a loved one there for, uh…support."

"Jasmine," she said, then broke down again. "I've always called my sister when I need someone."

Pitts leaned closer. "Is there a classmate, perhaps? Maybe a supervisor at your job?"

Ginger shook her head. "There's nobody I can call for this. I'll do it alone." She pushed the chair back from the table and reached for her purse. "If it's her, I need to know. I need to get her out of that cold, frightening place."

Daniels glanced discreetly at the other two detectives, letting them know he didn't envy them.

The solemn group passed Cassidy without a word, and she never looked up from her computer.

The ride to the ME's office only took a couple of minutes. They parked and entered through the front door used by the public. Jessalyn was waiting and quickly exited from behind the glass-enclosed reception area to meet them.

Unlike the accounts often shown on television or in gruesome movies, family and friends never actually view the deceased at this facility. The pathologists and investigators lacked any social work background and were in over their heads when bodies were uncovered in the cold, detached environment of the morgue. Protocol had been changed to simply viewing the photographs taken by investigators and autopsy assistants, although this was still a difficult task. It did seem much easier for everyone involved in the process. The deceased always looked better after being prepared by the funeral home, which was reiterated to the family left behind: *"You'd rather remember them that way, not the way they are here."*

"Please follow me," Jessalyn said, leading them slowly to the room designed specifically for that purpose. "Doctor Upshaw will be with you momentarily," she said professionally, giving no indication that she and Detective Pitts were anything more than colleagues. "Can I get anyone anything, water, perhaps?" she asked, looking at Ginger.

"That would be nice," Ginger answered as she nervously twisted the shoulder strap on her purse. Her eyes were dry but were red and swollen from her earlier tears. Her hands were trembling slightly, but she'd found some hidden strength during the car ride. "Will I be able to see her soon?" she asked. "I-I really want to get this over with."

"You won't actually see the body here. Doctor Upshaw will show you photographs, and you'll be able to let us know if it's Jasmine or not. Photographs are a lot less...traumatic," Pitts explained.

"Really? I thought I'd get to see her," Ginger said. "I need to see her."

Pitts cleared his throat. "It's important that we find out if it's Jasmine. Let's deal with that first."

Jessalyn tapped on the door, opened it, and handed the water to Ginger. She was much better with paperwork and receptionist duties than dealing with grief. She passed Travis Upshaw as she made her way back to her desk and dropped her gaze toward the floor. Just so awful.

Upshaw tucked the folder containing the eight-by-ten photos Tess had taken under his arm. He was grateful when the family didn't have to see gruesome pictures of a savage murder or suicide by gunshot. It was difficult, at best, to see a loved one gone. He realized the instant he saw the sister it was likely they would have their ID. He reached his hand across the table and introduced himself before taking a seat.

"I'm Doctor Upshaw," he began. "I'm sorry to meet you under such circumstances, but I understand you haven't been able to contact your sister in a few days."

"Yes." Ginger's lower lip and chin began to quiver. "I need to know if she's here."

"There's a high probability she is," he said, breaking the hard truth to her as kindly and gently as he could. "I have some pictures for you to look at. I know this isn't easy, and I must warn you that she won't look completely like herself. She is pale, with a tinge of blue, but it isn't a violent picture. You won't see any blood, cuts, or abrasions."

Ginger squeezed her purse to her chest and shook her head. "I understand, I-I'm ready."

Upshaw slid his chair closer to her and slowly opened the folder.

The first picture was not as close up as the ones to follow, but Ginger gasped when she saw it. "Oh no," she said softly. "That's her, Jasmine. Wh-what happened to her? Please! Please tell me everything."

Travis closed the file without pulling out the remainder of the photos. There was no need to upset the deceased's sister further. He had more information to share, and the headshots would only upset her more. "I'm afraid your sister was strangled," he said, then gave her a moment to let it sink in.

"Strangled, as in…murdered?" she asked, incredulous. "I-I don't understand. No one would've wanted to hurt, Jasmine. You must be mistaken, Doctor."

Travis looked up at Pitts and nodded for him to take over. His job was done, it was up to the detectives to find the killer. "I'm going to leave you with these police officers, Ginger. I've done my part. It's important that you help them do theirs now."

"Wait!" she all but screamed. "I want to see her. Where is she? Take me to her. She needs me," she said, her voice rising into a wailing crescendo.

Chapter Six

JaQuita sat across from Clara's desk with a legal pad in hand. Iris Hadley sat in the chair beside her, attempting to sneak a peek at the many scribbled notes and doodles on the first page.

"Stop it, Miss Iris," Quita scolded. "This is serious business. I was hired as a consultant, and I aim to do my job. I've noticed several things around here that just won't work, and we need to discuss them."

"Iris, the girl is right. There's no need for you to give her notes the once-over," Clara said, glaring at her old friend. "We obviously need some help if this business is going to be successful in today's crazy world. Now, Quita, what have you got for us?"

"Well, first of all—and most importantly—is the rate you're charging folks for your services. It isn't enough, and you're gonna put yourselves out of business. Heck, half the time, Miss Iris doesn't want to charge anybody a dime."

"That's because we get so many sad stories," Iris said defensively. "I know these poor people don't have money to pay us. They just need help to find their children's father, or when their kids are stealing their money for drugs. It's sad, I tell ya."

"You gotta quit being so emotional—plain and simple. They're customers, and we ain't running a charity, Miss Iris. If word gets out that we'll work for nothing, this business will fold in a month. In the streets, people mistake kindness for weakness."

"Well," Iris huffed. "I was just trying to do the right thing."

"You do the right thing for your friends and church folks, not your customers," Quita said.

"Don't be so defensive, Iris," Clara said. "Quita has a valid point. We aren't a government agency or a nonprofit. We're a real business, with real bills to pay. Do you have any suggestions, Quita?"

"Of course. For starters, let me answer all the calls and screen possible cases before they get to you. Some simply won't pay off, and they're a waste of time and resources. Also, we need to charge a consultation fee and get a retainer up front, just like lawyers do. Trust me, these folks have money for an attorney if it's gonna save their ass," she said before quickly cupping her right hand over her mouth. "Oh! Excuse me. That slipped out, but anyway, you get my point."

"But we're not lawyers," Iris said. "We can't expect someone to pay a consultation fee."

"That's where you're wrong," Quita interjected. "I've checked with several reputable private investigation firms in the Southeast, and that's exactly what they do. Otherwise, you'll spend all your time talking to people about what you can do for 'em, and you won't earn a dime. If they're serious, they won't mind plopping down a small consultation fee. Once they have money in the game, you know they won't just walk away."

"I understand," Clara said. "But we aren't reputable yet. We don't have any experience to bring to the table, and clients are going to want references and experience."

"But you've got something no other investigators do," Quita countered.

"And what's that?"

"You're old."

"No, sh—," Iris started before Clara cut her off.

"Iris, please hear her out. Actually, I'm quite impressed with what you've come up with so far, Quita. Tell us more."

"Well, you hired me to do a job, and this gig ain't so bad. So, I'm not gonna blow smoke up your, uh…well, you know what I'm saying. I think it'd be pretty cool if your business did well. Now, with that said, being old has its pros and cons. First, we have to stay away from any cases involving computers and cell phones. You don't know anything about that stuff, so if we come across a potential client who wants to tap into someone's browser history or recover someone's text messages, we'll recommend them to someone else. There's way too much involved in that type of thing, and you've got no time to learn it all now. Besides, all that changes so fast with new technology every day. New phones come out every six months, and computers too. You're good at other things, so we don't need to waste our time on things that aren't your specialty."

"Like what?" Iris asked, feigning interest.

"I know the truth hurts sometimes, Miss Iris, but I'm just trying to help. I may not have a good education, but I know about this type of stuff. I'm not trying to be bossy. No disrespect, but nobody would ever expect you two to be private eyes. I mean, c'mon! Seriously. But, that's the best part. It's your niche, as they say, the thing that makes you stand out from the others. We need to take cases like catching cheating spouses, investigating fraudulent workmen's comp claims, and surveillance. You two are a goldmine."

"How do you know all this stuff?" Iris asked suspiciously.

"You and Miss Clara hired me to be an adviser, so that's what I'm doing. I've been doing some research online, and I have gut instincts of my own. I really think this could work out if we all stay open-minded."

"Okay," Clara said. "What else have you got?"

"I suggest one-hundred, twenty-five bucks an hour."

"What! We could never get that kind of money. Where did you come up with that figure?" Clara asked, her eyes wide.

"Like I said, I've been Googling it."

"Doing what?" Iris asked. "Sounds painful."

"Very funny," Quita said, rolling her eyes at the old, snarky woman. "I've been doing some comparing with other agencies. The costs range from eighty to one-hundred, fifty dollars an hour. Those charging just eighty dollars also charge for expenses, which includes everything from gas to food to printing photos. That's a real pain in the ass. Sorry for the language, ladies, but I'm not gonna sugarcoat anything. If we go that route, we'd have to keep track of all those expenses, with receipts and everything like an accountant. That takes up time we don't need to waste because we can just charge more, to begin with, so it'll all be included in the price. The agencies that charge a hundred an hour just go ahead and figure expenses in their price. Then you don't have to haggle over the little stuff like filling up your tank. You know what I mean?"

"Yeah, we get it, but even if the average private investigator charges one-hundred dollars an hour," Clara chimed in. "How can we charge that much when we're so inexperienced? We're rookies. What might take them four hours could take us two days."

"Maybe, but you two have to work as a team. It's dangerous out there, and since you'll both be undercover, watching each other's backs, your customers are really getting a two-for-one deal. Of course, I can't go with you because that'd be a dead giveaway. Why would I be hanging out with two old white ladies in the 'hood?"

"Gee, that's nice," Iris blurted.

Quita shrugged. "Just keeping it real. What I'm really getting at is that your clients will be paying the same rate for two investigators as they'd pay for one anywhere else."

"I see your point," Iris interjected, with more enthusiasm than ever. "How do we get all these customers? Can your Googler help us with that?"

"Actually, yes. It's gonna take more than a sign on the window and a number in the Yellow Pages. That stuff's old-fashioned, and most people don't even use phone books anymore. You need a website, some business cards, and flyers, and a Facebook page, just to get started."

"That sounds expensive," Clara said. "We don't want to invest a great deal more money. We can't, really."

"It doesn't have to be top-notch just yet, but it has to be done. You'll need to get somebody to help us with the website. I can do the Facebook page, it's free. If you don't get up with the times, you're not gonna make it. It takes money to make money," Quita said, like some kind of budding entrepreneur. "I'm also thinking about talking to some of the other agencies."

"What for?" Clara asked. "They're our competition."

"Well, maybe if we agree to send them some cases we can't handle, they'll do the same for us. They call it quid pro quo."

"What does that mean?" Iris asked.

"You scratch my back, and I'll scratch yours."

"So, let's get this straight," Clara said. "We let you deal with the clients first. You talk to them on the phone, and if you think it's something we can handle, you pass them to us."

"Right."

"I think we can give it a try. What do we have to lose? It's not like we're turning customers away, right?"

Iris resisted the urge to continue the banter. "I'm going to put on a pot of coffee. It's just nine o'clock, and it appears it's gonna be a long day."

Just as she was pulling out the coffee filters, the phone rang, and Quita walked back to her desk to answer it. "Hadley and Samples, Private Investigations," she said, sounding quite professional. After a brief pause, she continued, "I'm sorry, but I need to find out more before I put you through to one of them. They're busy with cases at the moment. So, I have to determine if we can help you." She patted the top of her head coarsely with her right hand.

41

Clara and Iris had recently learned that the gesture relieved the itching and tightness on her scalp from her long braids. They waited intently as Quita argued with the person on the other end of the line.

"I understand you know them personally, but they're very busy women. It's my job to screen all calls before I send them through." She rolled her eyes in defiance and let out a heavy sigh. "Okay, okay...just a moment." She put the call on hold and turned to Clara. "It's Daisy from J and L Sub Shop. She says she's a friend of yours and needs a favor, says you owe her one."

Chapter Seven

Nettles and Pitts had spent the better part of the week interviewing fellow students and coworkers of nineteen-year-old Jasmine Baines, only to come up with nothing—not one thing out of the ordinary and nothing the least bit suspicious from anyone who knew her. It was frustrating, but it wouldn't be the first random act of violence that they'd worked.

It took her sister, Ginger, nine days to come up with the money to bury her. Both detectives donned suits and left work early to attend the memorial service. It was common for them to make such appearances on behalf of the victims of their cases. It never got easier, but they laid low and tried desperately to blend in with grieving family and friends. They were there to support the family and to pay their respects, but there was another reason: wakes and interments often told much more than one would think.

Although psychiatrists frequently reiterated the vast scope of how people displayed their grief, the officers recognized odd behavior when they saw it. They'd spoken with Ginger at length and hoped she would heed their words. It was important for her, even in her sorrow, to take note of everyone there, to make a mental note if she noticed any strangers among the bereaved or perhaps the conspicuous absence of someone who was important to her sister.

Both men took a seat on the second-to-last pew and did their best not to look like two detectives scoping out a group of grief-stricken, innocent people. They stood on cue as the family entered and took their seats in the front two rows marked with white ribbons. Ginger walked in with a middle-aged couple, each of them clutching one of her arms as she sobbed quietly into a cloth handkerchief. Pitts discreetly elbowed Nettles. They both silently wondered who they were, since Ginger had made it clear her parents were no longer part of her life. She'd made no mention of any aunt and uncle taking them in. Several young women about the same ages as Ginger and Jasmine, followed behind, dabbing their eyes in an attempt to salvage their eyeliner and mascara.

Bringing up the rear was a woman who appeared to be in her fifties but was likely much younger. She had the gaunt, deflated look of someone who had battled drug addiction for many years. Her hair was clean, although thin and unkempt. Her roots were gray, but the ends were bleached blonde. It appeared to have been quite some time since she'd last had a proper dye job. Nettles and Pitts assumed she was the girls' mother. She had red, puffy eyes, and, without a handkerchief to dab her tears, she used the sleeve of her wrinkled dress to wipe them from her face. Ginger had clearly chosen to leave her alone in her grief, and the detectives couldn't blame her. She'd had many chances to be the mother the girls needed and now those chances were lost, at least with Jasmine.

A minister followed two solemn hymns with a generic sermon and eulogy. He encouraged forgiveness for whoever had committed the heinous crime and prayed for comfort for Ginger's and Jasmine's friends. The service was over in twenty minutes.

Pitts had been through grim scenarios many times, but he still couldn't help thinking about how tragic the whole ordeal was, from the senseless murder to the brief funeral summarizing a short, unfulfilled life. He and Nettles would do everything they could to solve the case, but Pitts was aware that the odds were against them. Unless the system later identified the DNA, or the murderer was brazened enough to strike again, the chances of finding the killer were getting slimmer by the day.

The organ blared as the funeral director rolled the casket down the aisle, followed by the small group of family, then the congregation. It was a sparse crowd, mostly young people who either worked with Jasmine or attended the Art Institute. Both men were surprised to see Stuart Mason, the cemetery sexton among the mourners. They'd decided prior to the funeral not to attend the interment at the cemetery but changed their minds and lined up with the other vehicles to ride in the procession when they spotted his familiar face.

The cemetery was less than a mile away. A green velvet tent, bearing the funeral home name, was set up near the rear of the property, and three gravediggers waited beside their aged, rusty backhoe.

The minister bowed his head to say a brief prayer, then shook the hands of those seated under the tent. The cemetery workers hovered over the attendees in the hopes they'd leave in time for them to lower the casket, refill the gaping hole, and make it to lunch at a decent hour. Ginger placed her hand on the cold, metal coffin before being led away by the older couple.

Pitts and Nettles made their way over to the sexton. "Good afternoon, Mister Mason," Pitts said. "I wasn't expecting to see you here."

"Me neither, I saw the obituary in the paper and felt I should come. Figured it's the least I could do. I ain't been able to get that young girl off my mind. Can't even ride past that section of the cemetery."

"Yeah, it's a tough one," Nettles said, surprising Pitts with his sympathetic tone. "It's never easy when such a young life is taken."

"Have you found out anything…about the person who did this?" Stuart asked.

"Nope, still investigating. She was a good girl. We can't find anyone who would've wanted to lay a finger on her, let alone do this."

Stuart fumbled through his pocket for his pack of cigarettes. "You s'pose you could let me know when y'all find the son-of-a-bitch who did this? I don't think I'll ever forget it."

Nettles gave him a firm pat on the shoulder and assured him he would.

Chapter Eight

Clara and Iris exchanged a knowing glance. They did, indeed, owe Daisy a favor. She'd helped them when they were assisting the doctor's wife in her escape months earlier. Clara worked for the doctor, and the two ladies had risked their lives to help his young wife get away from him. In the end, he was shot and killed by the FBI, and sweet Lizzie was now living the life she deserved in Biloxi, Mississippi. It'd had a favorable ending, but both women were keenly and humbly aware it could've just as easily taken a devastating turn.

"I'll take it," Clara said as she picked up the receiver. "Good morning, Daisy. I understand you may need our services." She poised her pen over a notepad and listened intently. "Mm-hmm, yes…I understand," she said as she scribbled notes on the page. "We'll need to talk to her, Daisy. Can she come into the office?"

Iris leaned forward in anticipation, struggling to make some sense of her partner's sloppy notes.

Clara gave Iris a disapproving look and shooed her away like a bothersome fly. "I understand that she doesn't want to drive, but it won't work for us to go to her house. That'd be a dead giveaway. Can we meet her somewhere?" Clara asked as frustration began to show on her face. "Absolutely not, Daisy. We will not go as visitors to her Sunday school class. If she doesn't trust us, she's picked the wrong investigators, and—"

Quita reached for the phone, temporarily interrupting the conversation, but Clara held up her hand in protest.

"Okay, okay, we'll meet her at Sarah's Diner at noon. Yes, I'm aware that they have their chicken-and-dumplings special today." Clara wrote the time on the pad and in an attempt to end the call, promised to order the daily special.

"What was that all about?" Iris asked as soon as the receiver was placed back in its cradle.

"Apparently, Daisy's friend is convinced that her son's fiancée is seeing another man. She's determined to find proof so she can stop the wedding before it happens. I'm not sure if it's a case of infidelity or if she just doesn't approve of the girl. At any rate, it looks like we've got ourselves a case, ladies."

"This will be great practice," Quita interjected. "We've got about two-and-a-half hours before you have to meet her. That gives us just enough time to trade in those flip phones for a couple of iPhones."

"Why? There's absolutely nothing wrong with the phone I have," Iris said adamantly. "I have all my numbers stored in it, and I'm not going through that hassle again."

"How many numbers do you have in there, Iris?" Quita asked as she struggled against a grin.

"I don't recall," Iris said. "But it took me a long enough time to get them in that blasted gadget, and I see no reason to do it again."

"Well, I've got some good news for you," Quita said. "The Verizon store will download them from your old phone to your new one in a matter of seconds. Hassle-free, I promise."

"There is nothing wrong with our phones, Quita," Clara said. "I don't see any reason to spend unnecessary money."

"Oh, but it is necessary, Miss Clara. Not only will the new phones work like minicomputers, but they have cameras too. You'll be amazed by all they can do. Trust me on this one. Remember what I said? It takes money to make money."

Clara let out a defeated sigh. "Okay, fine, let's do it."

At 9:30 in the morning, they walked out of the Verizon store with new phones in hand and all their numbers properly stored.

"There, don't you feel better now?" Quita said, grinning at them.

"I'm not so sure about that," Iris said, looking at her phone in confusion. "Will one of these buttons teach me how to operate the thing? Or maybe I can just ask it with that voice business the man tried to show me."

Quita laughed. "Well, the business plan for your cell service will save you money," she insisted. "And you can always reach me for help, anytime, day or night."

"Not if we can't figure out how to call you on this newfangled nonsense!" Clara teased, waving her iPhone around in the air.

47

Chapter Nine

Detectives Pitts and Nettles sat in their cluttered cubicles, discussing their unsolved case. The office was unoccupied by other staff, so they talked freely from one workspace to the other.

"It's not good, Nettles," Pitts said as he rummaged through the scattered papers on his desk. "We've come up empty on every angle we've looked into. It had to be random. The poor girl was in the wrong place at the wrong time. Her debit and credit cards are clean with nothing glaringly different from the prior statements. Her friends and family don't know of anyone new in her life, and she never shared with anyone that she was afraid of anybody or anything. Her schedule hadn't changed, she never missed class, and she never called in to work. All the calls on her cell phone were placed to the same people she always called. She was a beautiful, smart girl and well-liked with no known enemies."

"I know. That's what concerns me," Nettles piped up.

"What, that she didn't have any enemies?"

"Yes, because that can't be true."

"How so?"

"Well, pretty girls always have enemies. Even if they don't know or deserve them. Girls are jealous, and guys resent girls they can't get. Besides, I can't get away from the thought of her being bundled up in that blanket in the cemetery."

"Yeah, that was odd. No one knows of her having a boyfriend, and I'm sure her sister would've been aware of it if she did. That knocks out the theory of an abusive boyfriend with conscience enough to cover her and leave her to be found somewhere."

"Maybe she had a stalker she wasn't aware of," Nettles suggested.

"But she was familiar with her coworkers and neighbors. Seems as though they would've noticed if someone was following her around or playing Peeping Tom."

"You know stalkers are a different breed, man, real sorry sons-of-bitches. They even have television shows about 'em now. Disgusting."

Before Pitts could answer, he was interrupted by the phone on his desk. "Pitts," he said, then paused momentarily. "Yeah, send her up."

"Who?" Nettles asked as he wheeled his desk chair around the cubicle, to the opening of Pitts' cramped space.

"Speak of the devil, I guess. Ginger's here. Maybe she has something else for us. I'm gonna meet her at the elevator. Bring your notepad, and I'll see you in the conference room."

Pitts was waiting at the elevator when the doors whooshed open. Ginger was the only occupant, and she stepped out quickly and extended her hand. She looked tired and much thinner than she had at the funeral.

Pitts met her small hand with his own and motioned in the direction of the meeting room. "Good morning," he said. "We can talk in here," he continued as he opened the door. "You remember Detective Nettles, don't you?"

"Yes," Ginger answered quietly as she rolled out a chair and sat down. "Do you have anything else on the case? Any new leads?"

"We were just discussing Jasmine's case," Pitts said. "Unfortunately, we don't have anything new. This crime appears to be random, which makes it more difficult to solve. We're waiting on the DNA results from the GBI, but they've got a long backlog. I'm sorry, but I can't even estimate a timeline right now," he continued as he leaned forward and made eye contact, in an attempt to display his sincerity. "We really want to solve this case, Ginger, but I have to be honest with you. Even with the DNA, we'll need a hit to determine who it belongs to. We're doing all we can, but I wanted to be truthful with you. I was hoping you might have something else to share with us."

Ginger shook her head and looked at him, her blue eyes weary and full of emotion. "I don't, it just doesn't make any sense, Detective. There was nothing odd going on with her. We were very close. She shared everything with me."

"Had she made any new friends recently?" Nettles asked.

"No, she liked everyone she worked with and the people from the Art Institute, but Jasmine rarely spent time with friends. She was so busy between her schoolwork and waitressing, that she had very little free time for socializing or dating. When she did have a day off or a break from school, she spent it with me. God, I miss her so much."

Nettles listened intently and paused briefly before continuing, "Ginger, if ya don't mind my asking. Who was the older couple who sat with you at the funeral?"

49

"Oh, they're Colleen and Charles Walker. They were our foster parents for the last few years we were in foster care. As I told you before, several couples showed interest in adopting Jasmine and me, but our mother always popped up and fought to stop it. We went from home to home until the Walkers took us in. I only lived with them for two years, but Jasmine stayed with them for three more years after I graduated. They were the closest thing to parents the two of us ever had. They kept in touch with us even after Jasmine graduated from high school and moved into her apartment. They're taking her death extremely hard."

Nettles squirmed uncomfortably in his chair. "Was that your mother who walked in behind you at the funeral?"

Embarrassment briefly flashed across the troubled woman's face, but then her eyes took on a hardened, fierce glare. "Yes, yes, it was. I'm not sure how she found out about it, but she didn't hear it from me. What nerve she had to show up to Jasmine's funeral! As if being murdered wasn't horrible enough for Jasmine, that woman had the audacity to come to her funeral and pretend to shed a tear."

Nettles and Pitts shared sideways glances as the three sat in awkward silence.

Finally, Pitts ventured out on the proverbial limb. "I can't begin to imagine what your life has been like," he started, "but in my personal opinion, her grief did appear sincere. Drug addicts do a lot of horrible things, especially to those they love, but perhaps one day, you two can mend some of the hurt."

The beautiful blue eyes shot a hateful glare at Pitts. "You're right," Ginger said coolly. "You can't imagine what our lives were like. That woman is nothing more to me than a stranger on the street."

A hard knock on the door interrupted the awkwardness of the moment. Katie Swanson peeked around the door, sticking her head in before stepping inside. She was one of the best administrative assistants in the department, but lately, her personality had been gravely lacking. She was six months pregnant with twins, and her belly resembled an oversized beach ball. Her swollen ankles were often the topic of her many complaints. On this day, her curly, brown locks were pulled carelessly into a bun with an ink pen stuck through the middle to hold it in place. She hadn't taken the time to apply makeup, and thick eyeglasses replaced her normal contact lenses. Her expression mirrored frustration.

"Good morning, Katie," Nettles said with an overabundance of enthusiasm that successfully pissed her off.

"What's good about it?" she hissed at him. "I'm trapped in this body from hell, and still have to work to pay my rent. Have you seen the size of my ankles?"

Nettles seemed pleased with himself and let out a hearty laugh.

Pitts could see where the conversation was going and realized it wasn't appropriate with Ginger sitting there, so he intervened. "What's up, Ms. Swanson?" he asked.

"Captain Burke is looking for you two. There's been a shooting over off Howell Mill."

"All right, tell him we'll be right there," Nettles said as he folded up his notepad and placed a pen in his front shirt pocket.

"I guess you're moving on to your next case then?" Ginger said as she looked over at Pitts.

"Ginger, this doesn't mean we've forgotten your sister. We'll continue to look into every lead, and there's always the possibility that we'll get a hit on that DNA. They were able to get a fairly large amount, and if we can link it to anyone out there, we'll get them," he reassured her.

He'd purposefully left out that the tissue found under Jasmine's nails was from clawing at both her attacker and her own neck in a desperate struggle for air and survival. That would've been a horrible thought for Ginger to live with but was actually a blessing in disguise for the detectives. If there was ever a match to the DNA, they'd have their killer, and the evidence would be overwhelming. But meanwhile, they had to grab their fedoras and head to their next murder investigation.

Chapter Ten

Armed with their new cell phones and extensive directions on how to use them, Clara and Iris left the office for their first day of official surveillance. Daisy's friend Nancy had given them pages and pages of information on her daughter-in-law-to-be, and it appeared they'd be busy with the case for several days.

"I just want you to know up front that you could be wasting your money," Iris told Nancy flatly. "There's no guarantee she's fooling around."

The warning had fallen on deaf ears. Nancy insisted the girl was up to no good. "She's just after my son's money, plain and simple," she reiterated over and over again.

"What does your son do for a living?" Clara asked.

"My Lewis is a very talented boy," his mother contended. "He paints and can repair just about anything. He does beautiful yard work, even some power washing. Has his own equipment for it, too."

Clara literally gasped when Iris dared to ask, "So your boy Lewis is a handyman? Is that what you're saying?"

Nancy's face turned crimson as she scrambled to explain, "My son's services are very much in demand."

"If he's a day laborer, of sorts, what does this girl have to gain by marrying him?" Iris persisted. "Is there a great deal of property and money involved?"

In the end, Nancy refused to delve into her delightful son's finances, but she did say she was certain they'd come up with something incriminating on his gold-digging bride-to-be.

The Buick had a full tank of gas, both women had used the little girls' room, and their thermoses were full of fresh coffee. Quita had given them all the advice she could and reiterated numerous times for them to call her if they had any questions. It was really an easy assignment, but it was their first experience with surveillance, and she couldn't help worrying about the endearing old investigators. She was growing quite fond of them and loved her new job.

"That Nancy's a real piece of work," Iris said as soon as they pulled out of the parking lot. "Sounds a little creepy if you ask me. Every mother has to let go sometimes. I bet that boy doesn't even have health insurance, just going from one honey-do job to the next. What would any woman want with a so-called man like that in the first place? I tell ya, my Freddie always took care of me. He had a steady paycheck with retirement and health and life insurance to boot. I did hair to give me something to do."

"Let's not be too judgmental, Iris," Clara said. "Maybe Nancy has some valid concerns, or maybe she doesn't, but this is a good experience for us to make some money. It may not be the most exciting case, but at least it gets us out of the office."

"I don't understand a thing about these phones," Iris mumbled as she poked and prodded her new iPhone. "Who comes up with this stuff? Who the hell needs a computer on their phone? We're just throwing good money after bad if you ask me."

"I'm not sure why everyone is so obsessed with them, but I trust Quita, and we've got a lot of updating to do. Just give it a chance, Iris. You are so hardheaded sometimes."

The long silence that followed let Clara know Iris was not happy with her. Quita had told them how to program the GPS, but they decided against it in the end. It was all too new for them. Instead, they had gone the rather old-school way, printing off a map and turn-by-turn directions from MapQuest, yet another thing Quita had shown them. Iris defiantly interjected when they needed to make a turn, slowly coming out of her tantrum.

"Summer works as a receptionist for a reputable insurance company," Clara said. "The fact that she works lets us know she isn't just looking for someone to take care of her."

"Maybe she doesn't want to continue working," Iris said.

"Well, I don't suspect she'll live too high off the hog with Nancy's son," Clara added as she spotted the insurance office and pulled into a parking space at the Dollar General across the street.

"Not a bad spot," Iris confessed as she pulled the pictures of Summer out of her purse and inspected them. "She's quite a looker. I don't understand what she sees in that son of Nancy's. From the pictures she showed us on her mantel, he isn't much to look at."

"Iris Hadley!" Clara exclaimed as she feigned a look of shock before chuckling out loud.

"Please, Clara. We may be old women, but we aren't blind, and we know if a man has what it takes. Now, I'm the first to admit that some bald, older fellas are handsome, but it's the stage in between that's a major turnoff. I don't see anything attractive about a ring of hair around a man's head when he's lost all of it off the top."

"At least he didn't attempt to sport a comb-over," Clara said, as both women burst into laughter.

"You know, this might not be so bad after all," Iris said as she settled back in her seat and removed her seatbelt.

"Not so quick," Clara said, looking across the street. "I think that's her coming out."

Both women craned their necks to get a better look.

"I think you're right," Iris said. "Yep, that's her, getting in that red two-door. Crank 'er up, Clara. We've got a live one!"

"Write the time down, Iris," Clara instructed as she slowly pulled the Sedan out to follow Summer.

"I'm in charge of the notes," Iris said. "You concentrate on driving and staying out of her field of vision like Quita said. Stay a few car lengths behind if you can."

Having no idea that she was being tailed, Summer casually pulled into the bank to make a transaction at the drive-thru window before stopping at a nearby Dairy Queen for lunch.

"I sure do wish we could grab a chili dog. Their onion rings aren't too bad either," Iris commented.

"We can't chance her seeing us. We've got a good visual on her now, and she's alone. We need to stay in the car, but if she meets someone later and gets distracted, we can go in."

For over an hour, the two women watched as Summer ate her burger and fries, refilled her drink twice, and talked on her cell phone.

"Oh, for the love of Pete," Iris groaned. "Since when do lunch breaks last the whole afternoon? That never happened in my day!"

"Does it matter?" Clara asked. "Do I need to remind you we're on the clock?"

"Right, anyway, here she comes," Iris said with a yawn.

Summer drove straight back to work, and the women parked in the Walmart parking lot a couple of blocks away.

"Nancy said she gets off at five o'clock," Clara said. "I say we ride by a few times and come back closer to closing time. What do you think?"

"I agree, I don't see why she'd take a long lunch if she was planning on leaving right away. I'll check in with Quita and let her know what's going on."

Later that night, after 10:00, Clara pulled into Iris's driveway and let her out.

"Want to come in for a glass of wine?" Iris invited.

"Not tonight, I'm exhausted. Honestly! I wasn't this tired when I worked on my feet every day."

"I know what you mean," Iris said. "We can discuss everything with Quita in the morning. I'm gonna take a hot bath and hit the sack."

"If I didn't know any better, I'd say our Girl Friday's growing on you," Clara said.

"She's a little too bossy for my taste," Iris said as she got out of the car.

Clara smiled as she drove two driveways down to her own house. It had been a good day and a good beginning for Hadley and Samples Investigations. She fell asleep with a satisfied smile on her face.

Chapter Eleven

Detective Pitts felt like kicking himself in the ass for letting Nettles drive to the crime scene. He certainly knew better based on their history of narrow escapes, as Nettles swerved aggressively in and out of traffic on Atlanta's many busy streets. "You know, Nettles, they're already dead. There's no need to rush. We won't be needed for CPR," he admonished.

"Just because you drive like my grandmother doesn't mean I have to. How can so many idiots be in one place?" he grumbled at the other drivers as he gripped the steering wheel and leaned forward in his seat. He blared his horn as if that might somehow make a difference. "It's not the growing population that contributes to this traffic. It's the DMV's fault. Why in the hell do they issue licenses to these people? Half these folks need to be taken in on traffic charges, I tell ya."

"I was just thinking the same thing myself," Pitts said snidely as he held onto the dashboard and braced himself. "I'm grateful you're on lead with this one. That's a lot less paperwork for me."

"Yeah, you got that right." Nettles pulled into the crowded strip mall. "Just had to happen right around lunchtime, though, didn't it?" he mumbled. "Now we'll have to deal with every *Nosy Nellie* out here."

"They're back there in the far corner," Pitts said, pointing in the direction of the crowd. "Geesh, already a bunch of onlookers. The first responders need to do a better job of crowd control."

Nettles honked his horn several times before the crowd parted to allow the unmarked car through. The victim appeared to be slumped in the driver's seat of a gold Chevrolet Caprice that sported an amateur paint job. It was the kind of large, older, four-door vehicle that was quite popular among young gang members.

Nettles muttered under his breath when he saw Dr. Gail Duffey. "Great, it would be her when I'm in the lead," he said sarcastically. "I can't stand that bi—"

"You never learned how to whisper, did you, Nettles? Or even keep things to yourself?" Pitts said as he scowled at his partner. He, along with everyone else in the department were well aware of the animosity between the two. The whole problem was that they were too much alike. Gail was a good medical examiner, but she was hotheaded and blunt, just like Nettles. The two often butted heads when they had cases together, and Pitts wasn't looking forward to this one.

"What've we got, Doc?" Nettles said as he pushed his weight through the throng of spectators.

Dr. Duffey was squatting down beside the victim, with the driver's door open. "Clean shot to the head and one to the chest. The headshot killed him instantly, but the chest would have done the job, too. Either way, his heart would've stopped before he ever reached the hospital."

Long, thick dreadlocks blocked the view of the black male's face. All the detectives could see was a limp arm hanging from the vehicle.

"Got any I.D.?" Pitts asked.

"Yeah," Gail answered without looking up. "His girlfriend's over there, along with another male, both passengers in the vehicle at the time of the shooting," she said as she pointed toward the growing crowd of bystanders. "She can give you the information. You can't miss her. I swear that baby's gonna pop out any minute."

"I'd better go talk to her then," Nettles said. "I glanced through the passenger-side window. There's a few dime-bags of weed on the floorboard. I'll get I.D. over here to take photos before we collect it."

Gail Duffey didn't respond but continued bagging the limp, lifeless hands, before standing back for the investigators to take their pictures. Duffey was in her mid-forties and had never been married. Nettles always said it was because she was a lesbian, but he had no proof. She had milky-white skin that clashed drastically with her dyed black hair, which she wore in a short, spiky style. Her eyebrows were plucked into thin, arched lines that made her appear as if she were questioning what everyone said to her. That, among other things, drove Nettles mad every time he had a conversation with her, so much so that he felt it was an attempt to personally mock him as if she fashioned her brows that way simply to irritate him. Duffey's expression often reflected frustration, which made her virtually unapproachable unless absolutely necessary—another quality she shared with her nemesis, Detective Nettles.

The girlfriend was indeed easy to spot. She was short, barely tipping five-two, and her swollen belly looked as though it might explode at any time. She was screaming piercingly into her cell phone while she massaged her back with her other hand.

Nettles tapped her on the shoulder and displayed his badge. "Ma'am, we need to speak with you. Can you disconnect the call?"

She was clearly unimpressed with the badge and his professional request to put the phone away. She turned her back and continued to scream profanities and harsh threats into the cell.

"Ma'am!" Nettles barked, his patience quickly wearing thin. "Get off the phone. We need to speak with you...now," he said, his tone harsh and his voice deep enough to finally get the frantic woman's attention.

"I'll call you back," she snapped, putting the phone in her knock-off designer purse and turning to face the detective. "Yeah? Like, what can you do for me *now*?" she snapped. "Tony's *dead*. Ain't nothin' nobody can do, not you or your cheap-ass badge."

Nettles gave Pitts the look he always gave him right before he went off, so Pitts stepped in front of him and took over. "Ma'am, we need to speak with you. It'd be best to do it here, but if not, we'll have to take you to the station. What's your pleasure?"

She turned and looked through the crowd until she spotted someone she knew. "G-boy!" she yelled. "Get over here, would ya? These bitches 'bout to take me to the station!"

Nettles reached for his cuffs, but Pitts waved him off. The crowd was growing, and the last thing they needed was an angry mob accusing them of police brutality.

The young man walked up slowly, holding his palms up and facing Pitts showing him, he was unarmed. "Yo, man, they killed him. They took Tony out, man."

"I understand you were in the car with him?" Pitts said.

"Yeah."

"Okay, in that case, we need to talk to you and the female. Can you step over here, or do we need to go down to the station? The sooner we get some details, the sooner we'll locate the shooter."

"I'll go over there." He pointed, then whispered something to the female.

She followed him, massaging her wide back with both hands as they walked.

Nettles stomped hurriedly back to the car. His face was red with contempt when he turned to face the two eyewitnesses. "What the hell's going on?" he asked. "I mean, you were with this fella, and you don't even want to help us find who's behind this. What gives?"

"We already know who's behind it," the young girl said blandly. "We'll take care of it ourselves. We don't need the cops."

The male shot her a hard look that indicated she needed to keep her mouth shut.

"What's your name, Ma'am?" Pitts asked.

"Platinum. I'm pregnant, in case you smart-ass detectives failed to detect that. I need to get back to the house."

"I can see that," Pitts continued. "But it doesn't get you out of answering our questions. Like I said before, we can talk here or at the precinct."

"What do ya want to know?" she asked, rolling her eyes.

"For starters, who the hell shot this man?" Nettles seethed. "And second, what's wrong with you? And finally, were you in the car with him or not?"

"I was," she said defiantly, but offered nothing further.

"I say we haul both their stubborn asses back to the station," Nettles said to Pitts. "I'm done with this."

"Yo, man, it ain't like that," the male said, stepping forward.

"Well, maybe you should tell us what it's like then," Nettles snapped. "What's your name? And I don't mean on the streets."

"Germaine…Germaine Wilkins. Tony was my homeboy. We've known each other since we was kids, man. This ain't right."

This time, it was the girl's turn to send a threatening glance. "You don't have to say anything to these clowns," she insisted, pressing her bulging belly in his direction. "We got this, G."

"That's it," Nettles said, motioning for one of the patrolmen. "We're about to take a ride, Ma'am, whether you like it or not."

Platinum was clearly not happy about it, but Pitts wasn't sure what was making her more nervous, going back to the station or leaving Germaine there to explain what had happened to Tony.

Once she was handcuffed and in the back of the patrol car, Germaine seemed more at ease. They walked toward the gold Caprice stopping just short of it. The bloody scene made him cringe, but he didn't insist on being questioned out of sight of it.

"So, what went down?" Nettles asked.

"We were riding around—ya know, just chillin'."

"Chillin' and getting rid of a few dime-bags?"

"Something like that. Tony's a good dude…er, he was, I mean. Nobody had a beef with him."

"Apparently somebody did," Nettles countered. "Who shot him?"

"Some dude, a Hispanic guy. He tapped on the window, and Tony rolled it down. I just thought he wanted some weed, ya know?"

"And that was when he started shooting?"

"No, he didn't say anything at first. Tony got pissed and asked what his problem was. That was when he pulled out the nine."

"As in nine-millimeter?"

"Yeah, a Glock with an extended clip. I saw it when he took it from his back waistband, but it was too late, man. I couldn't do nothing."

"Where were you sitting in the car?" Pitts asked.

"In the back, right behind Tony. There wasn't no way to stop him."

"So, Platinum was in the front?"

"Yep."

"How did the shooter miss her?"

"He wasn't after us, man. It was obvious he was out for Tony. He didn't even have a chance to get to his piece. Man, my boy was hit before he even saw it coming."

"Okay, I buy that," Nettles said. "What happened after he fired the shots?"

"It was so weird. Like, I was in shock or somethin'. He had that big clip, but he only fired two shots, like he knew to put one only in his head and chest. They was both kill shots if ya know what I mean. I watched it all. There wasn't even time to close my eyes."

"And where did this Hispanic shooter go after the shots?" Nettles pressed.

"He walked right over there to that cement wall, then jumped over it and was just…gone. He didn't run or nothin'. He just jumped over it and that was it."

"So, you didn't run after him?"

"No, I know I shoulda, but I still couldn't believe it. I jumped out of the car, but I knew Tony was dead. I couldn't help him," Germaine said.

"And what was Platinum doing? I can't believe this didn't throw her into labor," Pitts commented.

"She didn't freak out as bad as I did. She was shocked too, but like usual, hers came out as anger. She was screaming and cussing, even hittin' other cars in the parking lot."

"She didn't seem frightened?" Pitts asked incredulously. "What was her relationship with, Tony?"

"He's the baby daddy if that's what you're askin', but they weren't uh…how do people say it? Magmonomus?"

"You mean monogamous…exclusive?"

"Right, they just hung out, kicked it, and hooked up from time to time. Ya know?"

"So, she wasn't scared, didn't even cry over the death of her baby's father?"

"She's a tough one," Germaine said with a shrug. "I don't mean to make it sound like she don't care. I mean, I'm sure…she's upset, but everything comes outta her with anger or… look, man, I don't even know what I'm sayin'. So much was going on. It seems like the cops got here just a minute or two after it happened."

"This is a pretty popular place," Nettles said. "Especially at lunchtime. Do you have a license?"

"Yeah, but it's suspended."

"Then you shouldn't mind if I hold on to it for a few days," Nettles said, gesturing for Germaine to hand it over. "Where can I find you if I have any more questions?"

"The address on there's my granddaddy's. If I'm not there, Platinum knows where to find me."

"We need to finish this crime scene, Germaine. We'll be in touch. Thank you for your help," Pitts said.

The two detectives gave him a few minutes to disappear into the crowd before they spoke.

"I don't know about you, but I buy his story," Nettles said. "He seems genuinely upset."

"Yeah, he does. Did you notice how relieved he was when you had Platinum taken away? I get the feeling he's afraid of her."

"Me too. I'd better check with Duffey. She might be packing up."

"What've you got?" Pitts asked the ME as they walked up. "Pretty cut and dry?"

"Well, it was definitely a hit. He was taken off guard. Two shots were fired, both deadly. The second one was just for assurance, but the shooter knew right where to put it."

Nettles leaned over and examined the car's interior. It was a bloody mess, but the body had been removed and was en route to the Fulton

County Medical Examiner's Office. "I still see the weed, but where's the vic's weapon?"

"I didn't see any weapons," Duffey answered. "Other than the grass there wasn't much in the vehicle. We found a couple of CDs and left them there."

"That's odd," Nettles said. "The other male in the car said the vic didn't even have time to reach for his piece to defend himself. How many unarmed dope dealers do you know, Pitts?"

"None, maybe we should've kept Germaine around a little longer."

"I'll have the weed handed over as evidence. I'm anxious to get back and talk to that pregnant girl."

Pitts insisted on driving back to the office and much to his surprise, Nettles was too busy running the scene back and forth in his mind to argue about it.

Once they arrived, Officer Jackson was standing outside the interview room, wearing an agitated expression. "You two are gonna have your hands full with this one," he said, motioning toward the door in frustration. "She's a trip, cursed and spat the entire ride here. If I wasn't so damn hungry, I would've booked her."

"I appreciate you," Nettles said. "Go grab some grub, we'll take it from here."

Jackson saluted him and let out a chuckle. "Be careful, boys, she's a live one."

Platinum was on her cell phone when they entered the room but disconnected the call right away. "This ain't right. Y'all don't got no right to hold me here like I'm on lockdown. My lawyer's on his way."

Both detectives knew better but didn't say so.

Pitts started the interrogation. He always took his mother's sage advice. "You can catch more flies with honey than with vinegar." If the honey didn't do it, he'd send Nettles in with the vinegar. "You're not under arrest," he said. "We're trying to find your friend's killer, and I'm sure you're anxious to help us. Time is critical."

"Pssshhh," she spat, putting her hand up. "Why are you actin' like you give a damn about, Tony? We ain't nothin' to you cops. You'd just as soon we'd all shoot each other in the damn streets."

"That's not true. You said you know who the shooter is. I realize you may want to take justice into your own hands, but you're expecting a child. I'm sure you'd rather be free to raise that baby, rather than looking at him or her from behind bars. Surely you don't want your child to live without his daddy and his mom."

The thought of her impending delivery seemed to give her pause. She sat back in the chair and exhaled deeply. "You got a soda or something?"

Nettles jumped up and was back with a Coke in seconds.

"It was Lil' D, from the Rollin' 60s. He's been after Tony for selling weed in his territory. The Crips have always had a beef with the Bloods anyway. They don't need drugs to shoot somebody up."

Nettles couldn't hold his peace any longer. "So, you actually know the guy's name, and you're just now telling us? What the hell!?" he scolded loudly, wagging his index finger at her. "That doesn't make a damn bit of sense!"

"Look, man, I don't need some Crip shooting up me or my place. You must not know much about gang life. It's rough out there."

"In fact," Nettles said, as his face grew crimson, "I know a helluva lot about gang violence, and one thing I know for sure is that I've *never* seen a man shot up over a dime bag of weed."

"Okay, okay," Pitts said, scooting his chair closer to the young woman. "After Lil' D shot your friend, where'd he go?"

She shrugged. "Who knows? He got in his car and drove off. What'd you expect him to do wait for the cops to show up?"

"No, certainly not," Pitts answered calmly. "What kind of car was he driving?"

"I don't know, it was kinda big."

"Do you remember the color?"

"Dark, black maybe."

"Good, that helps a lot. There are over twenty surveillance cameras working in that immediate area. We'll have it all on tape."

There was no denying the nervousness that followed. Platinum's demeanor changed immediately, and she was desperate to get out of the station. "Look, I ain't gonna wait around here on the Crips to peg me as a snitch. I know the law, and you said yourself that I ain't under arrest. You can't hold me."

"No, we can't," Nettles said snidely, reaching for the cup of soda. "But we've got your prints and your DNA. I recommend that you stick around and don't leave the area."

Platinum slung her purse over her shoulder and stormed out, slamming the door behind her.

"This just doesn't add up," Pitts surmised. "Let's go talk to, Duffey."

"Why can't we just call her?" Nettles complained.

"Oh, quit whining, it's not becoming of you."

In lieu of forcing Nettles to deal with Gail, Pitts tossed him the keys, and they were at the ME's office in less than five minutes. They pulled around to the back and walked up to the loading dock.

Sugar buzzed them in. "What's up, gentlemen?" he asked.

"Not a lot, Sugar," Pitts said. "Just another day at the office."

"Another day at the office, my ass!" Nettles mumbled. "Got a man shot up in a crowded parking lot, and now we're dealing with a pregnant woman from hell."

"Yeah, when's Swanson having those twins anyway?"

"Not Swanson," Nettles answered, wiping the thick sheen of perspiration off his brow. "Believe it or not, there's one worse than her, and to top it off, Duffey's assigned to the case. Apparently, I'm not living right. What've I done to deserve all this?"

Sugar offered a good-natured laugh and patted Nettles on the back. "It's all good, my man. Gail's in her office. They haven't moved the body for autopsy yet."

"Thanks, Sugar," Pitts said.

Gail Duffey was seated behind her desk, filling out some paperwork. She looked up briefly, then returned her attention to what she was writing on one of the forms. "I wasn't expecting you so soon," she said as she continued scribbling. "The body's still in the cooler. I'm not a miracle worker, you know."

"Yeah, I'm pretty much aware of that," Nettles said sarcastically. "I have a few questions, then I need to see that body."

"You're welcome to it, but like I told you at the scene, it's going to be cut and dry two kill shots."

"Yeah, I know the cause of death. Did you get any shell casings?"

"Two bagged as evidence, both nine-millimeter target rounds. I didn't recover the slugs, so I'm sure they're still in the body. We'll dig them out in the autopsy."

"And when might that happen?" Nettles pressed, with little tact.

"I was hoping to finish this initial report, then—God forbid—grab a bite to eat. But it's clear you aren't gonna cut me any slack. What are you looking for, Nettles, that's so urgent I can't even have lunch like a normal person? We all know patience isn't your forte, but this isn't like you."

Nettles didn't take the bait which greatly surprised Pitts. He could only ascertain that his deep dislike for Platinum outweighed his disdain for Duffey.

"Well, the knocked-up girlfriend—and I'm using that term lightly—rubs me the wrong way. Her story is different from the one the other male passenger gave us, and I'm leaning toward his version. For some reason, she wants us to believe it's gang-related, but I don't buy it."

"Did you run the victim's rap sheet?"

"Yeah, he was a low-level dealer, weed, nothing more. He had a few minor brushes with the law while fighting with his buddies, suspended license, and no insurance. I don't get the feeling he was running with the Bloods. Did you notice any tatts or red colors?"

"No. Come to think of it I don't remember any red apparel. There were some tattoos though. Let's go take a look."

Sugar assisted Duffey in transferring the body from the cooler and body bag onto the autopsy table. Tony Hart had been a healthy young man by all appearances. He had a lean physique, with well-defined muscles. If he'd succumbed to drug use in the past, it'd been minimal. His skin bore no needle tracks, and his teeth were in good condition.

Pitts and Nettles joined Duffey in donning gloves and aprons, and Sugar assisted in removing the shirt.

"None of this ink seems to be gang-related," Duffey started. She ran her finger over his left hand, then reached over for his right. "How *original*," she said, pointing to the words *L-O-V-E* and *H-A-T-E* tattooed on his fingers. "And amateur at that."

"Looks like a spider web on his left elbow," Sugar added.

"Yeah, probably trying to get folks to believe he served serious time and gain a little street credit for his booming weed business," Nettles mocked. "Other than a few nights in County, he was never in much trouble. Some try to link the web tattoo to gangs, but that's rarely the case unless it's Aryan Brotherhood."

"He's got a pretty dark complexion," Duffey added. "So, it's almost difficult to see some of these. There's a teardrop under his eye and a cross on his left forearm. There are a couple of female names on his chest, but beyond that, nothing. I really don't see anything that indicates gang relations, not even the sports teams they often get tattooed."

"That's my thinking, too," Nettles said. "But humor me, Duffey. Check his shoelaces and see if they're red."

"Sugar, can you get his shoes?" she asked. "They're with his property."

The big man was back within a few minutes, carrying a pair of bloody Nikes that appeared to have the original laces.

"Thanks, Sugar," Nettles said. "No bandana, no gang tatts, nothing. This boy wasn't a Blood. His baby mama's lying. I wonder what that's about, Pitts."

"Who knows why people do what they do?" Pitts said. "Maybe she's afraid of the guy who did this. I know I'd be, and she's ready to give birth."

"That little girl isn't scared of the devil himself. I say we go find her and get to the bottom of this." Nettles then turned to Gail. "Appreciate it, Duffey. Call me when you've completed the autopsy."

"Make sure to get a bite to eat first," Pitts said, clearing his throat and looking scornfully at Nettles. "And what about you?" he asked his partner as they got in the car. "Wanna grab some grub?"

"Nah, I'll just hit up the machine," Nettles answered. "I wanna get back to the office so I can pull up the rap sheet on Platinum. I know we can get her on something."

"You're taking this a little personally, aren't you, Nettles? It's not like you."

"There's something about her, something that just doesn't sit right with me. What woman would be so callous when her boyfriend was shot right in front of her? It's like she doesn't give a shit that someone was firing a Glock inches from her pregnant belly."

"Yeah, that's a little odd."

"More than a little," Nettles said. "Let's go."

Pitts pulled into the parking lot and stepped out of the car. "I left my phone back at my desk. I'll grab it, then get a bite to eat."

The two detectives looked both ways, then started across the street. As soon as they took their first step onto the pavement, they heard tires squealing and a car accelerating.

"What the..." Nettles asked, but that was all he could get out before a spray of gunfire erupted, hitting both detectives, and sending their bodies reeling to the asphalt. Glock shell casings bounced across the pavement and concrete while the Hispanic male turned the corner and sped off.

Platinum sat up from crouching in the front seat. "Well, tell me you got 'em both," she demanded, her stormy eyes daring him to say anything different.

Chapter Twelve

When Clara and Iris arrived at the office at 8:30 in the morning, they were pleasantly surprised to see Quita had already opened and had the coffee brewing.

"Good morning," Clara said. "The coffee smells good."

"What took you two so long?" Quita asked. "I was hoping you'd call me last night. How'd it go with the surveillance?"

"Not nearly as exciting as I thought it'd be," Iris answered. "It was boring, and I was hungry. That was our day in a nutshell."

Quita gave her an exasperated look and turned to Clara. "Where did Summer go?"

"We waited across the street from the insurance office until she went to lunch. She went to the bank and Dairy Queen, then back to work until five o'clock. After that, it seems she had a fitting for her bridal gown, and she went by her girlfriend's apartment, where they watched a movie. At nine, she got in her car and went home."

"Could you tell if there was anyone else in the apartment besides the girlfriend?"

"The friend answered the door, and as it got darker outside, we could see in the blinds. They each had two glasses of wine and snacked on some cheese and crackers. It appeared to be two friends enjoying some time together."

"Where does Summer live?"

"With her parents, in a small house in Marietta. It was quite a tough drive for me, especially at night," Clara commented. "I hope we don't have to follow her back there again."

"If she's up to something, she'll do it in the next couple of days," Quita assured them. "The wedding is coming up, so we won't be stuck with this one for long. Do you think she suspected anyone was following her?"

"I don't think so," Iris chimed in. "She's not very observant. Are you saying we have to do the same thing again today?"

Quita laughed. "Yep, you sure do. That's how stakeouts work. They're not exciting like the cop movies. Who knows? Maybe the mother is on to something, and the girl is fooling around."

"It doesn't appear there's much in the way of money or status to gain from this Lewis fella," Iris retorted. "He's not a looker, nor does he have a good job. Matter of fact, he doesn't even have a stable job. He's just a handyman, the hand-to-mouth type. The best thing his mother could say about him was that he owns his own power washer."

"Iris, really," Clara said. "That's beside the point. Women pick men for many different reasons, some of which I'm afraid we'll never understand."

"You know," Quita said. "Iris has a good point."

Iris looked pleased and sat down at Quita's desk with her coffee. "I do, how do you figure?"

"Summer's pretty hot in those pictures Nancy gave you. She has a decent job with an insurance company, a stable nine-to-five, workin' no weekends or holidays, and she has her own wheels."

"Like I said, women go after men for many reasons," Clara repeated. "We can't discount she may actually love the guy. Stranger things have happened. Sometimes, young women just want to get married—plain and simple."

"I'm still not buying it," Quita countered. "Women aren't so into marrying these days, no offense to the older generation. Many don't even marry if they're pregnant. It's not a shotgun-wedding world anymore, ladies. I'm sure you watch television and read the papers. Women have their own jobs now, just like you two do. We don't need to rely on a man."

"Maybe she just wants to get out of her mama's house," Iris suggested. "She might make a decent wage, but I doubt she can fully support herself on a receptionist's salary."

"Still, a hot chick like that doesn't have to marry. Look at all the hotspots in Atlanta. She wouldn't have to buy herself a drink in any club, no matter how ritzy. Plus, there are sugar-daddy websites all over the Internet. If she wants an apartment, some man would easily front the money for it."

"Oh dear," Clara said. "I don't even want to think about that. I prefer to believe in old-fashioned notions, like she may actually love the man. I know love isn't out of style, at least not yet."

"Well, now that I think about it, there may be another theory we're overlooking," Quita suggested.

"What's that?" Iris asked.

"Maybe Lewis's mother has the money. How old is Nancy?"

"I'd say she's nearing eighty. What do you think, Iris?"

"That's about right, but she's clear-headed…and cynical as they come. We'll never convince her that Summer's not after her son's money, even if he doesn't even have a real job."

"It's not his money she's worried about," Quita said confidently. "I guarantee you she's loaded."

"But her house isn't anything special, and she has an old car. I wouldn't expect her property to be too valuable," Clara interjected.

"How much do you know about her?"

"Very little really, except that she's Daisy's friend."

"All right. I'm gonna look into her and her assets while you ladies are gone today. I bet we'll find something."

****

"Do we really have to sit in the car all day again?" Iris asked with a groan.

"Don't bother going till lunchtime, since you know she's not working till then," Quita suggested. "For now, let's practice taking pictures with your phones."

"My old Nikon works just fine. It takes great pictures from a distance," Clara said.

"Yeah, but we might need some up close."

"I'm afraid that's not a good idea. If anyone sees us snapping pictures in the room with them, it'll make them suspicious," Clara argued.

"You don't understand, Miss Clara. Look around the next time you're out at the mall or a restaurant. People take pictures everywhere now. Haven't you heard of selfies?"

"Actually, I have. What I don't understand is why everybody takes so many pictures these days. Just the other day, I saw some silly girl taking a picture of her cheeseburger! What for? It's gotten out of hand. Photos should be for capturing special occasions, not everything you eat or wear."

"People share them on social media. Anyway, no one will ever suspect a thing, since everybody takes pictures these days. Let's practice that for a while, and then we'll work on voice recording and video."

****

"Dairy Queen again?" Iris asked. "I know why she wants to get married. She's planning on letting herself go. I don't have anything against a good burger, but I couldn't do it every day."

Clara laughed at her old friend and nodded in agreement. "Perhaps it's just convenient. It's pretty close to her job."

"I suppose you're right," Iris said as she leaned back in her seat and rested her head on the headrest.

"Look!" Clara said as she patted Iris on the arm. "There's a man sitting down with her this time."

The two women squinted and concentrated on the small booth toward the rear of the restaurant. He was a middle-aged man, probably in his fifties, and quite the looker. Tall and broad-shouldered, he had a head full of wavy, salt-and-pepper hair, and a trim waistline. He sat across from her rather than next to her, opened a folder, and spread several papers across the small table.

"Looks like a business meeting to me," Iris said. "Although she'd be doing a whole lot better with that dapper gentleman than that grubby Lewis. He's a handsome man and look at that suit! It sure doesn't look cheap."

"I wonder what it's all about," Clara asked. "It looks official, but how many important meetings take place in a Dairy Queen?"

"I was thinking the same thing," Iris said. "It's odd, to say the least. Maybe I oughta go in there and order a chili dog. I could sit by them and pull up that voice thingamajig Quita showed us. I could record the conversation, and they'd never suspect a thing."

"That would be a good idea if they weren't the only ones near the back. I don't like it. They're clearly meeting about something. It'd be too noticeable if you walked all the way back there to sit down when there are so many other seats available."

"Yeah, I guess you're right. Looks like he's about to go, though," she said, pointing to the man who was gathering up the paperwork and standing to leave. "I say we follow this fella and see where he works. That might clue us in as to what they were meeting about."

"Good idea," Clara agreed. "He's going out the other side. Buckle up!"

They didn't have to follow the handsome stranger far. He pulled into the lot of the same insurance company where Summer worked.

"That's strange," Clara said. "If they had to discuss something, why not meet at work?"

"Must be something they don't want anyone at work to know about. Either way, it's fishy. We may be on to something."

"Get Quita on the phone and let her know what's happening. There may be something to this."

Summer hopped in her bright-red sports car and left the insurance agency at five o'clock sharp.

"You don't think we should follow her?" Iris asked.

"Quita thinks we should follow the man. He must work there since he hasn't come out yet."

"I hope she's making the right call."

It was after 6:00 when the man finally exited the building and locked it up. He walked around back and got into a silver Jaguar. He took no notice of Clara and Iris pulling out of the Dollar General lot to tail him.

"I think we need to be more aware of our surroundings," Iris said as Clara sped up to keep up with their subject.

"Why do you say that?" Clara asked.

"Neither of those two have even noticed us. We could be followed ourselves, and we wouldn't even know. I know I don't pay attention to anything that's going on around me."

"You've got to be kidding, Iris. You don't miss a thing."

"And how do you know that?"

"Because you give me a play-by-play of everything and everybody. No one is safe from your opinion. You notice every bad dye job, every unattractive haircut, every fuzzy permanent wave, every—"

"I was a hairdresser, for heaven's sake," Iris said defensively. "I'm supposed to notice those things."

"Let's get serious now. I'm going to need your help. The traffic is getting heavier, and I don't want to lose him."

For the next forty-five minutes, the women wove in and out of traffic, struggling to keep up with the expensive, flashy car. Just when the stress was getting to be too much for Clara, the man turned into a Mexican restaurant on Cheshire Bridge Road. He pulled in the closest space to the entrance while Clara drove around and parked out of his view. They gave him a few minutes to go in and be seated before they entered.

Again, he'd opted for a booth in the back, so Iris quietly requested that they be seated in the same area. The waiter nodded kindly, grabbed their menus, and led them to a booth adjacent to his table. Neither of the ladies so much as glanced in his direction; instead, they quickly started their own conversation. He looked up briefly but went back to scrolling through the messages on his phone when he realized it was simply two older women chatting.

Clara ordered a glass of water with lemon while Iris ordered the frozen margarita special. Clara shot a discerning look in her direction, but Iris simply shrugged.

"I'm not driving," she said. "Besides, it makes it more believable," she mouthed.

Clara nudged her forcibly with her foot under the table, but Iris refused to acknowledge it.

The women were nibbling on their chips and salsa and perusing the menu when, to their surprise and delight, Summer entered the restaurant and made a beeline for the handsome insurance man.

"Traffic was terrible," Summer complained. "I had to meet Lewis across town and use my debit card to fill the tank in his truck and lawnmower. That crazy mother of his cut him off since he insists on going through with the wedding."

The ears of Iris and Clara perked up, but they didn't dare remain silent.

"I think I'll have the shrimp tacos," Clara said. "What about you?"

"Oh, I don't know," Iris said, rummaging through her purse for her phone. "I'm not feeling seafood tonight. Maybe I'll have the cheese enchiladas," she continued as she pressed the voice memo button to record the conversation, just as Quita had taught them. "I wonder if my grandson will call me," Iris said, giving her friend a quick wink. "I guess I should keep my phone out, in case he does. I never get to talk to him."

It was obvious Summer and her friend were deep in their own conversation and couldn't care less about the two old women. Clara and Iris continued to nod and nibble as if they were still conversing but were doing their best to eavesdrop.

"Lewis is clueless," Summer said. "That boy hasn't worked a full day in his life. And to think his mother is suspicious of me getting his money! That's laughable."

"Don't be foolish," the man said sternly. "She's not as stupid as you think. She's well aware that anything he has, she's given him."

"What would make her think I want her money? Who would *ever* suspect she has any? Look at that old, rundown house. I bet you twenty bucks her sofa is as old as Lewis."

"You're making me nervous," the man continued. "Did you look at all those insurance papers?"

"Yeah," Summer said, picking up a chip and munching on it. "I'm starving, let's order."

The man didn't bother to mask his impatience with her. "I don't think you're taking this seriously enough. You've got to convince him to sign those life insurance forms right away. Once that old bat's out of the way, he'll get everything. Then, when he goes, you'll inherit the insurance money and her fortune. This is big, and you're acting like it's a walk in the park. You can't be too careful, Summer."

Iris and Clara held their breath as the plot unfolded. It went far beyond Summer having an affair. Not only was she after the son and his money, but she wanted Nancy's as well. The only way she was going to get it was for both of them to die.

Clara immediately delved into a deep conversation about replacing her aging heating and cooling system in her house while Summer and her partner-in-crime ordered steak fajitas and mixed drinks. Iris was blinking her eyes at such a rapid pace that Clara was compelled to kick her under the table once again. Iris nervously fanned herself with her menu. Clara knew they couldn't keep up the charade much longer.

"How do you plan to get him to sign the papers?" the insurance man asked.

"Oh, please, that's the least of our worries. I'll just kiss his neck while we're in the car and let his hand go almost up my shirt before I insist, we wait until our wedding night. He'll be so hot and bothered that he'll jump at the chance to sign. What I'm worried about is getting him to sign a will after that old wench is dead."

"There won't be a reason for a will. You'll be the surviving spouse."

Both Clara and Iris gasped as their hands flew up to their mouths.

Summer and the man quickly looked in their direction.

Iris grabbed her phone and shoved it in her purse. "Let's get out of here," she whispered.

"Good evening, ladies," the man said. "I don't mean to be rude, but it seems as if you were, uh…eavesdropping on our conversation," he said sternly. "Is there a reason for that?"

"I don't know what you're talking about, young man," Clara answered just as the waiter showed up with the food. "Thank you, Sir," she said to the waiter as she looked down at her plate and prayed the insurance man would let it go.

He slid his napkin from his lap and placed it on the table as he stood. "I'm going to need that phone, lady."

"My phone, but why? It was a gift from my grandson, so he can call me, and I—" Iris nervously stuttered. He clearly wasn't buying it.

"I'm not asking," he said as he moved closer.

"Granny!" Quita suddenly hollered from across the restaurant. She rushed over, accompanied by a bulky black man, sporting a nylon do-rag on his head, as well as a full, thick beard. "I was hoping you'd have supper with me and Rhadrick," Quita continued. "You haven't started eating yet, so you can come with us. Help Granny and her friend up, honey," she said to Rhadrick.

Rhadrick looked more than a little uncomfortable as he reached for Iris's arm.

"We haven't paid our bill yet," Iris stammered as she allowed the large man to assist her.

"I've got it," Clara said as she pulled two twenties from her purse and stood from the table.

"We've got unfinished business here," the insurance man said, moving between Iris and Clara. "Now give me that phone."

"I don't know who you think you are, or why you're trying to steal a phone from a stranger? But these sweet ladies are leaving, Mister," Quita's friend said firmly. "If you have a problem with it, we can take this outside. Now move aside."

The tall man in the expensive suit had clearly met his match and was well aware of it. He watched as the odd quartet exited the restaurant, climbed into an old, rusted Camaro, and sped off.

Chapter Thirteen

Captain Randall Burke ran out of the Homicide Division on Peachtree Street as fast as his aging knees would allow. It'd been years since he'd been in a foot race, and his body was rejecting his attempts to push it to the limit. As soon as he'd hung up his patrol uniform in exchange for street clothes, he hadn't begrudged himself any of the tempting snacks in the vending machine. Now, he regretted every donut and pack of chips he'd consumed.

Pressing his fist into his right side in hopes of soothing the piercing pain, Burke stopped to bend over and catch his breath. He watched in panic as his fellow cops rushed to the aid of the two downed detectives. Even pregnant Katie Swanson hurried past him to get to the bloody scene.

By the time the overexerted captain finally made it down the last set of steps, the troops had arrived. Red and blue lights illuminated the four lanes, and paramedics were kneeling by both of the injured men. All that was visible to Burke were their legs and two shoes that had traveled haplessly across the roadway. He'd never quite come to an understanding why shoes seemed to fly off the victims of violent crimes, but then again, he'd never questioned it, even though it happened often. Now his eyes remained fixated on the two loafers lying on the asphalt.

"Captain, are you okay?" Katie asked. "Captain, can you hear me?"

Burke shook his head from side to side as if to jolt himself back to the horror at hand. "Katie? Oh, my God! You shouldn't be down here. It'll send you into labor. Go back to the office."

"No way," she insisted. "It's you I'm worried about. You're so out of breath. I think you should sit down. I'm getting an EMT."

"Hell no, you're not!" Burke growled. "I need to get to them. Are they still alive?"

"Yes, but it's not good. Nettles is in the worst shape. They aren't sure if he'll make it to the hospital. They're working on him now."

"I've gotta get to my boys. What the hell happened? Who in their right mind would shoot two cops right in front of the police station?"

Against her better judgment, Katie took the overweight captain by his elbow and guided him to the scene of the crime. She was afraid he might have a heart attack when he saw his fallen men, but she was certain he would have one if he didn't. She motioned for one of the EMTs to take a look at Burke, and he grabbed the captain's bicep to help steady him.

"Why don't you let me take your blood pressure?" the paramedic asked calmly. "You look awfully red."

"That's because my men are down, you idiot!" he screamed as he pushed him away. "Get me through this crowd, and you won't have to worry about my blood pressure."

The two critically injured detectives were lying in close proximity of one another, their arms unintentionally overlapping. Thankfully, neither had been hit in the head, but the bullets had found their mark in center mass. Nettles was unconscious, but his eyes were open and blank. The small army of medics working on him were in a state of organized chaos. They quickly placed him on a backboard and moved him into a waiting ambulance, continuing to talk to him, despite his unresponsiveness.

"We've got you, man," one of them said calmly. "Ain't nothing Grady can't handle. We're almost there, and the doc's waiting on you. Hold tough, my man. You've got this."

That was the last thing the bystanders heard before the ambulance doors slammed shut and the high-pitched sirens screeched to part the crowd.

"Oh, Jesus," Captain Burke gasped. "He's got to make it. What are they saying about, Pitts?"

"I'm not sure," Katie answered as they walked closer to their wounded colleague.

The same pandemonium that'd ensued around Nettles was now happening with Pitts. A team of people trained to handle critically wounded patients worked quickly and efficiently. A mixture of both Pitts' and Nettles' blood pooled on the asphalt, Pitts' eyes were open but unfocused and confused. He appeared to be answering questions, but it was difficult to tell if he comprehended the brevity of the situation. Loud wheezing noises emanated from his chest, and a fine mist of blood escaped from his mouth with each labored breath. The diligent EMTs secured him on a backboard before placing him on a gurney that they rolled hastily to another waiting ambulance.

"I'm riding with him," Captain Burke yelled over the commotion.

"I wouldn't recommend—" the young paramedic attempted to suggest.

"Let him go," Katie insisted, cutting him off. "The best place for him right now is a hospital."

Captain Burke had barely made it into the front seat of the ambulance before it pushed forcefully through the growing mob. As was the case whenever a police officer was wounded, the ambulance was flanked by fellow officers. Their sirens and flashing lights signaled the urgency of the situation. Panicked drivers and passersby seemed to freeze from surprise rather than moving out of the path of the oncoming emergency vehicles.

Grady Memorial Hospital was little more than four minutes away, just under a mile, but with city traffic and so many onlookers, it was difficult to make it in record time. The positive side was that Grady remained the fifth-largest public hospital in the United States and housed the best level-one Trauma Center in the Southeast. Funded largely by Fulton and DeKalb County tax dollars, the hospital did remarkable things. Grady patients were predominantly indigent, the uninsured, and illegal immigrants with nowhere else to turn. But even the wealthy, flourishing citizens of Atlanta would only trust Grady for serious, life-threatening trauma.

Nettles' ambulance was in the lead, but Pitts' team quickly closed the gap, as did the several police cars behind them. The news choppers were already hovering overhead, broadcasting the caravan live for those watching from home. They traveled northwest, down Peachtree Street, toward Trinity Avenue, where officers on motorcycles had already blocked the streets at the traffic lights. They made the second right on Mitchell Street, then crawled ahead slowly, until they were able to make the left on Central. Captain Burke could feel his heart beating rapidly under his shirt, and although he was almost close enough to reach out and touch Edgewood Avenue, it seemed to take hours before they were able to make the right onto it.

By now, officers from several different jurisdictions had arrived and were waiting outside the Emergency Room bay in anticipation. It never ceased to amaze Burke at how quickly the brothers in blue assembled when one of their own was in trouble. Word had spread like wildfire over their radios, and anyone available had come to pledge their support.

The ambulances backed into the bay slowly and meticulously, to get their patients as close to the waiting arms of the trauma teams as possible. Before Captain Burke could unbuckle his seatbelt and step out of the ambulance, both men had been whisked away.

Somber colleagues from several different municipalities huddled silently together, feeling utterly helpless. Burke had that sick, empty feeling deep in his gut as he climbed the steps into the ER. Several of the medical staff were scurrying about, running in and out of curtained rooms. Just as he was looking for someone to guide him through the maze of cordoned-off areas, Burke heard a familiar voice.

"Hey, Cap, I need to talk to you. Let's find a quiet room," Katie Swanson said.

"How'd you get here? Like I told you before, this is the last place you need to be. God knows we don't need you going into labor, and there must be a hundred different diseases floating around this place."

She didn't respond verbally, but gently grabbed his elbow and led him through a door marked *For Staff Only*. They ended up in a narrow hallway that sparkled from a recent waxing and reeked of strong lemon cleanser.

"Where are we?" Burke asked as he looked around. "We aren't supposed to be back here. I need to check on them, Katie. The chief will want to make a statement to the press, and—"

"I need to talk to you, Captain," she insisted. "And this is the quietest place we're going to find. We need to contact Nettles' wife. Sandi teaches at Clancy Elementary. Do you want me to send a patrol car or try to reach another family member first? We need to do it soon, or she's going to see it on the news or hear it from somewhere else. Those leeches from the press are already on it, although thankfully, they won't have any names to release yet."

"Damn," Burke said as he pulled his glasses off and rubbed his fingers across his eyes. "I didn't even think of that. I appreciate you, Katie. A patrol car would scare her to death. But you're right, we can't waste any more time and take the chance that she'll hear it from another source. Would you mind riding over with Sammy in his car? He's out there somewhere. We don't have time to get one of the clergies on staff."

Katie patted his forearm. "I'll find him. I called Upshaw at the ME's office, and he and Jessalyn will be right over. Just promise me you'll find somewhere to sit down."

"I will," he lied. "Now, go, I need to see about my boys."

Chapter Fourteen

The Camaro sped through several intersections, turned onto Interstate 85, and headed south. Several minutes passed before anyone spoke.

Clara's hands were pressed against her chest as she struggled not to hyperventilate. "That was close," she said, her voice cracking. "How did you know, Quita?"

"I did some investigating of my own today," Quita answered. "It appears Nancy is quite a rich woman, a *stingy miser*, but rich just the same. The owner of the insurance agency Summer works for has a rap sheet a mile long. He's a con man who's managed to get out of as many felonies as he's been convicted of. Summer's not squeaky-clean herself. I'm sure Nancy and Lewis aren't their only targets."

"B-but," Iris stammered as she struggled to comprehend all that had happened. "How did you find us? Just in the nick of time, too. I thought I was going to have to stab that fella with a fork!"

"I had a locator put on your phones. I know it was kinda sneaky, but it worked. I worry about you ladies—looks like I made the right decision."

"A locator? My goodness. What'll they think of next?" Clara asked. "I just knew he was going to get his hands on our hard-earned evidence."

"Not from Rhadrick, here," Quita said as she patted him on his thick shoulder.

"We sure are glad you saved us," Iris said. "And it's nice to make your acquaintance, Rhadrick."

"You, too, Ma'am," he said, keeping his eyes on the road. "That coulda gone really bad."

"I'm not so sure it's over yet," Clara said. "What are we supposed to do with this evidence?"

"We better go to the police," Quita said. "I think we should have Nancy and Lewis meet us there. They need to know Summer has a bounty on their heads."

"Rhadrick, how do you know Quita?" Iris asked.

"She's my cousin, and I been lookin' after her since we were kids. When your mouth's bigger than you are, you gotta have somebody to look out for you."

"Well, we can't thank you enough. Could we trouble you for a lift to the station?"

"I'm on my way to one of the mini-precincts by Underground Atlanta now. I'm not sure what you ladies got on that phone, but that guy wanted it pretty bad. Don't know how long it'll take, 'cause they'll have to get a detective out. I work third shift, so I'm just gonna drop you off. I'm sure they'll help you get back to your car."

"Quita, will you stay with us?" Clara asked hopefully.

"I better," she answered. "It's probably gonna be a long night."

Rhadrick pulled up to the curb, jumped out, and pulled the front seat forward for the ladies to exit. "I gotta hand it to you," he said with a chuckle. "You ladies are somethin' else. If you ever need me, Quita's got my number."

"I think I'll get her to program it into my new phone," Iris said, giving the big man a flirtatious wink. "It's the latest iPhone, you know? Don't know what I'd do without it."

Chapter Fifteen

Captain Burke paced the waiting room like a caged tiger. The chief was on his way, but the doctors still hadn't come out to let anyone know about the men's conditions. The throng of law enforcement personnel was growing rapidly, and the mounting uncertainty was getting the best of them. A small hint of relief washed over Burke when he saw Travis Upshaw and Jessalyn pushing through the sea of blue uniforms to get to him. Jessalyn's eyes were red from crying, and her face wore an expression of disbelief. She fell into Burke's arms as soon as they reached him.

"What the hell is going on?" Travis asked. "I can't believe this happened right in front of your office. Tell me you've got some leads, Captain."

"Not yet," Burke answered. "And we still don't know anything about their injuries. It didn't look good when we left the scene."

The sound of conversation instantly muted, and Burke turned toward the door. Sammy was holding Sandi Nettles up while Katie tried to soothe her. The three made it to a row of connected chairs and eased the young wife onto one of them. Katie looked around until she spotted the captain, then gave him a nod to call him over.

Burke sat down beside Sandi and took her hand. "I'm so sorry, Mrs. Nettles. We haven't heard anything about your husband's condition yet. We're waiting for the doctor."

"I can't believe it," she said quietly. "I always knew there was a possibility this could happen, but I was never prepared for it."

"Captain," one of the officers interrupted. "It's the doctor."

Burke jumped to his feet and walked toward the physician. He noticed the doctor's demeanor was grim as he adjusted his scrubs. He had clearly pulled on fresh ones to face the anxious crowd. "What's going on, Doc?" Burke asked. "Are they still with us?"

"Are there any relatives here?" the surgeon asked his tone even not giving anything away. "Besides the law enforcement family," he quickly corrected himself.

"Yes, this is Detective Nettles' wife, Sandi," Burke said, nodding in her direction.

"With all due respect," the doctor continued, "I think it's best we talk to her down the hall. I'm sure you all understand she may need some time to let this register." He turned to look at Sandi, whose face was now ashen. "He's still with us, Ma'am, but we should talk."

Sammy stood up and grabbed her arm. "See, Mrs. Nettles. He's gonna be all right, he's a fighter."

"Please..." Sandi stammered. "Captain Burke and Katie, will you please come with me? I don't have anyone else here."

They followed the doctor down the long, narrow hallway, and the doctor opened a door marked _Quiet Room_. Burke had passed those types of rooms numerous times, and they never bore good news. He paced his breathing and steadied the officer's wife until she sank into one of the dark-orange, plastic seats.

The doctor sat across from her and adjusted his glasses on his nose. He cleared his throat and folded his hands together. "I'm Doctor Tucker. The good news is that your husband is still with us. As your friend said, he's quite the fighter. He has several critical injuries, but the most concerning at this point is the damage to his liver. He took a direct gunshot to the center of the organ.

"The liver is highly vascularized and is close to multiple large blood vessels. Our concern at this time is the profuse loss of blood volume..." He paused for a brief moment to ensure she was comprehending. Satisfied that she was, he continued, "We did a chest and abdominal ultrasonography and a _FAST_ sonography, which finds free-floating fluid in the right-upper and left-lower quadrants in the abdomen.

"He is headed to surgery now, and it will entail a liver resection to remove the source of bleeding and necrotic tissue. I must be honest with you, the odds are stacked against him. Your husband is extremely critical. If he does survive the surgery, there is also the danger of an abscess or postoperative hemorrhage. This, of course, is the most pressing injury. It will be addressed first before we are able to deal with any others." Dr. Tucker looked over at the captain, then back to Katie. "Do you have any questions?"

Sandi was now slumped over the right side of the chair with her head bowed. "I-I don't know what to do," she said. "I don't know what to do for him."

Dr. Tucker shifted in his seat. "If you're a praying woman, there's a chapel downstairs. His surgeon is one of the best we've got, and he's doing all he can, but ultimately, it's in God's hands now."

When the doctor stood to leave, Burke followed him out of the small, somber room. "Is there any news on, Detective Pitts?"

"Doctor Patel is working with him and should be out in just a few minutes. Apparently, he fared better than Detective Nettles, but he's in for a long road. Did you see any of his family here?"

"Yes…or at least the closest thing to family. Travis Upshaw, from the ME's office, is a close friend, and his girlfriend Jessalyn is out there, too."

Dr. Tucker pointed to another closed door. "If you can bring them down here, I'll see that Doctor Patel talks to you all as soon as possible."

Burke, Upshaw, and Jessalyn made their way to the small room and sat waiting impatiently. The only audible sounds were Jessalyn's faint sobbing into a wad of toilet paper that one of the officers had fetched out of the men's room for her. It seemed as though it had been days since the detectives had been shot, but in reality, it'd been little more than an hour. Burke literally felt the weight of despair from both the emotional and physical strain of the event.

A light tapping on the door was followed by Dr. Patel opening it and stepping inside. The room was furnished with six chairs, but it was so small that they all seemed to be stacked on top of one another. Travis and the captain both jumped to their feet when the doctor entered, but he swiftly motioned for them to take their seats. The three waiting for news looked at the physician with anticipation and trepidation. They knew all too well that once the words were spoken, it would become a reality, and there would be no taking them back.

"I'm Doctor Patel," he said as he sat down among them. "I understand you're Detective Pitts' family."

The three nodded, but no words formed on their lips.

"I understand you are all anxious to hear about his condition, so I want to give you a brief overview before he's taken into surgery. Detective Pitts has sustained several injuries, but the one we're dealing with now is a gunshot wound to his right lung. His blood pressure has dropped dramatically, and the oxygen in his blood is at dangerously low levels. To put it in layman's terms, he's in shock. In surgery, we will do one of two things. Either the surgeon can repair the lung, or he'll have to remove one or more lobes of that lung.

"He'll be on a ventilator overnight, but we'll try to remove the tube as soon as possible as several complications can occur if it's left in much longer than that. Among those are pneumonia and blood clots. A tube will need to be inserted through the chest wall, to evacuate air and any residual blood or body fluids from the chest cavity to keep the lung inflated. Such a tube is generally left in place for two to seven days, depending on the complexity of the surgery.

"After that, Detective Pitts will be treated with pain meds and antibiotics and will begin respiratory therapy. I also need to add that the detective received numerous gunshots. At this time, we believe the shot to the lung to be the most severe and threatening, but we'll know more once we go into surgery."

They sat silently for a few seconds after the doctor stopped speaking, looking at one another in shock.

Finally, Jessalyn nervously blurted out the question they all wanted the answer to, "Is he going to be okay? I mean, he's going to live, right?"

"His body has sustained a great deal of trauma, Ma'am," Dr. Patel answered warmly. "He's in for a long recovery, but he's in good hands. I'll be back to speak with you when we know more."

As the door closed quietly behind him, Travis Upshaw let out a sigh of relief. "It's not good, but it could be a helluva lot worse," he said as he patted Jessalyn on the shoulder. "That son-of-a-bitch knew exactly where to aim, in the chest and abdomen to do the most damage, barring the head of course."

"I just wish I could see him," Jessalyn said. "I'd like to let him know we're here and that I'm not leaving."

"He knows," Travis assured her. "Pitts knows he can count on us, right, Captain?"

Burke opened his mouth to answer but only managed a deep, guttural grunt. Perspiration had dampened his hair and was beading heavily on his forehead. His face had suddenly taken on a pale, ashen pallor, and he clawed at his chest to ease the pain.

"Quick!" Travis yelled to Jessalyn. "Get a doctor! Burke is having a heart attack."

Chapter Sixteen

"Okay, ladies," Quita said as she wheeled her office chair over to Clara's desk. "Looks like we've got another case."

Iris took a sip from her coffee mug and walked over. The past two days had been spent at the District Attorney's Office, and she was anxious for a change.

"I have to tell ya, I'm exhausted from being a despondent."

"What are you talking about?" Quita asked.

"Iris, the term you're looking for is *deponent*," Clara clarified.

"Whatever they called us it went on for four days. Frankly, I think they drew it out much longer than necessary."

"It was only two days, and depositions are an important part of the process," Clara countered. "Did you want those two to get away with their con games?"

"No, but we had it on tape, and I'm sure we'll have to go back through it again in court. I do declare, those attorneys were just trying to prove us incompetent. Don't let these gray hairs fool you, Quita. I've earned each and every one of 'em. Wisdom comes with age and experience, and I've got plenty of both. I thought I was going to have to tell that sassy little DA a thing or two."

"Oh, for heaven's sake, Iris," Clara interjected. "They were simply doing their jobs. It's important to dot every *I* and cross every *T*."

"Well, I suppose it didn't hurt that Nancy gave us a bonus," Quita said. "Of course, she has plenty to spare. You ladies did save her life, ya know."

Iris let out a chuckle. "You two wanna bet she won't let that homely Lewis out of her sight until she croaks?"

The three of them shared a good laugh.

"So…what have we got?" Clara asked.

"A workman's comp case. A roofing company is trying to catch one of their employees in the act of faking an injury. He claims he fell off a roof and hurt his back. It could cost them a lot, and they're pretty sure he's a fraud."

"So, we're back in the car again?" Iris asked with a groan. "For some reason, I figured we'd be doing more exciting things."

"More exciting than catching a pair of con artists attempting to murder a mother and her son to take all their money and cash in on the life insurance?" Clara asked. "That was a good thing we did, Iris."

"I suppose you're right," Iris said blandly.

"This is the info they faxed me," Quita began as she opened the folder. "This is our guy," she continued, pointing at a fuzzy picture of a young, white male in his early thirties. "His name is Bo McNeil, and he's employed by Hart Roofing. He's been there six weeks, but according to them, he's not the best man for the job. He was angry with his supervisor and told some other employees he knows how to get over."

"Get over?" Iris questioned.

"Yeah, get over. Um…it means to take advantage of the company," Quita explained.

"So, that's why they think he's a fraud?" Clara asked. "A lot of people complain about their bosses. I did it myself a time or two."

"That's only part of the reason. McNeil also has a real fishy work history, and nobody actually saw him fall off the roof."

"Surely they requested medical records from the doctor?" Iris interjected.

"Miss Iris, there are a lot of sketchy doctors out there. For the right price, they'll say whatever you ask 'em to, especially if they know they can pad their books with a guaranteed payment from workman's comp insurance. One scam just leads to another."

"Unbelievable. Well, what are we supposed to do? We aren't doctors."

"They don't want you to diagnose his injury," Quita continued. "They want you to show he ain't really injured."

"I'm not following you," Iris said, wrinkling her forehead in confusion.

"We just have to find him in some…compromising positions," Clara said to her old friend. "I saw this on 20/20. These guys aren't the brightest. Instead of lying low and enjoying the free money, they go out and about and do foolish things somebody with a back injury couldn't do."

"Exactly," Quita agreed. "He might go bowling or golfing or something like that."

"I see," Iris said. "So, where do we begin?"

"I've got his home address here," Quita said, pointing at a piece of paper in the file. "I also printed out the directions for you. You could use your iPhones if you weren't so stubborn, but I guess we'll have to keep practicing that. Anyway, he lives in College Park, about ten minutes south of the airport a straight shot down 85-South."

"Isn't that kind of a rough area?" Iris asked. "I see it on the news all the time, lots of burglaries and gang violence. Sounds a little dangerous."

"It's not the best place," Quita answered. "But I think you'll be okay. He lives in the house his parents owned before they died. It's an old, established neighborhood, still fairly safe—you know, one of those neighborhood watch communities."

"Two old women will stick out like a couple of sore thumbs," Clara retorted. "I don't know, Quita. Could be too risky."

"I had Rhadrick scope it out this morning on his way home from work. He thinks you'll be okay, as long as you're there during daylight and don't stop off anywhere. Make sure you gas up and eat before you hit the expressway."

"Oh, that's comforting," Iris said sarcastically.

"He drives a yellow Mustang," Quita continued. "You can't miss it. It was parked in the driveway this morning, so he must not bother putting it in the garage. If the car's there, he'll be inside. If not, he's gone somewhere. If you ride by and see the yellow car, just take a leisurely drive through the neighborhood for a bit. If he's gone, see if you can find someplace to park, where you don't look too suspicious. You can always call me if you get into trouble."

"And we're supposed to follow him until he does something a back injury should stop him from doing?" Iris asked.

"Exactly," Quita confirmed. "But we'll need lots of pictures. Hart Roofing is convinced if they confront him with solid evidence of fraud, he'll be quick to do a disappearing act."

"Well, I guess I'd better go to the little girls' room before we take off," Iris said, standing. "If we can't stop for gas or food, I'm sure we won't be able to take a potty break either."

Chapter Seventeen

At some point during the grueling day, Travis Upshaw, Jessalyn Brock, Katie Swanson, and Sandi Nettles made their way out to the rest of the crowd in the packed waiting room. The agonizing wait for the surgeons' updates would be easier to tolerate among those who shared the same concern and affection for their loved ones.

Captain Burke had been rushed into an operating room himself, for an emergency bypass surgery, after he'd collapsed in the quiet room. It'd been several hours since they'd heard anything further about the three downed peace officers. Family and friends were arriving one after the other, along with a steady flow of neighboring police officers. The hospital staff worked diligently to reroute other emergency room visitors to various parts of the hospital, only those who had some association with the fallen officers and Burke were allowed to occupy the designated waiting area.

It was strangely quiet, in spite of all the people, then again, there was little to be said. Silent prayers went up from many, but there was nothing else anyone could do but hope and wait. Katie Swanson hadn't even noticed the enormous swelling in her ankles and lower legs, her own ailments seemed trivial now. Sid, her husband had arrived an hour earlier, but even his pleading couldn't convince her to leave the hospital. He'd learned long ago that he couldn't compete with her strong bond within the PD. Sid was grateful his wife worked as administrative staff, but the allegiance to her coworkers couldn't have been more devout if she carried a shield and service weapon herself.

Finally, a stone-faced doctor entered the room but went unnoticed until he tapped on the doorframe. Everyone who was seated jumped to their feet in unison.

"Excuse me," he said noncommittedly. "I'm Doctor Carnes. Is the family of Detective Pritchard Pitts here?"

The surgeon was met with blank stares from his audience, and several seconds passed before Travis Upshaw could react. He realized the crowd was unaccustomed to hearing the detective's first name, and Pitts had made it a point to never share it with anyone other than Jessalyn and a few close friends. Even as a child, he preferred to go by his last name often joking that his mother had had a dreadful sense of humor when she gave him her maiden name as a first name.

"Good afternoon, Doctor," Travis said as he stepped forward with an outstretched hand. "I'm Travis Upshaw, from the ME's office, and one of the detective's closest friends. This is his girlfriend, Jessalyn," he continued as he motioned for her to join him.

She moved swiftly to his side and wiped a tear from her cheek. She'd never heard anyone refer to her as Pitts' girlfriend, and it felt warm and terrifying all at once. She resisted the urge to stand on her tiptoes so the doctor could see her better. "Is he still alive?" she asked softly.

"Yes," the doctor answered before turning to face the anxious crowd. "The detective has just come out of surgery. I'm happy to report that he survived the operation, but he still faces a long road to recovery. I'm sure you all understand I'd like to be excused to share the details with these folks." He then moved to the door and motioned for them to walk down the hall with him.

Jessalyn looked back and made quick eye contact with Sandi Nettles. She wanted nothing more than to grab her hand and take her with them, but she didn't want her to miss any news about her husband.

In the small box of a room once again, Jessalyn and Upshaw were limp from relief of Pitts surviving the surgery.

The surgeon seemed to sense their relief, so he wasted no time. "I understand that Doctor Patel filled you in on Mister Pitts' injuries?" He looked at them as they nodded in affirmation. "I'm a thoracic surgeon and was called in to operate on the damaged lung. We knew the damage was significant but were hoping we'd only have to remove one lobe of the right lung. Unfortunately, I had to perform a bilobectomy, which essentially means we removed two lobes. An incision was made in the side of the chest, between the ribs.

"The ribs were then spread apart so we could locate the affected lobes—the inferior and middle lobes in this case. The operation went as well as could be expected. Fortunately, Detective Pitts is in fairly decent shape for his age. That not only helped him survive the surgery, but it will also enable him to recover more quickly. He sustained two additional gunshot wounds, neither of which were life-threatening. Two bullets were removed, and the other will remain in his body, which poses less of a risk than trying to displace it…" He paused briefly to let the information sink in.

"I'm sure you have several questions, but first, I must make you aware that there is still potential for complications. As I'm sure Doctor Patel told you, there is a risk of bleeding and blood clots. He'll be placed in ICU, and we will use a ventilator overnight. The chest tube will be left in place for four to seven days. Although the surgery was a success, you must be prepared for the possibility of a setback." Dr. Carnes then leaned back in his seat as if opening the door for questions.

Jessalyn cleared her throat before she asked, "When can we see him?"

"In an hour or so, but only briefly. He won't be aware you're there. He'll be heavily sedated, and rest is crucial for his recovery."

Jessalyn nodded and wiped away another tear that was rolling slowly down her face.

"I understand the potential for complications, Doctor," Upshaw said, his voice wavering a bit. "But barring any other difficulties what kind of timeline are we looking at for recovery?"

"You're a doctor yourself," Dr. Carnes said. "You know all the factors that come into play with any surgery. However, like I said, he's in decent shape, and that will work to his benefit. This procedure typically keeps patients in the hospital for a week, give or take a day or two. We'll begin respiratory therapy as soon as possible and continue it after he's discharged. He'll have to avoid any strenuous activity for six to eight weeks, maybe more. I can't yet tell you what the limitations will be, but we may have to prevent anything from walking up stairs to jogging around the block. At any rate, he won't be back to work anytime soon. If he continues to show rapid improvement, he could be looking at some part-time desk duty in a couple of months."

"What about long-term?" Travis asked hesitantly.

"Again, every case is different. Some people suffer only a few long-term effects, while others live with shortness of breath and fatigue, requiring oxygen. I always tell my patients that they will know after a year." The doctor stood and offered a handshake as his good-bye.

Chapter Eighteen

Iris and Clara rode past Bo McNeil's house in College Park and spotted the bright-yellow Mustang in the driveway. The home was built in the seventies and had probably been quite a nice place back in the day. Now, it was nestled amidst other aging homes, all of which were showing visible signs of age and neglect. The exterior was red brick, like that of many other houses on the street, and the grass was in desperate need of mowing after the warm summer months. The shrubs were overgrown, and the roof had been patched in several places with shingles that didn't come close to matching the original shade of gray.

"I bet he hasn't done anything to the place since his folks died," Iris said. "What a waste. Bet his folks are rolling over in their graves."

"Yes, it's a real shame," Clara said. "I'm sure they worked hard to get the place and took good care of it. Anyway, it looks like he's home, so I'll just take a drive around the neighborhood."

The women drove slowly through the maze of similar streets, all of which led back to the main thoroughfare that held Bo's house. There didn't seem to be any pedestrians outside, and no one noticed their presence, so they had the opportunity to ride back and forth several times.

"Clara, we've been up and down this darned street at least four times," Iris complained. "Someone is bound to notice two old broads cruising around."

"Either everyone's at work, or they're not up yet. What time is it?"

Iris consulted her watch and looked back out the passenger window. "It's eleven-thirty. They must be at work."

Clara slowed to a stop a few houses down from Bo McNeil's. "That one says it's for rent or lease," she said aloud. "Let's check it out." She pulled into the driveway and placed the Buick in park.

"I don't know about this," Iris said, looking out the window at the vacant house. "This isn't exactly, *Mister Rogers' Neighborhood*, Clara…and Quita warned us not to stop *or* get out of the car."

"Look around you, Iris. It's a nice day, no one's out, and it's a sleepy little neighborhood. Let's walk around the yard a bit and look in some windows. It's innocent enough. People always stop and look at houses they may be interested in renting. That's why the sign's there."

Against her better judgment, Iris exited the vehicle and followed her friend. They peeked in several windows and commented on the blooming jonquils before they noticed Bo coming out of the garage and getting in his Mustang.

"We've got a live one," Iris said. "That looks like a fast machine. We'd better load up."

"He'll notice two old ladies. Just watch which direction he turns at the stop sign. A yellow sports car will be easy enough to spot in traffic."

"Thanks, *Captain Obvious*," Iris said sarcastically, a phrase she'd learned from Quita, who'd said it to her numerous times and explained it more than once.

"Captain *what?*"

"Never mind," Iris said, rolling her eyes.

The two got back in the car and buckled their seatbelts as Clara backed slowly out of the driveway.

"He took a left," Iris said. "That's the way we came in."

They were three cars behind Bo when he stopped at a red light, with his left blinker on.

"I bet he's going to merge onto the highway," Clara said. "Be my eyes, Iris. It's hard enough to deal with the traffic, I sure can't keep my eyes on him."

The light turned green, and Bo made a left, then took the turn lane to hop onto 85-North.

"You were right as rain, Clara. I'll keep him in sight. I just hope he doesn't have a lead foot. Mustangs are *muscle cars*, you know."

"Where in the world did you hear that?"

"I saw it on a calendar when I was getting my tires rotated. Of course, they had a bunch of food-deprived bikini models sitting on the hoods. People don't have any pride anymore."

"Focus, Iris! There are a lot of eighteen-wheelers on the road," Clara warned.

"Sorry. He's in the middle lane, four cars up. Doesn't appear to be speeding. I think we're good where we are."

They followed, staying a few cars behind and two lanes over until they merged onto 285-North. Clara felt confident that her four-door sedan was nondescript enough that it wouldn't raise any red flags. Not too far down the road, they exited at Camp Creek Parkway and made a left. Several red lights caught them, but they didn't lose sight of him.

"He's making a right," Iris said as she craned her neck. "Then a left into an apartment complex."

Clara followed safely behind as she observed him pulling into a parking space next to a U-Haul moving van.

"This can't be happening," Iris said. "It's manna from Heaven, I tell ya. He's gonna help someone move, with that supposedly wrecked back of his. Get out the camera, girl."

"Give me a minute," Clara said as she maneuvered the large car into a space far enough away where they wouldn't be seen.

Bo jogged up a set of stairs and disappeared into an apartment. The two ladies waited impatiently for over an hour before he emerged again, with a young lady and two other males in tow. They each held a beer in one hand and a cigarette in the other as they walked casually to the ten-foot box truck. The lady motioned for one of the men to roll the back door up, and they all stood for a moment as if assessing the available space. Bo finished his cigarette and flicked it onto the pavement, took a final slug from his can of beer, and lifted his hands as if to suggest it was time they get started.

As they walked back up the stairs to the apartment, Clara retrieved her Nikon, and Iris fumbled around with the buttons on her iPhone.

"Whew! I hope we get enough pictures to complete this job," Iris said. "I've really got to pee and it's lunchtime. If you ask me, Quita really underestimates these stakeouts."

Clara didn't offer a response, she was too busy aiming her camera at the apartment door and adjusting her lens for better focus. The other two men exited with a couch and struggled to carry the large piece of furniture down the stairway. Meanwhile, Bo supervised, waving his hands around in frustration.

"Oh no," Clara said. "If he's just supervising, we won't get anything. He's got to lift something!"

The women held their breath as they watched the two men struggling with the sofa. They made it to the landing but couldn't seem to turn it at an angle conducive for them to go any further. Clara couldn't make out what they were saying, but the conversation was clearly a heated one, their voices rising an octave every minute. Just when they were convinced that Bo wasn't going to get involved in the manual labor, he pushed one of the men aside, took the couch from him, and twisted and turned it until it was well above his head. Still talking loudly, he carried his end of the couch to the U-Haul, then easily lifted it onto the truck.

"Well, did you get that?" Iris asked in a whisper. "I got plenty. He lifted that thing like Superman. I don't think we'll need any more evidence."

"I got several photos, too," Clara confirmed. "I say we call it a day. I'm hungry, too. You're right about these stakeouts, Iris."

Chapter Nineteen

It'd been a grueling week filled with numerous touch-and-go occurrences. On the positive side, at the moment, all three law enforcement officers were still among the living.

Captain Burke had spent three days in the ICU, and another two in a regular room while he recuperated from the bypass surgery. There was no doubt his lifestyle would be drastically altered, but doctors expected a full recovery. Gone were the vending machine snacks, the fast-food, and the breaks spent smoking in the courtyard. Instead, he'd have to invite exercise and healthy eating into his life and avoid stress as much as his job would allow. The powers-that-be insisted he see an in-house psychologist, and no amount of resistance would modify their decision. In the end, Burke had to admit that it could only do him good. Not only was his heart surgery a blow to him, but the injuries to his detectives had taken an enormous toll on his mental state as well.

Detective Nettles was the most critical and still not out of the woods. The damage to his liver was extensive, and he'd been through several surgeries to help save the organ. It was still unclear whether he would require a transplant, and he'd yet to wake up enough to even comprehend that his wife was by his side.

Sandi Nettles hadn't left the hospital since the day of her husband's shooting. Family and friends took turns babysitting the couple's seven-year-old son, Ralph and the nurses were kind enough to allow her to shower on the premises. She was drained and close to getting sick herself, but no one could convince her to go home for a decent night's sleep. Sandi was determined to be there the moment her husband woke up *if* he ever did. The couple had a lot to live for, and Sandi was intent on letting him hear that from her.

One of the biggest surprises was that Dr. Gail Duffey arrived every day, during her own lunch break with a book and sandwich in hand, to relieve Sandi so she could get a bite to eat at the hospital cafeteria and decompress a bit with her friends. Duffey munched away on her packed lunches while she read to her colleague, who lay there in a fitful, perilous sleep. Some days she read from the newspaper, sometimes, she read articles from a medical journal, and once in a while, she even recited the dull and gruesome details of autopsy reports. Whatever she read the impromptu story hour for the unconscious officer became a welcomed respite for his worried, frazzled wife.

Detective Pitts, on the other hand, had morphed into a grumpy pain-in-the-ass. His surgery had gone well, and he only suffered a few complications, with the exception of some pain and being virtually bed bound. He desperately wanted to see his partner, and even more, he wanted the uncomfortable chest tube removed. He credited it as the main source of his discomfort. But most of all, he wanted to be discharged. No one was safe from his wrath, not the attentive nurses, Travis Upshaw, or even the sweet, dedicated Jessalyn Brock.

The respiratory therapist had finally had enough and slammed his fist on Pitts' lunch tray, rattling the dishes and spilling a bit of juice. "Has anyone ever told you what an *ungrateful* person you are?" the young man asked. "I work for two different hospitals and a nursing home, and I've never encountered anyone who acts as rudely as you do, even people who are a lot worse off…" He paused to give Pitts an opportunity to respond, but when he didn't, the therapist continued, "From what I see in your medical file, you're quite a lucky man. You could be six feet under right now."

The detective stared at him like a hungry great white would stare at an unwary swimmer's legs.

Cary Fisch held his breath for a few seconds. Perhaps he'd gone…a bit too far, he worried. He'd only been out of school for two years and was already burning out on the job. *Maybe it's my schedule? I've taken on so much recently.* Cary opened his mouth to apologize, but the detective beat him to it.

"You know, you're right," Pitts said surprisingly. He let out a long sigh and leaned back on his fluffed pillows. "I've been a real son-of-a-bitch, and I'm sorry."

Cary rolled a stool under himself and wheeled over to the bed.

Pitts cleared his throat and wiped coarsely at a tear that had escaped the rim of his eye. "It's tough, man…and I'm not talking about the gunshot wound. I don't give a rat's ass about losing over half of my lung," his voice caught with emotion, and he struggled to clear his throat again to continue. "I don't know how it is in the medical field," he said. "But when you're a cop, your partner's life means more than your own." Pitts winced briefly and shifted on the bed, trying to get more comfortable. "You don't know what I'd give to trade places with Nettles, right now. You say I'm lucky, but I'm not feeling it."

Cary felt a dense weight of guilt wash over him. It was wrong to take his own fatigue out on a patient, and he'd broken the first rule of Therapy 101. "Mister Pitts, I don't know what to say. I was out of line to speak to you like that. Perhaps you would feel more comfortable if I ask the nurses to assign you another respiratory therapist while you're here?"

The hardened detective let out a raspy laugh, only to spout off a chain of wicked profanities from the pain the laughter brought. "Hell no! I don't want anybody else. You're doing just fine, kid. In fact, I've never met anybody who has the balls to put me in my place like that. I know I'm not going to be any help to Nettles or anyone else if I'm lying in this bed feeling sorry for myself. Let's get on with this therapy so I can get the hell outta here."

A broad smile crossed the young medical professional's face. "Everyone's been walking on eggshells around you, thinking it'd be best for you. That's often the case with trauma patients who've gone through so much physically and mentally, but in your case…well, we were wrong. I understand that you want to visit your partner."

"Damn right, I do," Pitts said with great fervor as he struggled to sit up in the bed.

"Easy there, fella! I can't make any promises, but I'll talk to the doctor on duty and see if he'll allow you to go for a brief visit—*brief* being the keyword. I think it might do you some good to get out of this room. Just know you'll be tired, really exhausted, and you'll probably hurt like hell for most of the day."

"You're burnin' daylight, kid," Pitts said. "Go talk to that doctor."

"I'll be right back," Cary said, then hurried out of the room.

Pitts was waiting impatiently, like a kid at Christmas, when Cary and the doctor finally walked back in. "Well, fellas? What's it gonna be?" Pitts asked bluntly, prepared for a rebuttal should his request to visit Nettles were denied.

"I understand you're being a very difficult patient," the doctor said flatly. He took off his wire-rimmed glasses and stared at Pitts with the same condescending expression his middle-school English teacher had given him.

Pitts instantly felt the blood rush to his face but managed to maintain his composure. He stammered, "Yeah, uh...I was just apologizing for that. I admit this whole screwed-up situation has me a little angry, but I really want...no, I *need* to see my partner, Doc. We're like brothers, and exhausted or not, I know I'll feel better once I see him."

The doctor's expression softened, and he placed his spectacles back on his face. "Well, let's get you on your way then. Cary will wheelchair you up to ICU. I'll contact the nurses' station to let them know you're coming, but I must be very, very clear, Mister Pitts. You will not be allowed to stay more than five minutes, which is technically five minutes more than you should be there anyway. Mister Nettles is in critical condition, and we shouldn't disturb his rest or stir up too many memories of what happened. Any kind of stress will be very harmful to him, right now. Do you understand?"

"Yes, Doctor. I understand perfectly...and I really appreciate this."

"Good, don't make me regret my decision," he responded as he walked out of the room and shut the door behind him.

Chapter Twenty

It was after 3:00 when Clara and Iris finally made it back to the office. Quita was on the phone with a potential client and simply gave them a slight wave, without looking up from her scratchpad.

Both women hung up their jackets and took a seat behind their desks. Iris sighed loudly, stood up, then rifled through the supply closet until she found the Windex.

"How'd I know you were going to clean the front window?" Clara asked, without even looking over at her friend. "I knew it, just as sure as I'm sitting here."

"You should be thanking me," Iris said. "I never ask you to help clean this place. If it wasn't for me, it would look like a pigsty."

"You never even give me a chance. I think it's a nervous habit."

"It's not!" Iris spat defensively. "I'm just the responsible one, that's all."

Clara refused to continue the dialogue, choosing instead to lean back in her desk chair, close her eyes, and replay the events of the morning in her head.

Quita finally ended her call and placed the phone back on its cradle. "So, ladies, tell me…how did today go?"

"You don't have any idea how dangerous our jobs are," Iris started in. "You send us into the combat zone without food or water or even a toilet and expect us to work miracles!"

"Miss Iris, it isn't like I deployed you to Kuwait," Quita said, refusing to give in to the smile that threatened to form on her face. "Were you really in danger? Did anyone threaten you?"

"Not exactly," Iris answered flatly. "But one ever knows how these things will go. Fortunately for us, this one worked in our favor."

"How so?"

"We got the punk dead to rights. He went over to some girl's apartment to help her move. Couldn't have planned it better myself! I used my iPhone and caught him in the act of moving a very large couch. Of course, Clara had her trusty Nikon. We had it covered from both vantage points."

"Let me take a look," Quita said, walking over to take Iris's phone. She used her index finger to scroll through the numerous shots of Bo McNeil lifting his friend's couch. There must have been a hundred of him...shifting and angling the sofa to squeeze it down the cramped stairwell. "I have to say, you did an amazing job, Miss Iris. Next thing I know, you'll be workin' for the paparazzi."

"For Papa who? Is that some kind of pizza place?"

Quita laughed. "No, never mind. Anyway, there's no way he'll be able to stick to his injured back story now. I'm sure Hart Roofing will be glad we nailed him. That's another check for Hadley and Samples. We're getting a lot of calls. Seems word's gotten out on the streets..." She paused. "What's the matter, Miss Clara? You don't look too happy."

"I guess when we started this business, I expected to be making more of a difference," Clara said. "Spying on a fella moving his friend's couch isn't exactly what I had in mind."

Quita used her feet to roll her chair in front of Clara's desk. "You don't think saving an honest company a lot of money is helping somebody?" she asked. "What about saving Nancy's and Lewis's lives?"

"Well, we don't know for sure it would've come down to murder," Clara retorted.

"Well, at the very least, you two stopped a phony marriage and kept Summer from getting her hands on their money or cashing in on their life insurance. What you're doing is important. I know, 'cause my sister's baby isn't walking around diaper-less anymore. It may seem like a small thing, but she was really struggling. You and Miss Iris went over to that construction site and made Denard pay, and you didn't charge me a dime for your help. Not only that, but I landed a job out of it, too. Don't tell me you ain't changing things for the better."

Iris stopped cleaning the windows and walked over to sit down, touched by Quita's kind remarks. "I never really thought of it like that," she admitted.

"Denard hasn't missed one Friday. Last week, when I went to pick up the fifty bucks, he'd also left a Walmart bag full of baby wipes, lotion, socks, and a teething ring. You could've knocked me over with a feather!"

"That's really nice," Clara said. "I'm happy to hear that."

"I always knew he'd do the right thing," Iris commented. "He was actually quite respectful after all was said and done."

The three women sat in silence as they contemplated the cases they'd worked and the ones that lay ahead. The dinging of the bell jolted them out of their thoughts.

The young woman who walked through the door looked weary and forlorn. She attempted a smile, but it was obviously disingenuous.

Quita jumped to her feet to greet her. "Good afternoon. I'm JaQuita. How can I help you?"

"I'm not sure, really. In fact, I probably made a mistake in coming here. I really don't have any money to get the help I need, and—"

"Why don't you let us decide that honey," Clara said. "Please sit and tell us about your problem. I'm Clara Hadley, one of the owners. What's your name?"

The woman slowly made her way to Clara's desk, her face reflecting both exhaustion and deep-seated grief. "My name's Ginger, Ginger Baines. I-I didn't know where else to go," she said, her voice cracking with emotion.

Iris handed her a tissue. "Go on, dear," she coaxed.

"I've been riding around the city for a couple of hours and decided to come to this section of town, thinking your prices might be, uh…a little lower. I really need a private investigator, and I don't have much to spend." Her expression suddenly mirrored embarrassment. "No offense," she quickly added.

"None taken," Clara said. "Please tell us what you need help with."

"It's my sister, she was murdered!"

"Oh dear," Iris interjected. "Have you gone to the police?"

"Yes. They investigated every lead, but they've moved on now. Unless they get a hit on the DNA or someone calls in to confess, I'm afraid the file will sit in a box in some vast warehouse gathering dust along with all the other unsolved crimes."

"Have you remained in contact with the lead detective?" Clara pressed. "The squeaky wheel gets the grease, as they say."

"Yes, I revisited the two detectives who were assigned to the investigation, but they concluded it was most likely a random crime, which makes it more difficult to solve. I went back again this morning, thinking they might get tired of seeing me and that it would light a fire under them to keep the search ongoing, but it doesn't seem to be doing much good." Ginger let out a deep sigh and slumped back in the chair.

Quita handed her a bottle of water.

"What did they say?" Iris asked.

"Nothing, they're both out on medical leave," Ginger answered. "Apparently, the case will be reassigned, and they aren't even sure who that detective will be."

"*Both* of them are out on medical leave?" Clara asked.

"Yes, it was all over the news a couple of weeks ago," Ginger said. "Surely you saw it. They were gunned down right outside of Homicide headquarters."

"Oh, dear. Yes, I did see that, now that you mentioned it." Clara turned her glance to Iris. "One was Detective Pitts, the one who worked on Doctor Chatsworth's case."

"The doctor y'all busted?" Quita asked. "Someone shot him?"

"Yes," Clara continued. "Apparently, it was a drive-by, and both detectives were hit. It's a miracle they survived. I think one is still in critical condition, but Detective Pitts is recovering. That was the last I heard anyway."

"So, you know Detective Pitts?" Ginger asked, leaning forward in her chair. "Do you think you could talk to him? Will he give you any details he may have kept from me?"

"Oh, my," Clara said nervously, wringing her hands together. "Honey, we're just acquaintances, and I can't say he's very fond of me...or Iris."

"That's not so!" Iris interjected. "Why would you say such a thing, Clara?"

Clara shot her a sharp, knowing glance that didn't go unnoticed by Ginger or Quita. "I'm sure he'll be in recovery for quite a while," Clara said. "It will be difficult to contact him, if not impossible. I think you should stay in touch with the PD and push them to assign another detective to the case."

Ginger looked deflated. "Don't you understand?" she asked. "The case is cold. There are hundreds of unsolved murders in those archives, and my sister's is the newest. The Homicide Division has to work the warm ones that still have the potential of being solved." Ginger wiped the tissue across her forehead and the back of her neck. She would've welcomed the relief tears would have brought, but they were all spent, completely tapped out. All that remained were the raw emotions of loss.

Quita stood and paced in front of them, searching for the right words. "Miss Clara," she finally said. "You just finished telling me you don't feel like you've been making a real difference. Here's your chance. There's gotta be something you and Miss Iris can uncover."

"We're not detectives, Quita. We're merely private investigators and not seasoned ones at that. A murder investigation is way over our heads."

"Also, I'm broke," Ginger added. "I've already hit up every friend and nonprofit agency I can think of to help pay for Jasmine's funeral. I even dropped out of my classes this semester, so I can get more hours at my part-time job. I can pay some, but I know it won't be enough to cover your fee."

"Jasmine, you said?" Clara asked somberly.

"Yes, her name was Jasmine Baines. She was nineteen, a college student, and a waitress. She was murdered by some stranger who dumped her lifeless body in Oakland Cemetery. They left her in the morgue for two days before I even knew she was dead." She stopped and blew into the tissues the ladies had given her. "Jasmine was left all alone in that cold, sterile place, like some Jane Doe nobody cared about."

The rims of Ginger's eyes were red, but tears still failed her. It seemed a lifetime ago that the two detectives had driven her to the Medical Examiner's office to view the chilling photograph of her sister. Ginger recalled very little about Jasmine's face in that grotesque picture. It was the curls in her strawberry-blonde hair that had caught Ginger's eye, and she knew in an instant she was looking at Jasmine.

"Well, it's settled then," Clara said firmly. "We'll take the case. Of course, I can't promise anything, but we'll look into it. We have enough other work to keep us afloat financially, so this will be pro boner."

"Clara!" Iris shouted, shaking her head. "It's *pro bono!*"

"Oh, of course. Sorry, *Pro bono*...a freebie," Clara said, blushing. "That is if our office manager approves it."

"I certainly do," Quita said quickly. "And, Ginger, I promise these ladies won't let you down. They haven't lost a case yet...even if they aren't up on their Latin," she assured Ginger.

Chapter Twenty-One

Detective Pitts was somehow able to ignore the throbbing pain radiating from his rib cage as Cary Fisch wheeled him up to the ICU. He knew he'd feel better after seeing his partner. More than once, he'd wondered if Nettles was actually dead and they hadn't had the nerve to tell him. Now, he was going to see for himself.

The nurses at the centrally located counter in the epicenter of the unit nodded at him in greeting. They were all aware of the price the detective had paid for defending their city, and it was only right to acknowledge him in some way. After brief smiles, their eyes went directly back to their computers.

"He's right down here on the left," Cary said, speeding up the pace.

The room was enclosed in glass, and Pitts could make out Nettles' wife sitting by his bedside. He coughed slightly, so as not to startle her.

"Why look at you," she said excitedly. "You're a sight for sore eyes."

Pitts reached for her hand. "Sandi…" he began, but raw emotions wouldn't allow him to continue.

"It's okay," she said warmly. "It's all going to be just fine. Here," she said, motioning toward the bed. "Come closer to Matthew. He hasn't come to yet, but I'm certain he'll feel your presence. I'll leave you alone to talk with him." She bent down to kiss Pitts on the cheek. "It was a horrible thing that happened to you two, but you're both tougher than nails. It's clear your work here isn't done if the Lord saw fit to let you stay among the living."

Pitts struggled to swallow the lump in his throat, which was so large it threatened to strangle him. Fortunately, Sandi didn't wait on or expect a reply.

Cary patted him lightly on the shoulder. "I'll be right outside. Just call if you need me. Remember, you've only got a few minutes. If I keep you up here longer than that we may violate any future privileges."

Pitts simply nodded his words refusing to form.

After the glass door slid closed, Pitts looked around the room. It was a small, glassed-in cube, identical to the others on the floor. Medical equipment occupied every nook and cranny, leaving little room for visitors.

Nettles looked nothing like himself. He was in a deep sleep, with tubes and wires running from virtually every part of his body. His wavy, dark hair was slicked back as if it'd just been washed but still wasn't dry. He no longer resembled the robust man who'd shared Pitts' daily routine, but Pitts' eyes quickly moved to the one part of his friend he was sure to recognize: his hands. He reached for Nettles' thick right hand and held it in his own. Careful not to disturb the IV pushing fluids into Nettles' veins, Pitts studied his friend's hand.

A warm smile crossed his lips as he recalled the many times he'd witnessed Nettles wagging his index finger at someone who'd outraged him at a crime scene or the times he'd slammed the telephone receiver down on a superior who didn't agree with his theory on a homicide. Pritchard Pitts had spent many-a-days defending his partner's actions to the upper ranks, and he had no regrets about it. Nettles was one hell of a detective and a good, honest man.

He released Nettles' hand, then patted it a few times. "I wish it was me in this bed, old friend. God knows I'da taken those bullets for you if I could have, but I promise you this…I'll get the son-of-a-bitch who did this to us if it's the last thing I do."

As if on cue, Cary opened the sliding door and grabbed the handles of the wheelchair. He was well aware that his patient was emotional, so he didn't attempt any conversation. He hit the elevator button and backed in with the wheelchair when the doors opened.

"Thanks, man," Pitts said softly. "I appreciate the hell outta that."

"No problem," Cary said. "I'll make sure you get some pain and sleep meds when we get back to your room. I know you'll be hurting tonight, inside and out. That was the most activity you've had since you've been here."

"Maybe the pain pill," Pitts answered. "But I don't want the sleeping pill. I've got a lot to remember about the day we were shot. I need to start looking for whoever did this to us."

Chapter Twenty-Two

It was after 8:00 p.m., and Clara, Iris, and Quita were still at the office. They'd ordered Chinese and were taking a break. The story of Jasmine Baines's murder had touched each of them, and they were anxious to get started on the case. Quita had obtained a copy of the original police report, and they'd all slowly pored over it. They'd also found a small article in the *Atlanta Journal-Constitution*, but there was no follow-up story that they could find. They found it quite sad that murder was such a common occurrence in their city that a dead girl, left in a cemetery, could so quickly become yesterday's news before another hot topic stepped in to take its place. They'd been busy discussing how they might investigate the crime when their empty stomachs had gotten the best of them.

"I'm so glad you ladies agreed to take this one," Quita said.

"This coming from somebody who didn't want us to take any free cases," Iris said as she munched on an egg roll. "Or is it, pro boner cases, Clara?" she said, laughing at her friend.

"It isn't a crime to misspeak once in a while, Iris," Clara scolded. "If it was, you would've been behind bars a long time ago!"

"Let's just say we're learning from each other," Quita said. "I understand that you two wanna make a difference with your work, and I'm starting to feel the same way. I'll do all the research I can from the office, but you'll still have to take some paying jobs to keep this place afloat. Also, I know it's not the ideal time to bring this up, but I'm gonna need a few days off next week."

"Next week? But we'll be so busy," Clara said. "Is there any way you can put it off a few weeks? I really want to dig into this murder case."

"I don't want to take off at all, but I've got to find a new place to live."

Clara and Iris exchanged glances, they'd never even thought to question where she was living, and they felt guilty for not trying to get to know her better.

"What's the problem?" Clara asked.

"My apartment complex has been condemned—or at least I think that was the word they used. I guess the greedy manager stopped paying the sanitation company because trash is stacked a mile high around the

Dumpsters. Not only that, but there's also plumbing problems. He's a real slumlord if you ask me."

"Good Lord," Iris said. "Why have you been staying there if there isn't even any garbage pickup?"

Quita forced a laugh. "It's what I can afford," she answered. "Cheap apartments aren't easy to find these days, even in the worst neighborhoods, and I gotta have something on the bus line. I've only got two days to get my stuff out before they demolish the place, so I can't postpone my time off."

"Oh dear," Clara said. "I didn't realize your housing was so…serious of a problem. You can always stay at my place."

"That's really nice of you," Quita said. "But I need my own place. I wouldn't feel right staying with you."

"Like you said, cheap apartments aren't easy to find, and most aren't in good areas," Iris argued. "A pretty young woman like you needs to be in a safe part of town. Clara, what about the space above us? It's dirty and full of spider webs right now, but it's nothing a coat of paint couldn't cure. There's even a full bath up there."

"I don't know," Clara answered. "It's just been used for storage in the past, and it's awfully dusty. Not only that, but this isn't exactly a safe area either."

"It's not so bad," Iris suggested.

"How do you figure?" Clara asked.

"Let's think this through," Iris continued. "It's near the county jail, so there are cops driving by here at all hours. We have an alarm system, and I've heard that if somebody lives above a business, the insurance rates are lower. Personally, I think it'd be fun. What do you think, Quita? You sure wouldn't have to worry about using the bus to get to work anymore!"

Quita's eyes sparkled at the thought, but she'd known disappointment many times in her life, and she didn't want to get her hopes up. "You're right, I'd never be late to work."

"The bathroom might need some work," Clara warned. "There's no kitchen either."

"How much could a small kitchen area cost?" Iris asked. "We could start small, with a sink, microwave, and refrigerator, just the necessities. Hell, some college students live with a Styrofoam cooler and one of those hot plates, so I know we can set her up better than that!"

"I can have someone come take a look tomorrow," Clara said. "Do you think Rhadrick will be willing to help you move your stuff into a storage unit for a few days? We can get the upper space cleaned up and painted fairly quickly if we can find some cheap labor."

The smile on Quita's face was genuine. "I'm sure he would. I could stay with my sister for a few days, till it's done. She's on assistance and isn't allowed to have anyone living with her other than her son, but a few nights won't hurt. As far as I know, there are no laws about sisters having a couple of sleepovers."

"Then it's settled," Clara said as she took the last bite of her beef and broccoli. "First thing in the morning, see if you can find somebody who'll work with a limited budget. I think we should call it a night. I'll drop you off at your apartment so you can get to packing!"

Chapter Twenty-Three

Pitts began to regret turning down the sleep medication as it was a real struggle to fall asleep. The doctors had finally agreed to release him the following day, and he was anxious to get back to his apartment and sleep in his own bed. The plan was for him to continue respiratory therapy at home. A nurse would stop by daily for five days, before tapering her visits off to twice a week. Between the nurse's visits, Jessalyn stopping by to bring meals and fellow cops in and out, he remained in good spirits. The excitement of leaving the dreary hospital kept him tossing and turning until finally, he gave in to sleep sometime after midnight. Pitts' eyes darted rapidly from side to side under their lids as the dreams began...

The heavy rain was coming down in sheets as he and Nettles ran swiftly through the muddy cemetery. The tombstones seemed to jump out at them as they rushed to get to the young girl under the drenched, pink blanket. Her hands were uncovered, curled up in some macabre position that seemed to be beckoning them to her side. Her long, jagged nails were painted dark-red, and the polish turned to blood at her cuticles and ran down her slender hands. As Pitts knelt beside her, she grabbed his throat with unbearable force. Nettles pulled desperately at the gnarled hands, but nothing could force her to release her grasp. Pitts was struggling for air, gasping, wheezing, clawing at his own neck, and—

"Detective? Detective! Wake up, I need to talk to you."

Pitts bolted straight up in the bed just as a masculine hand covered his mouth.

"Take it easy, man. You can't scream now. I've gotta talk to you, but if you start yellin', I'm gonna bolt. Got it?"

Pitts nodded in agreement as he tried to clear his head from both the nightmare and his visitor. His mind was still hazy. It was the late hour, and the lights were dimmed, but there was enough light creeping in under the closed door and the machines that he could still make out everything in the room. Pitts was weak and unable to defend himself, but something in the tone of his late-night caller's voice suggested that he meant him no harm.

Pitts' vision slowly began to come into focus, and he leaned back on his pillows to ease the pain of his sudden movement. The face and voice were familiar, but he couldn't pinpoint the young man's identity. He was a black male, clean-shaven, with a medium build, his eyes filled with terror. He wore a dark stocking cap, pulled down to his eyebrows. His breathing was fast and panicked.

"I...man, I know you," Pitts started. "I know you from somewhere, but I can't place it."

"G-Boy," he whispered as he leaned closer to Pitts' face. His breath smelled of weed, beer, and some type of mint, perhaps an Altoid that had done him little good. "I mean, Germaine, Germaine Wilkins. You met me when my homeboy was shot over off Howell Mill."

"That's it." Pitts tried to lean back farther into his pillows, Germaine was so close to him that it was unsettling. "What are you doing here, man?" Pitts asked as his nerves started to get the best of him. *How did this guy know where to find me? Is he our shooter?*

"Look, dude, I'm not here to hurt you, if that's what you're thinkin'," Germaine insisted as he moved closer, closing the gap created by Pitts' retreat. His whispers were harsh and desperate, "I need you to listen, 'cause I gotta get the hell outta here. I'm going *ghost*."

"What?"

"Goin' *ghost*, man, gettin' the hell outta Dodge. I just don't want you cops thinkin' I got anything to do with Tony's shooting or what happened to you. Y'all need to—"

"Wait," Pitts interrupted. "Don't bolt yet, I need some answers. Obviously, something or someone's got you scared. Let me help you."

"Hell naw, man. Look at you, all shot up. I ain't waitin' 'round for the same shit to happen to me. I got a feelin' I wouldn't be as lucky as two cops. I'd end up on a slab 'stead of a hospital bed, and nobody would give a damn."

The adrenaline suddenly coursing through Pitts' veins cleared his head and vision almost instantly. Germaine knew something, and he had to keep him around as long as he could if only to pick whatever brain cells the man hadn't smoked away. Pitts prayed a nurse wouldn't come in to check his vitals because that'd send him running. "Hold on, Germaine," he begged. "Was your boy in a gang? Was the murder a rival shooting?"

"Hell no, Tony wasn't in no gang. He sold weed, that's it. He wasn't a bad guy. He just didn't want no nine-to-five."

"That pregnant girl said it was a gang killing." Pitts held his hand up to suggest Germaine back up a little, then sat up in bed. "I remember now," he said. "We went to the morgue to check his body for gang tatts, but we found nothing. Why'd she lie about it? Is she scared she'll be shot, too?"

The mention of the girl seemed to increase Germaine's fear. "Look, man, I don't know nothin' 'bout that bi...er, uh, girl. I just know Tony's dead and that you and your partner were shot. I ain't gonna wait around to be next." He then slowly backed away, his limbs jittery, bouncing back and forth like a bad audition for *So You Think You Can Dance*.

"Don't go, Germaine. Obviously, you came here to tell me something. No one knows you're here, right? Please, buddy, I need some help. I wanna solve your friend's murder and figure out who did this to us. It was pretty ballsy, shooting two cops right outside the station."

Germaine looked around the room nervously as if he feared someone had entered without his knowledge or that the place was bugged. "I just came to tell y'all that I didn't do *nothin'*. I'm leaving town, and I was afraid you'd come looking for me for more info on Tony's death."

"Germaine, there's more to it than that, or you wouldn't have gone to the trouble of sneaking in here at this hour. Something has the shit scared out of you, and I know it's not just the possibility of being blamed for Tony's murder. If that were true, you wouldn't come near a cop. It's that girl, Platinum, isn't it? She shot us, didn't she? Why?"

"Look, I'm outta here, but y'all need to watch your backs. Like most folks where I come from, I ain't real fond of cops, but you didn't deserve what you got. Plus, if somebody'll gun down two police in the street, they're capable of anything. Like you said, that was ballsy...or insane."

"But you know something, don't you? For starters, how'd you know where to find me?"

"You were shot with a nine, man. Where else would they take you but Grady?"

"Hmm, and how do you know it was a nine-milli?"

"I didn't say it was," Germaine said, his voice above a whisper now, the octave high and flustered. He tugged the stocking cap farther down on his head and turned up the collar of his leather jacket.

"Don't go," Pitts insisted. "I know you didn't do it, G-Boy. I need more information to—"

It was useless before he could finish his sentence, the frightened young man was gone, vanished just as quickly as he'd appeared. It left Pitts limp

111

and confused from the whole ordeal, with a hundred questions swirling through his pain-medicated head: *If he's really so afraid, why would he risk coming to the hospital? Am I still in danger? Something isn't right, I can feel it.*

Pitts laid back in the bed and ran the whole event back through his mind. Did it really even happen? His dream about the dead girl had been so vivid that he'd found it difficult to wake up from it. Maybe that ghostly visit from Germaine was only another part of the nightmare.

The door to his room opened slowly, and he heard the wheels from the blood pressure cart before he even saw it. Glancing at the clock on the wall, he noted it was 1:30 a.m.

"I'm surprised to see you awake," the middle-aged nurse said with a smile. "I figured you'd be fast asleep. Big day tomorrow, I hear?"

"Yeah, finally going home. Listen, I just had a guest."

"You did? That's odd. It's well beyond visiting hours."

"Did you happen to see anyone on the floor? It was a young, black male in a black leather jacket, stocking cap and faded jeans."

"I didn't see him, but I was at the nurses' station busy preparing meds for a room down the hall. If I had seen anyone, I would've run them off. We don't allow visitors at this hour. I'm surprised he got past security."

"Right. As a matter of fact, aren't the doors locked at night?" Pitts asked.

"Certainly, but the ER's always open. Maybe he came in that way and sneaked through the hospital. We have less staff in some areas at night, but it isn't usually a problem. Was he bothering you?"

Pitts wrinkled his forehead in concentration. "No, not really, but it was a strange visit, to say the least."

"Would you like for me to call security?"

"No, don't do that. I'm fine. He's gone now."

"Very well, let me check your vitals, and then hopefully you can get back to sleep." She fastened the Velcro cuff tightly around his bicep and punched the button on the machine.

"Jesus! That feels like it's gonna cut my arm off," Pitts complained. "I don't remember those things being that tight before y'all started using those machines."

"We get a lot of complaints about them," the nurse said. "But apparently, new technology is more reliable."

Pitts noticed a frown across her face. "What's the problem? Tell me I'm not an amputee now. I don't have time to fool around with a malpractice suit," he teased.

"No," she answered seriously as she reset the machine. "Your pressure is alarmingly high. Let me take it again. Are you sure that young man didn't upset you?"

"I'm fine," Pitts insisted, his tone a little sharper than intended. "I had a bad dream before he came in. I guess I'm a little nervous about going home."

She took his pressure again and vowed to return every thirty minutes to monitor it. Before she left, she poured a fresh glass of water for him and told him to drink it as it would do him good.

Something a little stronger would do me a whole lot more good, lady, Pitts thought as he reached for the water and took a long slug. As bland as it was, it felt good traveling down his parched throat. Nevertheless, his thoughts about the visitor continued to plague him.

If G-Boy took a chance to sneak into the hospital just to tell me to watch my back, there must be some truth to it. In fact, it only makes sense the shooter might come back to finish the job. If Germaine found me so easily, the attempted killer could do the same. Damn.

Pitts picked up the cell phone beside his bed. Normally, he would've called Captain Burke over any concerns, but it was out of the question. In fact, the shooter could technically be blamed for a trio of downed cops now. He scrolled through his contacts until he got to Lieutenant Costa's number.

"Costa," she said, answering on the second ring. Her voice was bright and alert as if it were 1:00 in the afternoon instead of 1:00 in the morning.

"Hey there, LT," Pitts answered. "Look, I'm sorry to bother you at this hour."

"No worries, Pitts. What's up, everything okay?"

He immediately picked up the alarm in her voice as well as her lame attempt to mask it with impossible perkiness. "Yeah, yeah, everything's fine. I was wondering if you could come by in the morning before you head into the office."

"Sure, but are you positive everything's all right? I thought I heard they're releasing you tomorrow."

"I am, but you know how disorganized that damn discharge procedure is. I'll be lucky to get out of here by noon."

She laughed, but her nervousness was evident in her chuckle. "I'll see you in the morning, but I can come by now if you need me to."

"That won't be necessary," he insisted. "We should probably both try to catch a few more Zs before the sun comes up."

"Will do. See you about eight o'clock," she said, disconnecting the call.

Chapter Twenty-Four

The past two days had been busy for Hadley and Samples Investigations. Quita had indeed found someone who was willing to work with a tight budget, and he'd been busy fixing up her new home. Fortunately for the business pocketbook, their main concerns about inept plumbing and electrical issues were unfounded. Although the building was old it was structurally sound and needed little work.

A fresh coat of bright paint worked wonders, and although it was essentially one large room, it gave off the appearance of a pricier loft. The bathtub was still functional, and the contractor re-glazed it and added an inexpensive, but charming, vanity and sink. With the savings they'd retained from not having to make any major repairs, the small kitchen became a reality. Even better, the resourceful Rhadrick found a deal on a refrigerator and donated it to the cause.

As Quita's new place started to come together, Clara and Iris decided to purchase a few pieces to spruce it up a bit. They loaded up in Rhadrick's Camaro and headed to IKEA, a place neither woman had ever heard of.

"Can you believe we actually had lunch in a furniture store?" Iris marveled. "Have you ever heard of such a thing?"

"You must've forgotten about eating in Rich's Magnolia Room at Greenbriar Mall," Clara piped up. "Many-a-Sundays, we flew over there right after church to catch the latest fashion show."

"Indeed," Iris recalled with a nostalgic smile. "I can still taste that marvelous chicken salad."

"Are you ladies talking about a food court?" Quita asked. "That's nothing new."

"Heavens no, dear," Clara answered. "It was a restaurant above Rich's department store and was quite a treat after a long day of shopping. It was decorated with paintings of large, beautiful magnolia blossoms, and ladies always felt special when they dined there. I declare I'd almost forgotten about it."

"Oh," Quita said, struggling to envision such a place in a mall. "I want to thank you, ladies, again for the furniture and the new place. I'll take real good care of it."

"I'm sure you will," Clara said lovingly. "I remember when Harold and I started out. We only had hand-me-down furniture, but we were very grateful for it and proud of our place. That was back when furniture lasted forever, and a fresh coat of paint gave it another chance at life."

"When Fred and I got married, my great-aunt Imogene gave us her couch because she'd purchased a new one. She never took the plastic cover off it, so there wasn't a spot anywhere. It was practically showroom new! We felt like we'd hit the jackpot," Iris said with a hearty laugh. "That thing lasted for thirty years. I swear, things were made differently back then, and people took care of what they had. I guess a lot has changed."

"It sure has," Quita agreed.

"Like sex for instance," Iris went on. "I can't believe young people these days are—"

"Iris!" Clara interrupted. "Do I need to remind you we're in mixed company? Think of poor Rhadrick, would you? We don't want to make the young man uncomfortable."

"Oh, for heaven's sake, Clara. Rhadrick knows about sex. It's a shame, I tell ya. It used to be between married folks, something that happened at home behind closed bedroom doors. No one spoke of it in public or on TV. Now it's out of control. There are women having sex on elevators and in public places. It's downright shameful. I saw something on a movie the other day I've never even heard of before."

"Why do I already know you're going to insist on sharing it with us?" Clara asked as she stared out the car window, praying her friend would change the subject.

"It seems people can become members of this Mile-High Club by having sex on an airplane—in the *bathroom*, I might add. I don't get it. Those bathrooms are so small, I don't hardly see how they'd fit. Not only that but what if there's a plane crash? It's pure foolishness, I tell ya."

Rhadrick let out a loud gut laugh and slammed his hands on the steering wheel. "Miss Iris, you're a mess. You're not just a trip, you're a whole vacation!"

"I'm not making this up! Who could even come up with such a thing? Have you ever been in an airplane bathroom? I can barely get my pants down in that miniature closet they call a restroom!"

"Iris, zip it!" Clara ordered. "That's enough, I really don't want to hear any more."

"It's just foolishness, I tell ya. This world is going to hell in a handbasket."

"How we went from chicken salad at the Magnolia Room to sex on a plane is beyond me," Clara said in a huff. "Let's talk about the murder and how we plan to get to the bottom of it. We've spent enough time on getting the apartment ready. Now it's time to get back to business."

"I agree," Quita said. "I've got a huge whiteboard back at the office. We can use it to map out our strategy."

"It won't be long, ladies," Rhadrick said, his voice still reflecting amusement. "Five more minutes and I'll have you back, safe and sound."

Chapter Twenty-Five

Pitts was awake at 7:00 a.m. He picked at his breakfast when it arrived but ate very little of it. The chest tube had been removed two days earlier, bringing much-anticipated relief. His blood pressure had come back down slowly throughout the night, but the periodic checks had prevented him from returning to a deep sleep, so he was exhausted.

He watched the local news but kept a continuous gaze on the clock. Eight o'clock came and went, and he wondered if Lieutenant Costa had forgotten his phone call from the previous night. Finally, at 9:30, she came through the door.

Her eyes reflected that she, too, had lost sleep, but her voice sounded alert. "What's up, Pitts? Sorry, I'm late."

"No problem, I was beginning to think you forgot."

"Nope, I'd never forget about you. A homicide was called in shortly after you phoned, and with half the division laid up here in the hospital…well, somebody had to step up to the plate."

Pitts flashed her a grin. "I'd be back in a minute if I could. This is the first time in my life I've been bedridden, and it's not a good feeling."

"I hear ya," Costa said. "Men are the worst patients, but you'll be back on your feet in no time. Anyway, what's up? You sounded pretty worried last night," she said as she slid a chair closer to his bed.

"First, have you got any leads on our shooter?"

"Not much, but there is something. We wanted to give you and Nettles a little time to heal before we started bombarding you with the details. You guys scared the hell out of us, you know. The two of you could've been toast, right there on the sidewalk. It's nothing short of a miracle you both survived those shots."

"So, I hear," Pitts said. "But I need to know what you've got."

"For starters, the bullets are an exact match to those used in that murder over off Howell Mill Road, the scene you and Nettles had just come from. I'm not sure how much you remember about that particular case. Doc says you might have a bad case of amnesia, with your entire memory of the day you were shot erased."

"I do have some memories of that day. In fact, they're just starting to come back. Did anyone see the shooter?"

"A couple of homeless guys told us they saw a black Dodge Charger speed by and spray you and Nettles with bullets. They hit the cement as soon as the shooting started, and it happened so fast they only made out the make and model of the car, no tag number or anything distinctive. No one else reported a speeding car in the surrounding area, and black Chargers are a dime a dozen in Atlanta. Of course, an APB was issued immediately, and several cars were pulled over, but that didn't turn up anything."

"I don't have any recollection of the shooting itself or the days immediately following," Pitts said. "But I called you because I had a visitor last night."

"Okay, who?"

"A guy name, Germaine Wilkins. He was in the car with Tony Hart, the homicide victim on Howell Mill."

"What the hell was he doing here?" Costa demanded. "And why the hell didn't you call dispatch?"

"I was sound asleep when he got here and in a daze from pain meds. For a minute, I thought I was dreaming the whole thing. He was scared, real scared. He said he was leaving the area and warned me to watch my back."

"Son-of-a-bitch, Pitts! And you didn't think to call somebody?"

"I called you," he answered defensively.

"If you'da told me someone from a homicide case had shown up at your bedside in the middle of the night, I'd have dispatched patrol and been up here myself. Have you lost your mind? He could've killed you!"

"But he didn't," Pitts continued. "It was strange. Something about that murder has him freaked out."

"Ya *think*? If someone in the car with me was murdered, I'd be freaked out, too."

"There was a girl with them, a real a piece of work. Her story didn't match Germaine's at all. We questioned her at the station but didn't have enough to keep her. Her street name's Platinum, and she's about ten months pregnant, from the looks of it."

"Yeah, I know. Her real name is, Monica Heard. I saw the recorded interview. She's a real tough cookie. She had her baby here at Grady four days ago and left without anyone seeing her, just abandoned the kid. The poor thing's addicted to crack, and last I heard, she's still going through withdrawals. She's in the NICU downstairs."

"We've got to find her," Pitts insisted. "She's got something to do with Tony's death and possibly the shots fired at Nettles and me, especially if the bullets came from the same weapon. I'm sure Germaine knows something about it. I know, because he slipped up and mentioned that I was shot with a nine which wasn't made public. I'm not sure where he went, but he's got some knowledge of what's going on, and it's no secret that he's scared to death of Platinum."

"We need to find them both," Costa agreed. "And we need to do it fast. Whoever shot you guys is still out there, and they may try again. If Germaine found you, the shooter can, too."

"Yeah, I was thinking the same thing."

"I'll get some eyes on the both of you."

"I have Germaine's driver's license back at the office. His grandparents' address is on it. Maybe they know something."

"Wait," Costa interrupted. "Give me a description of, Germaine."

"Well, I'd say he's an average-looking black male, with a medium complexion and a medium build. He's probably five-ten, about one-hundred and seventy pounds."

"And what was he wearing last night?"

"All black, a stocking cap, and a leather coat with the collar turned up," Pitts answered. "The night nurse said she didn't see—"

"Jesus," Costa interrupted. "I think we may have an ID on our newest homicide victim."

"What!?" Pitts asked in disbelief.

"He was shot in the head last night, found in a parking lot on Armstrong, right around the corner. Still had the stocking cap on his head. Like I said, the call came in about twenty minutes after you called me."

"Shit," Pitts said with a groan. "Then I guess he really did have a reason to skip town. You've got to find, Platinum, Lieutenant. I know she's got something to do with this. I'd bet my good lung on it."

Chapter Twenty-Six

Quita stood in front of the whiteboard with a red marker poised in her small hand. "Let's get this meeting started," she said. "I've put the investigation into four categories. Number one is her college, The Art Institute of Atlanta. I'm sure the detectives looked into any potential suspects there, but we've got to follow up. We also need to get her class schedule and talk to any friends and professors who might know about anything unusual.

"Secondly, there's her job at Greylon Steak House at Lenox Mall. I pulled the menu up online, and the place looks pretty expensive, not anything a bunch of college kids could afford. That kinda makes me wonder about a regular customer or something, some kind of creeper. Old men can be big tippers, and they use it to impress young women and lure them in. Some girls go for it, but others don't. It just depends on the girl, and how badly she needs the cash.

"Next, there's her apartment near the campus. Her sister said Jasmine never mentioned being afraid of anyone, but that doesn't mean there wasn't a stalker or someone with an obsessive crush on her. Apartments tend to have frequent turnovers, especially with college students, so Jasmine might not have noticed a new Peeping Tom in the area. Lastly, there's the cemetery, I'm wondering if there could be some connection with her killer. It was really weird that he left her there all wrapped up in a blanket. I can't stop thinking about it."

"You're right, and you've done a great job here, Quita," Clara interjected. "I know this took a lot of work and thought," she continued as she pointed to the board. "I'm proud of you, and I'm glad you're here to keep us in line."

Quita smiled briefly before getting back to business. "I don't know what went on between you and that Detective Pitts, but we need to talk to him. There's no sense in us doing double the work. If you can find out what he's already investigated, we won't waste time backtracking."

"You have a point there," Iris said. "Clara, we have to put our pride aside and give the man a call. Let's put the past behind us. That Chatsworth case is over, and the doctor's dead. I'm sure the detective is not interested in revisiting any of it."

"Why would he if the creep's dead?" Quita asked.

Again, Clara and Iris exchanged knowing, nervous glances.

"Okay, ladies, it's time you come clean. I'm not blind, you know. What's up with the looks?" Quita pressed. "Is there something I need to know?"

"Absolutely not," Clara answered, then turned to Iris. "You're right, it's time we talk to him. This isn't about us. It's about finding out who murdered that poor girl."

"Well, we can't go talk to him at the precinct. He's out on medical leave. How will we get in touch with him?" Iris asked. "For some reason, I don't think cops put their numbers in the book."

"We can visit his office," Clara suggested. "Hopefully, they'll have someone new on the case who'll share some of the information with us. We can leave our number and see if Detective Pitts calls us back. It's worth a shot."

"I suppose."

"In the meantime, let's get back to the cemetery. Why would the murderer kill someone, then wrap her up and leave her somewhere she was sure to be found?"

"I keep wondering that, too," Quita answered. "It sounds like somebody was in love or obsessed with her. She was very close to Ginger, though, so if she didn't share anything about a new boyfriend, it must've been a stalker."

"There are three places where he could've been watching her from a distance," Iris offered. "He could've been a fellow classmate, a coworker, a customer, or someone in her apartment complex. That's a broad area to investigate. Plus, it might not be someone who jumps out at us as a weirdo. This isn't gonna be easy."

"There are some things we can do online," Quita said. "For one thing, I can pull up any sex offenders near all those locations. But going back to the apartment, who knows how many times her neighbors have changed? How long did she live there?"

"She was in her first year of college, wasn't she?" Iris asked. "She couldn't have lived there long. I think it'd be best if you question the students and coworkers, Quita. You're young, you'll understand them, and they'll relate better to you."

"I don't have a problem with that." Quita straightened up in an attempt to appear taller and more confident, clearly, the suggestion pleased her. "First of all, we need to be on the same page as the homicide detectives. Why don't you ladies ride over to their office and see what you can do about that?"

Clara would've rather chewed glass than reconnect with Detective Pitts, but she knew a reunion was inevitable. "I think we should spend a little more time figuring out how to use that GPS thingamajig on our phones," she suggested. "We can't keep printing out directions and wasting all that ink and paper. Plus, Iris keeps leaving wadded-up maps all over my car seat."

Chapter Twenty-Seven

It felt good to be back in his apartment, but the ride over, along with the confirmation that it was indeed Germaine Wilkins who'd been murdered, had exhausted Pritchard Pitts. He was having a difficult time finding a comfortable position that would relieve his pain, and he was cantankerous as hell.

"I'm leaving you with it, Jessalyn," Travis Upshaw said as he quickly made his way to the door. "He's a real pain-in-the-ass."

"Hey! I heard that you know!" Pitts yelled from the bedroom. "Buzz me as soon as you're finished with that autopsy."

"I'll do nothing of the sort," Upshaw yelled back. "You're supposed to be resting, doctor's orders."

"I'll rest after I get answers…and somebody better make damn sure they're keeping an eye on Nettles!"

"They're on it," Upshaw confirmed. "And they're doing ride-bys all day in your complex. Now get some rest, Pritchard!" he yelled back, confident the use of his first name would piss Pitts off and shut him up.

"Get the hell outta here," Pitts responded.

"Good luck with *that*," Travis said to Jessalyn as he pointed to the bedroom.

Jessalyn giggled, but her heart wasn't in it. Truthfully, she was worried. She'd been so relieved when Pitts survived, but for some crazy reason, it had never occurred to her that his life could still be in danger. Whoever had fired those shots was still out there, and there was some reason they'd shot him and Nettles in the first place.

She shuffled around the small kitchen to make a sandwich and prepare some lemonade, then placed it all on a tray and walked back to the bedroom. "Feel like a little something to eat?"

"Not really," Pitts grumbled as he tossed and turned. "My side hurts like hell. No matter what I do, I can't seem to get comfortable."

"Let me fluff those pillows for you," she offered. "I'm sure the ride over is the culprit and climbing those stairs didn't help."

"I'm worried about you," Pitts said. "It might not be safe here."

"Oh, I'm sure it's fine. Travis said they're riding by often. Your service revolver is right there in the drawer," she said, pointing to the nightstand.

"I just don't get it," Pitts began. "I don't understand how Tony Hart's murder could have anything to do with us. A small-time weed dealer certainly wouldn't have any connections with Nettles and me. The more I find out about this shit, the less sense it makes."

Jessalyn pointed to the bed. "Mind if I sit down, or will it keep you from getting comfortable?"

"No, please do," Pitts answered, reaching over to smooth the comforter for her. "I don't think I'll be comfortable anytime soon."

"At least try to eat some of that sandwich, then I'll give you a pain pill." She scoped out the bed, slid his feet a little to the left, and sat down gently. "Why don't you tell me everything you remember about that day? Maybe more will come back to you if you talk about it."

"You mean the day we were shot?"

"Yeah."

"Well, it's all still so fuzzy. It's odd how the memories come back in bits and pieces. Sometimes, I'll remember something out of the blue, sort of like those flashbacks in movies."

"Start at the beginning of your day. You and Matthew were sent to the homicide on Howell Mill Road. Do you recall that?"

Pitts took a bite of the sandwich and closed his eyes as he chewed. A second later, he answered, "I was talking to the sister of that murdered girl, the one we found over at the cemetery. Nettles and I felt like shit about it. Ginger Baines…she's all alone now." Pitts grimaced, then took another bite of his sandwich. "That's my second bite. You promised a pain pill. I'll hold that thought while you go get it."

"Fair enough," Jessalyn responded, leaving briefly to retrieve his medication from a drawer in the kitchen. She returned quickly with the small pill and held his glass for him to drink from the straw. Once the medication was swallowed, she eased back onto the bed and waited for him to continue.

"The Baines girls are products of the foster care system. Their mom's still alive, but from the looks of her at the funeral, she's still battling a lifelong drug addiction."

"That's so sad," Jessalyn said. "I felt so horrible for her the day she came to identify her sister another tragedy among many."

125

"Yeah, well, anyway, she came by the office to see if we had any more leads. I was trying to be truthful with her—you know, giving her the real odds of us solving the case. It's really not good, Jessalyn," Pitts said, his forehead wrinkling with regret.

"Maybe you should try to take a nap. Give that pill a few minutes to kick in."

"No," he insisted. "I wanna talk about it..." Pitts paused for several seconds his gaze seemingly focused on something far away.

For a moment, Jessalyn wondered if he'd continue, and eventually, he did.

"Ginger looked bad like she hadn't been eating or sleeping. Katie came in to let us know Captain Burke was looking for us because there'd been a shooting. Ginger looked crushed as if it was all finally hitting her that we had to move on to another case. It made me sick to my stomach, but at the same time, I was relieved to be sent to the call, because it meant I wouldn't have to look at her crestfallen face anymore. I'm a real son-of-a-bitch, huh? I mean, what kind of person thinks like that?"

"You're human, Pitts," Jessalyn said softly. "You deal with death on a daily basis, along with all the emotions it entails. It has to get to you, especially with young people." She was concerned about pressing him, but he seemed to be recalling the day well, and she was hesitant to stop him. "So, Captain Burke sent you to the scene?"

"Yep, I remember being pissed at myself for allowing Nettles to drive. He scares the hell outta me when he's behind the wheel." Pitts chuckled briefly, recalling his friend before the unexpected shooting happened and changed their lives. "A young, black male was shot in his car. His girlfriend and a male friend were in the car with him. Those two weren't hit, which I found a little odd, but there was weed in the car, so I figured maybe someone just had a beef with him." Pitts closed his eyes again and inhaled, slowly and deeply.

Jessalyn adjusted his covers and remained silent, hoping he'd doze off in some semblance of sleep. She knew his side had to be aching. It certainly hadn't been easy for him to climb the stairs to his second-floor apartment.

He grinned as he recalled the argumentative banter that'd taken place between Gail Duffey and Nettles. "They've never liked each other," Pitts said. "They're just too much alike. That's the whole problem."

126

Jessalyn considered telling him about Gail spending her lunch breaks reading to Nettles but feared the change in conversation might derail his thoughts, so she kept it to herself.

"We tried to talk to the girl, Platinum. She was pregnant, just about to pop, but she didn't want anything to do with us. I thought that was odd because Tony had just been murdered right beside her. She was so disrespectful and belligerent. Nettles wanted to wring her neck. The other male in the car was Germaine Wilkins. He was respectful enough, but we could tell he was afraid of, Platinum."

"Afraid of a pregnant woman?"

"She wasn't your average damsel-in-distress. In fact, she made Katie Swanson look like a happy, glowing mother-to-be. Trust me when I tell you that's no easy task. Platinum was about to explode from the pregnancy, but she had a mouth on her."

"Do you think she shot, Tony?"

"No," Pitts continued. "But she damn sure knows who did. Anyway, Nettles finally had enough of her at the crime scene and told one of the officers to take her back to our office. Only when the two were separated did Germaine start to relax. It was evident he was relieved she was gone. We completely believed his story about the shooting. I mean, he'd woulda been a fool to lie about it with all those witnesses around, to say nothing of the surveillance cameras..." He paused for a moment, twisted his body in the bed, and groaned. "I'm thinking it's gonna take more than one pain pill."

"You know I would if I could, but I can't give you another one yet," Jessalyn insisted. "You need to rest. All this conversation may be too much for you."

"Nah, I need to keep talking while the memories are flowing," Pitts said. "I'm not sleepy."

Jessalyn nodded, then patted his leg gently. "Do whatever makes you feel comfortable."

Pitts took another bite of his sandwich, then handed her the plate, letting her know he was done with it. "Germaine said the shooter was a Hispanic male. He and Tony assumed the man was just tapping on their car window because he wanted to buy some weed, but when Tony rolled the window down, the guy basically executed him. Two kill shots, right in the head and chest."

"Oh, my Lord," Jessalyn said.

"Shit," Pitts said. "What am I thinking, talking to you like this?"

"No, it's okay," she assured him. "I see things like this on the news, but it's still hard to believe people do such things."

"I'll try to tone it down a bit," Pitts said apologetically. "So, anyway, this Hispanic dude wasn't playing around. He meant business. Germaine said he just jumped over a cement wall and disappeared. We've got nothing solid on a getaway car and nothing to identify him by."

"And no one saw where he went?"

"Nope, not even with that large lunch crowd mingling around. Everybody took cover as soon as they heard gunshots. All we know is his ethnicity and a generic height and build. A getaway car would've given us much more to go on."

"Okay, so they didn't know the killer?" Jessalyn asked. "Why would Germaine be afraid of Platinum?"

"I just said Germaine didn't know the killer. Nettles and I believed his story. Back at the office, we questioned the girl. Platinum was livid with us for taking her from the scene and making her wait. She was so belligerent that we had to cuff her just so we could question her."

"Even after her friend was just murdered?" Jessalyn asked in disbelief. "Didn't she want to help you find the killer?"

"Tony was more than a friend. He was her baby daddy."

"Oh."

"Well, because of that, one would assume she'd be willing to do anything to help our investigation, but it was like we were keeping her from something more important. We didn't have any evidence that she was involved, so we couldn't hold her or arrest her. We were just hoping she'd give us something."

"What was her story?"

"She tried to get us to believe the whole shooting was gang-related, something between Bloods and Crips, but there's no evidence to support it. As far as we know, Tony had no gang affiliation whatsoever. She also told us the shooter left in a vehicle."

"Wow, that really does contradict Germaine's story," Jessalyn said.

"Yeah, it was when we reminded her of the numerous surveillance tapes that she realized she'd said too much. She insisted on leaving then, and there was nothing we could do about it."

"And what about, Germaine? You said he came to warn you."

"Yep, because he was scared shitless, so afraid that he snuck into my hospital room in the middle of the night. It didn't help because they found him shot in the head a short time later. He was murdered just like the killer tried to murder Nettles and me," Pitts said, cringing from the pain.

"Okay, that's enough," Jessalyn said as she stood and pulled the covers up around his neck. "Get some sleep. We're both safe now, and I'm sure the department will get to the bottom of this soon. Until then you need rest and time to heal."

Chapter Twenty-Eight

Clara pulled into the crowded parking lot on Peachtree Street, across from the Homicide Division of the Atlanta Police Department. It was a chilly day, but the sun was out, and there wasn't a cloud in the sky.

Iris got out of the car and walked around to the rear of the vehicle.

Clara found her bent over, holding on to the bumper. "For crying out loud. What are you doing, Iris?" she asked her friend.

"What do you *think* I'm doing?" she asked. "I'm looking for the number assigned to the parking space. You didn't pull up far enough for me to read it. Don't you know how these unmanned parking lots work?"

Clara's face turned pink as she felt the heat of embarrassment stinging her face. "No, I don't," she reluctantly conceded. "Where's the fella who's supposed to collect our money?"

"Parking lots started the self-pay system long before stores came up with that ridiculous self-checkout foolishness. It's all about cutting out the working man's salary, saving more money for the CEO."

"Do parking lots even have CEOs, Iris? I mean, seriously."

"They're just like that slumlord that poor Quita had to deal with. I'm not kidding. They only care about fattening their wallets," Iris insisted as she stood up and stretched her back. "Fifty-eight."

"Fifty-eight *what?*"

"We're in number fifty-eight. Now we just go up and put our money in that slot. That way if by some highly improbable chance the parking lot boss comes by to check, we'll be covered."

"That's ridiculous! Surely someone else parked here earlier today and already put money in it. Why do we need to put more in?"

"The parking lot boss wants us to believe he has superpowers and can tell that we haven't paid our fair share, Clara. Either that or someone comes along and marks the tires periodically. Hell, I don't know. It can't hurt to put the money in, and we're just burning daylight arguing about it."

"Fine," Clara responded as she pulled out her wallet and walked over to the kiosk. "Well, isn't this something?" she said as she turned to face Iris. "Seems you're just as outdated as I am. It appears that parking lot boss you seem to know so well has discontinued the slots. Apparently, he's much wiser than I gave him credit for. Now he requires customers to swipe a credit or debit card, at which point the machine spits out a printed receipt, that we must then walk back to said parking space and place it conveniently on our dashboard. Should his *superpowers* fail him, he can literally come by and verify our payment."

"Fifty-eight."

"What?"

"You said to walk back to said parking space. I already told you it's number fifty-eight."

Clara spun around in a huff, swiped her credit card, and snatched the receipt from the machine. She loved her old friend, but some days, she felt it'd be much easier to just strangle her.

Iris had to almost jog to keep up with her partner, but she knew she'd pushed Clara far enough, so she remained quiet until they entered the building.

An older gentleman in a police uniform sat behind a desk flanked by metal detectors on either side. He had a scowl on his face, indicating he wasn't appreciative of the cushy desk job in his final years of employment. "What can I do for you ladies?" he asked blandly.

"Good afternoon," Clara began. "We're actually here to speak with whoever is working the Jasmine Baines murder case. It's my understanding that Detective Pitts was investigating but is currently out on medical leave."

He looked at Clara, then over at Iris, as if he were sizing them up. Apparently, he aimed to be intimidating, but little did he know that he'd chosen the wrong two women for that to be even remotely effective.

"Excuse me…Officer Laye, is it?" Iris asked, emphatically eyeballing his name tag. "Is there some type of problem?"

"Are you ladies relatives of the deceased?"

"No, Sir, we are not," Iris said as she began the ritual of digging through her purse to retrieve and flash her badge.

"We're private investigators hired by the family," Clara spoke up. "I assume the case has been reassigned since both investigating officers were injured. We'd like to discuss it with whoever is in charge."

Officer Laye tried hard to hide his shock and amusement. It was almost break time, and he could tell the old women were going to be trouble if he continued to stall them. "Please take a seat over there," he said as he pointed to a bench near the door. "I'll make a few calls and see what I can do."

"Very well," Iris said. "We have a full afternoon and need to move this along."

Officer Laye resisted the urge to roll his eyes at her, then picked up a phone and looked away. *I'm too damn close to retirement to have any more complaints filed against me for rudeness,* he told himself as he dialed. *These old broads aren't about to get me in trouble and screw with my pension.*

After numerous conversations with several people on the floors above, Officer Laye hung up the receiver. "Lieutenant Costa has agreed to meet with you briefly up on the sixth floor. Someone will meet you at the elevator and take you to her office," he said as he motioned them toward metal detectors.

They placed their purses on the conveyor belt and waited at the other end as he perused them.

The officer finally opened the glass door and motioned toward the end of the hall. "The elevator's right down there on the left. You can't miss it."

"Thank you so much, Officer Laye," Iris chirped flirtatiously.

"What do you think you're doing?" Clara asked as soon as they got out of earshot.

"There's nothing wrong with a little innocent flirting," Iris replied. "He might be more accommodating next time."

"Give me strength, Lord. Give me strength," Clara mumbled under her breath.

The elevator doors opened on the sixth floor, and a very pregnant woman greeted them. Her voice was friendly, but her face was twisted in a grimace. "Hello, ladies," she said. "My name's Katie Swanson, and I'm an admin with the Homicide Division. I understand you're here to see Lieutenant Costa."

"Yes, we are," Iris said. "Goodness gracious! You look like you might burst any minute, darling."

"Iris!" Clara exclaimed, mortified that her friend would make such a dreadful remark.

Katie was far from offended and laughed warmly. "Oh, you have no idea how much I wish I would," she said, happy to have an audience for her woes. "I've got twins in here, and three more months to writhe in agony. *Three!*" she emphasized by flashing three fingers at them. "I must've done something terrible in a past life to deserve this. Anyway, would you ladies excuse me for a moment?" she asked, flagging down another young woman walking down the hallway.

The women waited patiently as she made her way over to them.

"I suppose you're waiting on that paperwork from upstairs?" she asked.

"You know it," Katie answered. "Pardon me, ladies," she said, looking at Iris and Clara. "This is Cassidy Moore. She's an administrative assistant as well, and I try to keep her happy. Many times, I rely on her paperwork to complete my own."

"Hello," Cassidy said, flashing a quick smile. "Katie, I'll get that to you as soon as I put out these other fires. As usual, you aren't my only emergency." She continued down the hallway.

"She's really very sweet," Katie explained. "We're a bit overworked and quite understaffed. Anyway, this is the office you're looking for." The door was open, but Katie tapped on the doorframe first.

"Yeah, I'm here," a voice said from inside. "I'm not sure you'll find me under all this paperwork though. Might need to get the *Jaws of Life* to pull me out."

Flashing a sheepish smile, Katie motioned for the women to enter while she leaned against the doorway. "Lieutenant, these ladies are here to see you. Clara and Iris," she said, waving her hand in their direction to invite them in. "Will that be all, Lieutenant?"

"Yes, Katie. Thanks so much." The lieutenant looked up at the two women. "Good morning or afternoon, whichever it is now," she said as she glanced down at her watch. "I'm Lieutenant Costa. Let me get some of these files out of the way so you can sit down," she said as she maneuvered her way around the small office. "Sorry about the mess, but it never gets any better. There you go. Please have a seat."

Clara and Iris both sat down, their knees almost touching the desk in front of them.

"You know, everybody around here thinks it's a big deal that I have my own office, but there's actually more workspace in the cubicles. On the upside, though, at least I have a door to slam when I feel like it...which is often around here."

Both women smiled as if they completely understood her situation.

"Anyway, I really don't have much time, so I hope you don't mind me cutting right to the chase. What can I do for you today?"

Iris leaned forward to speak, but Clara beat her to it. "We're private investigators and have been hired by the family of Jasmine Baines to look into her murder."

If the lieutenant was shocked, she certainly didn't show it. She sat and looked at them kindly, listening intently.

"We understand that the two detectives assigned to the case were injured recently, and we were wondering if you've given the case to another detective."

"Not yet, but it's certainly on my agenda. The Pitts and Nettles situation not only left us shorthanded but also gave us another investigation to contend with. Not only that, but we're short a captain, too."

"I'm sorry to hear that. We were hoping to speak to someone about the investigation up to this point. We'd hate to waste valuable time reinventing the wheel, so to speak."

"I certainly understand where you're coming from…Clara, is it?"

"Yes, Clara Samples."

"Officer Nettles is still hospitalized, and his condition is far from favorable. Pitts has been discharged, but he's got months of recovery ahead. I'm afraid neither of them will be able to sit down with you."

"We've actually dealt with Detective Pitts in the past," Clara confessed. "Would it be possible for you to pass our phone number along to him, in case he feels like discussing the case?"

"I'm sure you understand that I don't want to bother him while he recuperates. He's been through a great deal, and although Pitts is a hardworking, dedicated detective who values the outcome of all his cases, it's imperative we give him time to rest and heal."

Clara tried to hide her disappointment. "I respect that, Lieutenant Costa."

"Well," Iris began as she placed her purse on the floor beside her and tapped her index finger on a stack of files. "I'm sure the file must be around here somewhere. Perhaps you can let us look it over? Then we can be on our way."

The lieutenant leaned back in her chair and let out a belly laugh that lasted far too long for Iris's taste.

"I don't know what's so funny," Iris said haughtily.

"No disrespect intended," Costa said as she wiped tears from her eyes. "But you two ladies are a sight, and I don't doubt your age works to your advantage in many instances. However, here at the Atlanta PD, we have to operate under strict protocols. Under no circumstances could I allow you to review an official police file on an open case. If either of the detectives were available, I'm sure they'd be glad to help, but that isn't possible. All I can suggest is that you speak with Doctor Travis Upshaw, at the Medical Examiner's office, just a couple blocks from here. He and Detective Pitts work together on a lot of cases, and if my memory serves me correctly, Upshaw performed the autopsy on Ms. Baines. If you'd like, I can give him a call and see if he's available to speak with you."

Clara and Iris nodded, eager for any help they could get.

"We'd appreciate that," Clara said.

Lieutenant Costa spent several minutes on the phone, before hanging up and scribbling an address on a scratchpad. "He said he can speak with you now, as long as you get there within the next few minutes. I'm not sure how much help Upshaw will be, but it's the best advice I can give you, right now." She passed the address over to Iris. "It's a straight shot, you can't miss it."

Clara stood and reached her hand over the desk. "Thank you for your time, Lieutenant. Our prayers will continue to go up for your wounded officers."

"We appreciate that. Can you ladies find your way back to the elevator?"

"Yes," Clara answered as she and Iris made their way out of the cramped space.

"I say we pretend to be lost and try to find the file room," Iris whispered.

"Have you lost your mind?" Clara asked. "I have no intention of being booked into the city jail today. Not only that, but we don't want to burn our bridges, Iris. If we're going to stay in this business, we'll surely need the lieutenant again."

The ride down to the lobby was a quiet one, but Iris perked up when she saw Officer Laye. "We're off to another case," she said with a wink. "Have a nice day, handsome."

"And that has to stop, too," Clara said firmly.

"Just trying not to burn our bridges, dear," Iris taunted. "If we're gonna stay in this business, we may eventually need a Laye, no pun intended."

"I refuse to even give that a response," Clara said smugly.

Iris grabbed her friend's hand leading her across the street. "C'mon, Clara, life is short."

"Oh, life is short all right, Iris. We may as well learn to dance in the rain."

Chapter Twenty-Nine

The cabin door opened, revealing a dense haze looming over the ground as if someone had hooked up a fog machine for a Hollywood movie set. A full moon hung overhead but was partially covered by thunderclouds that promised an impending storm.

Kori Reeves wasn't sure of the exact time, but she estimated it was approaching midnight. She'd been drugged earlier in the evening and loaded in the trunk of a silver BMW. He had carried her into the small cabin while she was still too groggy to recall what had happened to her.

She rubbed her wrists vigorously thankful her captor had removed the abrasive rope from her arms and ankles. Her thoughts were still fuzzy as he came into focus. "I-I don't understand. What's happening, and wh-why did you bring me here?" she stammered.

"You're a bright, young woman, Kori. Can't you figure it out?"

"But you…it doesn't make sense. I don't understand why you drugged me."

"It wouldn't have been any fun if you weren't sedated. I would've had to fight you all the way up the highway."

"Where are we?" Kori asked, beginning to realize the full scope of danger she was in. She looked around the cabin and shivered from the cold. The fire in the hearth had yet to warm the space, and Kori could see the frost from her kidnapper's breath. It was a small, but quaint bungalow, decorated in red and black lodge décor. Still unsure of the time, she knew wherever they were, they'd gotten there by car, limiting the miles they could've traveled. More than likely, they were somewhere in the North Georgia Mountains.

"To answer your question, my dear, we're far from the hustle and bustle of the big city," he said, flashing a sinister grin. "Here, the air is pure, and no one can hear us."

Kori closed her eyes in an attempt to concentrate and formulate an escape plan. He hadn't killed her yet, which meant he either planned to keep her locked away for a long time, or he wanted to toy with her first, like a cat tossing a helpless mouse around in its mouth before devouring it.

Either way, she had to get away from him. Her memory was still muddled, as hard as she tried to put the day back in chronological order, things just wouldn't line up. There were brief flashes of recollection of her fingers feeling around the inside of the trunk in the darkness, then of him carrying her inside, but the rest was simply blacked out. She didn't even recall him removing her restraints, the ropes that had brought her so much discomfort. Kori rubbed her scratched wrists again, just to ensure it wasn't all a dream.

"Still sleepy?" he asked, almost kindly.

"Yes. What did you give me?"

"Just a little something to make you come willingly. Are you hungry?"

Kori saw a chance to play along. *If he's going to feed me, he obviously doesn't plan to kill me, at least not for the next few minutes*, she thought. "Yes, I am. What time is it?"

"Way past your bedtime, little girl," he taunted. "Don't you still live with your parents? I bet they're really pissed at you by now?"

"My parents know I'd never worry them unnecessarily. I'm sure they've already sent out a search party for me."

"Really?" he asked, seemingly amused at the thought. "Well, even if they have, I doubt anyone will think to look here," he said matter-of-factly as he rummaged through a cabinet filled with pots and pans. "How do you feel about scrambled eggs?"

"Do I have a choice?"

"Trying to be rebellious, are we? I highly recommend you eat the eggs. You'll need the protein for energy."

"Energy for what? What are you going to do to me?" Kori asked, trying desperately to hide the fear in her voice. She knew she needed to feel and sound confident, but it was certainly a struggle to do so.

"Oh, nothing to worry about just yet. We'll have lots of fun before it's over."

Chapter Thirty

Clara and Iris walked through the front entrance of the Medical Examiner's office and were met by Dr. Travis Upshaw himself.

"We didn't expect you to be waiting for us in the lobby," Clara commented. "We certainly appreciate you making time for us."

"Our receptionist is out today, and I didn't want you to have to wander around searching for me." Upshaw glanced down at his watch and continued. "I only have a few minutes before a staff meeting—you know, one of those unnecessary meetings to discuss the next unnecessary meeting." He chuckled to himself. "If you'll follow me, we can talk in my office." He took off, his long legs leaping into a fast pace, leaving Clara and Iris struggling to keep up. Upshaw wound his way through a maze of freshly waxed, shiny hallways before stopping in front of a closed door. He retrieved his work badge from his pocket, swiped it across a pad, and opened the door. "Come on in, ladies," he said as he held the door open. "Welcome to my humble abode. It's not much, but it's home about ninety percent of the time." He shuffled a few piles of paperwork around, making room for them to sit down.

"We're starting to see a pattern here," Clara commented. "It looks like the County needs to hire a few filing clerks."

"If anyone moves even one of these sheets of paper, I'd never find anything," Upshaw said. "I call it *organized chaos*. Anyway, what can I do for you ladies?"

"We've been hired by the family of Jasmine Baines to investigate her murder. We understand you performed her autopsy."

"Yes, and it wasn't pretty. It was a very sad situation."

The group was interrupted by a knock at the door.

"Yeah? It's open," Upshaw called out.

The door opened slowly, and Sugar stepped inside. His vast size caused both women to gasp.

"My goodness," Iris spat out in surprise. "How's the weather up there?"

If Clara could've gone through the floor from embarrassment, she would've welcomed the opportunity.

Sugar, on the other hand, was quite amused. He let out a strong laugh that came from his gut and leaned over to slap his thick thigh. "Ya know, Ma'am, I haven't heard that one in at least five minutes!"

Travis Upshaw laughed, too, but Clara wasn't sure if it was because of Iris's comment or if the large man's laughter was contagious. "Sugar, allow me to introduce you to a couple of real-life private eyes, Clara Samples and Iris Hadley."

"Nice to make your acquaintance," he said, his eyes still reflecting amusement. "Name's Stanley Peters, but my friends call me Sugar."

"It's nice to meet you, too," Clara said.

"You're one healthy fella," Iris said, springing to her feet. "Let me just stand up and see how I look next to you." She pressed her small body close to his enormous one, and her face was about level with his belly button. "Would you look at this, Clara?" she squealed. "It's like standing next to one of those basketball players. Which one does that *Icy Hot* commercial we like so much? Is it Shaq?"

Clara wished she could close her eyes and become invisible, but everyone else seemed to be enjoying the show.

Iris patted Sugar on his muscled forearm before returning to her seat, shaking her head in amazement.

"Sorry to pop in on ya, Upshaw," Sugar apologized. "I wasn't aware you had visitors, especially not such delightful female callers."

Upshaw smiled. "No worries. What can I do for you?"

"I just need this release signed for Watkins Funeral Home. They're on the way with the hearse now, and I thought it was already signed. Guess I shouldn't have opted for decaf this mornin' after all."

"No problem," Upshaw said, picking up a pen and gesturing for the clipboard. When Sugar passed it over, he quickly scrawled his signature across it. "There you go."

"Thanks, man, and it was good meeting you two."

"Sorry, ladies," Upshaw said after Sugar walked out. "Now, back to Jasmine Baines. It was a real tragedy. If you've been hired to look into the case, I'm sure you're already aware of the official cause of death. Her sister was given the death certificate."

"Yes, we've seen it," Clara confirmed, trying to bring some credibility back to the visit. "It's our understanding that you worked with Detective Pitts on the case."

"Yes. In fact, we often work together, but as you know, I'm a pathologist. I do very little investigating if any. I simply travel to the scene where the body is located, scope out the environment in which it is found, and ensure that it's transported here and autopsied. We do have an investigative unit that takes crime scene photos and such, mostly to determine if the death was natural or of a suspicious nature. Ultimately, it's up to the homicide detectives to continue the investigation and solve the case, but we do pass on any evidence found during the autopsy."

"As we shared with Lieutenant Costa earlier, we don't want to waste valuable time reinventing the wheel. We certainly understand the legalities of turning over a homicide file to us, but we'd like to speak with anyone who can give us any information that's already been gathered. Do you suppose we could talk to your investigators who took the crime scene photos?" Clara asked.

"I don't have a problem with that," Travis said. "But I don't see how it'd be of much help. Tess Dyer was on call that day and rode with me to the crime scene. I stayed with her until the body was transported back here. I can give you as much information as she could. Tess photographed the location where Jasmine was laid as well as the surrounding area. She came back here with me and took the remaining photos needed during the autopsy."

"Where Jasmine's body was laid?" Iris parroted. "Interesting."

"I don't get what you're saying," Clara said.

"You caught that, did you?" Travis asked. "You're pretty astute."

"Would either of you care to fill me in?" Clara asked.

"He said where the body was laid," Iris said. "You believe she was murdered somewhere else and moved to the cemetery."

"She was most definitely killed somewhere else and left there for hours. She was strangled and left lying on her stomach long enough for lividity to set in the tissues and blanch those areas. Later, her body was moved to the cemetery and left there, wrapped in a blanket. When we uncovered her, she was on her back which exposed those white areas of lividity."

"How long does a body have to lie in one particular position for blanching to occur?" Clara asked.

"Several hours," Travis answered.

"So, someone left her in one location for hours, then decided to cover her and move her somewhere she was sure to be found. That's odd, don't you think?"

"Yes, it is, but in this business, we see a lot of odd things. It never ceases to amaze me."

"So, what's your take on her being wrapped in a blanket?" Iris asked. "It sounds like an act of compassion."

"That was our theory. I'm no psychiatrist or criminal profiler, but it does seem as if someone didn't want her lying in the elements to decompose. There could be many reasons for it, but it could've been a boyfriend or even someone secretly obsessed with her."

"Have you ever seen such a thing before?" Clara asked.

"From time to time, although in different scenarios. Most were cases of parents losing their patience and shaking their children to death or husbands who beat their wives a little too hard. In cases like that, the victims were often lovingly tended to, but the killers often call the police and confess, out of remorse. I've never known anyone to be murdered, then covered, then moved somewhere else."

"Do you see many strangulations? It sounds very personal," Clara persisted.

"Believe it or not, we don't. Wait. Let me rephrase that. We don't see many manual strangulations. We get suicide by hanging, asphyxiation by smothering, or ligature strangulations, but manual ones are rare."

"By manual, you mean somebody did it with their hands, right? Wouldn't it take a very strong person to do that?" Iris conjectured.

"Well, actually—"

"So, you're assuming it's a male?" Iris said, cutting him off, trying to put two and two together a little too quickly.

"Actually, it doesn't take a great deal of pressure to cause unconsciousness. On average, about eleven pounds of pressure must be placed on both carotid arteries for ten seconds to accomplish that. If the pressure was released, the victim would regain consciousness within a few seconds. It takes three times as much pressure to close off the trachea, and the strangulation would have to persist for several minutes to cause brain death."

"Someone would have to be strong enough to overpower the victim and continue to strangle them then," Clara commented. "It sounds like a male to me."

"She was certainly overpowered," Travis said. "Jasmine had several self-inflicted claw marks on her neck. There were also nail marks from our killer as well as bruises where his thumbs were placed as he strangled her."

"Oh, my goodness. That poor child," Clara said. "It's horrible to think about."

Travis looked down at his watch. "I'm sorry, ladies, but duty calls. That's basically all I've got for you anyway. Once identification is made, and the autopsy completed, I'm out of the loop unless I get called in to testify at trial."

"We appreciate all you've given us," Clara said. "I hate to be an aggravation, but we really need to talk with, Detective Pitts. You seem to know him fairly well. Is there any way you could pass our number along? I understand he's recuperating at home, but I'm only asking that you give him our number. If he doesn't return our call, we'll understand."

"I appreciate the job you have to do, but he's not well. In fact, he's far from it. The last thing Pitts needs right now is to get involved with a case again."

"Maybe it'd take his mind off his injuries," Iris suggested. "Surely it can't hurt for you to pass on our information, Doc. If he doesn't respond, no harm, no foul."

The two women watched as Dr. Upshaw struggled with his conscience. In the end, he gave in. "Okay, ya got me. Do you have a card?"

Iris began rambling through her purse, but Clara already had a card in her hand. "Will you give me your word that you'll share it with him?" she asked as she passed it across the desk.

"I'll give it to him, but I can't make any promises that he'll call you back."

"Fair enough," Clara said as she stood to leave. "Thank you."

Chapter Thirty-One

"Could you close the door?" Kori asked, shivering violently from the cold. "I'm freezing."

He walked out of the kitchen with a large plate of scrambled eggs. "I think it feels nice, kind of energizing," he said.

His deep voice was as smooth as velvet, and Kori recalled the first time they'd met. He was sinfully handsome, and she'd admired him from a distance. The crush formed instantly, a crush that was certainly shared by many others. She was younger than his other would-be suitors. A college student, she still lived at home with her folks. She was sure nothing would ever transpire between them since he was quite a bit older and very successful. *What would he ever see in a girl like me?* Now, another thought hit her: *What a fool I was to so willingly jump into that shiny, sleek sports car.*

"Better eat up," his voice boomed. He reached his arms toward the ceiling and stretched like a cat. "The night is young, isn't it?"

"What are you going to do to me?" she asked again.

"We're just going to have a little fun, Kori, that's all. You're young and adventurous, aren't you?"

"Why'd you drug me? I got in the car with you on my own."

"Yes, but for some reason, I didn't think you'd be so willing to play the game."

"What *game*? I'm so tired, so confused."

"Then you should eat the eggs before they get cold. This brew will do you good, caffeinate you, and warm you up," he said as he handed her a mug of black coffee.

She placed the brim of the hot cup against her lips. The coffee smelled strong and tasted like sludge, and she couldn't help scrunching up her nose in disgust. "*Please* just let me rest."

"Two minutes. That's all I'm going to give you to finish your meal. Quit complaining about being tired and chug that coffee. Believe me, if you don't, you'll wish you had."

Something in his tone suggested truth in his statement, and it frightened her. Kori picked up the fork and ate as quickly as she could, shoving the food in so hastily that pieces of egg fell from her mouth and onto her shirt. She gulped down as much of the coffee as she could stand, but it scalded her mouth and continued to burn as it slid down her throat.

He reached over and grabbed the plate from her trembling hands. "That's it. Time's up. Now, off we go!"

"Where?" she asked timidly.

"I'm feeling a little generous this evening, so I've decided to give you a bonus. Normally, I'd allow you a ten-minute head start, but in lieu of your weariness, I'm going to give you an additional five. That's a grand total of fifteen minutes!" he said in a booming voice as if imitating an animated game show host.

"A head start, is it a race of some sort?"

"The rules are very simple, my dear. You have a fifteen-minute head start through the woods. Should you be elusive enough to lose me, you win. Should I catch up with you, you're dead. See, simple!"

"You can't be serious," Kori's voice cracked, and the tears began to flow. "You're kidding, right?"

"I'm completely serious. Dry those tears, honey. The clock starts right now!"

Chapter Thirty-Two

Detective Pitts was mindlessly watching *The Price Is Right* when he heard a knock on his apartment door. "Yeah, who is it?" he yelled from the couch.

"It's Costa. Can you make it to the door?"

"Yeah, just gimme a sec'," He tried to stand slowly in an effort to find a position that'd cause the least pain.

"That took you long enough," she said when he finally reached the door. "You look like hell. Has anyone else had the nerve to tell you that?"

"Nice to see you, too, LT. To what do I owe the pleasure?"

"Do I need a reason to pop in on a friend?"

"When did you start calling me *that*?" Pitts asked with a laugh.

"Get over yourself," Costa said. "How's it coming, still in pain?"

"Yeah, but it's better. I'm just sick of not being able to get around. I'm not cut out to be a damn invalid."

"The man I knew would much rather watch TV than fill out paperwork."

"Score one for the lieutenant."

"Want me to fix you something to eat?"

"Nah, Jessalyn's been making dinner for me every night, and the guys have been dropping in with lunch. I'm good. How's the investigation going?"

"That's one of the reasons I stopped by—not that I wouldn't have stopped in to check on you anyway. Monica Heard is still MIA, but she can't hide for long."

"Monica who?"

"Heard, aka Platinum."

"Oh. Well, that chick is no Monica. Her street name is more fitting. What all do you have on her?"

"She's twenty-two, born and raised in Southwest Atlanta, Adamsville, to be exact. She was born to a teenage, drug-addicted mother who dumped her off on her grandmother so she could party. Her mother never came back for her. I don't know where Heard is now, but her grandmother still lives over off Boulder Park Drive. We spoke with her yesterday, but she's washed her hands of her granddaughter, or at least that's what she claims. Monica started getting wild in middle school and got to be too much for Grandma to handle. She basically came and went as she pleased, and dropped out of high school at the ripe, old age of sixteen. The grandmother seemed genuinely upset about the murder of Tony Hart. Although she was aware of his drug dealings, she always thought he was good to Monica."

"Do you think she knows where Platinum is? Is there any chance she'll return to Granny's house?"

"I don't think she will, but that's just my personal opinion. The grandmother is old, living off food stamps and a small Social Security check. She doesn't have anything to offer Monica. One thing's for sure. Grandma wants no part of that newborn baby. She says she's done raising kids."

"So, where's the baby now?" Pitts asked.

"Still over at Grady, going through withdrawals. When she's well enough, they'll put her in the system, but nobody wants to adopt a drug-addicted newborn. There are too many long-term effects. Sad situation. But who knows? Maybe Monica will develop some kind of conscience and go back for the baby."

"That'll never happen. That girl is *evil*. Don't let her mother's actions allow her to play the victim. She's responsible for all she's done. I'm telling you, Platinum had something to do with Nettles and me getting shot."

"She has a record, but it's about like Tony Hart's, just small-time stuff—shoplifting, drugs, driving without a license, and so on. Friends of Hart's say she's been hanging out with a new crowd, a group of Hispanics who just moved into the area."

"That's it! Germaine Wilkins told us that day at the murder scene that a Hispanic guy shot Tony. We've got to find Platinum. Is anyone on the gang task force looking at Mexican gangs in that area?"

"Yeah, continuously. If it's those guys over near Lakewood, then Platinum's in way over her head. That would explain why Germaine was so afraid. The DEA, ATF, and INS are all investigating the drugs being trafficked in from Mexico and Miami. I-20 and I-85 lead right to the middle of the city, making it a convenient distribution point. There are some stash houses over in Clayton County being raided as we speak."

147

"Well, like you said, Platinum's just small-time, and so was Tony. How the hell did she get involved with the Mexican drug cartel? It's not like she could just walk up and introduce herself."

"You're right about that, but if they're looking for a place to store, package, and distribute large quantities, they'd need someone from the neighborhood. Maybe Tony and Germaine didn't want to go along with it."

"So, what's the plan?" Pitts asked.

"We find Platinum. Maybe she'll roll over on the shooter. Who knows?"

Pitts opened his mouth to respond but was interrupted by his cell phone. "Hold up a sec'. It's Upshaw," he said as he answered the call. "What's up?" He paused briefly. "Really? That's interesting. Those two are something else." After another pause, he sighed. "I don't have time for two old busybodies but give me the number. Who knows? Maybe I'll get bored enough to deal with them eventually." Pitts reached for a pen and wrote the number on a greasy McDonald's bag that had held the prior day's lunch. "Okay, well, thanks, man. Come by soon. Being cooped up like this is for the birds. Even your ugly mug would be a welcome sight."

"Let me guess," Lieutenant Costa said. "The two private eyes begged Upshaw to call you, too."

"Yeah, apparently so. He promised them he'd call me, and he never breaks promises to the elderly."

"What a nice quality to have," Costa said, rolling her eyes. "They were persistent, those two. I've gotta give 'em that."

"They came to see you, too?" Pitts asked as a grin spread across his face.

"Yep, they're investigating the murder of Jasmine Baines. How do you know them?"

"I met them on another case I was working. I think they were involved much deeper than they claimed, but it all worked out in the end."

"You mean criminally involved?"

"Let's just say it was, um…a means to an end. They're good people. I heard they opened a private investigation firm over off Bankhead Highway. Talk about being in over your head."

"Oh, I don't know," Costa said. "I think those two may just be naïve enough for it to work to their advantage. You really need to concentrate on getting stronger. You don't need the stress, Pitts. Leave the old ladies alone."

Chapter Thirty-Three

Kori Reeves looked at her kidnapper in disbelief. *This has to be a dream? It can't really be happening.*

"I didn't stutter, did I?" he asked, his booming voice assaulting her ears once again. "Tick-tock, tick-tock, the mouse ran up the clock…oops! My apologies. That's hickory-dickory-dock. At any rate, I'm sure you get the picture."

She suddenly wished she'd skipped the eggs altogether and had forced the whole cup of coffee down instead. Her body was sluggish as if she'd just been awakened from a sound sleep. She used the arms of the chair to push herself up, then ran through the open front door and into the night.

Large oaks and magnolias loomed in the distance. A gravel driveway led from the front of the house, then disappeared from view. Kori knew better than to follow the driveway, he'd be sure to spot her more clearly out in the open. The driveway would eventually lead to a road of some sort, so she decided to make her way through the woods and hopefully loop around until she intersected with a thoroughfare.

Her chest began to burn from inhaling the frigid air, so she slowed to a stop, bent down, and placed her hands on her knees to catch her breath. She had to think clearly, to prevent herself from making a deadly mistake. She took slow, deep breaths, then stood to assess her surroundings. It was definitely rugged terrain, but the heavy underbrush and hardwoods offered a great deal of cover. The years of layered pine needles silenced her footsteps, but they were also slick and could hinder her progress, especially if it rained.

Kori paused for just a moment to evaluate her clothing. Her hoodie offered both warmth and a cover for her head and neck. It would be some protection as she moved through the wooded area, as would her jeans, long athletic socks, and sneakers. She moved her hands to her waistline, relieved to discover she'd taken the time to put on a belt before leaving for class. *That might come in handy later,* she thought.

She figured it was about forty-five degrees, so there was some concern about hypothermia, especially if rain moved in. She'd be at even greater risk if her clothing got wet.

Nevertheless, in spite of the odds, a sudden calm washed over her as she recalled tagging along with her mom, a den mother for her brother Kaleb's Cub Scout troop. The other sisters had played with paper dolls and colored while they waited, but Kori enjoyed listening to the various guest speakers her mother recruited to educate the young boys about camping and the outdoors. She never let Kaleb know, but it fascinated her. She kept it to herself as it would have infuriated him, and Kaleb would've demanded their mother leave Kori at home in the future. She was glad she'd listened in, all the information she'd retained would come in handy now.

She looked up at the massive, low-lying thunderheads that promised a hard, raging rain. She'd have to seek some sort of shelter, but at the moment, her prime concern was getting as far from the house as her fifteen-minute head start would allow.

Chapter Thirty-Four

Quita was already downstairs in the office when Clara and Iris arrived, and the two couldn't help but notice that she looked worn out. "Good morning, ladies," she said, somewhat unenthusiastically, as she fumbled with the coffee maker.

"Good morning, Quita." Clara hung up her coat and placed her purse in the bottom drawer of her desk. "You look a little tired, dear. Is everything all right?"

"Yes, I'm fine…just a little overworked, I guess. We've been getting a ton of calls, and I've been visiting the college in the afternoons and hanging out in the restaurant at night. I understand you completed that latest workmen's comp case with the cook who slipped in the wet kitchen."

"That was a joke," Iris said. "I tell ya, people like him ruin a good thing for the ones who really do get injured. By the way, we just picked up the pictures from Walgreens. Clara has the folder."

"How's your investigation going?" Clara asked, handing the folder to Quita. "You're working so hard on the murder case for Jasmine. Maybe you should stay in the office for a few days. Too much fieldwork will take a toll on you, sweetie."

"No, we have to hit these murder cases hard and fast," Quita said as if she had a great deal of experience. "These college kids come and go, just like tenants at an apartment. She was well-liked at school, but she wasn't very social and didn't take part in any…extracurricular activities or clubs or anything. An occasional group project forced Jasmine to spend time with her classmates outside of class, but otherwise, she saw very little of them after the bell rang. The professors I talked to said she was a dedicated student."

"Any particular boy who caught her interest?" Iris asked.

"Actually a lot of her classmates were willing to talk to me, but nobody mentioned anything about a boyfriend or any guy showing her unwanted attention. The one thing they all agree on is that Jasmine was all about her schoolwork. I really didn't get the vibe that any of 'em really know much about her."

"Well, in that case, maybe we're barking up the wrong tree there," Iris continued. "What about that fancy restaurant?"

"A couple of waiters and waitresses talked to me, but they didn't give me a lot of time. They're all about their tips, and there to hustle. The bartender's pretty cool. He let me sit at the bar and didn't charge me for the sodas I drank. He's a young, white guy, in his mid-twenties, not a creep or anything. His name is, Joey. A regular crowd of businessmen hang out at his bar every night. The waitresses like him because he's friendly but professional with them—not to mention good-looking."

"Okay, and what did this Joey have to say about Jasmine?" Iris asked.

"He said she was cool. He didn't know her very well but recalled that a lot of the regulars asked to be seated at her tables. According to him, she never stayed late to hang out with the employees after work, and she never flirted with anyone."

"Did he seem upset by that?" Clara asked. "The lack of flirting, I mean."

"I'm not feeling that he lacks female attention," Quita answered. "I think he was pretty upfront with me. He even warned me about questioning people too much. Apparently, the manager's very protective of his clientele's confidentiality. Joey did seem to feel bad about Jasmine's murder and said I could sit at the bar anytime. He said he'll refill my glass as long as I keep a low profile and act like a normal customer."

"That's pretty nice of him," Iris said. "Are you sure he's not a little too anxious to help?"

"I like to think I can read people," Quita said. "I'm telling ya, I don't get a bad feeling from him. I'm thinking I should show up a few nights a week, just to get a read on who comes in on a regular basis. Can't hurt. What about you two? Has that detective called you back yet?"

"No," Clara answered. "I'm not getting my hopes up that he will. Detective Pitts was shot, and I'm sure the last thing he's concerned about right now is a cold case. It was worth a try, but we'll just have to work it from the angles you outlined."

"We still have the apartment complex to check out," Quita continued. "I've ridden by there several times, day and night, tryin' to get a feel of it. It's really just your average, cheap housing, occupied mostly by college kids."

"Would it be odd for someone to reside there if they don't attend school?" Iris asked.

"Not really," Quita answered. "School or not, young people all tend to live in the same areas, *cheap* being the keyword."

The phone rang as Quita sat down at her desk with a cup of fresh coffee.

"Y'all are killing me," she said as she turned to answer it. "They're both in a meeting at the moment," she said into the receiver, rolling her sleepy eyes at Clara and Iris. "May I ask who's calling?" She paused briefly before spinning around in her chair and waving madly at both of them. "Hold please." She looked over at Clara and Iris, her eyes wide. "Speak of the devil! I've got that detective on the line. He asked for either of you."

"Clara, you take it," Iris said. "I hate to admit it, but you're the best talker when it comes to important things."

Clara nodded, took a deep breath, exhaled slowly, and reached for the phone. "Clara Samples, here. How may I help you?" Her face was flushed with nervousness, but it softened as the conversation continued.

Iris and Quita hung on every word she spoke, anxious to hear the details.

"That'd be very nice of you, Detective," Clara said warmly. "Are you sure it won't be too much trouble?"

Iris heaved a loud sigh, indicating her fear of Clara ruining an opportunity.

"Very well, Detective Pitts," Clara continued as she scribbled his address on her notepad. "We'll see you in an hour."

Chapter Thirty-Five

Platinum huddled in the corner of the cold, dank basement, in nothing but a pair of panties and a foul-smelling men's sweatshirt. The euphoria from the last hit of crack cocaine had long since worn off, leaving her edgy and depressed. She wasn't sure if it was day or night, or when she had last eaten a meal. The baby she'd deserted at the hospital had been pushed to the back of her mind, her only concern now was her next high. After that, she'd worry about what to do with the rest of her life.

Damn Tony anyhow. All he had to do was go along with the Mexicans who wanted to use his place. I was tired of living off small-time money. We coulda made a lotta dough, had a better life. It's like he didn't want something better for his kid, him, or that punk Germaine. All they had to do was keep their mouths shut. Now look how messed up everything is because of those stubborn fools! Shivering from head to toe, she pulled her legs closer to her chest.

The door at the top of the stairs opened, and the light filtered down to her.

She squinted, having been in the dark for so long. "Who is it?" Platinum yelled. The heavy footsteps suggested a male. She remained curled up in a ball but lifted her head to see who it was. She quickly sobered up at the sight of the large man suddenly standing over her. "Who are you?" she asked bluntly.

"I'm here to take you away. You'll be trouble for us."

"Where's Felipe?" Platinum asked nervously. "I wanna see him."

"You run nothing here," the large man spat. "I take you to Mateo now. Get up," he ordered, throwing a robe at her. "You stink."

Platinum stood unsteadily and reached for the garment. "I'm not going anywhere with you. I'm getting outta here. Whoever you are, you've got no right to—"

He grabbed her arm forcibly and squeezed it firmly. Platinum let out a yelp and struggled to free herself. She was down from her high, and reality was setting in. She was in way over her head and had nothing more to offer them. The memory of Tony's shooting flashed through her mind for the first time, and the thought of him slumped over the steering wheel sickened her so much that she bent forward and vomited on the floor.

The man had no sympathy for her and dragged her up the stairs, across the kitchen floor, and to a dark van in the garage. Felipe was in the back and Platinum landed on him when she was pushed inside.

"What the…" Platinum started, but she was quickly silenced by the expression on Felipe's face, his eyes were dead, reflecting no recognition of her. "Felipe, snap out of it," she whispered. "They're gonna kill us. You've gotta do something."

He blinked rapidly but didn't answer. Felipe had come to terms with what was to come, but Platinum had no idea of what lay ahead. She was as greedy and merciless as the cartel, but she couldn't begin to imagine the depths of what they were going to be put through. He knew now that it'd been a huge mistake to let her talk him into shooting the cops. It had brought unwanted heat down on them. Mateo was not happy, and when Mateo wasn't happy, somebody had to pay.

Chapter Thirty-Six

Kori wound her way through the woods, weaving in and out of bushes with briars and thorns large enough to hinder her progress. She had little doubt that they were in the North Georgia Mountains. She pulled her hood up and tied it tightly so that most of her face was covered. Her main concern was to ensure she wasn't running in circles, heading back toward her would-be killer. The only sound she heard as she ran were her own heavy breaths as she pushed her body to put the most distance between herself and the man who was relentlessly pursuing her.

She would've much preferred a full moon to provide some light, but the thunderclouds prevented visibility. Her one solace was that if it was difficult for her to see, his chase would be difficult as well—unless he was extremely familiar with the terrain. Kori looked in every direction desperate for some light to indicate another residence or business in the area, but there wasn't any.

Her best hope was to intersect with some type of roadway on which motorists traveled, she would have to rely on a good Samaritan—the kindness of a stranger passing by if she could find any at all. *He can't own this whole mountain.*

Kori forced herself to concentrate on making as much progress through the forest as she could, dispelling all questions and thoughts as to why it was happening to her in the first place. *Focus, Kori, you can do this. Just concentrate on your surroundings, like the Cub Scout leaders said.*

She slowed for a brief rest to give her racing pulse and labored breathing time to slow and stabilize. Her lungs were stinging from the cold, and her thighs and calves ached. Her mind was still hazy, but her body was beginning to get its strength back. In the cloudy darkness, it was hard to decipher whether she was heading up or down the mountain. She could only continue maneuvering her way through small gorges, unsure of what progress she was making toward civilization if she were making any progress at all.

The other sounds of the night didn't frighten her, the symphony of crickets and owls meant she was still among the living. The clouds were becoming darker, changing from a gray fog to dark shadows lingering just overhead. The air was no longer dry but filled with a fine mist. Kori knew the rain was imminent and had to prepare for it. If she got wet, there would be little hope of surviving hypothermia.

Her first priority, for that reason, was to make some type of shelter. She hadn't passed any caves or indentations in the mountain that could provide her with cover from the elements, so she was left to put her few survival skills to work. Unsure of how much time she had before the rain or her predator moved in, she could only hope to accomplish a simple lean-to. Luckily, she encountered several downed trees, so she chose one next to the side of a ravine. Rummaging around quickly, she gathered all the limbs she could find and rested them diagonally against the large, fallen trunk.

She diligently scooped up armfuls of dry, brittle leaves that'd recently fallen from the large oaks and threw them into her makeshift shelter. When it was filled to capacity, she squinted into the darkness, trying to locate all the pine boughs she could. She worked quickly to cover her living quarters, then crawled inside and blanketed herself with leaves, just as the first few drops of rain started to come down from the heavens.

The storm came fast, a relentless tumult, while Kori lay among the leaves for warmth. Violent flashes of lightning bolted across the sky, followed by raucous thunder. Closing her eyes, she worried about her parents. She knew they were still up, unable to sleep, frantic with their daughter missing at that late hour with no word from her. She closed her eyes and envisioned her warm bed, the one her mother had bought for her when she'd started middle school. Kori had complained of her old twin bed with its childish bedspread, until her mother finally agreed it was time for a double, with a white, eyelet comforter. Kori recalled being so proud of that bed, which made her feel more like a teenager than a little girl.

Oh, what I'd give to be back there now, she thought, under that cozy blanket.

The adrenaline that had given her the strength and stamina to continue through the woods was wearing off, but the sedative he'd given her hadn't. The sounds of the storm and the rain methodically hitting the pine boughs threatened to lullaby her to sleep, in spite of her predicament. For several minutes, Kori struggled against the weight of her eyelids before finally giving in to her weariness and toppling into a deep slumber.

****

Kim Carter

He'd kept his word and waited exactly fifteen minutes before leaving the cabin in search of Kori Reeves. He strode swiftly through the same woods he'd spent years of his boyhood. The terrain was difficult at best, but for a young woman who'd never been out of the city, he knew it'd be next to impossible to navigate. He supposed it was cheating, to some extent, but he didn't really care. She'd be like the rest, wandering aimlessly around in circles, in that labyrinth of trees that all seemed to resemble each other. He was sure he'd soon happen upon his prey, and she would be exhausted and confused, huddled under one of those trees and pleading for mercy. It was starting to become too predictable, and he began to think of new games he could play.

As skilled as he was at traversing them the woods still posed somewhat of a challenge, especially in the dark and rain. With all the pine needles on the ground, it was hard to track her. He'd have to predict her strategy and bank on some of her clothing getting caught in the briars.

She'll leave telltale signs. They all do, he consoled himself as he stomped over broken branches and crunching leaves.

He'd underestimated when the storm would start and was now too far out on the property to get back in time to bypass it. His heavy coat, made for conditions such as these would protect him from the torrential downpour, but he had no intention of wading through the icy rainstorm.

I won't allow you to be the cause of a bad cold, Kori. I think I'll teach you a little lesson. Because of your parents, I was going to let you be found, but now you've pissed me off. I was looking forward to seeing them on the news, pleading for your return, crying those salty tears for the camera, then watching them crumble when someone found your body. Now, we'll just let them wonder, for years to come. See what you've done to your poor mom and dad, Kori? As for you, I'll just step back inside and let you scramble around in the elements until morning, he thought with a wicked sneer. *Yep, I think I'll let last weekend's hunt win the honor of being discovered. Then I'll let a few years pass before I allow anyone else to be found. Surely you understand the importance of keeping things...low key. At any rate, come on down, Nina Culver! You're the next contestant who'll be found!*

Chapter Thirty-Seven

Clara and Iris stood at Detective Pitts' door, tightly clutching their notepads, as they built up the nerve to go ahead with the meeting.

"Oh, this is ridiculous," Iris whispered. "Just knock already."

Clara took a deep breath and tapped three times with the brass door knocker.

"Yeah? Come on in," a male voice yelled.

The women exchanged looks before Clara reached for the knob and turned.

"Detective Pitts?" she questioned as she peeked around the door. "It's Clara Samples."

"Come in!" he yelled again. "I'm over on the couch. I've been up enough for one day, and I guess my butler and maid are out for the week," he said snidely.

She eased the door open just wide enough to enter, and both ladies quickly squeezed through.

Pitts was sitting on the couch, with his feet crossed on the coffee table and a flannel throw blanket draped across his lap. "Sorry about that," he said. "It's hard to get up and down, so I don't do it any more than I have to. Have a seat."

Iris sat in the recliner while Clara took the vacant end of the couch. "We appreciate you seeing us," Clara began. "I understand you're out on medical leave."

"Yes, I am," Pitts answered as he lightly patted his right side. "They had to remove most of my lung. My partner and I were shot right in front of our office."

"We saw it on the news. It's hard to believe someone would be so bold."

"This world's getting worse by the day, but I know you ladies aren't just here on a courtesy call. I understand you're working on the Baines murder? I've gotta say, I'm a little surprised to hear that you two opened a P.I. business."

Clara and Iris diverted their eyes, not comfortable enough to make eye contact. They knew the detective had had his own suspicions about them while investigating Dr. Chatsworth, and they both hoped he'd just let it go.

"If you think I'm pursuing anything further on the Chatsworth case, ladies, you're wrong. I'm not so sure you two weren't involved in more than meets the eye, but whatever it was is better left unearthed. As far as I'm concerned, justice was served when that son-of-a-bitch was killed by the FBI."

Both women were visibly relieved, but neither offered a comment.

Pitts let them exhale deeply before he continued, "I really hate that we couldn't solve the Baines case before all this went down. My biggest fear was that Jasmine was a random target. Those are the most difficult to solve because, without DNA or a fingerprint match, we're basically stuck waiting around for the perp to strike again."

"So, you weren't able to come up with anything?" Iris asked. "No suspects at all?"

"Nothing," he said, shaking his head. "Of course, we looked at every obvious angle—her college, her apartment, and her job—but as hard as we dug, we didn't come up with anything. Sadly, there wasn't much to look into. Jasmine didn't have any close friends except her older sister. They grew up in the foster system, so I guess it makes sense that she was so...guarded. From what everybody told us, she didn't date or party. All she did was study and work. I am curious about one thing, though."

"What is that, Detective?" Clara asked.

"Who hired you, ladies, to investigate?"

"Her sister, Ginger," Clara answered. "Why do you ask?"

"Well, it's just that she had to beg, borrow, and steal to have her sister buried. I'm wondering how she came up with the money for your, uh...services."

"She didn't," Clara said. "We felt so bad for her that we have to help. We aren't really in this for the money anyway, and we've got a few other cases that will allow us to keep the lights on."

"I see," Pitts said as he scooted farther back on the couch. "Telling her about her sister's murder really broke us up. Ginger came back in to see us the morning we were shot. In fact, it was just before we left to go to a homicide scene. I sensed that she was a bit disgruntled with us and felt like we'd given up on solving the murder. In our defense, though, we're always working more than one case. We take them all very seriously, but when a lead grows cold… well, when that happens, there's not much we can do."

"I think Ginger understands that," Clara said. "It's still a difficult pill to swallow. I'm sure every friend and relative affected by a murder feels their loved one should take priority. We wanted to talk to you because we didn't want to waste time retracing your steps."

"That's a good idea. As you know, time is of the essence in a murder investigation. Where do you want me to start?"

"How about at the beginning?" Iris chimed in as if it was obvious. "Who found her body?"

"Stuart Mason, the sexton over at Oakland Cemetery. He found her when he got to work that morning while doing his rounds on a golf cart."

"Any reason to suspect him?" Iris continued.

"No, not really. Mister Mason was real upset and jittery. That always makes my partner suspicious, but I think he was genuinely distraught. I mean, the man works in a cemetery, not a morgue. That's the last place somebody would dump a body. Hell, he's worked there for over forty years, and he's never seen that before. Plus, he's an older gentleman, with a bad case of arthritis. I can't see him carrying a dead body around a cemetery."

"Strange," Iris said as she opened her notepad to scribble down the sexton's name. "Why would anybody dump a body in a cemetery?"

"That was our first thought. It's odd to dump a body in a graveyard, especially one as large and busy as Oakland. There can really only be one answer to that. The killer knew she'd be found. Maybe he couldn't bear the thought of her just…decomposing somewhere."

"Maybe it's not that at all," Clara said. "Is there any significance to the area where she was dumped? Was she related to anyone buried nearby?"

"I thought of that, too," Pitts said with a sly grin.

"Well, you know what they say about great minds," Iris said, winking at him.

"I guess I haven't given you ladies enough credit. Anyway, I had the crime scene investigators from the Medical Examiner's office and the PD take photos of the surrounding area. We couldn't come up with any correlation between Jasmine and anyone who was interred there. The only other living family member is their mother. She showed up at the funeral and looks pretty rough. Ginger told us she's a long-time drug user, and she certainly looked the part."

"So, if there's family buried in that cemetery, Ginger doesn't know anything about it?" Clara asked.

"No, not that I'm aware of. At the funeral, we saw an older couple with her. We asked about them, and she said they had been foster parents to her and Jasmine for their last few years in the system. I can't recall their names right off, but we didn't find it significant. They appeared to be nice people and were very emotional about her death. They must've cared deeply for her."

"Do you think their mother could've done it?" Iris asked.

"I can't come up with a motive," Pitts said, shrugging his shoulders, then wincing from the pain. "I mean, she hasn't had much to do with them through the years, other than to block any opportunities for adoption. Ginger said they hadn't heard from her since Jasmine graduated from high school. Their mother knew very little about either of the girls, and I can't imagine Jasmine going anywhere with her. There was very little love lost between them. They despised her, and I can't say I blame 'em."

"Maybe she resented them for how they'd treated her," Iris piped in. "Perhaps she didn't want them to be successful? So, she killed her youngest. That might explain why the girl was all wrapped up in a blanket and left somewhere to be found. In some sick way, it sounds sort of...*motherly*."

"Yeah, we rolled that idea around in our heads a few times, too," Pitts said. "Frankly, I can't see it. The mother doesn't have a car or any mode of transportation, and I can't imagine Jasmine agreeing to meet up with her."

"What if the mother knew where she lived?"

"Our CSI team went over her studio apartment with a fine-toothed comb. I don't believe Jasmine was murdered there, and no one supports the idea that a woman her mother's age ever visited. It isn't that heavy drug users are above crime of this type, but I don't believe it was her. Her mother is thin and malnourished, and the person who did this had to be strong enough to overpower Jasmine."

"Okay, that makes sense," Iris said. "However, if they didn't have any dealings with their mother. How did she find out Jasmine was dead? Did your office call her?"

"That's a good question," Pitts answered. "In fact, Ginger was adamant that she hadn't told her mother, and from the looks of it, the lady hasn't exactly been sitting around reading the daily news. I'm not even sure they knew how to contact her in case of an emergency—or that they cared to know. Nettles and I didn't call her, we weren't privy to that info either. I'll ask Jessalyn. Maybe they found something in the system at the ME's office. Jessalyn always goes the extra mile."

"Yes, it might be of some importance to find out who notified the mother," Clara said. "Did you happen to see who drove her to the funeral, since you say she doesn't have a vehicle? If she's as strung out as you say she is, she wouldn't have the money to catch a cab."

Pitts took a deep breath and massaged his side. "I hate to admit it, but we really never pursued that angle. I'll look into it, though." He groaned from the massage, then continued, "Tell me, ladies…how are you two going to tackle this investigation from here on out, any thoughts?"

"We have our assistant looking into the restaurant where she worked and scouting out the apartment. She's young and can get a better feel for it than we can. We'd stick out like sore thumbs, two old bitties in places like that. We haven't come up with any new suspects at this point, though. I'm banking on a regular customer at her job, or a transient moving from one cheap apartment to the next," Clara said.

"Let's go back to the cemetery again," Iris interjected. "Surely, they lock the gates at night. So, how did someone get in to dump a body?"

"We did inquire about that," Pitts answered. "The main gate is locked every night and opened in the morning, but the side gate on Memorial Drive is left unlocked. Apparently, a group of walkers comes in the mornings, and they requested access before the sexton arrives. It isn't advertised, though. It's just word-of-mouth among those spandex-wearing, health-nut types. They're always early risers. I have to admit, it's a nice place to walk, morbid as it might be."

"So, the side gate is closed but not locked?" Iris continued to press.

"Yes, but the average Joe Blow wouldn't be aware of that."

"It's still odd," Iris said. "I mean, if I was gonna dump a body, I'd think it through a little beforehand. I'd assume a gated cemetery so large and frequently visited wouldn't have twenty-four-hour access. So, why try to dump a body there?"

"You're exactly right, Iris," Clara said. "I agree with you a hundred percent. It has to be someone familiar with the cemetery. Maybe it's a regular walker, or maybe it is the sexton. What did you say his name is, Detective?"

"Stuart Mason, he's about your age, I figure, but again, I didn't get any killer vibes from him. I think he's very dedicated to his job and this murder really caught him off guard."

"I might just have the woman for the job," Clara said with a broad grin. "It seems, Iris, here, enjoys being a flirt. Maybe she could get to know Mister Mason a little better."

"Hey, I only flirted with a fine, upstanding cop in case we need some inside scoop in the future," Iris said defensively. "Don't go trying to set me up with an old graveyard housekeeper who drives around on a golf cart, and just might be a *murderer!*"

"He might not be our guy," Clara said with a laugh. "I'm simply suggesting we start getting up early to exercise. Should we run into, Stuart Mason. Perhaps you can give him one of those flirtatious winks you're so famous for?"

Chapter Thirty-Eight

The old, dark van backed out of the driveway and eased down the neighborhood street. Platinum sat up and leaned heavily against the paneled door. Using the toe of her sneaker, she nudged Felipe to get his attention. His eyes still had that faraway look as if he were somehow willing himself to another place.

"Felipe?" Platinum whispered. "What the hell's wrong with you?"

The fixated stare lingered for a couple of seconds until he turned his head slightly in her direction. His eyes soon followed and met hers, but he said nothing.

"Where're they taking us?" she demanded.

"You don't wanna know," he finally uttered.

"Snap the fuck out of it," she hissed. "If they were gonna kill us, we'd already be dead."

Felipe shook his head and closed his eyes. "We'd be *lucky* to be dead, right now," he whispered. "I never shoulda let you talk me into shooting those cops. It brought too much heat. We were stupid, and Mateo is pissed. Killing us is an understatement of what they're gonna do, you stupid bitch!"

"We had to do it," Platinum whispered as she leaned closer to him, her spittle dampening his face as she hissed. "Germaine gave 'em your description, you fool. They woulda nailed you for killing, Tony."

"Like they could ever I.D. a Mexican. They can't tell us one from the other with so many around. They had nothing, no car, weapon, nothing that woulda led them to me."

"I made the right call. Don't you realize our stories didn't add up?"

"It was the right call to keep your ass out of jail."

The blank stare returned, and Platinum let out a frustrated sigh. Hunger pangs began to gnaw at her empty stomach, and she wasn't fond of the feeling. She glanced around the van. It was staged to resemble a work vehicle transporting menial laborers. Paint-stained tarps were tossed around carelessly amid various tools and paintbrushes, but if anyone took a closer look at the van, they'd easily notice it was a far cry from what it appeared to be.

Boxes of vacuum-sealed bags were present, along with bottles of bleach and rubbing alcohol. It was the easiest way to transport large quantities of marijuana without the stench drawing attention. They'd used Platinum in an assembly line many times when they needed to get the fresh product out to local dealers. She'd scrubbed her hands over and over before filling the plastic bags with weed, then vacuum-sealing them. That part of the process was followed with more handwashing, bleaching and wiping the bags with rubbing alcohol, before re-bagging several more times.

It was all quite exhausting and it pissed her off. The Mexicans chose the trashiest neighborhoods and rundown homes for the production and bagging of their drugs. The environment was often cold and filthy. Platinum felt far above such crude working conditions, but her ego and pride were soon forgotten when they'd paid her in drugs and cash.

Platinum allowed her mind to drift back to Tony if for no other reason than to stifle the persistent rumbling in her belly. He was a nice guy, but she always knew he'd never make big money. When they finally had a real chance at making a major change for their better, he punked out. "*I don't like Mexicans,*" he told her adamantly. "*I jus' don't trust 'em,*" he reiterated, again and again.

Platinum was convinced he was simply weak. He never wanted to work for somebody else. He was too scared of going to prison. Now, it was all water under the bridge, and Tony was six feet, just like his friend G-Boy. Platinum looked back at Felipe. He was the first to approach her when the cartel started scouting out the area. Having grown up in Los Angeles, he spoke English well. He was shorter than she preferred but was well built and always had a wad of cash.

Felipe was low-level cartel but was cartel nonetheless, and that meant something to her. He was as close to a real somebody as she'd ever been around. After all, the cartel was the new mob, and even television couldn't get enough of it. Now, he was a mindless, defeated goon, lying next to her on the floor of a dirty drug wagon, on the way to his doom right along with her.

Felipe looked back at Platinum and marveled at her ignorance. *If she was born in another place and time, she might have been a pretty, young woman,* he thought, *but the streets put an end to that.*

They'd hardened both her appearance and her character. He wanted to pity her, but he couldn't bring himself to do it. Platinum was like so many other young women he'd come in contact with as the cartel began moving through the U.S.: greedy, ruthless, and desperate for the things she'd never have. Ultimately, he knew he was really to blame for the fix they were in. He'd gotten caught up in the moment and allowed her to influence him. Mateo's first rule of the game was no one ever got high off their own supply, and when Felipe broke that cardinal rule, it severely clouded his judgment. He'd gotten so close to locking down the neighborhood necessary for them to move the product that was coming through in droves, but Tony Hart was arrogant and got in his way. Felipe wanted the money, but he wanted it on his terms, and he wanted to control Platinum.

Apparently, Tony's love for her went way back, and he wasn't willing to let her loose to see another side of life. What he didn't count on was that Platinum wouldn't bat an eye when it came to cutting him loose. Felipe was high enough to go along with the murder, but once he came down from his hit, he realized the grave mistake they'd made. Somehow, Platinum had convinced him that getting rid of the two cops would solve the problem, but it only compounded it, bringing down a shitload of heat on both the local dealers and the Hispanics sent over by the cartel to work the area.

Now, countless gang task forces, the FBI, the GBI, the ATF, and every other agency Felipe could think of were coming down on them. The drug trade from Miami, Houston, and Mexico was being affected, and scores of shipments were being stopped and confiscated along the interstates. The cartel wasn't concerned about the transporters going to prison or the vehicles that were seized, they simply wanted their product back on the street. The search-and-seizure efforts were costing them money, and anyone even potentially responsible for that had to be swiftly and harshly dealt with. It went with the territory, and everyone involved knew the risks, but the locals who naïvely fell for the quick money had no idea of the horrors they were up against.

In the housing projects in the U.S., getting shot over a drug deal was something that happened often, but the cartel worked with far more brutal means than bullets. The ignorant dealers in the States had a disillusioned fantasy of the Mexican drug cartels and almost idolized the fictional characters they'd built them up to be. Unfortunately for Platinum, she was one of those who'd succumbed to her fantasies about what and who they really were.

"Who's this Mateo cat anyway?" she asked. "Who the hell does he think he is?"

"You really don't get it, do you?" Felipe asked. "They're gonna torture us till we're close to death, but they won't let us die. They'll keep torturing us. When they finally let us die, they'll roll our fucking heads down the interstate and hang our naked bodies under a bridge, just to send a message."

"Get the hell outta here," Platinum said. "That crazy shit only happens in Mexico and in the damn movies, Felipe. This is America."

"Yeah, crazy or not, shit just got real. You don't shoot cops in America and get away with it. They came down hard on the cartel, and now they're seizing their supply coming off the interstates. We brought all that down on them. *Don't you get it?*! It's so bad that Mateo came in from Mexico City to personally oversee our demise. He'll make an example of us one nobody will soon forget."

Platinum rolled her eyes and forced a snicker, but the fear on her face was evident. The bitter, horrifying truth was beginning to register with her, and the last thing on her mind now was filling her empty stomach.

Chapter Thirty-Nine

The fire had successfully heated up the small cabin, making it cozy and warm. He slipped off his coat and hat, shook the rain off them, then laid both items across the back of a rocking chair on the front porch. He was furious, rarely did he allow anyone to get under his skin, but he detested being cold. He hated getting wet even more. His waterproof hiking boots were the next item to come off, along with the thick, wool socks. He went to the bedroom and retrieved his slippers, then paced wildly across the wooden floor of the small den.

It's all your fault, Kori. You know that, don't you? Now I've got a mess, trying to find you in this weather so I can finish the job and hide your body. You blew it for yourself, you selfish little girl.

He put water in the kettle and lit the stove, the tasks of the night necessitated coffee. One of the best things about the cabin was that Wi-Fi and phone service were never installed, freeing him from the harassment of the ills of the world. When he was here, he could fully leave the mad rush of his life behind. There weren't any thoughts of work or the idiots he worked with, no struggles over what suit to wear or which tie would make the most impact on his career. Such trivial bullshit.

While he waited for the water to boil, he turned on his battery-operated radio to listen to the weather forecast. He had forewarning of the storm coming through but hadn't expected one so severe. Now, he hoped Mother Nature's wrath would quickly blow over and present little more than a minor inconvenience.

Aggravated by the mindless banter between the radio hosts, he poured himself a cup of strong, black coffee and sat in the recliner, anxious for them to turn their attention to the storm at hand. He was glad when they finally did just that and announced, with feigned enthusiasm, *"It appears we're in for a long night, folks. This thunderstorm is promising to stick around for several hours. The portion of the state north of Ellijay, Dahlonega, Cleveland, and Toccoa is taking the biggest hit, and this will continue until early tomorrow afternoon. Snuggle up out there and throw some logs on the fire. I'll now brave the elements and leave the broadcast in the hands of our lovely Cameron Diggs. Stay tuned for the latest weather and news, as Cameron will be live with up-to-the-minute reports."*

He was tempted to throw the radio across the room, but he'd done that once before, and it had proven to be more trouble than it was worth. Instead, he hit the power button forcefully. In the silence, broken only by the rain pelting the cabin and the logs crackling in the fire, his mind raced with random, manic thoughts as he struggled to rein them in.

If Kori had failed to find a decent tree to huddle under, she might very well be dead before he found her, which wasn't necessarily a problem for him. He'd never particularly liked her, so he felt no allegiance to serving as her killer. The decision to eternally leave her hidden was one he'd stick to. Once his mind was made up, there was no turning back. Her opportunity to make the news was over, so now he had to go with Plan B.

He'd always liked Nina Culver, for no particular reason other than her bright, pleasant nature. Of course, that faded quickly when she'd realized what fate had in store for her. Just like Kori, she had a family. His mind drifted back to Jasmine Baines, quite a beauty. Sadly, for him, allowing her body to be found hadn't brought the media coverage he'd hoped for. Jasmine's only family was the sister she was always whining and worrying about, but Ginger was far too distraught over the murder to be interviewed on TV. It was quite a letdown, and a mistake he wouldn't make again.

No more orphans, he told himself. *Even pretty girls are too easily forgotten without grieving parents to keep the media outlets rolling with their anguished pleas for justice.*

Nina would be the last one he'd allow to be found for the next several years. The profilers would scratch their heads and chase their tails, then assume he'd moved on to another part of the country. The media would soon find another story to cover, one as rich with emotion as the last had been, and the world would go back to spinning on its proverbial axis.

He got up from the recliner and walked to the door. He could hear the rain coming down in sheets but aware he had to get moving if he was going to retrieve Nina's body and dump her before dawn. He'd have to take the old Jeep stored in the barn, rush back to the city, and be back in time for sunrise. It was doable as long as the torrential downpour didn't slow his progress on the expressway.

Waiting patiently for the warm coffee to take effect, he stood, stretched, and put on dry clothes. He didn't expect to get wet again, after all, the barn was only fifty yards away. There were plenty of tarps to conceal

Nina's body, and the odds of a cop pulling him over in a storm were nil. One thing he wasn't looking forward to was pulling her up from the underground bunker in the barn. The hay would be damp and smell like an old, wet dog. The weather had been cold, so she wouldn't decompose too badly, but she'd be heavy, and even with the rope and hoist, it would be an aggravation. He hated Plan B, but it was the only plan he had.

Chapter Forty

At 5:30 a.m., Iris knocked on Clara's door.

"It's awfully early, Iris. I can't imagine people walking at this hour," Clara said as she opened the door. She handed an insulated travel cup of coffee to her friend, then locked the door behind her. "I think we'd better put our purses in the trunk. People are breaking into cars to steal things left in plain sight. I heard about it on the news."

"I declare, common sense is dead," Iris moaned. "Who in their right mind would leave their purse or laptop on the seat for someone to see anyway? It's just too tempting for criminals."

"Yes, it's a shame we live in a day and age when anybody could be tempted enough by material things to break into a car to steal them," Clara said as she opened the trunk and placed her purse inside. "I remember back when we could almost leave our windows down and the keys in the car without a worry in the world."

"Since when did we start leaving our bags behind anyway?" Iris asked. "I planned to carry mine with me. I started carrying a pocketbook in my teens, and I feel naked without it."

"You can't be serious, Iris. How many walkers have purses slung over their shoulders? We're going undercover here. We can't risk looking ridiculous."

"I hope you aren't planning on tromping all over that place, for heaven's sake. I haven't even had my morning coffee, yet, to say nothing of my cheese toast. I'm not even fully awake."

Clara pointed to the trunk and waited as Iris unwillingly placed her purse inside. "Now get in the car, Iris," she ordered firmly. "And stop whining."

They were halfway through their first cups of coffee when Iris spoke again. "What do you s'pose has all these people up at this hour?" she asked, looking around the busy street. "Fred wouldn't have believed it, I tell ya. He always said the drive into Atlanta was the most peaceful part of his day. There wasn't so much congestion back then and no one had ever heard of bumper-to-bumper traffic. I think we've gotten ourselves overpopulated."

Clara sighed and reasoned, "The city's built up a lot since Fred was a commuter, Iris. Atlanta has the largest airport, and there are several major corporations here. Times change, and it doesn't have to be a bad thing. It's good to see so many people on their way to work."

"Well, I still think driving to work in the wee hours is preposterous. Here we are, retired and driving to a cemetery to exercise. Fred must be rollin' over in his grave."

"We're really going into work, too, basically another day at the office for us. Would you rather be sitting in the car somewhere doing surveillance?"

"Absolutely not! A little of those stakeouts goes a long way. They certainly glorify surveillance duty on those cop shows. Now we know how overrated it is. Then again, they usually get to sit in the car all night with some hot officer in a uniform, and I'm stuck with you."

"Gee, thanks, Iris."

"Anyway, what's the plan?" Iris asked.

"I say we go in and get a feel for the place, maybe strike up a friendly conversation with a few people and walk around a bit. We're not going to do any of that power walking, though. Pitts said there are benches everywhere, so we can pretend to rest and do some people-watching."

"Definitely no power walking! I'm wearing brand-new sneakers, and I don't need any blisters. I'd think people out this early in the morning must be serious about getting their exercise. I doubt any of them are gonna want to talk religion or politics."

"I'm not talking a full-fledged conversation," Clara said. "I hate to break this to you, Iris, but I have a feeling this is going to require more than one early-morning walk. We have to get familiar with the regulars, so prepare yourself to put a little mileage on those sneakers."

Iris wrapped her scarf around her neck and buttoned the top button of her coat. "At least surveillance in your car is warm," she grumbled.

Clara pulled the car into the gravel parking lot on Oakland Avenue. There were several other cars there, indicating they weren't alone. "Okay, let's hit it and get it," Clara said. "We have to start somewhere, and if your gut tells us we'll find our killer here, we have to go with it."

Iris rubbed her middle. "My gut's also reminding me about that cheese toast you made me miss."

"Come on, Iris."

The two ladies walked to the side access on Memorial Drive and opened the gate leading to the pedestrian entrance. Indeed, they weren't alone. The women hid their surprise at the number of walkers quickly passing by. Clara estimated a dozen people, ranging in age from their early twenties to mid-sixties. Most appeared to be alone, with earphones in their ears, and not wearing nearly as much clothing as Clara and Iris had on. Their cheeks were pink, and their breath came out as billowing clouds. They zoomed past the older ladies without so much as an acknowledgment of their presence.

"This may be tougher than we thought," Clara said. "Let's just start with a leisurely stroll. The exercise will be good for us."

They walked at an unhurried pace, talking between themselves as they took in the beautiful scenery around them. After about ten minutes, they decided to utilize one of the many benches. The walkers were alone for the most part and appeared very serious about their workouts, with the exception of two middle-aged women and a young couple who walked side by side. After about thirty minutes of people walking laps around them, the women received a few nods. It wasn't exactly a slew of hearty welcomes, but Iris and Clara considered it a good start.

Clara looked down at her watch. "I say we go get some breakfast and come back when they open. The sexton should be here by then."

"You won't get an argument from me," Iris said. "I think we've seen at least two different groups come and go. Tomorrow may bring others, but we can see who comes back."

"Exactly," Clara agreed. "Maybe we should use a rotation schedule, give or take thirty minutes or so each day."

"Good idea," Iris said. "Want to hit IHOP? I could go for an omelet."

After a filling breakfast and almost a whole pot of coffee, the ladies finally felt warm and satisfied. The parking lot at the cemetery was empty when they returned, except for a couple of cars parked near the back. Clara figured they belonged to the cemetery workers, kind enough to leave the closer parking spots for visitors.

The main entrance was open, so both women leisurely strolled inside. They paused to admire the wide array of trees, hedges, and flora. The historic cemetery was indeed an impressive place.

Iris was reading a plaque aloud to Clara when an older gentleman pulled up on a golf cart. "Good morning," he said cheerfully. "You ladies are out bright and early."

"Actually," Iris began in an overly friendly tone. "We were here even earlier. We got word through the grapevine in our Golden Oldies group that this is the place to be."

The remark drew a hearty chuckle from the sexton. "I'm not so sure that's true."

Iris looked insulted, an expression that brought a quick apology. "I suppose that did sound a little odd," she conceded with a forced smile. "It's just that my friend and I enjoy a good workout, and this is a beautiful place to walk."

"Yes, it is. Allow me to introduce myself. Name's Stuart Mason, the sexton here."

"I'm Iris, and this here's Clara, my bestie, as the youngins say. What exactly does a sexton do?"

Stuart puffed his chest out a little before he recited his dossier. "I'm in charge of the place," he began. "I've got lots of duties, but ultimately, I'm the overseer," he said as he waved his hand over the general layout of the cemetery. "Quite a beauty, isn't she?"

Iris was a little perplexed by his personification of a graveyard, but she smiled sweetly anyway. "Looks like you're doing a good job. The plants are beautiful. I bet you work all the time."

"Now, now! All work and no play make Stuart a dull boy," he said with a chuckle.

Clara wanted to roll her eyes at the flirtatious banter between the two of them but managed to restrain herself.

"I have a staff," Stuart continued. "We've got forty-eight acres to tend," he said, waving his hand across the property again as if it personally belonged to him. "Why don't you hop on, and I'll give you the grand tour, show you both the highlights of the place?" he suggested, patting the seat beside him with his arthritic hand.

"We wouldn't want to impose, Mister Mason," Clara said quickly. "It's obvious you're quite busy."

Iris shot her a quick look. "Why, Clara, this man's offering to show us the place. If we plan to walk here on a regular basis, surely it can't hurt."

"It's not a problem," Stuart insisted. "I always start my day off with a ride-through. You ladies are welcome to tag along."

"Very well," Clara said.

"Thank you for giving us the VIP treatment, Mister Mason. If you don't mind, I'll just ride up front with you," Iris said, flashing him a grin.

Clara had to admit he was quite knowledgeable about the cemetery, and she enjoyed hearing about its history. She recognized the area where Jasmine had been found, based on the names etched in the surrounding tombstones. She'd hoped Stuart Mason would mention it, but he didn't, in fact, it wasn't lost on her that he turned his head and ignored the area altogether as if purposefully excluding it from his tour.

That's so odd, Clara thought. She had no idea how to interpret it.

Either it bothered him so deeply that he couldn't bring himself to look at the space, or he'd dumped poor Jasmine himself and couldn't bear to think of it. She desperately wanted to bring it up to see how he would react, but she ultimately decided against it. They were just getting to know the sexton, and if he was involved, the topic would only scare him off and drive him away.

After thirty minutes, he pulled up next to the bell tower and invited them in for coffee.

"We really shouldn't," Iris said. "We've already had plenty and need to get back home. The house isn't gonna clean itself. Also, I'm in the middle of crocheting another afghan. Guess my life isn't nearly as exciting as yours, Mister Mason."

"Stuart, please. I hope to see you, ladies, again sometime," he said to Iris, without even looking back in Clara's direction. "I don't know if I will if you're only up at sunrise to walk with those early-morning folks. I usually don't get here until after they leave."

"Oh, we'll swap it up," Iris insisted. "Some mornings are early, but once in a while, we sleep in, depending on how late I stay up to crochet. Lots of people look forward to my *afghans*, so it keeps me pretty busy. I've got to admit, we were a little surprised to find that you leave that gate open. It seems a little...dangerous. Does anyone ever bother anything?"

"Nope," Stuart quickly answered. "I've been workin' here for forty years, and we've yet to have anyone vandalize the place. As you saw this morning, the walkers and joggers are simply here to get their exercise in, and this is one of the safest places in the city to do that. They don't have to worry 'bout traffic, stoplights, or sidewalks in need of repair. Other than those power walkers, it's pretty harmless. I always wonder how those folks walk that fast! I know it's a cemetery, but it's really pretty here if I do say so myself. Not only that, but considerin' that the residents are so quiet, it's pretty darn peaceful."

"Well, that makes me feel better," Iris said. "I hate to burden you, Stuart, but would you mind giving us a lift back to the gate? These sneakers are new, and I don't have them broken in yet. I feel a blister coming on. I guess that's the price I pay for working out," she added with that flirtatious wink that made Clara want to pinch her.

"It'd be my pleasure," Stuart said. "Have a nice day," he politely said a few minutes later, when he dropped them off at Clara's car.

"You too, Mister Mason," Clara offered before turning to open her door.

"I have a car, too," Iris said emphatically. "I drive all over. It's just Clara's turn today. We save on gas that way."

He smiled and nodded, then drove back toward the cemetery entrance without another word.

They closed their car doors, and Clara cranked the engine. When Iris reached over to turn on the radio, Clara smacked her hand.

"Hey! What was that for?" Iris asked.

"What was all that talk about afghans? And who in the hell would work their daily schedule around crocheting anyway?"

"Aw! You said *hell*, Clara Samples. What's gotten into you? Are you jealous because Stuart seemed so taken with me? You're the one who insisted I flirt with the man."

"Of course not! You just say the craziest things sometimes, Iris. I'm beginning to wonder about your mind."

"My *mind*? You can't be serious. I'm sharp as a tack! We're old, Clara. Most people our age don't go around acting like that, Murder She Wrote woman, do they? Do I need to remind you that most people's grannies have big old baskets of yarn lying around? I couldn't very well tell the man we're private investigators, working undercover. He's still a working man. I had to impress him with something."

"So, you went with crocheting? That's original."

"I do declare, you're practically turning green with envy!" Iris said with a laugh. "Anyway, I've had my coffee and an omelet, and I feel good. Maybe it was the walking? At any rate, I'm not going to let you spoil my mood by baiting me into one of those silly arguments you seem to enjoy."

Clara had to laugh, realizing she was, perhaps, being a little too hard on her friend. She just never knew what Iris was going to come up with and what was going to come out of her mouth. That made her nervous. She had to admit that Iris had played the part well. "I apologize, Iris. I just get concerned sometimes. This job can be dangerous, and I worry."

Iris reached over and patted her old friend's hand. "I know, Clara, I know. What's your gut feeling about the sexton?"

"I'm not really sure. He seems nice enough, and he's quite proud of his job, which he certainly does well. I noticed the site where Jasmine was dumped. He rode by it quickly and didn't mention it at all. It was almost as if he made an effort to turn his head away."

"And what do you make of that?" Iris asked.

"I'm not sure. It could mean several things, and first impressions aren't always right. Let's give it some time."

"I agree," Iris said with a smile. "Let's go by the office and check-in with, Quita. At least we have each other in the field, but she's all alone out there. I worry about that girl. She's such a tiny little thing. Maybe we should take her an omelet or two."

"Really?" Clara asked. "I never would've guessed that you worry about anything…except maybe your backlog on afghans," she said with a laugh.

Chapter Forty-One

The hunger pangs that had been gnawing so persistently at Platinum's stomach vanished the second she realized the brevity of the predicament she was in. Unlike Felipe, who was resigned to his fate, she was close to hysteria. The shaking began in her hands, and soon, her entire body followed suit.

"We've gotta do something," she whispered to Felipe. "We can't just sit here while he takes us to our deaths."

"And what do you propose we do? Open the door and jump?"

"Well, if what you say is true, that'd be a helluva lot better than getting our heads cut off!" She turned to the back door of the van and struggled to open it, but it was useless. It was fastened with an industrial lock and neither had the strength to budge it. "Don't just sit there, you idiot," Platinum hissed. "Help me think of something."

"You're wasting your energy. They're way smarter than we are."

"So, you're just gonna sit here and do nothing?" Platinum asked in disbelief. She'd just delivered her daughter a few days earlier and was weak from blood loss and lack of nutrients, as well as her drug use. Still, as faint and woozy as she felt, she was determined to live.

The old cargo van, paneled on the sides and with solid back doors, was not manufactured with any windows, so the two of them had no idea where they were headed. Platinum listened intently but couldn't hear any other vehicles on the roadway. She suspected they weren't on the interstate, but since she didn't hear any gravel under the tires, she assumed they were on a paved road and took that as a positive sign.

"If we can remove part of this panel, we can bust the taillights out," she whispered. "Somebody will spot that if they come up behind us."

"Do you really think he won't notice if we start kicking things back here?" Felipe asked.

"The way I see it, we don't have anything to lose." Platinum ran her fingers around the edges of the door until she found a place to ease them up under the panel. "Just keep an eye out," she whispered, as she struggled to pull it loose. When she felt it give a bit, she tugged as hard as she could.

Much to her relief and surprise, it tore away from the door with a crack. Her efforts to move away weren't quick enough, and the van skidded to a stop.

Felipe and Platinum heard the jingling of keys before their kidnapper found the appropriate one and opened one of the back doors. Felipe immediately returned to his blank, resigned-to-his-fate stare, while Platinum cowered from the burly man. He reached in and grabbed her hair, pulling her from the van. She screamed and kicked with all her might, but Platinum was little competition for his size and strength.

"You're a stubborn one, aren't you?" he growled through his teeth. "I'll teach you a lesson you won't forget."

She took a solid swing at him, but that was all she would remember before his large fist cracked against her face repeatedly. When she collapsed on the ground, he stomped her limp body over and over again.

The sounds were sickening to Felipe, and the beating woke something up in him, for the first time since he'd been thrown in the van, he wanted to live.

Maybe Platinum was on to something in trying to knock out those taillights, he thought.

She'd already loosened the panel and the rest could be done slowly and meticulously. Felipe leaned out of the van and looked at the attacker. "If you kill her now, it won't just be our heads that roll. Mateo didn't come all the way from Mexico City just to view a dead body," he reasoned.

The man stopped instantly and gave Felipe a hard stare. He knew he was right, the girl wasn't worth it. She'd almost gotten the best of him, but she was still alive. She would look like hell when he arrived with her, but he was determined to deliver his cargo with a pulse. He picked up her limp body and shoved her back inside like a sack of cement.

Felipe pulled her close to him and wiped the blood from her face. "Stupid, stupid girl," he whispered in her ear. "I hope you're right about the taillights, or we're dead for sure."

Platinum didn't hear a word, the first punch had rendered her unconscious.

Chapter Forty-Two

A loud clap of thunder woke Kori from her sleep. Unlike earlier, she found herself clear-headed and fully recalled where she was. Her clothing was damp, but not as wet as she'd feared it would be. It was still raining but had eased up a great deal and was now just a slow drizzle. She was cold, and her mouth was as dry as cotton. The dark, low-lying thunderheads seemed to be passing over, and a glimpse of the moon gave off some silvery light.

She reached under her hoodie and unhooked her bra, slipped her arms out of the sweatshirt and pulled her bra straps down. She pushed her bra out through the pine boughs, until it was saturated with the rainwater, then sucked on it to relieve her parched mouth and throat. She repeated that process several more times, grateful for whatever hydration she could get.

It was still dark, and she was unsure of how long she'd slept. From the looks of it, dawn was just around the corner. The rain had come in so quickly that Kori had been forced to assemble her makeshift shelter in lieu of making progress through the woods.

Surely, he's closer now, she thought. She knew she had to move on and leave the lean-to lodging behind.

She placed the bra in the waistband of her jeans, knowing it would come in handy later. There were likely streams or riverbeds in the woodlands, but she knew better than to drink from them. Rainwater was her only safe option for drinking.

Okay, Kori, you've got this. Remember the things you learned from Kaleb's Cub Scout troop. People are counting on you.

After her quick pep talk, she pushed the pine branches back and made her way out of the shelter. She listened intently but didn't hear anything around her. The canopy of tree leaves and branches proved to be a barrier that kept much of the rain out, which she appreciated. Her mind went back to a thin, wiry man with a handlebar mustache, one who'd spoken to Kaleb's group about the North Star, also known as Polaris. She recalled it was the brightest star and was part of the Little Dipper constellation.

Even among the lingering clouds in the night sky, Kori could see Polaris shining there, flickering brighter than all the rest. She needed to follow it, even if she went in the wrong direction, at least that would keep her from running in circles, and she'd hopefully move farther and farther away from her kidnapper.

Perhaps I'll come upon someone else or a road by sunrise? she hoped.

She couldn't believe her feet had remained dry, a much-needed blessing. She hoped her sneakers would prevent her socks from getting wet. She didn't want to struggle with blisters on top of all her other hardships.

Following the North Star, she made as much progress as she could through the rough terrain. Downed trees, briars, gullies, and large rocks made her commute all the more precarious, as they were slippery from the rain and difficult to climb. The last thing she needed was an injury.

Only when her body demanded it, did she pause to rest. The rain had slowed enough that she could no longer wet her bra to quench her thirst. Her body ached from exerting herself, but she felt a renewed energy that kept her from resting for long periods of time.

Continuing, she found herself in a heavily wooded area that was so thick with trees that she couldn't feel any raindrops at all. Kori was looking up at the dense canopy when she felt something beneath her feet give way. Pain seared through her right calf as she stumbled and fell. She discovered that her foot had gone through a rusted sheet of metal, and as she carefully pulled her leg out of it, the sight of the blood-soaked denim was frightening. She rolled her pant leg up to look at the wound, and as soon as she saw it, she realized it meant trouble. The large gash was deep enough to cause an infection, but her greatest concern at the moment was the profuse bleeding. Her belt could act as a tourniquet, but that'd be a last resort, she was sure her best bet, for the time being, was to apply pressure. She struggled desperately to rip her jeans, but that effort proved futile, even with the large tear that should've aided in the process.

Kori reached to her waistband and pulled out her bra, wrapped it around the large cut, and tied it tightly enough to add pressure and hopefully assist in stopping the bleeding. She realized the injury could be a deal-breaker, and at the very least, it'd slow her progress substantially.

As she sat on the ground, she looked around the area. How did this sheet of metal get out here anyway? she wondered. Kori grimaced as she struggled to stand. Tears flowed from her eyes as the pain radiated up her leg. She prayed aloud that her instincts were leading her in the right direction as she hobbled around the surrounding space. Squinting, she finally spotted what she was hoping and praying for.

Kori bent down, grabbed a long stick, and used it as a crutch to limp over to the gray, mildewed tarp. A laugh escaped her lips as she pulled the cover off to reveal an old, abandoned still. It was definitely out of use, the years of neglect apparent in the layers of flaking rust. The majority of the structure was still there, although it appeared various parts had been pilfered through the years, perhaps to fashion other stills together. The heavily forested area made for a great hiding place to manufacture moonshine.

Kori recalled her father's stories of his grandfather running *white lightning*, as they often referred to it, for an elderly couple in South Georgia. It was the perfect cover as the older pair were well known as upstanding citizens who occupied a pew every time the church doors were opened. Kori's great-grandfather drove from Atlanta to pick up the illegal alcohol and bootlegged it in the big city. He eventually made enough money to buy a car, quite an accomplishment back in the day. The moonshine was never sold anywhere down South, in fear that the couple would be implicated for its production. According to her father, they died with community honors, still believed to be good, church-goin' folks, never having been implicated in their liquor runs.

The presence of the still meant there was a possibility of other supplies or maybe even an underground shelter. After all, the moonshine had to be stored somewhere before it was transported, or at least that was what Kori's father had explained to her. She knew if there was a storage area, it wouldn't be too far from the still, and that gave her some hope for a hiding place out of the weather.

The pain was worsening, and the bra tied around her calf was saturated with blood. She had to get off her feet soon. The still had obviously been deserted for years, so the opening to any underground shelter was likely covered with pine needles and leaves. She used her homemade crutch to test the ground for anything out of the ordinary.

It took at least thirty minutes of painful poking and prodding before her stick hit something solid. Kori dropped to her knees, seething through her teeth as the pain increased. She pushed the wet pine straw aside with her hands and saw the glint of an old Master Lock. She limped back to the still, hoping to find a pipe or something she could smash it with, but everything was so rusty and heavy that it would've done her more harm than good. She did manage to find a large rock and quickly made her way back to the storage bunker. No matter how many times she pounded on the lock, it didn't seem to make a difference, but the wood was old, and the moistness of the leaves and debris had caused it to rot. She began beating on the rotted wood near the hinges, which proved successful, but her hands were bleeding by the time she was able to pull the piece of wood back.

The morning sun began to peek over the horizon, but the sky was quickly darkening again with the threat of more rain. Kori could make out a ladder, but the hole was pitch-black, and she was unsure of what lay beneath her. Still, considering the oncoming rain, she had little choice. "Maybe I'll find a lantern or something down there," she muttered to herself.

She feared that the rungs of the old ladder would also be rotted and give way but was pleased to find that it was still in surprisingly good condition. She eased her way down it, wincing in pain as she descended. It was longer than expected, and it was slow going with her hurt leg, but eventually, her feet touched the dirt floor.

The air in the space was stagnant and smelled earthy, like red clay. Kori bent down to touch her injured leg and realized the bra and surrounding denim was completely soaked, indicating that the bleeding hadn't stopped. She wasn't sure how bad it was but knew she needed to find some source of light to take a look at it before she dozed off again. The last thing she wanted to do was bleed out in the bottom of an old bunker, with nobody any the wiser of where she was. "I will not die down here," she told herself resolutely.

She hesitantly felt around with her fingers, careful not to touch anything too fast. Kori didn't have any idea what was down there, and she didn't need another cut or abrasion. She touched something that felt like an old kerosene lantern, but it would be useless without matches. Her fingers slid across an old metal tin with a flip clasp, and she quickly opened it and felt around to determine what it held.

When she realized it was a first aid kit, full of bandages, she released a heavy sigh and tried to calm down. *Matches. I've got to find matches.* She crawled around the fairly large space until she lightly bumped her head on a set of shelves. There were several more tins, and one was the size of a coffee can, but it felt quite light. She pulled back the plastic lid, and to her delight, found several books of matches inside it.

"Yes!" she squealed.

Kori closed her eyes and offered up a silent prayer as she struck the match across the flint on the side of the box. The flame illuminated a small area, just enough to allow her to see the shelf in front of her.

The supplies were sparse: bottled water and several tins, which she was anxious to open. The match burned out, and she quickly lit another one, before turning to find the kerosene lamp. She burned through three more matches while she struggled to remove the glass globe. When she finally lit the cotton wick, soft light instantly filled the small, dirt room.

She leaned against the shelf and cried until there were no tears left. Then, Kori pulled herself back together, removed the saturated bra from around her calf, and assessed her injury. It wasn't good, and it likely needed several stitches and strong antibiotics, but that wasn't an option. There were eight gallon-size containers of liquid along the wall, so she opened one and smelled it to make sure it was water instead of moonshine. Satisfied that there was nothing alcoholic in the contents, she took a long drink from the jug, and although she wanted more, she was afraid it might make her sick to drink too much at once.

She rummaged through the first aid kit. It contained several useful items, but there really wasn't a lot to choose from. She did find a roll of gauze, which she could use after she cleaned her wound. She slowly poured water over the cut, then wiped it with the inside of her sweatshirt. The pain was excruciating, and she bit her bottom lip to keep from screaming. After she'd cleaned it as best she could, she dabbed on some antibiotic cream from the kit and placed a layer of clean gauze on it. She desperately wanted to see what the other tins held, but she was in too much pain to move.

She needed rest and her leg needed to be elevated. Every move she made seemed to agitate the wound, so Kori decided to roll over on her side, pull a dusty, old tarp over herself, and close her eyes for a much-needed nap.

Chapter Forty-Three

Clara and Iris were back at the office by noon and found Quita at her computer, busily researching something. She was grateful for the break and quickly logged off the Internet.

"I've been dying to know how it went at the cemetery," she said before laughing at the unintentional pun. "Well, maybe not dying."

"We were up with the chickens," Iris said as she plopped down at her desk. "You'd be shocked to see how many nuts are up at that time of morning."

"Well, you'd be shocked by all the people coming and going out of Jasmine's apartment complex all hours of the night. I'm exhausted myself."

"Any suspects?" Clara asked. "We're not very comfortable with you being out at night."

"I always have my cell with me, and I've been taking Rhadrick to work so I can borrow his car. It's all good, and there's no need to worry about me. As for suspects, I don't have anybody in mind yet. Everyone who lives there has lots of friends, and they're always coming and going. I haven't noticed any prowlers or weirdos, though, and everyone seems to have someone with them or at least lives there. It wouldn't surprise me if it was someone who passed her in the parking lot, found her attractive, and then came back later. There's literally no way to figure out who's been there. I mean, just think about it.

"You got three or four young people living in a studio apartment. They each have friends, and those friends have friends. Not only that, but they're constantly making new friends at the local club. It's insane. Anyway, during my stakeouts, I've had a good view of her place, and I haven't seen nothin' out of the ordinary. The maintenance guy started painting her apartment so they can rent it out to somebody else, and Ginger's already removed all of Jasmine's personal belongings. I asked her if she found anything suspicious, like a note from an admirer or something, but she said she's seen nothin' of the sort."

"What about the restaurant where Jasmine worked?" Clara asked. "How's that going?"

"Joey, that cute bartender, has kept his word about letting me sit at the bar and refilling my glass at no charge. When Jasmine's regulars show up, he gives me a heads-up. So far, I haven't seen anything strange. There are a few older couples, an office crowd that meets once a week after work, and a lady in her mid-forties, who always meets her online dates there. Apparently, she enjoys expensive meals on somebody else's dime. Whatever floats your boat, I guess."

"Tell us more about this, Joey," Iris pressed. "He seems awfully helpful. Doesn't that make you uneasy?"

"Not at all. Joey's cool, real respectful to me and the women who work there. Everyone seems to like him except the manager. What a prick! Oops, sorry, Miss Clara."

"Oh, she can handle it," Iris said flippantly. "Tell us about this manager. What don't you like about him?"

"Everything. For one thing, he's arrogant. I'd say he's probably in his thirties, maybe close to forty. He's a decent-looking guy, I guess, but he's not as hot as he thinks he is. He acts like the wealthy folks who come in there to eat, real uppity and snobbish."

"What's his name?" Iris asked.

"Connor something. He's such a suck-up, too. You should see him schmoozing the customers, but then he turns around and treats the employees like crap. Nothing they do is ever good enough."

"Not that I'm taking up for him but managing a restaurant like that one is quite a task," Clara said. "I'm sure his salary is nothing to sneeze at, and with so many movies being filmed in Georgia, Atlanta's seen its fair share of the rich and famous coming through. Word-of-mouth is crucial in any business, restaurants included, so he has to earn brownie points with those customers. So, you get bad vibes from him?"

"No, I get punch-him-in-the-throat vibes," Quita clarified. "I understand what you're saying about the customers, but there's still no need to be nasty to the waiters and waitresses."

"Do you think he could've had something going with Jasmine?"

"No way," Quita said adamantly. "He's far too arrogant to date a lowly waitress, and she was too young to have been interested in him."

"I'm still wondering about the bartender," Iris said. "Keep an eye on him. Maybe Clara and I should go eat dinner there tonight? Just to scope the place out."

"Wouldn't be a bad idea," Quita said. "My days are numbered there, I'm sure. If Connor finds out I haven't been paying for my drinks, he'll kick me out, and poor Joey could lose his job, which he doesn't deserve. Now, tell me about your day."

Iris moaned and bent over to unlace her tennis shoes. "I'll start with some free advice. Never wear new sneakers on your first day of exercising. I'm sure I have a blister the size of Texas under these socks."

"Good grief, Iris, quit complaining!" Clara criticized. "It's really a popular place, Quita, for a cemetery. Several different groups showed up while we were there. They appear to be regulars, just there to get some exercise. No one was lurking in the shadows, scoping out their next victim."

"So, are you going back tomorrow?"

"You know she's gonna make me go back, blisters and all," Iris said.

"As I recall," Clara said. "It was you who suspected someone from the cemetery."

"Did you meet the cemetery worker? What's his name and that weird job of his? Uh…sex-something?" Quita asked.

"He's called a sexton," Iris said. "He was very accommodating, wasn't he, *Clara?*"

"Yes, he was, especially when you turned on your charm. I don't know how to feel about him. We'll have to get to know him a little better, won't we, *Iris?*"

They were interrupted by the phone.

Quita answered it, then placed the caller on hold. "It's for either of you. It's Detective Pitts."

"I'll take it," Clara said as she reached for the phone on her desk. "Good afternoon, Detective." She listened intently as he spoke, taking notes from time to time, which drove Iris crazy. Finally, she bid him goodbye and hung up.

"Well, does he have something new or what?" Iris asked.

"He checked with the young lady at the morgue, but she wasn't the one who contacted Jasmine's mother about her death. Apparently, it was the former foster parents. They called her and provided her with cab fare to attend the funeral. They'd maintained contact with her through the years while they had the girls. They felt it was only right to let her know of her daughter's death. They even gave her a hundred dollars for a hotel room, but they haven't seen her since."

"I'm not surprised," Iris said. "Those junkies are like that."

"Iris, must you be so cruel?"

"I'm not! Haven't you ever seen those intervention shows? They don't give a rat's—"

"Stop right there, Miss Iris," Quita said. "If I gotta watch my mouth around Miss Clara, so do you."

Clara shook her head and continued, "I suppose that shoots down the theory that the mother was involved."

"I don't know if that's a deal-breaker, but I'm thinking she's not our culprit. Then again, I could be wrong."

"What about the foster parents?" Quita asked.

"There's no reason to suspect them," Clara answered. "They loved both girls and wouldn't have anything to gain by killing Jasmine."

"Totally random then?" Quita asked. "If that's the case, we may never solve this."

"I hate to think like that," Iris said sadly. "Let's not give up just yet. I say we keep walking at the cemetery. It can't hurt. We'll have dinner at the restaurant tonight, Quita, to give you a break. Clearly, you've overstayed your welcome, and we need to get you out of there before anyone suspects anything."

"I can pop back in every few days," Quita suggested. "I'm not ready to turn it loose just yet."

"Okay, ladies," Clara said. "Let's all take a break and get back to work later. If we're going to dine out tonight, we'll need it. Also, Iris, it'll give you a chance to soak your feet."

****

Even after a long nap and a hot bath, Clara was still easily stressed while driving. "I hate to admit it, but I think I'm getting too old to drive at night, especially in this traffic. There comes a time when we just have to admit it."

"Nonsense. You're doing a great job, Clara. You used to really make me nervous, but now I'm totally at ease with your driving. Maybe I'm getting used to it or I'm just older now and at peace with meeting Jesus."

"Gee, that makes me feel better."

"I'm looking forward to setting my eyes on this bartender. I've got bad vibes about him, even if Quita doesn't."

"You just think he has the hots for Quita, and that makes you nervous."

"She's young, Clara. Young folks want to believe the best in people. That's probably what got little Jasmine killed."

"You know better than that. Quita's got a great deal of common sense, to say nothing of her street sense. She's a bright girl."

"Yes, she is, and that worries me. Everyone slips up from time to time, especially when a handsome man is offering free drinks."

"Free soda, Iris," Clara corrected. "You might not admit that you care about her, especially since you didn't want to hire her in the first place, but I know you do."

"I was never against it," Iris insisted. "In fact, I've always dreamt of having a daughter of my own."

Clara smiled as her heart warmed. Her friend was always so defensive, but Clara had known her far too long to be fooled by her guarded exterior. "Do you think we should let the valet park it?"

"Have you seen the parking decks at this mall?" Iris asked. "Good Lord, I can't walk at five o'clock in the morning and trek across this parking lot, too. I have Band-Aids on my heels as it is, and I'm wearing flats, not my slippers. Whip this Buick into valet parking."

Clara apprehensively handed her keys to what appeared to be a twelve-year-old with a bad case of acne.

"Take care of her," Iris spouted at him. "She's the best one between us. You wouldn't wanna be responsible for two old ladies being stuck in the nursing home without wheels to escape, would ya?"

"No, Ma'am," he answered nervously.

"You think you're funny, but you're not, Iris."

Iris chuckled. "We're on the downhill slide, Clara. Learn to laugh a little."

By seven o'clock, the steakhouse was doing a booming business. Clara was grateful she'd taken Quita's advice and made a reservation. The hostess was a beautiful woman who Clara estimated to be in her early thirties. She was clearly experienced and well versed in dealing with patrons who didn't bat an eye at dropping a hundred dollars apiece on a steak dinner.

"Good evening, Mrs. Samples." The woman smiled, revealing fluorescent white teeth. "We have your table ready, and we're delighted you've chosen to dine with us tonight. Have you been here before?"

"A couple of times," Iris interjected. "Is Jasmine working tonight? She's quite delightful. We'd prefer her section if it's available."

"I'm sorry, but she's no longer with us," the pretty woman said, without the slightest change in her tone or demeanor.

"Really, she completed her degree at the Art Institute already? My, my, how time flies," Iris added.

"I trust this table is suitable," the hostess said as she placed the leather-bound menus down in front of two chairs. She clearly didn't intend to offer any further conversation about Jasmine.

"This will be fine," Clara said.

"Just one more thing…" Iris said before the hostess walked away. "Would it be possible for the bartender to come over? I'd love a suggestion from him. They're always coming up with new cocktails."

"Certainly, I'll see that Joseph visits your table promptly," she said. "Wendy will be your waitress tonight."

Both women nodded at her, then waited until she was out of sight before speaking to each other.

"She sure clammed up about, Jasmine, huh?" Iris said. "Did you notice that?"

"I didn't expect her to tell us she was murdered. That would've been awkward."

"I suppose you're right. I guess I didn't think about it like that." Iris cleared her throat and nodded her head to the right.

Clara turned around to see what she was indicating, and that movement drew a scolding by Iris.

"Don't turn around," she hissed. "That was so obvious, Clara."

"Why do you do that?"

"What?"

"Draw my attention to something, then expect me not to look," Clara said just as the bartender showed up beside their table.

"Good evening, ladies," he said, bowing and then politely shaking their hands. "I'm Joey, the bartender. I understand you'd like a cocktail suggestion."

"Very nice to make your acquaintance, Joey," Iris said as her demeanor quickly changed to one of refinement. "I'd like to try something new. What would you suggest?"

"One of our most popular drinks is the mojito. Have you ever tried one?"

"No, please, tell me about it."

"It has five ingredients, including a rum base, lime juice, sprigs of mint, sugar, and soda water. It's served on the rocks, and I highly recommend it."

"That sounds delightful," Iris said. "I think I'll take one."

"I'll bring it right over."

"By the way," Iris continued, "We were very disappointed to find out that Jasmine no longer works here. Did she finish her degree?"

Joey looked at them strangely. "Did you know, Jasmine? Forgive me, but I don't recall having seen you, ladies, in here before."

"We've only dined here a couple of times," Iris said. "She was our waitress on both occasions. She's a very nice, unforgettable young lady."

"Yes, she is, and we miss her," he affirmed. "I'll be right back with your mojito, Ma'am."

Just as Joey was turning to leave their table, a man in an expensive suit showed up from out of nowhere. "Good evening, ladies," he said, extending his hand to them, one after the other. "I'm Connor, the manager. Is everything all right over here?" he asked, casting Joey a scolding look as if he was a puppy that'd just soiled the rug.

"Oh, yes," Clara answered. "Joey was just giving Iris a drink suggestion."

"He's one of our best," Connor said, changing his expression and patting Joey on the shoulder. He then nodded in the direction of the bar. Joey quickly took the hint and scurried back to his post. "Your waitress should be here shortly, ladies. If you have any concerns, please let me know."

"We were just mentioning how much we were looking forward to Jasmine Baines serving us. She's such a nice young lady," Clara said. "I'm sure she's missed here, by staff and patrons alike."

"Yes, we were very sorry to hear about Jasmine," Connor commented, almost in a whisper.

"Sorry, about what? Is something wrong?" Iris asked.

"Oh, I, uh…I apologize. I assumed you heard. It was in the paper."

"What was? Please tell us what happened to her," Iris pressed, playing dumb.

"Jasmine was murdered," he said softly to avoid being overheard by the other patrons. "I'm sorry to be the one to tell you."

"Oh!" Iris said, moving her hand to her mouth, as if in shock. "Oh, my goodness. Do they know who killed her?"

"Not that I'm aware of," Connor answered. "Please excuse me, ladies. I need to check on a few things in the kitchen. I certainly hope this won't affect your experience with us tonight. Do have a nice evening." He was gone, just as quickly and suspiciously as he'd arrived at their table.

"That was weird," Iris said. "Joey sure wasn't going to tell us anything. Did you notice how he talked about Jasmine in the present tense, saying she *is* a nice young lady? I don't trust him. At least Connor told us she was dead."

"I have to say I'm surprised he told us, especially since the hostess and bartender both refused to open up about it. Look," Clara said, pointing toward the bar.

"Oh, my," Iris said, shaking her head as she caught a glimpse of Quita, sitting at the end of the bar.

"Doesn't she look beautiful in that black dress?"

"Beautiful?" Iris said. "That's cut way too low in the front. No wonder that creep is filling her glass for free."

"It's not too low," Clara said. "She looks lovely."

"I don't trust that, Joey. I'm tempted to go get Quita and bring her over here with us. At least the two of *us* won't be looking down her top."

"You'll do nothing of the sort," Clara said sternly. "Let's just enjoy our meal and head home."

A short time later, Iris was in the middle of her wood-grilled salmon filet, while Clara enjoyed her lamb chop.

Iris cleared her throat again, causing Clara to turn her head.

"Would you stop it?" Iris said. "For a private investigator, you're mighty obvious!"

"Who are we looking at...or not supposed to look at?" Clara asked.

"That hunk who just walked in. I've seen him somewhere before."

Clara turned around in her chair to look toward the door.

"Seriously?" Iris asked sarcastically.

"How else am I supposed to see, Iris?" Clara asked. She studied the handsome gentleman and was overcome with déjà vu of her own. "I know I've seen him, but I'm not sure where."

"That's a sharp suit he's wearing. Looks like money. Quita seems to be checking him out, too. Turn around and keep eating, Clara. I can see him from here."

"Is he alone?" Clara asked as she turned her attention back to the lamb chop.

"He's having a friendly conversation with the hostess, but he appears to be solo. Hey, Connor is walking over to shake his hand. He seems to be making quite the fuss over him. Now the hostess is seating him at a small table. She only has one menu in her hand, so he must be dining alone."

"Interesting," Clara said, "Atlanta is full of handsome, young men, but I do wonder why he looks so familiar."

Wendy, their waitress, returned to ask if they wanted to look at the dessert menu, both women declined, too full for another bite. She was about Jasmine's age and very cute, although not quite as beautiful. She was an excellent waitress, professional and accommodating.

Clara used her credit card to pay the bill and left Wendy a generous tip. She wanted to question her about her former coworker but decided they'd already interrogated enough people for the evening.

Both women looked over at the handsome, well-dressed stranger once more as they made their way to the front to leave, but neither could place him.

Clara smiled pleasantly at the hostess, then groaned quietly when she saw Iris making a beeline for the bar. She followed behind her, with no idea of what her friend had up her sleeve.

Iris stepped up to the bar near Quita but didn't make eye contact or acknowledge her. She knocked on the bar with a balled fist to get Joey's attention.

Clara held her breath and willed herself not to intervene.

Joey passed a mixed drink to a customer, then made his way over to Iris.

"Hello, young man. I just didn't want to leave without telling you how much I enjoyed that mojito you recommended."

"I'm glad, the mint really makes it."

"Indeed," Iris agreed before turning to Quita. "That's a lovely dress, dear," she said. "It's just a little low, don't you think? Young ladies have to be careful these days, especially around handsome bartenders like this one," she said as she playfully pointed at Joey. "Have a good evening," she finished, then turned her head and sashayed out of the steakhouse.

Chapter Forty-Four

The large Hispanic man, who'd never given his name, got back in the driver seat, wiped Platinum's blood off his hands with an old rag, cranked the van, and pulled back on the roadway.

Felipe assessed Platinum's injuries, which were pretty severe. She was clearly no match for the hefty brute who'd beaten her so mercilessly. Her eyes had already swollen shut, and with the exception of the few moans that escaped when Felipe touched her wounds, she didn't respond at all.

Using his shirttail, he wiped the blood off her face. She needed stitches over one eye, but Felipe was more concerned about her abdominal area, where her attacker had stomped repeatedly. Her middle was swollen and bruised, Felipe was certain that she was suffering from internal bleeding. He was no medical professional, but he knew if she didn't get to one soon, she wasn't going to make it. He brushed her blood-soaked hair away from her face and laid her head on a tarp. Every touch caused her great pain, and there was nothing he could do but try to make her comfortable.

He leaned his back against the side of the van and listened as intently as he could. The driver was turning right, and it sounded as if he was merging onto the interstate. Felipe realized he had to work fast to break through the taillight which might prove to be their only chance at escape. For all he knew, they'd get off the highway and travel on a deserted road where no other vehicles would spot the damaged lights.

He was grateful for the loud noise of the passing eighteen-wheelers, as well as the rickety shakes and rattles of the van itself. It camouflaged the sounds of his escape attempt. Keeping his eyes on the driver, he felt around until he found a long-handled screwdriver. He began punching it through the bulb and reflector of the taillight behind the driver. Unless he got suspicious and looked in his rearview mirror, Felipe was out of sight.

Confident he wasn't making too much noise, Felipe smiled when the tool finally pushed through. He continued to break out a larger hole, then took a brief break to search for other items to throw out the small opening, hoping it would draw enough attention from other motorists to cause concern.

Felipe pretended to be kneeling over Platinum's body to console her and tend to her injuries, but all the while, he was busying his hands with discreetly gathering any small tools that could be pushed out of the opening he'd created. He quickly collected several paintbrushes, a socket wrench, and four paint sample strips.

He moved back toward the taillight and leaned against it with his back, placing his hands behind him so he could push the items through one at a time. He waited for a horn to blow or for any kind of acknowledgment that the items had been seen, but he heard nothing of the sort. For all intents and purposes, Felipe seemed dead to the world, and before long, he was sure he would be, *literally*.

Not ready to give up, he waited several minutes before moving back toward Platinum again, hoping to gather more things to toss out. She groaned and moved her left hand as if reaching for him. He took it in his own and leaned down next to her. Her eyes were swollen shut, preventing her from seeing him, and he wasn't sure if she could hear him, but he spoke to her gently and encouraged her to fight. It was then that he heard a sound he had dreaded in the past but was now music to his ears. The police siren was so loud it sounded as if the cruiser was right on their bumper.

"Son-of-a-bitch!" the driver yelled as he slammed his fists on the steering wheel. "I don't believe it!"

Felipe felt such a surge of relief that he was almost nauseous. Completely expecting the driver to pull over, he was surprised, when instead, he accelerated and pushed the van to its top speed. The driver was pounding on the horn with his fist while maneuvering in and out of traffic with his other hand.

The sounds of other blowing horns and screeching tires were accompanied by the persistent noises of several police sirens. They were now involved in a full-fledged car chase one Felipe was sure would end quickly.

What the driver did next shouldn't have come as a surprise to Felipe, but it did, leaving him no choice but to brace himself for the worst. He should have known better, anyone who knew Mateo was aware he wouldn't have expected anything less from one of his men.

The van continued to accelerate, then surged through the traffic and veered steadily to the right. The last thing Felipe heard was the huge Mexican reciting a prayer in Spanish as the van left the roadway and wrapped around a large pine tree.

Chapter Forty-Five

This time, Iris donned her oldest pair of Reeboks, the ones she normally wore to work in her flower garden. She was quickly tiring of their mornings at the cemetery. It was getting much too cold, and she had to miss many of her favorite television shows to go to bed early. "This is getting old fast, Clara," Iris said. "I enjoy an occasional early morning, but this is ridiculous."

"It's only our third day, Iris, be patient."

"Are you sure it's just been three days? Feels more like a month."

"Yes, I'm sure," Clara confirmed.

They were sitting on one of the benches in the middle of the cemetery, nodding to the walkers as they passed. Some had shown up all three days, others once or twice, but they took stock of every face that passed them.

"Well, looky there," Iris said as she sat up straight and craned her neck. "There's that hunk from the restaurant, or at least I think that's him. He's not wearing the expensive suit, but if that's not him, they could be twins."

Clara looked at the man who was walking briskly in their direction. "I believe you're right, Iris, but let's wait until he gets a little closer. I don't think he saw us the other night, but just in case, don't make eye contact. Let's keep talking, so he doesn't realize we're giving him the once-over."

As he walked closer, the women immersed themselves in a deep conversation about the tombstone directly across the path. He didn't acknowledge them as he passed, appearing to be engrossed in whatever he was listening to on his headset.

"Maybe we've seen him in a movie," Iris said. "His looks are distinctive."

"What are the odds that we'd run into him at both places?"

"I don't know. Coincidences happen, I suppose," Iris said, looking down at her watch. "Let's call it a day. Quita said she wants to talk to us this morning about a couple of new cases."

"You're right," Clara said as she stood to leave. "I hate to admit it, but I'm ready for the weekend. These early mornings are wearing me out, too."

As they neared the Memorial Drive entrance, Stuart Mason drove up on his golf cart. He immediately smiled and waved at them.

Iris referred back to her watch again. "Mister Mason, it's seven-thirty," she said. "I didn't expect you to open up this early."

"I change it up from time to time, but I've got to admit, I have my reasons for being here. Truthfully, I was hopin' to run into the two of you. I didn't figure you'd come back after your early walk to see me." He looked away briefly as a flush of pink crossed his cheeks. "Could I interest you in a cup of coffee?"

Clara thought of speaking up and giving him an excuse, but they needed to find out more about him, and it seemed the ideal opportunity. After all, he'd approached them and not the other way around, that meant he wouldn't be suspicious of any of their questions.

"I'd love a hot cup if you don't mind a third wheel," Clara said.

"Great. What about you, Ms. Iris?" he asked.

"Are you kidding? I'd love it, I'm just about frozen to death."

"Well, hop on," he said, motioning to the golf cart. "I've got a fresh pot brewing in the bell tower."

As they rode through the cemetery, Stuart pointed out areas that were soon to be revitalized, paths that would soon have new stones placed, and walkways that had seen better days and would be dug up to have their bricks replaced.

He slowed to a stop at the whitewashed, two-story, brick building. "This serves as our visitor's center and my office. It also houses a small gift shop. It's not opened to the public until ten a.m.," he said as he pulled the keys from a retractable wire on his waistband and unlocked the front door.

"The coffee smells delicious, Mister Mason," Iris complimented, inhaling the enticing aroma deeply. "It's exactly what I need, I tell ya. It's getting too cold to walk outside. I may have to put it off a while and take it back up in the spring."

"Stuart," he said.

"Pardon me?" Iris asked.

"Stuart, if ya don't mind, I'd prefer first names. I've never been very formal."

"Neither have I, Stuart," Iris said. "This is a quaint little place."

"Yeah, I used to live on the floor above, but it got too outdated. I miss it." He fumbled through a metal cabinet until he found disposable cups, cream, and sugar. He poured three cups of coffee and offered them a seat across from his desk. "This is my favorite part of the day," he said warmly. "It's so peaceful here. The walkers are usually gone by the time I arrive, and the dew is still on the ground. I make my rounds before the other staff arrives, then plot out my day."

"Sounds like a stress-free job," Iris said. "I loved my job as a hairdresser, too. I even had my own shop. After my husband, Fred, died, my heart just wasn't in it—or in anything else, for that matter—so I've been retired for several years now. Clara, here, just recently retired. Her work kept her busy after she lost her Harold. I guess that sorta thing hits everybody differently."

"I never married," Stuart said. "I can't even imagine what it's like. Living in the bell tower kept me on the premises most of the time, and I've never been one for socializing. I'm kind of a loner. I like peace and quiet."

"You seem happy," Clara said. "That's what's important. How long have you worked here? Didn't you say over forty years?"

"Yep, forty-one as of this December," he answered proudly. "I've always enjoyed my job, but lookin' back on it, I do wish I'd made room in my life for a family. It gets lonely from time to time. I dread the day they make me retire. I expect that day to come sooner rather than later."

"Oh, I'm sure they wouldn't put a prize bull like you out to pasture," Iris said. "It's hard to find good help these days."

Stuart pondered her comment, leaning back in his chair. "I'm more of a supervisor than a worker nowadays. I let the youngins do all the back-breaking work."

"Don't blame you one bit," Clara said before blowing on her coffee and taking a sip. "Is this the cemetery I read about in the paper, where a murdered girl was found?" she asked nonchalantly.

Both Iris and Clara noticed the blood drain from his face, and instantly, his swollen, curled fingers reached for his front shirt pocket and fumbled around for a cigarette. "I know it's not socially acceptable anymore," he began. "But do you ladies mind if I have a smoke?"

"Not at all," Iris said. "Goodness, Clara, why would you bring up such a dreadful subject?"

"Please forgive me, Stuart," Clara said. "I just recalled reading the article and wasn't sure if it was here at Oakland. I didn't mean to be insensitive."

"I'm sure you didn't," Stuart said after a brief pause. He took a long drag from the cigarette and inhaled deeply. "It was here, and I'm actually

199

the one who found her. I never woulda dreamed something so horrible could ever happen here. It was the worst day of my life."

"I'm terribly sorry and apologize for bringing it up."

"No, it's okay. I know you didn't mean to upset me. This is a graveyard, but they're usually...well, you know...underground. A dead body was the last thing I expected to find lying on the ground that morning, 'specially the way she was." He inhaled again and stared at the ceiling while he exhaled slowly. "I saw her picture at the funeral. She was a beautiful young girl, but I didn't actually see her that day. I couldn't bear to look too close and she was wrapped in a blanket when I came across her. My first thought wasn't that I'd found a person, but then I saw her foot hanging out, and realized it was a young woman. This world is changing. Who'd do such a thing to a young person, a woman, no less?"

"I was wondering that myself, and I also wondered why they left her here," Clara pressed. "It's so odd. Undoubtedly, they wanted her to be found."

"There are a lot of walkers in the mornings, but you'd be surprised at how many visitors we have here daily. Whoever put her there knew somebody would find her."

"When could they have brought her?" Clara asked. "In the middle of the night?"

Stuart shrugged and shook his head. "It had to be before I got here. I do my rounds every night before I leave. So, I woulda noticed if she was here then."

"I don't see how one of the walkers didn't spot her," Iris said. "They traipse all over every inch of this place."

"The road leading back to where she was found was under construction at the time. It was still drivable, but we were doing some repair work. I came in early several days and instructed them not to walk in those areas. It woulda been a liability for us, and since the walkers are technically supposed to be locked out at that hour, they were okay with following my instructions."

"Do you suppose it could've been one of your walkers?" Clara asked.

"Oh no," Stuart insisted, with great conviction in his voice. "I may not know their names, but I know their faces, and I also know they're good folks."

"For heaven's sake," Iris said. "This makes for terrible conversation, you two. Can we change the subject?"

"Certainly," Stuart said. "My apologies to you, Ms. Iris."

"It's okay," she answered. "I don't even read the paper anymore. It's all bad news." She looked at her watch again. "I hate to leave so soon, but I have a hair appointment this morning. Did you forget about that, Clara?"

"I sure did," Clara said, glancing at the watch on her own arm. "We don't want to upset our beautician. She won't schedule us for a month if we miss an appointment."

"I've certainly enjoyed it, ladies. Can we do this again sometime? I always look forward to company."

"How about the same time, same place, next Monday?" Iris suggested. "I think I'm going to take the rest of the week off and let my blister heal."

"It's a date," Stuart said, then stood to walk them out.

Chapter Forty-Six

Clara and Iris were having breakfast at a diner near their office when Iris's phone began to ring. She dug through her jumbled purse frantically but couldn't find it before it stopped ringing. "What a nuisance these portable phones are!" she exclaimed. "What can possibly be so important that it can't wait until I get home?"

"Have you forgotten that we have a business to run, Iris?" Clara asked.

"Quita handles all our calls at the office, and none of our clients have my cell number. It can't be an emergency."

"Well, who does have your number?"

"My niece in Florida and she's fine. My doctor's got it, and clearly, I'm fine. My pharmacy has it, but I already picked up my prescriptions for the month. It wouldn't be my dry cleaner because I haven't taken anything there for years. You don't have your phone to your ear, right now, and the only other one is Quit...oh."

"Gee, Iris, for someone so worried about investigating this murder. You sure aren't available for our office manager when she needs you."

"I know. Let's get out of here, and I'll call her back."

Iris picked up the tab for breakfast and walked with Clara to the car, mumbling about the burden of taking calls at all hours.

As soon as Clara cranked the engine, the buzzing from Iris's purse began again. Pulling it out, Iris studied the glowing phone. "How in the hell do you answer this contraption?" she snapped. "I can never remember which button to push."

Clara pointed to the name on the front. "It is Quita, I knew it," she said before connecting the call and placing it on speaker. "Go ahead, Iris."

"Hello?" Iris answered.

"What in the world is going on?" Quita demanded. "I've been trying to reach you for hours!"

"I just heard the phone five minutes ago and couldn't find it in my purse. I'm answering it now, aren't I?" Iris said defensively.

"You didn't notice the five missed calls on your phone? Where have you been?"

"The same place Clara drags me to every morning, the cemetery."

"You make it sound like it's been months. It's only the third day," Quita said sarcastically.

"So, I've heard. Anyway, what's the problem?"

"For starters, you're not answering your phone, which kinda defeats the purpose of a mobile phone. You could be in trouble, and I'd never know it. Didn't you have the phone with you at the cemetery?"

"Yes, as a matter of fact, I did," Iris was quick to answer. "However, it was locked in the trunk of Clara's car because she insists someone will steal it."

"Stop it, both of you," Clara interjected. "We put our purses in the trunk because we're supposed to be exercising, and no one carries a purse when they work out. They're out of sight in the trunk, less likely to be stolen. Now, is everything okay, Quita? Why did you call?"

"Other than me being worried out of my mind that someone has killed you both?" she asked. "Honestly, it took ten years off my life."

"We had coffee with the sexton," Iris added.

"Great. You might've had a coffee date with a murderer, and you didn't have your phone on you!"

"He's not a murderer," Iris said. "He's just a lonesome man."

"Enough," Clara interrupted. "We're only ten minutes away from the office, Quita. Are you there?"

"Yes. We had a meeting scheduled, remember? Our client list is building up, and they're gonna take their business elsewhere if we don't get to work on their cases."

"See you in ten minutes," Clara affirmed, then disconnected the call.

"Well, look who's getting too big for her britches," Iris said.

"I think it's nice that she worries about us."

"There's no need for it," Iris retorted. "We're grown women, and we were taking care of ourselves before she was even born. Quita's the one runnin' around at night, showing her cleavage."

"Let it go, Iris."

Quita was sitting at her desk pouting when Clara and Iris got there.

"I'm sorry, dear," Clara said sincerely. "Honestly, cell phones are new to us. We'll catch on soon."

The apology was appreciated and seemed to lighten Quita's spirits. "We're swamped," she said. "We can't continue to spend so much time on the Baines case. It's interfering with the growth and reputation of the business. I know it's important to you both, but we aren't getting any answers."

Clara and Iris both pulled a chair up to Quita's desk.

"I hate to let Ginger down," Iris said.

"I know how you feel," Clara said. "But let's think about it. We've got no suspects to speak of, and we aren't detectives. What makes us think we can solve a murder, anyway?"

The three of them sat silently, each pondering what else they could have done. Suddenly, their thoughts were disturbed by the ringing of the phone.

Quita answered it, then politely said, "Hold, please," and handed the receiver to Clara. "It's Detective Pitts, right on cue."

"Hello, Detective," she said, then paused to listen. "Okay, I understand. We'll be right over. We have our assistant with us. I hope that isn't a problem." After another pause, she finished, "Very well then. We're leaving now."

"What was that all about?" Iris asked.

"I'm not sure," Clara said. "He wants to talk to us in person. He asked that we come to his apartment."

"Maybe he's found out something," Quita said.

"Well, he has no problem with you joining us," Clara said. "Can you drive? I'm so tired of traffic."

"I'd be glad to," Quita said.

A few minutes later, Clara knocked on the apartment door, then stuck her head in and called for Pitts.

"In here!" he called from his usual place on the couch.

"How are you?" Clara asked as they walked in.

"Better…at least health-wise," he said. "But we need to talk."

"What's going on? Do you have something on the murder?" Quita asked.

"Forgive me," Clara said. "This is our office manager, JaQuita. She's been doing a lot of work on this case."

"Nice to meet ya," Pitts said. "Sorry to drag you, ladies, over here again, but I can't drive, and my girl's at work."

"Yes, Jessalyn. I remember," Clara said with a soft smile.

"Yeah, well, I'm not to supposed to be working any cases or even talking to you all, per my boss, Lieutenant Costa. You've met her. Anyway, she wants me to rest and get well, which I understand, but police work is in my blood. I just can't let it go."

Quita was growing impatient. "Do you have a lead, Detective?"

"Not really. I do have something else, though. Please have a seat."

They sat down quickly, without taking their eyes off him, each anxious to hear his news.

"Okay," Quita said. "If you don't have a lead, what've you got?"

"Another dead girl," he said slowly.

"What!" Iris asked in shock.

"They just found another young girl, wrapped in a blanket and dumped at Westview Cemetery."

"Oh, my God," Iris exclaimed. "It has to be connected, with the same modem operandus. It must be a serial killer!"

"That's modus operandi, Ma'am," the detective corrected.

"Whatever."

He continued, "The media isn't aware of the girls being wrapped up. We insisted they not share that detail. The news generally only hears a portion of the story. Otherwise, it can compromise our case or spark copycat killers."

"Do you have an I.D. on her?" Quita asked. "Is she connected to, Jasmine Baines?"

"No identification yet, but there have been two missing person's reports from the metro area. Both girls about her age. As you might imagine, the department has two very frantic families on their hands."

"If Lieutenant Costa doesn't want you on the case. How'd you find out about it?" Clara asked.

"Travis Upshaw. You met him."

"Yes, and he was very helpful," Iris said.

"Well, he was called to the scene and is performing the autopsy as we speak. If you ladies can give me a ride, he promised to speak with us when he's done. We'll just have to sneak in the back."

"We don't have a problem with that," Iris said. "Any idea what the connection between the cemeteries could be? Is dumping them there symbolic in some way?"

"I'm not sure," Pitts answered. "Upshaw also offered to meet us at the cemetery later this afternoon, after the CSI crew leaves. He'll show us where they found her body."

"Clara and Iris said you thought Jasmine's murder was random," Quita chimed in. "If that's true, Atlanta may have a big problem on their hands. My grandma was always so protective of me and my sister when we were little. She said something about the Missing and Murdered Children's Case, which I don't remember."

"Yeah, you weren't even born yet. It was before my time, too, but I've heard a lot about it through the years. Those murders took place from the summer of 1979 to the spring of 1981."

"I remember that like it was yesterday," Clara said. "It paralyzed the city and made national news. Is Wayne Williams still alive?"

"Yes," Pitts answered. "He's filed several appeals through the years, even had the mitochondrial DNA of his dog's fur tested. It was found on a couple of the victims. As you know, it didn't exonerate him."

"So, they got the guy who did it?" Quita asked, becoming more interested now.

"Yes, Quita," Iris said. "However, there's been much controversy over the years as to whether or not he was actually guilty."

"Not that, so much," Pitts interjected. "There was certainly the evidence to prove he committed some of the murders, but there's doubt that he committed all of them," he clarified.

"How many children were killed?" Quita asked.

"The murders occurred over a two-year period," Pitts continued. "Even though the press often refers to them as the Atlanta Child Murders, some of the victims were young adults. To answer your question, twenty-eight African Americans were killed. It's certainly possible that he didn't commit all those murders, but there was a common thread."

"What?"

"Most of the victims were found in a small vicinity of the city."

"How'd they die?" she asked, concern growing on her face.

"As I recall—and you can correct me if I'm wrong, Clara—most of them died of asphyxiation. They were strangled. A few of the causes were undetermined, and a couple died from blunt-force trauma to the head. One suffered a gunshot wound."

"What if we have a copycat now?" Quita asked.

"These girls were young," Pitts agreed. "However, it's highly unlikely to be a copycat of the Williams' case. It was so long ago, and these victims were Caucasian. I'm no profiler, but almost all serial killers kill within their own race. We can't really put it in that category," Pitts said. "Maybe we can discover a common thread, a mutual male friend who felt disrespected by both women. It's best to wait until we hear from Travis with the details."

"Better get your boots, ladies," Iris said.

"What for, Iris?" Clara asked, looking at her strangely.

"Because this is getting pretty deep!"

Pitts' cell phone rang, and he picked it up off the end table. "Speak of the devil," he said. "What's up, Upshaw? Got anything yet?" Pitts listened intently, then said, "We'll be right over. I'll be coming in the back, as you know." He ended the call and looked over at his three visitors. "Let's roll, ladies," Pitts said. "Upshaw's ready for us."

Quita drove, and Pitts rode up front to give her directions to the loading dock around the back.

"Have you met, Sugar?" Pitts asked, turning to Clara.

"We sure did," Iris said. "What a delightful man."

"Yeah, they broke the mold with ol' Sugar. Could one of you get him to come help me? Getting down those stairs at my apartment took it out of me."

"I'll get him," Iris said, happy to see Sugar again.

A couple of minutes later, Iris came out the back door, with Sugar right beside her. A broad smile formed on his lips when he saw Detective Pitts.

Sugar opened the car door and leaned down. "Good to see ya, Pitts," he said. "How're you doin', man?"

"I've been better," Pitts answered. "We're trying to sneak in to meet with, Upshaw. Can you help me out?"

"Sure, no problem. I see you're hanging out with good company these days."

"Ah, they'll do," Pitts said with a grin. "They certainly keep me entertained."

"I know that!" Sugar agreed. He glanced over at Quita. "I'm sorry, we haven't met. Name's Stanley Peters."

"Otherwise known as Sugar," Pitts explained. "Sugar, this is Quita, the manager of this wild group."

"It's a pleasure," Sugar said as he pulled Pitts from the car and all but carried him to the dock.

Travis Upshaw was waiting for them in the back. He greeted Clara and Iris, introduced himself to Quita, and gave Pitts a gentle bear hug. "Let's go on back to my office. I instructed Jessalyn to buzz my office if anyone comes in. Don't want to get you busted by the PD, Pitts. I still haven't determined whether or not it's a good idea to let you get involved in this."

Pitts offered a snort for a reply.

"Want me to put you on one of the autopsy tables and roll you around there?" Sugar asked.

"Hell no!" Pitts said. "You're doing a fine job. Just be a little easier on my right side."

"Hey, beggars can't be choosers," Sugar said.

Some effort toward organization had been put forth in Upshaw's office since Clara and Iris's last visit, and he had ample seating for all of them.

"Well, what've you got, Travis?" Pitts asked. "The suspense is killing me."

"Sorry it took me so long to get back with you, but it hasn't been a good day. We've had two sets of parents here, both praying it isn't their daughter. Unfortunately, one family's prayers weren't answered. Our victim is twenty-one-year-old, Nina Culver, an only child from a well-to-do family."

"A college student?" Pitts asked.

"She attended college for one year out of state but got into some minor trouble, some underage drinking, and marijuana use. Her folks made her come back home to pull her out of the party environment, but she quickly turned to Heroin and OxyContin. Her mom and dad did all they could to help her get clean, sparing no expense. Apparently, the last rehab worked wonders."

"Did she know, Jasmine Baines?" Pitts asked.

"Detective Scoggins is looking into that, but I seriously doubt it. They were from opposite sides of the tracks. Nina was older and had everything handed to her on a silver platter, whereas Jasmine had to work hard and was driven. From what I understand, Natalie really had no plans for her future other than hooking back up with her friends, who had access to drugs."

"Did you say, Scoggins? They're sure scraping the bottom of the barrel with this investigation. Doesn't Costa realize we might have a serial killer on our hands?"

"Costa's having a hard time, right now. She's short two detectives. Just count your blessings I called you. They'll have my ass in a sling if anyone finds out."

"I appreciate it," Pitts said sincerely. "Do you have a cause of death?"

"Yep, manual strangulation just like the Baines murder. She was dead for several days before she was dumped but thank God for the cooler temps because decomp' was minimal. I did find something interesting, though, several blossoms from a mountain laurel shrub. I'm no botanist, but I could swear that's what they are."

"Doesn't that plant bloom from mid-spring to early summer?" Clara asked.

"Yes, Ma'am, but these are old blossoms, long since fallen off the bush. They only survived because they were sheltered by damp pine needles. They're pretty damaged, but they've got that distinctive coral-red color to them, my mother's favorite color. I also found a couple of green, oval leaves. Do you know much about mountain laurel?"

"A little," Clara said. "It's also one of my favorites, but I've never had much success growing it. It does best in cooler, mountainous regions."

"Exactly," Travis agreed. "Mom always enjoyed them when we went to North Georgia on the weekends. They usually thrive in areas with a cooler winter, which forces their dormancy until early spring. They tend to flourish when temps dip to at least fifteen degrees which rarely happens this far south."

"You're right. They're naturally found on rocky slopes. I've seen them grow over ten feet tall in the mountains. They cover large areas in the forest and prefer some shade."

"So, what you're both saying is that these blooms came from somewhere other than the metro Atlanta area?" Pitts asked.

"That's my theory," Upshaw stated. "I'm sure there are exceptions, but I'm thinking she was killed somewhere in North Georgia. I can't imagine our killer coming from an area much farther than that. It'd be too risky. Plus, Nina's body was in good condition, which would make sense if she was up in the mountains, where it's much cooler."

"But how would he get the girls to go with him that far from Atlanta?"

"So, we're assuming it's a male?" Iris asked.

"It makes the most sense," Travis said. "Like I said before, manual strangulation doesn't necessarily take that much pressure, but it does require overpowering someone. In my opinion, most females couldn't pull it off. It's also extremely uncommon for a female to kill someone in that manner."

"It has to be somebody the girls trusted," Quita said. "I can't imagine them getting in a car with anyone that weirded them out. Do you think they knew the guy?"

"It's possible, maybe even probable," Pitts said. "But we've found no link between the girls. If we could find one, that'd be huge."

"Maybe it's a cop," Quita suggested. "It wouldn't be the first time."

"I'm sure the Culver girl has a rap sheet," Upshaw said. "Her parents' money could've kept her out of jail time, but it wouldn't expunge any arrests from her record. I doubt Jasmine has one, but it's certainly worth looking into, Pitts."

"I agree, I'll get someone on it immediately. But I'm damn sure not gonna talk to Scoggins about it. He'd go straight to Costa. He'd love to see me out of the loop and out of a job, that jealous son-of-a-bitch."

"Do you still want to see where the body was found?"

"Absolutely," Pitts answered. "When can you meet us out there?"

"How about four o'clock this afternoon. I'm sure they'll be scouring the scene for at least another hour. That'll give me some time to take care of all this paperwork."

"Yeah, and me some time to rest," Pitts answered.

As if to mock his remark, his cell phone rang.

"Shhh," he said as he put his finger to his lips. "It's Costa." He then returned to his phone and answered casually, "Pitts here." The two exchanged pleasantries, then Pitts listened intently to what she was telling him. His face went pale, followed by hot pink. "Really? I'll be damned," he said before going quiet again. "Who's with her?" After another pause, he yelled, "You don't know that!" He blushed again, this time from an obvious reprimand. "Sorry, Lieutenant. You just don't know what she's capable of. I swear, she's the devil." His breathing was heavy, and perspiration was beading on his forehead.

Travis motioned for Pitts to calm down, but he threw up his middle finger.

"Yes, I'm at home," Pitts lied, "And no, I won't come up there. Just promise me somebody's with Nettles." Pitts disconnected the call and asked for a bottle of water from the small fridge in Upshaw's office. He took two lengthy sips before saying anything else.

"What was that all about?" Upshaw asked.

"They've got Platinum, aka Monica Heard."

"Who?" Iris asked.

"The crazy woman who shot Nettles and me, and the one who had her boyfriend shot. Apparently, she was in with the Mexican drug cartel."

"The cartel?" Iris asked excitedly. "You were shot by the cartel?"

"Basically," Pitts said as he took another slug of water. "It's not as big-time as it sounds. They roll into town and take over low-income areas, where they can pay off small-time dealers in exchange for using their houses as bases for their illicit dealings. I'm guessing Platinum jumped at the chance for some fast money, but the dude who knocked her up didn't want any part of it, so she had him taken out. That was followed by the shooting of Nettles and me because she knew we didn't buy her story. What Platinum wasn't counting on was that the cartel means business, unlike her little dime-bag-dealing boyfriend."

"How'd they find her?" Upshaw asked.

"Apparently, the cartel picked her and her Hispanic boyfriend up somewhere. State Patrol got behind them, with Cobb County PD backup. The driver was keenly aware of what the cartel would do to him if he was captured. So, he pulled a kamikaze move and wrapped his vehicle around a tree. He was dead at the scene, but Platinum and the Hispanic guy she runs with are at Grady."

"What's their condition?"

"Platinum took a near-fatal beating before the wreck even happened and sustained additional injuries after the crash. She's hanging on by a thread. The guy's in the same boat. I'm banking on him being the shooter."

"How do you feel, Pitts? This is…a lot to deal with," Travis pressed.

"Mixed feelings," Pitts mumbled as he accepted another bottle of water. "I'd like nothing more than to see them both dead and rotting in hell, but I also wanna see them face justice."

The room remained silent for several seconds, giving Pitts time to let it all sink in.

When he finished the second bottle of water, he pushed himself up. "I need some rest," he finally said. "Can you call, Sugar? I need his help."

Chapter Forty-Seven

It had been days since she'd crawled down into the bunker, but Kori was unsure of how many had actually passed. Her fever had spiked, and in between sleep, mixed with vivid, frightening dreams, she'd tried to make sense of her situation. The deep wound to her calf was infected, but she'd expected it. The laceration was severe, and the metal that had snagged her flesh was rusty. The antibiotic cream was helpful for the scratches and cuts she'd received from tree limbs and briars, but it wasn't strong enough to do anything for her most daunting wound.

She washed the gash thoroughly several times a day, but it was still dark red and swollen, so badly that she was unable to stand. She could, however, slide across the small area to get water and light the kerosene lanterns.

Going through the many tins had helped to take her mind off the situation, and she'd rationed them to two at a time, between naps. So far, she'd found canned meat and dried fruit, which had sustained her, along with peppermint and Juicy Fruit gum. What she enjoyed most were the personal letters from a woman to her husband, undoubtedly the owner of the still. She assumed the woman had written to him, so he'd have a piece of home while he was busy making moonshine, and she found the whole thing quite romantic.

According to Esther's letters to her husband, Hilliard his summers were spent in the mountains, where he produced large batches of moonshine for sale throughout the year. It was the safest time when the large pines and oaks offered safe cover from the authorities. They'd hoped to build a cabin on the land when he retired, but in the meantime, it was used to subsidize their income. Each June, Hilliard took his three weeks of vacation from his railroad job and spent it there. That left Esther at home to tend to their animals alone, from the heartbroken words in the letters, it was clear she'd missed him terribly.

From the looks of the supplies Kori had found, it hadn't been more than a couple of years since Hilliard had last been in the bunker. The still was clearly out of use, rusted, and partially dismantled. Kori wondered if

Hilliard or his wife had died before they were ever able to build their cabin in the woods.

She folded the last of the letters and put them back in their appropriate envelopes. Having nothing else to take her mind off her predicament, she was forced to deal with it. Her kidnapper hadn't found her yet, but that didn't necessarily mean he wasn't looking. She knew if she stayed where she was, one of two things were bound to happen, and neither outcome was pleasant. Either she'd die from the infection, or he'd find her. He'd never leave her undiscovered for fear she might escape and tell the authorities.

Kori had to make a move, but she wasn't even able to stand, much less ascend the ladder. Even if she did make it out of the bunker, she could never make it out of the woods. *Maybe he went back to work in Atlanta?* she thought. *If so, I could go back to his cabin.* She tried to remain positive, but tears stung her eyes as she realized just how desperate she was. *Who am I fooling? I have no idea where I am. Do I sit down here and wait for him to find me, or do I drag myself through the woods?*

Chapter Forty-Eight

Pitts was worn out when the three women returned to his apartment to take him to the cemetery. Although he'd been working hard to move around more, the trip to the ME's office and the news of Platinum's capture had taken its toll on him.

"Maybe you should sit this one out," Iris suggested. "You don't look so good."

"I'll be fine, I need to go to the scene. Who knows what it'll tell us?"

"You're exhausted and clearly in pain," Clara scorned. "This could set back your recovery."

"I'll rest tonight," he insisted. "Quita, go ahead and start the car. I'll be down in a couple of minutes. I don't want Upshaw to have to wait on us."

They went to the car and waited while Pitts slowly eased himself down the steep staircase for the second time that day. By the time he plopped himself down in the car, he was moaning from the pain.

"Did you take a pain pill?" Iris asked.

"Yeah, a couple of hours ago. I've got another one in my pocket. Can you pull into a gas station and grab me a water, Quita?"

"Sure, but aren't you supposed to take those a few hours apart?"

"I've been weaning myself off them the last few days. Two of 'em in a two-hour span isn't going to kill me this one time."

"Famous last words," Iris said.

Pitts ignored the comment and pointed out the first convenience store they came to.

Quita ran in and out, with water in hand, and was quickly back on the road. "I don't know where I'm going," she said.

"Hit I-20 up here. We're not far."

They rode in silence until they pulled into the cemetery.

"This looks a lot like Oakland," Clara said.

"I think it's a good bit larger," Pitts said. "Quita, follow the path around to the mausoleum. Upshaw's supposed to meet us there."

She drove through the large cemetery and circled around until the large, stone building loomed in front of them.

"Wow! When you mentioned a mausoleum, I didn't think it would be this big," Clara said, looking at the structure in awe. "I had no idea this was here."

Quita eased the Buick up the ramp and into the parking area adjacent to the building. Travis was already there, standing at the entrance. Pitts got out and motioned him over for help, but another man came out of an attached wing, pushing a wheelchair.

"Heard you might need this," the man said. "Name's Sandy, Sandy Mason, I'm the sexton."

Clara, Iris, and Pritchard Pitts stood silent, their mouths agape at the man who was a dead ringer for Stuart, the sexton of Oakland Cemetery.

"Is everything okay?" Sandy asked his three mute visitors.

"Oh, I'm sorry," Pitts said as he pulled himself together. "It's just…you must be related to Stuart Mason, over at Oakland."

"You know my brother?" he asked.

"Yes, I was on another case over there recently. I'm sure you've heard about it. A young girl was left there as well."

"Yes, I heard," he confirmed. "Strangest thing, isn't it? We've never had any problems here even with things going down in the surrounding area."

"Were you the one who found her body, Mister Mason?" Pitts asked.

"No, one of my men did. I came in late today, had a doctor's appointment first thing this mornin'. He was pretty upset, so I sent him home for the day after the detectives talked to him for a couple of hours. He was emotionally spent as I'm sure you'd expect."

"Yes, I'm sure he was. This is quite a distance from the main entrance. Do you lock the place up at night?"

"Always, as a matter of routine," Sandy said firmly. "I don't know many folks who'd want to break into a cemetery. The only problem we've ever had is having to come back and unlock the gate to let people out. It's a big place, and sometimes we miss folks who've stuck around past closing time. Apparently, this time was different. The lock was easily manipulated. When the employee arrived to open up, the gate was closed. He didn't really notice anything out of the ordinary until he went to open the lock and discovered it wasn't there. He found it lyin' on the ground."

"Why do you suppose someone would dump a body in a cemetery?" Pitts asked.

"I got no idea, sir."

Pitts studied the sexton for a moment. He was much younger than his brother, by at least a decade, Pitts estimated. Although the resemblance was initially alarming, upon closer inspection, he noticed many differences. He wasn't as soft-spoken as Stuart and seemed far more confident and self-assured. Sandy wasn't as vulnerable as his brother, nor did he appear to be as upset over the death. Pitts surmised it was probably because he wasn't the one who'd found her.

Travis walked over and took the handles of the wheelchair from the sexton. "We really appreciate this, man," he said. "I'll make sure I get it back to you when we're finished."

"Not a problem," Sandy said. "If I'm not in my office, just feel free to leave it here. I'll get to it, eventually." He turned and walked back to the small wing of the mausoleum where he'd come from.

"I don't know what to make of that," Pitts said quietly, referring to the relationship between the two sextons. "We'll talk about it later. Where was she found, Upshaw?"

Travis pushed the wheelchair toward the nearest entrance. The building resembled some sort of Civil War fortress, so much so that Clara half-expected to see a cannon. The entrance consisted of a covered porch that opened to another small room with an arched entryway. There, they spotted a wooden door that was surely locked after hours.

"They found her here," Upshaw said, pointing at the ground near the entryway. "She was under this covered area, just shy of the locked door."

Clara looked up and noted a scripture from the Book of Genesis inscribed in the marble. "*The Lord watch between me and thee when we are absent one from another,*" she read aloud, then motioned Quita over. "Can you take a picture of that with your phone?" she asked. "It could be significant."

Quita nodded and pulled out her cell.

"There are several other places he could've left her if he wanted her to be found quickly," Pitts said. "Why not leave her near the main entrance instead of coming all the way back here?"

"I don't know," Travis said with a shrug. "Your guess is as good as mine. The blanket was almost identical to the one wrapped around Jasmine, even the same color and material."

"We're definitely dealing with the same perp," Pitts said. "We've got to find the link between the girls."

"Shouldn't we go inside?" Iris asked. "Maybe we'll find something that'll catch our eye. Although I don't have any idea what it would be."

"Why not? Might as well since we're here. Once I get back home, I may never come out again," Pitts said.

When they walked through the wooden door, the group was stunned. In sharp contradiction to the stony, fort-like exterior, the interior was magnificent. The sunlight burst through splendid stained-glass windows, adorned in jeweled tones. A chapel, off to their left, resembled a miniature version of the National Cathedral in Washington, D.C. Marble hallways led to various tombs and family crypts, and marble banisters led to three different floors.

"This is something," Iris commented. "I wonder why, after breaking through the initial lock and driving all the way back here, he didn't bring her inside."

"It *is* a beautiful place," Clara said.

"It gives me the creeps," Quita said flatly. "We've seen what we needed to see. Let's get out of here," she said with a shiver.

"She's right," Pitts agreed. "I've gotta lie down and wait for this pain to subside. We need to focus on finding a connection between the victims. That might be the missing link we need to solve this case."

"Yeah, and I've got to get back to the office," Travis said. "Scoggins called me. The family of Kori Reeves is holding a press conference at six tonight."

"Who's Kori Reeves?" Pitts asked.

"That other missing girl. God, I hope we don't find her in a cemetery, wrapped in a blanket."

217

Chapter Forty-Nine

It was 5:15 when Quita pulled the Buick back into the office parking lot.

"I'm bushed," Iris said. "Can we just come back in the morning and pick up where we left off?"

"Sounds good to me," Clara said. "Iris, why don't we go home, take a warm bath, and put on our pajamas? I'll pull some of my spaghetti sauce out of the freezer, and you can drive up to my house. It'll be like old times before we started this business and got so busy."

"That sounds delightful," Iris said. "I'll bring the wine."

"If we hurry, we can catch those parents on the six o'clock news. Quita, you're free to join us. We have plenty."

"I'd love to," she answered. "But I promised to take Rhadrick out to dinner tonight. It's his night off, and I wanna thank him for letting me borrow his car."

"That's awfully nice," Iris said.

"He's a great cousin and friend. It's the least I can do."

"I think we'll just head on home then," Clara said. "There's no need to go back in the office. It's been a long day."

"Okay, ladies. Have a good one," Quita said as she headed up to her apartment above the office.

It was 5:58 when Iris rang the doorbell two houses up from her own.

Clara opened the door wearing her chenille robe and motioned Iris inside. "I've got the TV on in the kitchen," she said. "The sauce is simmering, but it'll be a while before it's ready."

Iris made her way to the kitchen and reached into a drawer to retrieve a wine opener. The glasses were already sitting on the table.

"Detective Pitts called and said it's going to be on Channel forty-six. I guess the other networks didn't bother," Clara said.

"Shoot, I was hoping Fox Five would show it. That's my favorite news show. I love seeing what outfit that beautiful, Cynne Simpson's wearing every night," Iris said.

"Well, I'm sure she'll look as lovely as always. I want to hear what this family has to say. I certainly hope there's no similarity to the other cases. If there is, it might not end well for them."

They both took a seat at the kitchen table and sipped from their wine as they waited for the story to air. They sat through grim reports of a police chase that resulted in an accident at a major intersection, a bomb threat at a local school, and a teacher being arrested for having sex with a student.

"I don't know why we even watch the news," Iris said when a commercial came on. "I honestly believe it's the same newscast in every major city, just different names, and faces."

Clara got up to stir the sauce and put the water on to boil for her pasta. She was looking for a loaf of French bread in the freezer when she heard Iris squeal, "Clara! Oh, my goodness, get over here. It's him!"

"Him who?" Clara asked, pulling the bread out from under a pack of ground beef.

"Him, that hunk! There he is."

Clara turned around and stared at the TV. Sure enough, it was the handsome gentleman they'd seen at the restaurant and among the cemetery walkers.

"He's an investigative reporter," Iris said excitedly. "I knew we'd seen him somewhere before."

"Shhh," Clara said. "The family's about to speak."

A couple in their mid-forties stood before a wooden podium, with a large, black microphone protruding toward their faces. A handsome younger man, about thirty stood beside them. The rims of their eyes were red, and their expressions reflected deep inconsolable sorrow.

The husband stepped forward and cleared his throat. "We want to thank the network for allowing us to speak on the air. Friday night, our twenty-year-old daughter, Kori Reeves did not return home after her classes at Georgia State. It's very out of character for her not to contact us if she's going to be late. In fact, I can't remember her ever being late," he said as his voice cracked with emotion. The tears started, but he continued through his grief. "Kori has still not come home or contacted us. Something is very, very wrong, and we now plead with the public to look at her picture and let us know if you have *any* information about her whereabouts. If you have seen, Kori, or know anything at all, please contact the Atlanta Police Department." His emotions got the better of him, and he started to weep.

The cameras quickly changed angles, and the hunk's face filled the screen, along with a picture of a young lady. "We are asking the public for any information on the disappearance of, Kori Reeves," he said, his deep voice smooth and melodic. "She is five-six, one-hundred and twenty-five pounds, with light-brown hair and blue eyes. If you have any information on her whereabouts, please contact the APD at the number posted below. This is Dan Kimball, reporting live from Atlanta."

"What are the odds of that, Mister Kimball showing up at the restaurant where Jasmine worked and the cemetery she was found in?" Iris asked as she switched the TV to Fox Five. "Oh, she's wearing a pink suit today,"

"What?" Clara asked as she placed the noodles in the boiling water.

"Cynne! She looks good in light pink. I swear, she's not big as a bean. I hope she doesn't worry herself dieting."

"Iris, please. Can you focus, just for a minute? The detectives need to interview that family extensively. I just pray there's no connection."

"Well, I suppose it's a good sign that Kori's body hasn't been found."

"That last young lady was dead for a week before she was found. It's not a good sign, I'm terribly troubled by it."

"You know I'm the last person to mention surveillance," Iris said. "However, I think we may need to tail this Dan Kimball fella. As I see it, he's up to his eyeballs in this mess, and not just to get the scoop."

Chapter Fifty

No matter how hard he tried, Pitts couldn't get comfortable. After rolling around in his bed for over an hour in an attempt to find the perfect position, he finally gave up and moved back to the couch. Jessalyn had shown up after work and was frying chicken in the kitchen.

"You know, now that I think about it. I don't think I've eaten anything today, Jess," Pitts said.

"Well, it's not because there's nothing here," she said as she peeked her head around from the kitchen. "I left you plenty of things to choose from in the fridge."

"I know, and I appreciate it. I guess I just forgot."

"Only because you're running around playing detective. You overexerted yourself, Pitts, and I'm sure you overdosed on pain pills. That's not good, especially on an empty stomach. If Lieutenant Costa finds out you and those ladies met with Travis, she'll have all your stubborn heads on a platter."

"She's not going to find out," Pitts assured her. "Besides, what does she know? She's got Scoggins working the most recent case, for God's sake. What the hell can that screw-off do? That's like putting a seven-year-old in charge."

"So, what you're saying is that if it's not you and Nettles, the case can't possibly be solved," she said with a laugh.

"No, I'm not saying that at all! Did you talk to Sandi Nettles today?" he asked, steering the conversation in another direction.

"Yes, briefly. They're reducing some of Matthew's meds, and he's been a little more alert. The transplant is still up in the air, but his liver is stabilized. Sandi asks about you every time I speak with her. I know she'd love to see you."

"When I get better."

"You must be better now if you can hang out with private eyes all day."

"I think you're jealous!" Pitts said.

"Of those two? Give me a break."

The banter was broken up by a loud knock on the door.

"Who is it?" Pitts yelled.

"Jeez, you're bellowing," Jessalyn said as she wiped her hands on a dishtowel. "Let me get it." She stood on her tiptoes and looked through the peephole before opening the door. "Hello there, Lieutenant," she said, almost with a smirk. "Pitts is right around the corner."

Pitts rolled his eyes before the lieutenant was within eyesight of him. He was tired, his side ached, and the last thing he needed was a visit from Costa.

"You look worse than you did a week ago," Costa spouted off as she sat down in the recliner. "Have you been back to the doctor?"

"Nice to see you, too. I was shot, remember? It's not like I've been down with the flu. Damn, gimme a few days, would ya, LT? Are you this hard on Nettles?"

"And such a *pleasure* to be around, too," Costa said sarcastically. "Anyway, I just stopped by because I thought you might want the latest on your case—the *shooting*, I mean, not the flu."

"Everybody's a comedian. What've you got?"

She tossed a file on the coffee table. Pitts leaned over to pick it up.

"They're both in pretty bad shape, but they'll make it. Don't know which side of the fence you're on with that, but they'll both go to trial."

"I have to admit, I wavered on it for a minute, but ultimately, I'd love to see them rot in the State Pen. Have you been able to interrogate either of them?"

"Felipe is scared shitless of the cartel. He was grateful to be arrested. He's in administrative segregation at Fulton County, but the feds are biting at the bit to get their hands on him. Brandon Webb wants to go for the death penalty in the Tony Hart shooting, and there will be a hefty sentence for yours and Nettles' shooting, to be served consecutively."

"That's good to hear. I'm surprised the DA's willing to let his assistant take the case, though. He so enjoys the media spotlight."

"He's going through a divorce. Apparently, it's getting pretty ugly. She's going for the jugular and threatening to go to the press with some personal issues. He can't afford to be immersed in a death penalty case, right now."

"Webb's a good attorney. If he's putting the death penalty on the table, he must be serious about the case. What about, Platinum, has she confessed?"

"Her doctors aren't letting us anywhere near her yet. It's a miracle she survived. She had a great deal of internal bleeding from the beating which required surgery. Not to mention she also sustained some serious injuries in the wreck. She looks like hell, even more so than before. Her eyes are still swollen shut, and she'll remain in ICU for at least another couple of days."

"What about her baby?"

"Believe it or not, Tony Hart's mother went to court for custody. Who knows what the long-term effects from Monica's drug use will be? Poor kid."

"Please spare me the Monica reference."

"It is her name, Pitts. You'd better get used to it because you'll hear it in court."

Chapter Fifty-One

Iris was silent as they drove back to the cemetery the following morning at 5:00 a.m. She'd wanted to argue with Clara about going, but knew it'd be their best bet to run into the hunky reporter again. If he was there, they hoped to have a chance to follow him when he left. If he didn't show up, they'd have to find him some other way.

They didn't want to call Quita so early in the morning, so Clara figured out how to send her a text. She was proud of herself because it was her first attempt, but neither woman was sure it had even gone through.

They sipped slowly from their hot coffee as Clara drove down the interstate.

"What do you think the odds are that we'll see him the second day in a row?" Iris asked.

"Who knows? Let's keep our fingers crossed. There have been too many coincidences already. I can't get it off my mind. He's young, handsome, and successful. I can't imagine any young woman not being taken by him."

"Yep and his smooth voice alone would've reeled me in at that age."

"At that age? He's reeling you in at *our* age, Iris."

"Hey, I know a hunk when I see one! Still, that's not to say I'd join the Mile-High Club with him."

"It's too early for this," Clara said. "Honestly, is *that* all you think about?"

"What?"

"Sex! And who says *hunk* anymore, anyway? I think that term went out in the sixties."

"I think it was actually the seventies," Iris argued.

"Whatever, it's outdated either way."

"*Outdated*, how does a word become outdated? I can understand a phone or a computer, but a word?"

Clara gripped the steering wheel and took deep breaths instead of responding.

They pulled into the parking lot and went through the normal routine of placing their purses in the trunk. Wrapped up in thick coats and scarves, the ladies walked to the bench that was situated in the middle of the cemetery. It was the perfect spot, situated at the center of all the activity, with the most walker traffic. They waved jovially to the people who offered greetings and made light conversation as they sat.

An hour later, they were debating whether to head to the office.

"Look, Hunk at ten o'clock. Wait. Don't you dare look."

"Okay, I won't," Clara assured her. "Are you positive it's him?"

"Yep, and he's wearing the same thing he wore yesterday or close to it. He's got those earbuds in again, and he's walking really fast."

"Let's give him fifteen minutes, then head to the car," Clara suggested. "We aren't sure if he's parked in the lot or on a side street, so we'll have to find a central place to see all angles when he leaves."

Ten minutes later, they both agreed to head back to the car. They weren't sure how long it'd take to find a good surveillance spot.

"We need a view of the pedestrian gate," Clara said as she pulled out of the lot and onto Oakland Avenue. "That's the only way out of the cemetery. We'll have to hope for the best from there."

The women drove past the gate and made a right onto a side street to wind back around and face the exit.

"Dollars to donuts, I bet that's his," Iris said as she pointed to a shiny red sports car. "A TV personality like that has to drive a snazzy little number."

"Okay," Clara said. "I'm going to pull over here and try to blend in with the cars parked on the street. Let's hope you're right. We'll lose him if he heads in the other direction."

"There's no frost on the windshield," Iris said. "That means the car was driven this morning."

"You're right," Clara agreed. "Let's hope he's not as perceptive about our car."

They sat for twenty more minutes before they spotted Dan Kimball walking toward the red car. He held out his key chain and pointed it in the direction of the door to unlock it. Both women scooted down in their seats, hoping to avoid his gaze. He cranked the engine, then stood beside the vehicle and stretched his arms and legs for several minutes before actually climbing in.

"Keep an eye on him, Iris," Clara said. "I'm so nervous. I'm not sure I can do this."

"You've got this, girl," Iris exclaimed. "You're as reliable as a Goodyear tire, Clara Samples, and you've never gone flat on me! Okay, he's pulling out and has his blinker on to turn left." Iris paused and wrinkled her forehead in confusion.

"What is it?"

"Who uses a blinker at this time of the morning in a residential neighborhood?"

"Probably just habit," Clara said as she eased the Buick onto the street. "I'm going to try to stay back as far as I can. Just don't lose sight of him."

Even with the traffic growing thicker from the morning commute, they remained several cars behind but managed to maintain sight of him.

"I do declare, he's going to IHOP," Iris said. "It's our lucky day, surveillance with food."

Clara pulled into the lot and parked several spaces down, toward the back of the restaurant. "We shouldn't go in," Clara said. "It's far too risky. He's bound to have seen us at the cemetery. We were there two days in a row."

"How did I know you were going to shoot that idea down?" Iris said with a moan.

Dan got out of his car, made a quick call on his cell, and stretched his legs some more, lunging back and forth and then stretching from side to side.

"What in the world?" Iris asked. "Is something wrong with him?"

"I think it's what runners do," Clara said. "They always stretch before and after exercise."

"Whatever," Iris said sarcastically.

Another small car pulled into the lot and parked in the available spot nearest Dan. He threw up his hand in a wave and walked over to open the driver's door. A young woman got out, and the two exchanged a light hug.

"Looks like he has a breakfast date," Iris said.

"Look closer," Clara said. "She looks awfully familiar. I can't place her, though," she said with frustration. "It's a sign of getting old, Iris. I remember faces, but not names or associations. Does she look familiar to you?"

"Yes, but I can't place her either. Are you sure we shouldn't go in?"

"No, it's too risky. Let's just wait here."

Dan Kimball and his date scanned the parking lot as if they were looking for someone.

"I don't like it," Clara said instantly. "They might be meeting someone else. Maybe they know Dan was followed. I think it's time we get out of here."

"What?" Iris asked. "You can't be serious. We've come this far, and we don't want to lose him now."

"I'm sorry, Iris. Maybe you're right, but I never doubt my gut, and it's telling me to go. As soon as they go inside, I'm driving back to the office."

Chapter Fifty-Two

Against her better judgment, Jessalyn Brock took the morning off to take Pitts to see the assistant DA. She couldn't bear to tell him no after he'd spent most of the prior evening pleading with her to do so. Not only that, but Jessalyn knew if she didn't do it herself, Pitts would find another way.

Pitts was toweling off from his long, hot shower when his phone rang. "Pitts here," he answered.

"Good morning, Pritchard," Sandi Nettles said in her soft, kind voice. She was the only person who ever referred to him by his first name, and the only one he allowed to do it, simply because he found it impossible to tell her not to. Sandi was such a sweet soul, and he couldn't bear to scold her for anything.

"Morning, Sandi," Pitts said, genuinely happy to hear her voice. "How are you?"

"I'm doing well, thank you, but I'm actually calling to check on you. I've been so concerned about you."

"Yes, Jessalyn said you've been asking about me. I'm sorry I haven't been to the hospital to visit. This recovery has kicked my ass."

"I'm so sorry for what you've gone through. I won't keep you. I just wanted to let you know that you're on my mind. I'll tell Matthew I spoke with you."

"How is he?"

"He's coming along. It's been a tough road, but I think it's safe to say he's out of the woods. Who knows what the future holds? For now, God's grace is sustaining us."

"Good to hear. How are *you*, Sandi? How are you and Ralph?"

"I'm exhausted, but that's to be expected. Ralph is seven, so much of this is too difficult for his young mind to comprehend. I suppose we should be grateful for that. Right now, he's the center of attention wherever he stays, so he's faring pretty well. Thank you for asking. Again, I won't keep you. I just wanted to tell you I'm praying for your recovery and that I love you."

"Love you, too," Pitts said before he disconnected the call.

"I'm so glad you finally spoke with her," Jessalyn said when she walked in and caught the tail end of the call.

Pitts shook his head. "For the life of me, I can't figure out how in the hell Nettles snagged that woman. They're as different as night and day."

"He just got lucky," she said. "Let me help you get dressed. Your breakfast is on the table. I called the office and told them I'll be a couple of hours late. I've missed a lot of work lately, so I need to go in after we see Brandon."

Pitts allowed her to help him dress, ate a hearty breakfast, and took his meds. By then, he felt as if he'd already put in a full day but was still determined to meet with Brandon Webb. He wanted to know everything Brandon knew about the case.

As usual, the damn staircase down to the parking lot was difficult, but Pitts conquered it slowly and made it to the car. The courthouse was less than ten minutes away, and a sheriff's deputy was waiting for him outside with a wheelchair.

"Thanks, man," Pitts said. "This is just what the doctor ordered."

"Jessalyn called ahead, I was happy to help," he said.

Pitts recognized his face but didn't know his name, so he referred to the bar on his chest. "How's it going, Trenton?" he asked as if he'd known his last name all along.

"Pretty good, Pitts. Sorry about the shooting. I heard Webb's going for the death penalty, and I'm glad to hear it."

"Yeah, me too. Let's go on up to his office. Jessalyn is parking and will meet me up there."

It was nice to be back out in public, even though, he was still very weak. All the officers who passed him stopped to speak and shake his hand. It felt as if he hadn't seen them in years.

Deputy Trenton pushed the button on the elevator, and it arrived instantly. They rode six floors up, and Pitts' escort wheeled him around the corner and into the plush office of the district attorney.

"My, my, aren't you a sight for sore eyes," Irene Edwards said. She jumped up from her desk and waddled over to kiss his cheek. "I've been so worried about you and Matthew," she said as she brushed away the lipstick she'd left behind on his cheek.

Irene was close to retirement, and everyone dreaded the day she'd finally have to call it quits. She was as wide as she was tall, about five feet in either direction. Not only was she a competent secretary, but she was also an astonishingly talented cook. She baked wonderful cakes and pastries for office birthdays, and everybody enjoyed a delicious, homemade snack whenever they visited the DA's office. Pitts loved her as much as everyone else did.

"You're just as handsome as ever," Irene said. "Brandon's filing a motion in court, right now, but he'll be back in a few minutes. Can I get you some coffee? Perhaps a chocolate chip cookie?"

"All of the above," Pitts said with a grin. "Is Milton in his office?"

"Yes, Warren's in there, but he's on the phone with his wife again," she whispered, referring to District Attorney Warren Milton. "Lord have mercy, what a mess. She's taking him to the cleaners, and he's a bundle of nerves. Anyway, I'll get your snack, and if the light is off on his phone when I get back, I'll see if he has a minute for you."

"Okay. Thanks, Irene."

Pitts only had to wait a minute before she returned with his coffee and a napkin full of warm, soft cookies. He bit into one immediately. "Mmm, mmm, mmm. You never disappoint, Irene."

"The light's off," she whispered, then picked up the receiver and buzzed her boss. "Yes, Warren, Detective Pitts is out here. He's wondering if you might have a moment for him?" She paused briefly, then answered, "Wonderful, I'll wheel him in." She then leaned down to whisper in Pitts' ear. "Don't mention the divorce," she said, her breath warm on the side of his face. "Granted, it's common knowledge, but it's a raw nerve. I'd just leave it alone if I were you."

Pitts nodded in agreement.

"Well, would you look here?" Warren exclaimed as he got up from his desk. "I have to tell you, Pitts, I had my doubts about you and Nettles making it," he said while Irene let herself out.

"You and me both," Pitts answered. He took stock of Warren Milton's appearance. He was a tall, well-built man, and even at forty-five, he displayed the physique of an active athlete from his football days at Clemson University, before he headed to UGA for law school. Milton's downfall had always been women, and despite his efforts to stay true to his various wives at various intervals, he always failed miserably when it came to fidelity. The stress of his present situation was apparent on his face, but Pitts pretended not to notice.

"Yeah, I put Brandon Webb on your case," Milton said. "He's the best I've got, other than me, of course," he said, then faked a chuckle. "My plate's pretty full, right now, but I've got confidence in Webb. It doesn't hurt that your shooter is singing like a bird either."

"Webb's a good guy," Pitts said. "I'm sure he's got this."

"Yes, I do," Brandon said from behind him. "I appreciate the vote of confidence, Detective."

"Hey! Where'd you come from?" Pitts asked as he turned around in the wheelchair.

Brandon reached his hand to meet Pitts'. "Just got back from filing a motion, Irene said I'd find you in here."

"I just wanted to stop in and see how the case is going."

"It's pretty early, Pitts," Brandon said, looking up at his boss. "But we both think it looks good," he continued as he nodded to the DA for assurance. "Felipe Nunez is happy to tell his side of the story and is more than willing to implicate, Monica Heard. It's a slam-dunk for a conviction. I'm just hoping the jury will think it warrants the death penalty."

"Yeah, me too," Pitts said. "Have you talked to her?" he asked, unable to bring himself to call the woman by her given name.

"Her doctor won't consent to us interviewing her, yet. That's cool with me. I don't want the defense to doubt her ability to understand our questioning later. Nunez is dropping the dime on her anyway, so her ship is sunk."

"I've got to head to a meeting, boys. It was good to see you, Pitts," Milton said as he reached for his blazer.

"Apparently, they pay lawyers more than they pay us lowly cops," Pitts said sarcastically. "I've never owned a suit that sharp."

"It's all about first impressions," Warren Milton said. "Yes, indeed…good first impressions."

Chapter Fifty-Three

"I sure do wish you two would've waited around," Quita said after Clara and Iris told her about their exciting morning. "I'd like to know where he went after that?"

"Clara was acting strange about the whole situation," Iris tattled. "It's just not like her."

"You, more than anyone I know, preach the importance of gut instincts, Quita," Clara said in her own defense. "I can't put my finger on it, but I felt like he must have noticed us at the cemetery. We stick out like sore thumbs when we're there that time of day."

"Speaking of the cemetery, how weird is it that the two sextons are brothers?" Quita asked.

"It's not so odd for brothers to work in the same profession," Clara said. "What is odd, though, is that a dead girl turned up at each cemetery."

"You're both missing the point," Iris said. "They're not the oddballs. Whoever is dumping the bodies is. The killer obviously chose cemeteries as his dumping grounds, and both cemeteries are located in the same city. I honestly don't think the Mason brothers are involved. I mean, think about it. They've both made a career out of working at graveyards. Dumping a body at one of their workplaces would automatically draw attention to them and dumping two would be crazy on their part."

"Murdering a young woman is crazy in itself," Clara said. "Whoever dumped the girls at the cemeteries did it for one of two reasons. Either he wanted to make a statement, or he just wanted them to be found. Personally, I'm going with the first theory."

"What kind of statement would leaving a dead body in a cemetery make?" Iris pressed.

"That's the million-dollar question," Clara said. "This is a major city, with many places where a body would be guaranteed to be discovered. A cemetery adds another dimension to it. It's just so symbolic, all about death."

"You're getting deep, Clara," Iris said. "Also a little creepy if you don't mind me saying so. Are you sure you didn't have too much wine last night?"

Before Clara could shush her friend, the phone rang, and Quita quickly answered it. "Do you mind if I put you on speaker?" she asked. "It's Detective Pitts," she announced to Clara and Iris as she pushed the button to share the call with them. "Go ahead, Detective. We're all here."

"Listen, ladies," he began, "I just met with the DA and the assistant DA about the guy who shot me and my partner. Jessalyn brought me, but she's gotta get back to work. If she drops me off at your office, can you drive me back to my apartment later? The way I see it, we've got some things to talk about."

"Sure thing," Quita answered. "We'll be here."

Pitts was at their office within a few minutes. He was tired but looked much better than he had the day before. Clara offered him her desk chair, which he gratefully accepted, then he listened intently as they excitedly told him about their morning adventure with the newsman.

"I don't watch that channel, and don't know any reporter by that name," Pitts said. "I'm familiar with most of them since we have run-ins with the press on a regular basis. The media loves to follow crime, and viewers can't get enough when it comes to murder. He must be fairly new if I've never heard of him."

"Okay," Quita said. "Let's add new to the area, along with being at the restaurant where Jasmine worked and at the cemetery where she was left."

"And aware that the side door was unlocked for entry," Iris added. "Clara, maybe the woman we recognized is a reporter, too. That might be why she looks so familiar."

"You're probably right," Clara agreed.

"I hope Scoggins is delving into the other missing girl, that Kori," Pitts said. "I missed the newscast last night because my side hurt so badly. It was three o'clock in the morning before I found a comfortable position, and even that wasn't so comfortable."

"We were thinking the same thing about the missing girl," Clara said. "I also can't get the mountain Laurel out of my head. If the killer is taking girls up in the mountains, he may not be local at all."

"What exactly is mountain Laurel?" Quita asked.

"It sort of resembles an azalea or a rhododendron," Clara said. "It's definitely colder up in North Georgia, but my goodness, that's a third of the state! There's no way to pinpoint where it came from."

"Ladies, I'm afraid our only way to solve this case is to find a link between those girls," Pitts said. "I can't think of one to save my life."

"I'll pull up their social media accounts," Quita said. "Maybe they had mutual friends on Facebook."

"How can a dead person have one of those social media things?" Iris asked, confused.

"It takes a while for the sites to shut their pages down, even when they're notified of a death," Quita explained. "That could work to our advantage."

"Good idea," Pitts said. "I'll call my friend in missing persons. Maybe she'll do some sneaking around for me."

Quita began tapping away on her desktop while Pitts scrolled through his cell phone for the number.

"Good morning. How's everything there?" he asked when someone picked up the call. "Yeah, I've heard you're pretty busy these days." He paused briefly, then said, "Shhh, don't say my name. I'm supposed to be in bed recuperating, and Costa is on me like white on rice. If she finds out I'm calling, she'll wring my neck! Anyway, have guys got any news on that Reeves girl? The one they had a press conference about last night?" He paused briefly as he listened to the response. "Damn, tell me, has Scoggins's lazy-ass even been up there at all? He'd better be working hard on this." He listened for a few more minutes before saying, "Thanks so much, Cassidy. I appreciate it…and I'd appreciate it even more if you don't tell anybody I called. I'd like to stay out of the doghouse, if at all possible."

"Who was that?" Clara asked, wearing a confused expression. "I think I remember hearing that name before."

"Oh, that was Cassidy Moore. She's the receptionist on the floor above mine."

"That's it!" Clara exclaimed. "That was who we saw with the reporter! I knew I'd seen her before, but I couldn't place her. We met her when we went to meet with your lieutenant. Some young woman met us at the elevator to take us to her office, and she ran into this Cassidy. I remember because she asked for some kind of paperwork to complete her reports. She seemed a little irritated, but the other young woman tried to smooth it over to us. She explained that Cassidy's paperwork often had to be completed first and that she was under some pressure."

"Yeah, Cassidy's a good worker," Pitts said. "She does most of the paperwork up there, and she also answers the phones, which can be a real headache, let me tell ya. Every time some bratty kid misses his curfew, a parent calls her in hysterics. She also gets the calls about elderly persons who wander away from assisted-living facilities and the toddlers who get out of their yards. I guess the pressure would get to anybody from time to time. We've talked about it before, but Cassidy's a nice girl."

"Maybe she was meeting with him about a case he's investigating," Iris said. "That'd make sense."

"I don't think she'd do that," Pitts responded. "We're not really allowed to speak privately with the press. There are appointed spokespeople for that. Hell, if they let the average investigator or office personnel speak to the media, we'd have a worse mess on our hands than we have now."

"Then why was she with him?" Clara asked.

"Maybe she's dating the guy," Pitts said. "Who knows? It's a free country."

"But they were looking around the parking lot like they were concerned they might be seen together," Clara added, with uneasiness evident in her voice.

"Oh, Clara," Iris said. "If they were worried about that, they would've gone somewhere more private than an IHOP. You're overreacting. Maybe they were meeting another couple for breakfast. Like Pitts said, it's a free country, and there's no crime in pancakes."

"No," Clara insisted, "I know there's more to it than that. I'm sorry, but I just have a gut feeling, even if I can't explain why."

"Don't apologize for how you feel, Miss Clara," Quita said. "We'll get to the bottom of it. Don't you worry."

Chapter Fifty-Four

"I think we need to go back to the mausoleum," Clara said as the four of them shared a pizza at the office.

"Why would you want to do that?" Iris asked as she picked a pepperoni off and popped it in her mouth. "Haven't you had enough of cemeteries this week?"

"I want to look at some of the names on the crypts. Maybe something will ring a bell, or a last name will match some of the tombstones at Oakland, the ones near where Jasmine's body was found."

"You could call the sexton," Pitts suggested. "I'm sure he'd fax you a list of those who were interred there."

"I don't want to call his attention to us," Clara said. "I'm still not convinced that those brothers aren't connected somehow. I really don't know what my reasoning is for wanting to go back, I just feel I need to. Those cemeteries must have some significance to this case. As I was telling Quita and Iris earlier, those bodies could've been dumped in a thousand different places if the concern was them being found. I didn't overanalyze it so much when we only had one body at a cemetery, but two takes it to another level."

"I'm with Clara," Quita spoke up. "If she feels something needs to be investigated further, she has to have a reason. I'll drive you over, Clara."

"Not without me, you won't!" Iris insisted. "I don't want to stay here and get stuck answering the phone."

"I'll ride along with you ladies, as long as you can drop me off at my apartment when we're done. I need to rest. Being out two days in a row has taken a toll."

"No problem," Clara said.

Pitts glanced down at his cell when it rang. "Shit, it's Costa. Doesn't that woman have anything to do other than monitor me?" he grumbled as he punched his phone with his index finger to connect the call. "Pitts." He rolled his eyes as he listened to her. "No, you don't need to come over, Lieutenant. Just spit it out. How bad can it be? Unless something has happened to Nettles, I can handle it by phone." After another eye-roll, he spoke again. "Yes, I'm sitting down," he spat in the phone, his growing impatience reaching its peak. Pitts' face then turned crimson, and he inhaled deeply. "You've gotta be shitting me!" he screamed into the phone. "What idiot put him in the general population? Who's running that circus over there anyway? I hope they lock that idiot up and throw away the key. How could somebody be so incompetent?" he continued to scream.

Clara stared at him, horrified, afraid his blood pressure might reach stroke level.

"I am calm," Pitts yelled. "No, do not—and I repeat, do not—come over here. I need to be alone," he said, then disconnected the call and threw his cell phone against the wall.

The three women sat silently, afraid to speak. Pitts was visibly beside himself with anger, and they didn't want his wrath turned toward them.

After several minutes of awkward silence, Clara asked, "Are you okay, Detective?"

"No, I'm not," he said, surprisingly calmer than his outburst a few minutes earlier. "The guy who shot Nettles and me was just murdered in the Fulton County jail—the admitted shooter, let me add. That means his confession and testimony against the woman who ordered him to shoot us is now inadmissible in court. Isn't that something?"

"I'm sorry to hear that," Clara said quietly. "It's understandable for you to be so angry about it." The instant she said it, she regretted it and half-expected him to turn on her. Clara couldn't possibly understand his pain and pretending that she could relate to it was cruel at best. "Please allow me to retract my last comment. I can't understand how you feel. I'm just sorry you have to deal with it."

"Thanks," Pitts said. "The cartel wanted him dead, and the staff at the jail knew it. To let him out of isolation and into the general population was nothing short of ignorant on their part. Hell, for all I know, the staff took a bribe to make him accessible."

"Why did the cartel want him dead?" Quita asked.

"Because he was gonna spill the beans about their operation in Atlanta. According to Costa, he was one happy camper to be in jail."

"Who'd be happy to be in jail?" Iris asked.

"Somebody who'd rather be above ground than six feet under it. Unfortunately for, Felipe Nunez, his joy was short-lived," Pitts said sarcastically.

Chapter Fifty-Five

Kori Reeves huddled under the filthy tarp in the underground bunker. Her temperature was so high that her clothes were drenched with sweat. She'd eaten the last of the potted meat a couple of hours earlier, and it had caused her to vomit profusely. The infection from her wound had worsened to the point that if she didn't receive medical attention within the next few hours, she'd certainly succumb to septicity.

She had remained in the bunker initially because she was afraid her kidnapper would find her, but now she had to take a chance and leave. Her numerous attempts to pull her body up the ladder had proven unsuccessful. She'd rested for a while and given herself a serious talk. She had to make it work this time. If she could get up the ladder, she'd crawl until she either found help or died. In the end, it was her only choice.

Kori wiped her face with a piece of molded tarp and slid over to the bottom rung of the ladder. After praying aloud for strength, she pulled the upper half of her body up. The pain coursing through her leg was so sharp that she could hardly bear it, but she pressed on. Closing her eyes, as if to block out the task before her, she continued to pull, until she was able to place her left foot on the bottom rung.

Unsure of how long it had taken her, and almost near delirium, she reached over her head and felt the wooden door above her. Kori's body shook from both the pain and the sheer weakness of her sickened body, but after several tries, she was able to push it open. She hadn't even considered what time of day it was and was grateful to discover it was dark outside. Reaching deep inside herself for extra strength, she managed to slide her body out and onto the cold ground.

The sky was clear, and the stars twinkled like beautiful diamonds. For a moment, Kori forgot all about the pain and just stared up at their beauty. *Polaris! Find the North Star, Kori.*

Suddenly, there it was, in all its glory, as if waiting to lead her. She dragged herself in the direction of the star that she knew was away from the killer's cabin.

At times, Kori felt as though it had been hours since she'd begun crawling on her belly, but at other times, she wondered if it had simply been minutes. She realized she was becoming delirious, and she probably had been for some time now. The cold was stinging her face, but the rest of her body seemed immune to it. She pulled her body across the ground, in the direction of the bright star above.

Kori suddenly saw shepherds holding their long, crooked staffs beside them. She squinted and caught sight of a donkey, a lamb, and a wooden manger. There were men with jeweled crowns on their heads and a beautiful young woman holding a suckling infant. *It's Baby Jesus! The star is shining so brightly that I can see His precious face. And is that Joseph taking the gifts from the Wise Men?*

There was a wet sensation on Kori's face, and she reached up to wipe it away. As soon as she did, her ears were assaulted with a loud sound she couldn't decipher.

"What are you barking at, Henry?" she heard an older woman yelling. "What's out there, boy?"

Kori lifted her head and yelled as loudly as her broken body would allow. "Please! Please, I'm over here. Help!"

She listened as slow footsteps came closer and closer, but she could no longer lift her head to see who was making the footfalls.

"Oh, good Lord, child. Where did you come from?" the woman asked as she wiped Kori's face with her apron.

Kori could smell fried chicken and suddenly felt alive.

"Where'd you come from?" the lady asked again. "Ain't nobody else on this mountain 'cept for my grandson, and he's only here on the weekends."

Chapter Fifty-Six

Quita pulled Clara's Buick into Pitts' apartment complex and did her best to help him up the stairs. "You need a beer," she said as she used his keys to open his door. "Your blood pressure must be sky-high. You've got to chill. Let us deal with the cemetery."

Pitts thought about responding, then decided against it. There was far too much weighing on him at the moment, and he didn't want to unload on her, especially since he knew she meant well. "Thanks for the lift," he offered instead. "I'm gonna lie down. I guess I'm safe, now that my shooter is dead."

Quita handed him the keys and closed the door behind him. He'd had a rough few weeks, and she wished him all the best before she departed. She took the cement stairs two at a time to make sure she got Iris and Clara to the cemetery before it closed for the day. She was a little concerned about Clara, who seemed to be taking the investigation a little too close to heart. She hoped visiting the mausoleum again might help.

"Okay, ladies," she said. "We've got about twenty minutes to look around before we have to head back to the front gate," Quita instructed. "I seriously don't want to get locked in this creepy place. Maybe we should split up since we have our phones. If you see anything you think you should take a picture of, do it. It's better to have it than to regret not taking it later."

They nodded in agreement, even though none of them really knew what they were looking for, they just hoped it would jump out at them if they saw it.

"It's five-twenty," Quita said. "Meet me at the entrance at ten till," she said sternly. "They lock the front gate at six, so we'll be cutting it close."

Clara and Iris nodded, then quickly dispersed. Clara had her mind set on checking out the family crypts. They were cordoned off with fancy, braided ropes that could be unlatched. Each was labeled with a family surname and could entomb up to a dozen relatives. She was hoping a common thread would somehow tie all three girls together.

Quita chose to walk into the chapel. It was so peaceful and reminded her of the few times she'd gone to church with her grandmother. Beyond that, she'd only seen it on television. She sat in one of the wooden pews up front, close to the pulpit. She ran her hand over the crushed, red velvet cushion that stretched from one end of the pew to the other. Marble columns extended from the floor up to the thirty-foot ceilings, and she marveled at their beauty. Quita watched as the sunlight grew dimmer through the stained-glass windows, contemplating what she should pray for. After much thought, she decided it was best not to ask for anything. Instead, she wanted to thank God for the many blessings she'd recently received. Other than her sister and her cousin Rhadrick, she never would have dreamt she'd have more family, such a meaningful job, and a home of her own.

Yes, I've got plenty of blessings to thank Him for before I go askin' for anymore, she reasoned.

Iris, on the other hand, decided to take the road less traveled. She knew Clara would check out anything within eyesight of the door, so she took the spiral staircase to the bottom floor. She took deliberate steps, careful not to take a tumble down the marble stairs. It was similar to the first floor with the same layout of crypts. The last thing on her mind was trying to discover something in the mausoleum that might solve a murder investigation. Instead, she meandered along, taking in names and dates of birth and death.

Just as she rounded the corner to go down another hallway, she heard voices. They were soft at first, then grew louder the closer she got. Iris slipped her espadrilles off and reached down to pick them up with her hands. Leaning against the marble crypts, she edged closer to the voices.

"Why'd you have to leave the body at another cemetery?" the female voice questioned. "Talk about a stupid thing to do!"

"It was far from stupid," the deep male voice responded. "They're both beautiful resting places. It was appropriate."

"Have you lost your mind?" the female continued. "Now the media's gotten hold of it, and they're not going to let it go."

"What better way to bring peace to the grieving family?" he asked.

Iris felt her heart beating under her shirt and placed her hand over it to keep the two from hearing it. She felt light-headed but mentally talked herself through it. Just as she edged a little closer to hear the remainder of the conversation, her worst fear came true.

"Iris?" she heard Quita yell. "We can't be late. Where are you? Are you down here?"

Quita's light footsteps could easily be heard as she made her way through the maze of waxed hallways. Iris shut her eyes and tried to think of a way to get out of the situation. She backed away from the voices and was near the end of the aisle when someone grabbed her shoulder. She screamed before even realizing it.

"It's just me," Quita said. "What are you doing down here?"

"Yes, what are you doing down here?" the smooth voice of the investigative reporter asked. "And how long have you been here?"

The two women turned around to find themselves face to face with a possible suspect.

"I-I just got down here," she lied. "What's going on?" Iris asked as she continued to back up, pulling Quita with her.

"Why don't I believe you?" Dan Kimball asked. "I recognize you from Oakland Cemetery, where I walk in the mornings. Why are you following me?" he demanded in a low, threatening voice. He continued to move toward her, slowly, like a wild animal sneaking up on its prey.

"We know who you are," Quita said. "We will go to the police. Don't bully old women, it's not becoming."

"I can't let you do that," he said as his strides grew quicker. "I won't allow it."

Quita ran to the bottom of the stairway and yelled as loudly as she could, "Clara, make a break for it! We've got the killer! Call the police!" She then ran back to Iris, who was lying on the floor. "Oh, my God!" Quita screamed. "Did you break your hip?"

"No, child, I didn't break my hip! I take four calcium pills a day. My hip wouldn't break if a train ran over it. Now go get that son-of-a-bitch. We can't let him get away."

Quita ran up the stairway as quickly as she could. She slowed at the top of the stairs and listened intently, but she heard nothing. Her first instinct was to run through the hallways on the first floor, but something told her to go up one more flight. Her legs led her there, even against her mind's better judgment. Her sneakers squeaked and squealed on the waxed floor, so she slipped out of them and made her way around the corner in her sock feet. That floor seemed a little smaller than the others, and there were areas under construction. An old metal table on an extendable lift reminded her of an autopsy table, and her body shivered at the thought. She grabbed a heavy wrench from the floor, the only makeshift weapon she could get her hands on.

Quita heard whispers and followed them. She wondered why they hadn't run out the first-floor door, but then it hit her, *Why, would they try to get away? We obviously know who they are, and they don't want any of us to get out of here alive.*

Chapter Fifty-Seven

Pitts decided to forgo the pain medication and went straight to his liquor cabinet instead. *Maybe Quita had a point*, he thought. *I need to relax*. He hadn't had so much as a beer since he'd returned from the hospital and decided a little alcohol might be more effective than his meds.

He pushed past the Jim Beam and Tito's Vodka and went straight for the Jose Cuervo. He rarely pulled out the Tequila, but he couldn't think of a better time to drown his sorrows. He grabbed a shot glass from the cabinet, and he pulled a Miller Lite from the fridge to chase it down, along with the half of the sandwich leftover from the day before, to absorb some of the alcohol.

Pitts plopped down on the couch, placed his spirits on the coffee table, turned on the television, and was just about to pour a shot of liquor when he heard someone banging on the door. Jessalyn and Upshaw both had keys, and he didn't give a damn about anyone else, so he tried to ignore it.

The knocking persisted, but he refused to acknowledge it.

"Pitts, we know you're in there," Costa yelled. "It's Webb and me, and we're not leaving until you open the door."

"Go away, nobody's home!" Pitts yelled back.

"Quit being a baby," Costa said. "We just want to talk to you."

"You're not off to a good start," Pitts countered. "You're not exactly winning me over with your glowing personality."

"Open the damn door," she yelled. "Don't think I won't knock it down myself."

"Shit, all right. I'm coming," Pitts mumbled. He opened the door, then rudely turned his back to his visitors and returned to the couch. "What happened to me staying home and recuperating? You're running my blood pressure up," he said angrily.

"I wanted to check on you," she said.

"I told you not to come, I'm fine."

"I know you're upset," Costa said softly as she sat down beside him. "I thought speaking with Brandon might help. We're still gonna get her, Pitts."

"Right, Nunez is dead and can't testify against her. All we've got is evidence that he committed both crimes. Do I need to remind you that we have Platinum on tape, in the parking lot when Tony Hart's murder occurred? If it ever goes to trial, she'll have the jury eating out of her hands. No one ever loved her, and she fell in with the cartel, with no idea how bad they were."

"It won't happen like that," Costa insisted.

"Really, how many times have you seen it happen, Webb?" Pitts asked, turning to Brandon for affirmation.

The assistant DA turned his gaze to the floor. Pitts knew how the system worked just as well as he did, there was no point in lying to him. "Look, man, you know I'll do everything in my power to put her away for a long, long time."

"Yeah! Well, what have you got? Go ahead, tell me. Nobody's gonna testify against, Platinum. She's just as evil as the cartel. Germaine Wilkins was petrified of her, that should tell you something. The man grew up in a drug-infested, crime-riddled neighborhood he never batted an eye at, for God's sake, but he shook like a leaf at the thought of her."

"One thing I know for certain," Brandon said firmly. "Is that a leopard never changes their spots. Trust me, she'll screw up again."

"So, we just wait around for her to unload another clip into us?" Pitts asked, rage growing in his voice. "Can't you get the DA on it? I figured Milton would be begging to stand in front of the media and rave about how he's gonna stop the cartel from transporting drugs into our fine city!"

"Pitts, that's enough," Costa said. "None of this is Webb's fault."

Pitts poured a shot glass and slugged the caramel-colored liquid back in one gulp. He closed his eyes and opened his mouth as the fire ran down his throat and came back up again. It almost took his breath away, but he was instantly calmer. "Look, I'm sorry, Webb. I just can't believe the jail let this happen. I want her locked away forever, man. She almost killed us, and Nettles is…well, he's…" Pitts was aware that his voice was giving way to emotion, so he popped the lid on the beer and took a slug from it.

Brandon sat down on the recliner and reached for the Tequila. "Mind if I have a shot?"

"Hell no. The shot glasses are in the kitchen."

"Just pass yours over," he said. When Pitts complied, Brandon poured a full one and turned it up. His facial expression never changed as he swallowed the strong liquor. "I know a cop's life isn't easy, but you should try being a prosecutor," he said. "It's no walk in the park."

"I suppose you're right," Pitts said.

"Listen, I'm going to give this all my attention. I'd love to pass it on to Milton, but he's going through a shitstorm, right now. I'm sure you've heard about it, and if you haven't, you will soon enough. His wife is going for the throat, threatening to ruin him."

"That's rough," Pitts said. "Why does Milton keep getting married if he knows he can't keep it in his pants?"

"I can't figure that one out either," Brandon said with a laugh. "This one might change his ideas on any future nuptials, though. She's not about to walk away peacefully. When I left the office, he was in an uproar. Her attorney just sent over a letter demanding their two vacation homes and Milton lost it."

"Two? Damn, I realize y'all are attorneys, but I didn't realize you made that kind of money. His house in the city is nothing to sneeze at, but two vacation homes, seriously?"

"Ha! I bet my salary doesn't even match yours," Brandon said. "Milton's father was an attorney and had his own firm. The only way to make money is to be in the private sector. Milton inherited a lot when his parents died, including the family getaways. At the rate he's going, though, he won't have much of an inheritance left."

The wheels began to turn in Pitts' mind, but he didn't dare give that away. "I appreciate you coming by," he said, then turned to face the lieutenant. "Sorry for being so rude, Costa," he said. "I just need some rest. I'll come to terms with it eventually. I appreciate you, Lieutenant," he finished, then gave her a wink.

"You'd better rest up," Costa threatened. "I've got my eyes on you," she said as she motioned with her index and middle finger, pointing first to her eyes, then to Pitts.

"I know you do, Costa," Pitts said with a laugh. "I know you do."

"Can you excuse us for just a minute, Lieutenant?" Brandon Webb asked.

"No problem, I'll go crank up the car."

Webb waited until he heard Costa close the apartment door. "Hey, don't sweat this Monica Heard thing too bad," he said to Pitts, as he poured himself another shot and tossed it back. "I'm sure the cartel will take care of her. They always handle their business."

Chapter Fifty-Eight

Quita tried to hear them talking but couldn't make out the conversation. She inched slowly toward the end of the hallway and peeked around the last row of crypts. It was there that she spotted them at the door leading out onto a balcony.

She slowly started moving backward. They weren't looking for her, and that freed her to head back downstairs to get Iris, so they could make a run for it. She was sure Clara had managed to call for help by now, and they had to get out of there.

She was almost to the stairs when she heard a loud ding and noticed that the old elevator was stopping on her floor. Afraid to turn around, she simply held her breath. The doors opened, and Quita opened her eyes to find Iris standing behind the old, wrought-iron folding gate that covered the front of the elevator.

"What are you doing, Iris?" Quita whispered. "Stay there. We'll ride it to the first floor and try to get away. They're out on the balcony."

"Not anymore," Dan Kimball said, shocking Quita to the point of a gasp. "Step out of that elevator," he said to Iris.

Iris unfolded the door and stepped out, limping from her fall. "You just threw an old lady to the ground!" she snapped at him. "Did that make you feel like a man?"

Quita grabbed Iris's elbow and held her back. "We're supposed to be escaping," she whispered. "Now is not the time to prove a point."

"Hush! I'm buying time here," she whispered back to Quita before turning to face the man she had previously referred to as a hunk. "There are laws against attacking the elderly, young man. I'll see to it that you rot in prison."

He stepped toward Iris. "You're a feisty old bag, aren't you?" he said as he grabbed her forearm.

"Ouch! You're hurting me," Iris said.

"Let go of her!" Quita barked. "I swear I'll kill you if you don't get your hands off her, right now!" she screamed as she lifted the large wrench over her head.

"Let the woman go, Dan," a male voice said.

Quita and Iris turned to see Sandy Mason and Clara at the top of the stairs. Iris leaned heavily on Quita, fearing she might faint. "It's okay, Miss Iris," Quita said, pulling her friend close to her. "Help has arrived...I think."

"That's enough," Sandy said. "What's going on here, Cassidy?"

"You *know* these two?" Iris asked.

"Of course, I do," Sandy answered. "What man wouldn't know his own children?"

"What!" Quita said, thinking she hadn't heard him right. "They've been killing young girls and dumping their bodies in the cemeteries."

"You're mistaken," Sandy insisted.

"But I heard them talking about it," Iris said. "Cassidy just told Dan he was a fool to dump the bodies here."

Sandy Mason's eyelids began to blink rapidly. "There's clearly been a misunderstanding here. Tell them, Cassidy, Dan..."

The siblings looked down at the floor, like young children who'd been caught in a fib.

"Tell them!" Sandy demanded. "Tell them you aren't murderers!"

"We wouldn't kill anybody," Cassidy said softly. "Neither of us would ever hurt a fly."

"Why are they making up these cruel accusations?" the sexton asked. "What are they talking about, Dan?"

"I didn't want to see another family go through what you and Mom did," Dan said, his voice no longer smooth and confident.

"Spit it out!" his father demanded. "What did you do?"

Dan Kimball leaned against the wall, and his knees buckled. He slid down to the floor and wept. Cassidy sat beside him and reached for his hand.

"They may need an attorney," Clara suggested.

"I won't ask you again!" Sandy said firmly. His voice was demanding, but tears rolled slowly down his cheeks.

"I got a call," Cassidy said. "An anonymous caller phoned the missing person's line and reported that he'd dumped a body next to the landfill. He wanted us to find her."

"How did her body get from the landfill to the cemetery?"

Dan was now a blubbering mess, sobbing uncontrollably.

Cassidy patted his hand, then stood to look her father in the eyes. "I remembered the grief our family went through when Sarah was taken from us. It was the *not knowing* that hurt the most. I prayed every night that she'd be found before Mom died, but she wasn't. If only Mom could've had that peace before she passed away."

"Sarah's disappearance was a terrible thing," Sandy said. "But it's something we've learned to live with. Did you go pick up that girl's body?"

"The caller said she'd be nude and strangled, and I couldn't stand the thought of it. I called Dan and told him about it, and he felt the same way I did. We didn't want the family to find her in a landfill, dumped there like garbage, with all her clothes off. If we'd found Sarah like that, it would've killed us."

"So, you decided to wrap her in a clean blanket and place her somewhere peaceful?" Clara asked.

"Exactly," Cassidy said, as the tears began to flow. "Dan went to get her. I never dreamt he'd put her in the cemetery, though. I guess he felt it was appropriate."

"You took ten years off of your Uncle Stuart's life, to say nothing of tampering with evidence at the scene," Sandy said. "Then you did it again!"

"She was dumped in front of an elementary school," she said between sobs. "For God's sake, we couldn't leave her there. Do you know how that would've affected those children when they heard about it? They'd be frightened for the rest of their lives, just like Dan and I were when our sister disappeared. Not one night went by that we didn't have nightmares. Don't you understand, Daddy? Don't you see why we did it?"

Sandy Mason reached for his daughter and held her close, both of them sobbing. "I love you, Cassidy. I guess I never realized that Sarah's disappearance really stripped you and Dan of your childhoods. I was only thinking of her. Please forgive me!"

Sandy turned to Clara. "Please," he said. "Use my office to call the police. We aren't going anywhere. We'll be right here when they arrive."

Chapter Fifty-Nine

Pitts put a call through to Detective Scoggins as soon as Costa and Webb were out of the parking lot.

"Scoggins here."

"Yeah, this is Pitts. I need your help with a few things."

"Okay..." Scoggins said, sounding suspicious.

"I heard you got the Nina Culver case."

"Yep, but I'm headed out the door, right now. I just got a call from dispatch. Can I hit you up later?"

"No worries," Pitts said. "You can reach me on my cell. I'm still out on medical leave."

"I'll catch you later then," Scoggins said.

Pitts needed answers, but he wasn't sure whom to trust. Costa would stop him in his tracks if she found out he was investigating. So, she was out of the question, and not everyone in the department was trustworthy. There really was only one person he could call.

He picked up a notepad and scribbled down all the things he needed her to look into. *Maybe I'll just ask her out to dinner outside of the office? So, we can discuss all this, he thought. It will take her by surprise, but she's a strong woman and she'll find a way to deal with it. Yep, out of the office. That's the best idea.*

****

It had been a long, frightening, sad day for Clara, Iris, and Quita. They'd gone from being certain they had their killer to watching the emotional heartache of a family who'd suffered for far too long.

"I wonder what'll happen to them," Iris said.

"Regardless of their good intentions, they did compromise evidence that could've helped police find the killer before he struck again. Maybe they'll have a sympathetic judge who'll get them the help they need," Clara said.

"I've never felt so many emotions in one day," Quita admitted. "I don't think I'll ever be able to fall asleep tonight."

"You were pretty serious with that wrench, weren't ya, girl?" Iris asked playfully.

"I just knew we had the murderer," Quita answered.

"I've still got some of that frozen spaghetti sauce in my freezer," Clara said. "What about a sleepover, gals? I have the latest Sandra Bullock movie."

"You had me at spaghetti sauce," Quita said. "Can we sleep in tomorrow?"

"I don't see why not," Clara answered. "You're the boss, it's your call."

Chapter Sixty

Pitts had been up all night, delving into the mind of the killer. He had always prided himself on never being shocked by anything, but clearly, this case had thrown him a curve.

He finally drifted off to sleep around four o'clock in the morning but was up again by 8:00. He took a long, hot shower and got dressed. He'd told Jessalyn to stay at her place the night before because he needed to work.

At nine o'clock, Pitts picked up his cell phone, called his lieutenant, and asked her to come pick him up immediately. He waited on the couch, with the television off, his mind in a whirlwind.

Pitts waited until it was almost time for Costa to pull in before he locked up his apartment and maneuvered down the stairs. He was either numb from the course of events, or he was getting stronger.

Clearly, Costa wasn't happy when she pulled in. "I really don't have time for this," she spat. "Whatever you need can wait. I've been pulling my hair out at the office. I've never been so behind."

"Just trust me on this one," Pitts insisted.

"Okay, just tell me where we're headed…and if you know any shortcuts."

"To the DA's office."

"What for, what's this about?" she said, turning to look at him. "Webb already assured you he's doing all he can, so—"

"Trust me on this, Lieutenant."

Costa opened her mouth to offer a rebuttal, but her cell rang and cut her off. She sighed loudly and pulled it from its case on her belt. "Costa," she snapped.

Pitts could make out Scoggins's voice on the other end of the line but didn't know what he was saying.

"You can't be serious!" Costa said. "I guess some problems just take care of themselves," she said. "At least the streets will be safer," she uttered before hanging up and placing her phone back in its case. "I guess we can turn around now."

"Why is that?"

"Looks like the cartel took care of your girl last night. During the shift change, a nurse found her with a pillow over her face," Costa said nonchalantly as she turned on her blinker to head back to Pitts' apartment.

"Platinum has nothing to do with this. Keep going."

"Whatever you say, Pitts." Costa shrugged, continuing toward their destination. "Anyway, how do you feel about it?"

"About what?"

"Monica Heard, what else? Are you okay, Pitts?"

"I guess it hasn't sunk in yet. She wasn't a good person. I don't doubt she would've continued down the same path for the rest of her screwed-up life. I guess I'm just sad for her baby, Tony Hart, and even Germaine Wilkins."

"Wow, I've never known you to be so…emotional," Costa said. "I don't really know what to say."

"It's a tough world out there, LT. Good people die, and bad people keep going as if none of it matters."

"Damn, did you and Jessalyn break up or something?"

"No," Pitts snapped. "I just get tired of all the bullshit sometimes."

"Well, we're here," Costa said as she pulled into an empty spot by the curb.

The elevator door opened, and Pitts walked straight to Warren Milton's office. Irene Edwards was on a call, but she immediately placed the phone back in its cradle when she saw them. She looked exhausted, and Pitts knew she hadn't slept any better the night before than he had. He secretly hoped she'd soon retire and move somewhere sunny, like Florida.

"Good morning, Irene. Are Webb and Milton here?" Pitts asked.

"Yes, they're both in Milton's office. I told them you and Lieutenant Costa were on your way. They're expecting you."

Costa turned and looked at Pitts but didn't ask any questions.

"I called for backup," Irene whispered before she opened the DA's door to let them in.

"Good morning, gentlemen," Pitts said, then helped himself to a chair. "I won't be long."

"Pitts, I understand you're not happy with how things turned out," Milton said. "Brandon shared it with me this morning. I'm sorry, but I really can't take the case. I'm—"

"I know. You're busy with your divorce and don't want to lose those two vacation homes."

Milton looked puzzled but didn't argue the point. "It's a bad time for me."

"As you know, Milton, we think we're dealing with a serial killer. I've been racking my brain, trying to come up with some connection between these girls. To save my life, I couldn't find one."

"Pitts, these men are busy," Costa said. "This isn't the time or place."

"Just give me a minute," Pitts said as he held up his hand to quiet her. "See, the one clue we had from the last autopsy were some Laurel blossoms. They're only found in the mountains, you know. It's kinda hard to get them to thrive here where it's warmer."

"Thank you for the agriculture lesson, Pitts, but I do hope you'll get to your point shortly," Milton said.

"I most certainly will. When I found out your wife was threatening to go to the press with a family secret, I must admit, I got a little curious. Then, when Brandon told me about your two vacation homes, I got even more curious. A good friend with a few connections to some secure info looked up the location of your getaways. I was a little let down about what was found. You don't own a house in the mountains at all. Imagine our frustration when we found out I was on the wrong track."

Warren Milton's face was beet red, and he slammed his fist down on his desk. "Were you in on this, Costa? Because I'll have your job, too, if—"

"Hold up a minute," Pitts said, cutting him off. "Just bear with me. I still wasn't convinced there wasn't a connection, so we looked at the office case logs. It seems Jasmine Baines, recently deceased, gave a deposition to this office a few weeks ago about sexual harassment she'd witnessed on her job. Apparently, the manager was making unwanted advances to a male bartender. She never mentioned it to her sister because she didn't want to worry her. Meanwhile, Nina Culver had made numerous plea bargains with this office for drug offenses her parents were desperate to buy their way out of. Then there's Kori Reeves, the missing girl whose parents were recently on the news, begging for help to find her. Well, I found it interesting that she applied and interviewed for a summer internship with this office."

District Attorney Milton had clearly had enough. "I've heard all I intend to from you, Detective. I don't know anything about those girls or their dealings with this office. I've got no idea where you're going with this but you're way out of line, Pitts."

"I know you don't know anything about those girls, Milton because you didn't handle their cases. Someone on your staff, however, dealt with all three of them."

Warren Milton sat back behind his desk. "Who?" he demanded.

"Do you care to tell him, Brandon?" Pitts asked.

Brandon said nothing and stood still as a statue.

"Mister Webb was the only member of your staff who spoke with those girls. He also has a little inheritance of his own. Care to share that with us, Webb?"

"You can't prove a thing," Brandon finally said. "I didn't do anything to those girls."

Pitts' phone dinged, indicating a text. He glanced down at it and shook his head. "Are you sure you don't want to get an attorney?"

"I don't need a damn attorney, but you, on the other hand, need a shrink! You're out of your mind, Pitts. Maybe you've been taking too many painkillers."

"Kori Reeves just arrived, via ambulance at a hospital in Dahlonega. She crawled to your grandmother's house for help."

Brandon fell back into a chair and placed his face in his hands. "I'm sick of always being second best, Milton," he said, turning to face his boss. "I was always the last one picked for kickball, the last to get into a fraternity, the last in my class to land a job, and now I'm the damn assistant DA. Those girls were just using me to get what they wanted—a plea bargain, a job, their boss to be fired. They all deserved it—every, last one of them!"

"Lieutenant Costa," Pitts said. "Please open the door, Irene already called for backup."

Several APD officers burst in and two placed cuffs on the assistant DA.

"I wouldn't have killed the bitch who had you shot if I'd known you were going to treat me like this," Webb leaned over and whispered as he passed by Pitts.

Epilogue

Pitts, Clara, Iris, Quita, and Rhadrick sat in the office of Hadley and Samples, Private Investigations. Clara and Iris had splurged on a nice bottle of wine, and Pitts had brought a cooler of beer for Rhadrick and himself.

"Well, this time next week, Nettles will be out of the hospital," Pitts said. "He'll never believe all the stories I have to tell him."

"I'm sure he'll be happy to be back in his own home," Iris said.

"Yes, he will. Not only that, but I get to go back to work next month," Pitts added. "Strictly desk duty, but it's a start."

"That's good," Quita said. "We can use somebody on the inside."

"What are you ladies working on next?" Pitts asked.

"Who knows?" Clara said. "In the meantime, though, there's quite a demand for little, old ladies who are willing to do some surveillance. Apparently, no one would ever suspect us of being private eyes."

"No kidding," Rhadrick said with a grin.

"Quita," Clara said with a warm smile. "Iris has something for you."

Quita reached for the red gingham gift bag. "I was wondering what's in here. Can I take a peak, Miss Iris?"

"I don't see why not," Iris said. "Since your name is on the tag."

Quita moved the tissue paper and pulled out a small box. She opened it slowly and let out a squeal of delight.

"What is it, Quita?" Pitts asked.

"Oh, nothing really," Iris said. "It's just the keys to an old lady's Honda Accord that's seen better days. I catch a ride into work with Clara every day, and it's just sitting in my garage, gathering dust."

Quita jumped up to hug Iris. "I can't believe it! My own wheels."

"Let me make one thing very clear," Iris said. "I can drive! I simply choose to catch a lift with an old friend."

"I have some good news to share," Quita said. "I bet you two won't believe it."

"What's that?" Clara asked.

"We've been invited to a wedding. My sister and Denard are gonna tie the knot. Can you believe it? My nephew will be raised by both his parents!"

"You're right, I don't believe it!" Iris said happily.

"Apparently, your very first case was a success," Quita said. "He hasn't missed a Friday payment yet!"

"I love happy endings," Iris said, only to be interrupted by the ringing phone.

"Hadley and Samples, Private Investigations," Quita said. She paused briefly before a broad grin formed on her face. "Sure, I'd like that. See ya then." She hung up, still beaming. "Wow! The good news just keeps coming," she said to her friends. "I actually have a date Friday night."

"A *date*?" Iris asked. "It's not with that no-good bartender, is it?"

"Nope, it's with Stanley Peters."

"Wait. *Sugar*?" Iris squealed. "Woo-hoo, let's raise our glasses, folks," she said. "Here's to happy endings!"

Sneak Peek

Sneak Peek at Sweet Dreams Baby Belle

Lizzie Headrick thought she had finally met her Prince Charming in Dr. Grant Chatsworth. She was young and in love, and their quick courtship ended with the four-carat diamond engagement ring of her dreams.

Now residing in one of Buckhead's finest estates, Lizzie soon learns all that glitters is not gold. Her handsome husband, a renowned cardiac surgeon, and developer of a new congestive heart failure drug was becoming cruel and controlling. She finds herself captive in the vast expanse of his estate without a phone or car, and under the watchful eye of Flossie who runs the household.

When Lizzie discovers that Cardiac Care Research, his drug development company, is a Ponzi scheme, she realizes her life could be in danger if she doesn't somehow escape the gated mansion on the hill.

Her only hope is to get to Biloxi, Mississippi and seek refuge with her sister, Maggie. Maggie and her husband, Leland, quickly find a safe harbor for Lizzie in a house on the bayou. However, the house at the end of the street might not be the quiet retreat Lizzie was hoping for.

As the confines of her hideaway close in on her, she retreats to the small historical cemetery next door where the small, damaged tombstone of a child soon catches her eye and captures her heart. Just when Lizzie Chatsworth thinks her world can't get any more complicated, she finds herself in the middle of a mystery from the 1800s that is pulling her in and demanding she seeks justice.

As her husband's empire begins to crumble, he's more determined than ever to find Lizzie and eliminate her. But, will the mystery of the small tombstone end Lizzie's life first?

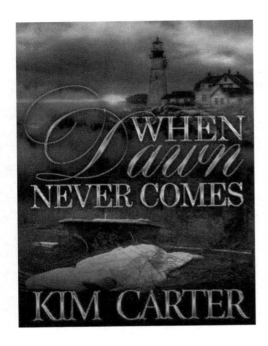

Sneak Peek at When Dawn Never Comes

Jordan Maxwell, a twenty-seven-year-old freelance journalist, ventures to New York City to make a name for herself. Being that both of her parents are dead, she struggles to get by living in one of the worst neighborhoods in the city. In a twist of fate, Jordan finds herself the sole heir to her great-uncle's estate in Solomon Cove, Maine.

She packs her bags and heads to Maine where she soon realizes her rags-to-riches journey entails much more than she bargained for.

Crime was unheard of in the small fishing village of Solomon Cove, a town where everyone knows everyone. It was the last place anyone expected crime, especially murder. However, the tides turn for this quaint town when the body of a young girl comes crashing in with the waves.

As the victims continue to mount, Jordan starts to believe the murders are connected to her and the family she never knew. Digging deeper into the past, Jordan must protect herself before she becomes the serial killer's next target.

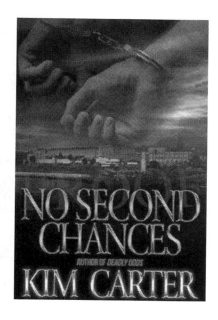

Sneak Peek at No Second Chances

Falling from a life of wealth and substance, to inside one of America's most notorious prisons, prominent orthopedic surgeon Phil Sawyer is incarcerated for the voluntary manslaughter of his wife. While confined, he finds himself on the trail of a serial killer that infiltrates the walls of San Quentin. After finding himself in the infirmary for getting involved in an incident that didn't concern him, Phil struggles with the decision to stick his neck out. But he can't ignore the rise in suspicious deaths among the African American inmates.

Using the aid of an empathetic nurse and help from the outside, he tries to identify the unexplained cause of their cardiac arrests. He finds himself out on early release and heads to Solomon Cove, a peaceful town in Maine. But, could the tranquil town all be a façade, or has the serial killer made their way across the country to seek revenge?

From wealthy Los Angeles to the justice in San Quentin, and the serene landscapes of Maine, you will applaud the friendships and hear the cry as you ride the roller coaster of emotions this story will bring.

Sneak Peek of Deadly Odds

Two worlds collide in this edge-of-your-seat thriller. Georgia bounty hunter Nathaniel Collier finds himself in perilous danger as he hunts down the notorious Mad Dog Consuelos.

As Nathaniel draws near, Consuelos strikes again leaving behind a bloody path of violence. Collier, along with Gracie, Mad Dog's daughter, takes the brunt of the assault, leaving them struggling to survive for weeks in the hospital.

Meanwhile, Atlanta PD officer Reid Langley decides to leave the violent city behind and take a cushy job as sheriff in the small town of Hayden, Wyoming. All appears to go as uneventful as planned until a serial killer shows up to wreak havoc on the safe-haven Reid is determined to protect. Just when he thinks he has all that he can handle, Reid finds himself harboring his old friend, a nurse, and an innocent young girl.

The battle is on as this group of characters embarks on a race against time to locate a serial killer and to track down the elusive Consuelos before he can take his revenge.

Sneak Peek of And The Forecast Called For Rain

Detective Jose Ramirez and the Sierra Hills Police Department are scrambling for leads on a killer who has already struck five times, each time leaving his signature trademark: large butcher knives piercing the abdomens of his young female victims.

Profiling the killer is proving to be difficult, and Detective Ramirez knows that it's only a matter of time before their perpetrator strikes again.

As if Ramirez isn't frustrated enough, to his dismay, he is assigned a partner. Officer Daniel Chatham, a handsome, young man, fresh out of grad school has pulled some strings to join the division and becomes Ramirez's, right-hand man. The lead detective's anger slowly begins to dissipate as he discovers the book-smart kid can be quite the asset.

Utilizing Ramirez's experience, Chatham's sharp mind, and quick thinking, and the insight of Erin Sommers, a beautiful, young journalist, the three make a powerful team gaining on their criminal.

Kim Carter

It's raining… it's pouring, and a killer is on the loose in the rainy Sierra Hills of Washington State. No one is who they seem, and the plot thickens with every turn. You'll never guess the ending of this enigmatic tale.

About The Author

Kim is an author of suspense, mystery and thriller novels. She was a finalist in the 2018 Killer Nashville Silver Falchion Award and recipient of the 2017 Readers' Choice Award for her book Murder Among The Tombstones. This is the first book in her Clara and Iris Mystery series. The characters in this series are a couple of overly curious widows who become private investigators and were inspired by Kim's mother and her mom's best friend.

Her other titles include: When Dawn Never Comes, Deadly Odds, No Second Chances, And The Forecast Called For Rain, and Sweet Dreams, Baby Belle.

Kim's writing career started after she suffered an illness that made her housebound for a couple of years. An avid reader of mystery novels, she embarked on writing as a means of filling her time. Kim shared those early writings with friends and family who encouraged her to pursue writing professionally. Her health struggles and successes have been chronicled on The Lifetime Television in early 2000, The Atlanta-Journal Constitution, Women's Day Magazine, and Guidepost.

Prior to her illness, Kim worked in many different capacities in the county government ranging from Park Director with Parks and Recreation to the Grant Department with Human Services. But, ultimately, it was her job as a correctional officer that provided her the opportunity to interact with a variety of people from all walks of life. Her experiences ran the gamete of inspiring success stories to tragic endings, much like her mysteries.

She self-published her first book No Second Chances. One of the guest speakers at the launch party she had at the Performing Arts Center in Newnan, Georgia included her close friend retired Atlanta Police Chief Eldrin Bell. This connection would become helpful as she started doing more research for other books, this time working with a small publishing house.

Kim started networking and made connections with the Fulton County Medical Examiner's Office. Her research has taken her many places including morgues, death row, and the occasional midnight visit to cemeteries.

She is a college graduate of Saint Leo University, has a Bachelor's Degree of Arts in Sociology. Kim and her husband have three grown children and live just outside of Atlanta, Georgia.

Get In Touch With Kim Carter:

Website: https://www.kimcarterauthor.com/

Email: kimcarterauthor@gmail.com

Facebook: https://www.facebook.com/kimcarterauthor/

Instagram:
https://www.instagram.com/kimcarterauthor/?hl=en

About.Me: https://about.me/kimcarter.mysteryauthor

Amazon Author Page:
https://www.amazon.com/Kim-Carter/e/B019QSNFI0/

GoodReads:
https://www.goodreads.com/author/show/4075351.Kim_Carter

Twitter: https://twitter.com/KimCarterAuthor

Google+: https://plus.google.com/105425029849895301377

For speaking engagements, interviews, and book copies, please get in touch with Raven South Publishing at info@ravensouthpublishing.com.

Kim Carter

I hope you enjoyed reading Murder Among The Tombstones. I'd appreciate it if you would post a review on the site you purchased it from, as well as on Amazon and Goodreads. I'm grateful for everyone that I receive. Feel free to contact me on Facebook and my website if you have any questions or thoughts about the stories. I love hearing from readers.

Very best regards,

Kim Carter

Facebook: kimcarterauthor
www.kimcarterauthour.com

kimcarterauthor@gmail.com

Made in the USA
Columbia, SC
06 January 2022